States

of

Grace

STATES
OF
GRACE

A NOVEL OF SAINT-GERMAIN

Chelsea Quinn Yarbro

TOR®

A TOM DOHERTY ASSOCIATES BOOK
NEW YORK

STATES OF GRACE

Copyright © 2005 by Chelsea Quinn Yarbro

A Tor Book
Published by Tom Doherty Associates, LLC
175 Fifth Avenue
New York, NY 10010

www.tor.com

Tor® is a registered trademark of Tom Doherty Associates, LLC.

Library of Congress Cataloging-in-Publication Data

Yarbro, Chelsea Quinn, 1942–
    States of grace : a novel of Saint-Germain / Chelsea Quinn Yarbro.
        p. cm.
    "A Tom Doherty Associates book."
    ISBN-13: 978-0-765-31392-8
    ISBN-10: 0-765-31392-8
    1. Saint-Germain, comte de, d. 1784—Fiction. 2. Women musicians—Crimes against—Fiction. 3.
Inquisition—Fiction. 4. Vampires—Fiction. I. Title.

PS3575.A7S73 2005
813'.54—dc22   2005041937

First Hardcover Edition: September 2005
First Trade Paperback Edition: October 2006

Printed in the United States of America

0 9 8 7 6 5 4 3 2 1

For

Anne Eudey,

a Virgil in the labyrinthine world

of California politics

Author's Notes

The title of this story refers to the religio-political unrest gripping Europe, and the justification that was rigorously promulgated as part of it, as well as the volatile social conditions to which it contributed: Europe in the mid-sixteenth century was caught up in the Reformation and a host of regional conflicts that would seriously prolong and escalate the Wars of Religion. Luther's movement, as well as a handful of others, in fact, were becoming more than regional disruptions, attracting significant followings unlike earlier Christian heresies, and had taken on the alarming aspects of being lasting revolutionary movements: In England, the debate between Henry VIII and the Pope reached a point of no return. While parts of modern Germany, Alsace-Lorraine, and Switzerland attempted a posture of limited tolerance to religious reform, the Inquisition in Spain went into high gear to keep the fatal taint of heresy from contaminating the country, and in so doing, created some very real schisms among the Hapsburgs, who controlled both Austro-Hungary and Spain and, by extension through the Spanish Crown, modern Holland and Belgium. The posture of the Austrian branch was fairly religiously tolerant; the Spanish branch was just the opposite. With so much social restructuring, the Hanseatic League was finally losing its commercial grip on the northern European and Scandinavian ports, opening trade to many more commercial ventures, including ones in the New World.

Of equal, but less obvious impact was the expansion of publishing throughout Europe, with centers in Germany (major presses at Heidelberg), Holland (major presses at Antwerp and Amsterdam), and northern Italy (principal presses at Venice); the debates of the day were regularly reinforced and fueled by the proliferation of books and the increasing mutation of religious observances. This was strengthened by the failure of the Ottomites to take Vienna, and their subsequent loss of territory in eastern Europe and a wedge of the Balkans, ending in a centuries-long stalemate the residue of which conflict is still with us today. Publishing had a number of less obvious but equally important consequences: Publishing began to regularize language, defining form and syntax as never before, codifying dialect and regionalisms as offshoots of central language, such as the difference between the Venetian dialect as compared to Italian, and the proliferation of languages in northwestern Europe during the time in question; insofar as possible, the linguistics of the day are used in this book: Venezia, Venezian, and the usual Venezian tendency to drop the last vowel or syllable of a name—Sen, not Seno—and the end of certain nouns—gondolier, Consiglier, and so forth. Period spellings and usages are found in the text when they are consistent: Fiorenze (modern Florence) is an example of this. Publishing increased literacy, especially in cities where reading was more of an asset than it was in the country, and spurred the cause of education; and publishing fed the growing importance of record-keeping by making such records more generally available and concise.

The social ferment touched on issues other than religion: peasants' revolts were not uncommon in this period, and somewhat less common but as significant were the occasional guild revolts in cities, some of which resulted in strikes and riots as the demand for reorganization of outmoded social conventions and traditions became more pervasive. Many of those traditions dated back five hundred years and more. Due to the religious changes in various parts of western Europe, there was a dramatic upsurge in refugees seeking the safety of coreligionists, which brought about significant demographic changes throughout the century. All of these factors impact this novel in a variety of ways, from tangential to directly confrontational.

Another small-but-monumental social shift in the sixteenth century was the standardization of time: clocks became more reliable, and the perception of time went from cyclical to linear. By the 1580s, pocket watches were a common accessory for members of the merchant and upper classes, and elaborate clocks were more and more the objects of choice for setting off a town's center. It may not seem like much on the surface, but it changed banking and commerce as well as providing more reliable measurements, which in turn created the intellectual climate that supported empiricism and what became the scientific method.

❖   ❖   ❖

Thanks are due to D. J. Ahntoe for his information on sixteenth-century commerce and commercial law; to Meredith Deller for her expertise on the evolution of language in Europe; to Edwin Haws for his material on the various Protestant movements in Catholic Christendom; to Barry Nimmo for letting me borrow half a dozen books on specific aspects of this period; and to Ed Traegar for access to his maps of western Europe in the sixteenth century.

Thanks are also due to the Luckes, Gaye, Brian, Megan, Alice, Bill, Patrick, Steve, Randy, with extra to Maureen; to my readers, Ginny Brovard, L. L. Louis, and Susan Kinsolving, who read it for clarity; and to Libba Campbell and Celia Montoya, who read it for errors; to the Lord Ruthven Assembly and the Transylvanian Society of Dracula, especially Elizabeth, Stephanie, Sharon, and Katie; to the Web-promo top gun, Wiley Saichek; to the folks of CQYarbro Yahoo group; to Lindig Harris for the *Yclept Yarbro* newsletter; to Irene Kraas, my agent, and her affiliates for their long support of this series; to Melissa Singer, my editor, and Tom Doherty, the mastermind at Tor; to the booksellers who have championed Saint-Germain; and to you, the readers, who make it all possible.

CHELSEA QUINN YARBRO
October, 2004

PART I

PIER-ARIANA SALIER

*T*ext of a letter from Marcantonio Rosseli, apothecary in Verona, to his cousin, Pier-Ariana Salier in Venezia, delivered by private messenger ten days after it was written.

To the daughter of my aunt Gioella, of revered memory, Marcantonio Rosseli sends his most faithful greetings, and his congratulations on your securing the patronage of the eminent foreigner, Conte Franzicco Ragoczy di Santo-Germano, and the hope that neither you nor he will have cause to regret the association.

You tell me he has secured you a casetta near San Zaccaria, and that you have been provided virginals and a lute on which to play your songs, as well as the promise of publication of the best of them. To have so much distinction, and you only twenty-five, much younger than most patroned musicians: it is a very great honor, as I am sure you know. The terms of his patronage are most generous gifts, and I trust you will be at pains to deserve them. Few musicians ever have such good fortune as you have encountered, and as far as I am aware, none of those musicians who have achieved such success have been women. This requires your gratitude and careful performance of your talents, for to do anything less would shame your present benefits as well as deprive you of all opportunities in the future, for once known as feckless, no musician, and certainly no woman, can do other than fall in the eyes of the world.

It may be, as you suggested, that more than music is required of you, and if that is the case, then I urge you to make a formal agreement regarding how you are to conduct yourself. If di Santo-Germano were a Venezian, it would be another matter, but since he is not, you must be prudent and see that your patronage cannot be rescinded on a whim. Conte or not, Santo-Germano—however grand it may be—is not in La Serenissima Repubblica Veneziana, and so long as that is the case, his title is more courtesy than binding responsibility. You need terms of settlement as to what he will provide you, and be sure that such monies or property that he provides is secured in such a way that his absence will not adversely impact your situation.

For your own protection, be sure you maintain notes on di Santo-Germano's activities, in case you are ever required to appear before the Doge in regard to di Santo-Germano's affairs. You do not want any suspicions that fall upon him to fall upon you as well, and such a record would relieve you of any taint of wrong-doing. If di Santo-Germano did not own a press, it might be less important, but since il Conte is engaged in publishing, who knows what scandalous material he may decide to foist upon the world. The Maggior Consiglio takes a dim view of our own Veneziani undertaking to publish questionable material—they will be all the more stringent with a foreigner, noble or not, if he should go beyond the acceptable bounds established by the Doge.

I am sending you a gift of lace to mark this fortunate occasion, and I will write to my father on your behalf, so that he need not send you money for as long as di Santo-Germano attends to your keep. He will be glad for you, I am sure, and for the sake of your mother, he may send to di Santo-Germano to learn more of your arrangements with him. I pray you may flourish with such a patron, and that you will gain a favorable reputation, unattended by the notoriety that so often adheres to musicians in general, and to women in particular, for that would leech away the many advantages that now lie before you.

> *Your most affectionate cousin,*
> *Marcantonio Rosseli*
> *apothecary of Verona*

By my own hand at sunset, on this, the 9th day of February, 1530 Anno Domini

1

"Conte!" the young page Niccola exclaimed sleepily as he stumbled to his feet, rubbing his eyes and trying to appear fully awake. He saw his master step from the shadows into the light of the four blazing torches, a man who seemed to be about forty-five, attractive without being beautiful in the current fashion, his bearing confident but lacking cockiness or arrogance; instead he evinced a self-composure that was both compelling and daunting at once. He was magnificently dressed in black damask silk, a wide fur collar on his broad-shouldered French dogaline-and-doublet, his eclipse device shining on a dark-red satin sash. His dark hair was shorter than the prevailing fashion in Venezia, its loose, dark waves falling just to the edge of his collar, and he was clean-shaven; it was past midnight and most of Venezia lay in darkness, dozing on the out-going tide.

Franzicco Ragoczy di Santo-Germano removed his plumed black hat as he came through the hastily opened door and fixed his astonishing dark eyes on the drowsy page; behind him, the Campo San Luca was limned in the pale wash of light from a gibbous moon, the darkness deeper by contrast to the milky lume. A cold, hard wind polished the night to a jewel-like shine. "Have there been any callers while I was out?"

"A messenger from your warehouses called to leave an inventory from the *Gilded Angel*, which arrived in port yesterday morning," said Niccola. "No one else. At least, no one I admitted." He put his hand on his chest. "I will not let villains into this house. And I suppose anyone who might call was at the Collegio."

Di Santo-Germano frowned a little. "Nothing from Ulrico Baradin?"

"No, Conte; I'm sorry." The youngster flinched, as if expecting a rebuke or a blow.

The Conte's expression immediately softened. "You have no reason to be sorry. You have done nothing wrong, Niccola, nor has he." He paced his loggia, his black, leg-hugging boots giving sharp reports of his progress. "Who will be on duty in the morning?"

"You mean my duty?" Niccola asked, his uncertainty flaring again.

"Yes: your duty. Who is assigned to man the door?"

Niccola was glad he had the answer. "That would be Enrici; since Rinaldo broke his arm, Enrici has—"

"So long as Enrici does not neglect his other duties, he is a fine choice."

"Rinaldo is grateful to you for setting his arm; he says it is healing straight," Niccola reported as if revealing great news.

"That is good to know: Rinaldo should be ready to resume his work in another ten days, I would think, if his splint holds." Di Santo-Germano stopped by one of the torches and stared at the flame, his dark eyes fixed on some other vision. Finally he blinked, asking, "Is Ruggier still up, do you know?"

"He is in your study, or he was an hour ago," said Niccola in a rush of relief. "He was out earlier, but returned."

Di Santo-Germano started toward the stairs at the far end of the loggia, but stopped. "Niccola, have I ever struck you?"

"No, Conte, never," said the page.

"And have you ever been beaten by anyone in this household?"

"No, Conte," Niccola said, becoming more contrite.

"Then why do you behave at every turn as if you expect such usage?" di Santo-Germano asked, truly curious.

"Because, Conte, it is the custom," said Niccola, his voice dropping with every word.

"Niccola," said di Santo-Germano in a voice that commanded attention; the youth looked up. "It is not the custom with me."

Niccola nodded. "Si, Conte," he muttered, and turned away.

With a single shake of his head, di Santo-Germano made for the stairs, going up them two at a time, for though they were steep, they were also fairly shallow. As he climbed, he tugged off his embroidered gloves of black Fiorenzan leather and thrust them into his broad, ruby-studded belt. At the top of the flight, di Santo-Germano stepped into an odd little hall where two corridors met at right angles; an antique red-lacquer chest and two chairs stood in the broadest part of the hall, the chairs beneath a clerestory window. Taking the corridor leading south, di Santo-Germano went down to the end of it to a beautifully carved door; he opened the latch and entered his study.

"There you are," said the middle-aged man with sandy hair and pale-blue eyes; he spoke a dialect of Roman Latin that had not been heard in more than a thousand years. He was dressed in well-tailored servants' livery of rucked-and-padded dove-gray wool doublet over a white-muslin camisa, distinguished with a silver-edged black shoulder-sash that indicated his high rank in the household; the Conte's eclipse device was embroidered on his sleeve, as it was on all the livery in the household.

"Were you worried?" di Santo-Germano asked in the same tongue as he tossed his hat onto the handsome writing table against the western wall, in front of ceiling-high bookshelves. It was one of three tables in the large, well-appointed room, and it held only a sheaf of papers, an inkpad and standish, and a supply of quills. On the eastern wall, atop a heavy trestle-table, there was an astrolabe, a trio of retorts, two alembics, a beam-scale, a saw-clock, and two large, locked chests. The third table was lower than the other two, and placed in front of the fireplace in the southern wall, opposite the door, to provide a place to entertain guests. On it a pair of handsome branched, bronze candlesticks of Eastern design stood, squat beeswax candles surmounting them both. An upholstered settee and a pair of matched chairs were set around this table.

"No; since Doge Gritti provided you an escort to the Collegio, I assumed all was well," said Ruggier.

"Why would that ease you?" di Santo-Germano asked with an ironic lift of one fine brow. "I would have thought such distinction would have alarmed you, given what we have experienced in the past." In their nearly fifteen hundred years together, di Santo-Germano had been escorted away to an uncertain future nearly a dozen times, as both of them were well aware.

"Ah, but in those cases your escorts were soldiers, not clerks, and Venezia is supposed to be at peace. As far as I or anyone knows, no accusations have been made against you, and there is official toleration of foreigners in La Serenissima," said Ruggier sagely, laying down the two volumes he had been inspecting. "The rest of this edition should be ready in a day or two."

"Excellent," di Santo-Germano approved, his demeanor lightening as he stared at the books. "I take it Giovanni sent those over by messenger while I was out." He wondered why Niccola had not mentioned the arrival of the books, but said nothing of this omission.

"No; I went to find out how much more paper will be needed, and he gave them to me. I brought them back to this house." Ruggier held one of the books out.

Di Santo-Germano took it, running his hand over it as if seeking to absorb its contents by touch alone. "This is very good. The embossing is precise and elegant. The gilding of the page-edges is not overdone, and the trim is very even." He opened the cover and turned to the title page: *The Far East, Its Peoples and Customs,* it read in Latin. *By Germanim Ragoczy.*

"What did you tell the Collegio?" Ruggier regarded di Santo-Germano with interest.

"That I will submit all the books we publish to them for their approval, as I am required to do. I said this second book was a work by my cousin—which they could all comprehend, having cousins of their own—and since Venezia is the city of Marco Polo, I thought it would be most appropriate to publish a book on the parts of the world he explored so long ago, and about which he dictated so many—" He stopped. "You know what I said, or near enough, and fortunately, the Collegio accepted it."

Ruggier set down the book he held. "They believed you?"

"Of course they did," said di Santo-Germano. "I flattered them shamelessly, and praised their erudition: what could they do but accept my terms?"

"You sound disappointed," said Ruggier.

Di Santo-Germano shrugged. "I may be," he allowed, and expanded on this, saying, "It is one thing to be able to set up a press without hindrance, but it is another to gain the good opinion of those under whose auspices the press exists through expected courtship, and appreciation expressed in gifts and gold. When it is necessary to adulate and bribe in order to gain acceptance, some of the satisfaction of producing books is lost."

"You have done that before," Ruggier pointed out. "Why is this any different?"

"Perhaps I'm growing tired of the hypocrisy of it," said di Santo-Germano.

"I think it is that you believe the merit of the works you publish should be obvious, and not require your skill at courtesy to make them unobjectionable," said Ruggier with a knowing nod. "You resent the lack of appreciation."

"Astounding, isn't it?" di Santo-Germano remarked with a crack of self-taunting laughter. "At my age, too, and with all that has happened, I cannot entirely rid myself of such idealism." He had no reason to remind Ruggier that he had been born over thirty-five hundred years ago.

Ruggier stacked the two new books together. "Idealism of any kind after so much time isn't entirely unfortunate, my master."

"No, probably not," said di Santo-Germano, making no effort to disguise his doubts; he went on in a brisker tone, "I understand from Niccola that the inventory from the *Gilded Angel* has been sent over from the warehouse."

Accepting this change of subject with the philosophical resignation borne of long association, Ruggier went to retrieve a sheaf of papers. "Yes. Captain Carazza has made a notation that they were chased by corsairs a day out of Antioch. Two ships, working together, pursued them for a full five hours. According to Captain Carazza, the weather, which was very rough and blustery, is all that saved them; in heavy seas, his merchants' galleon fared better than the corsairs' lighter craft."

"From which we assume that someone in Antioch told the pirates about what the ship carried and when it would sail," said di Santo-Germano, giving his attention to the pages he was handed. "Three barrels of wine were lost—as a diversionary tactic, do you think?"

"I don't know," said Ruggier, "but it wouldn't surprise me."

"It is one thing to lose a few barrels of wine, and another to lose an entire ship, along with its cargo and crew," said di Santo-Germano, a touch of grimness about his mouth. "I prefer the former."

"As who would not," said Ruggier.

"Given what some of the Collegio were suggesting, I cannot guess," said di Santo-Germano. "They are trying to find a way to persuade the Sultan to ban the taking of hostages for ransom."

Ruggier looked shocked. "Don't they know that will mean any captive will become an Ottomite's slave? Or simply be killed?"

"Apparently not," said di Santo-Germano. "Although I pointed this out to them as tactfully as I could."

"Did they listen at all?" Ruggier asked, knowing the answer from di Santo-Germano's demeanor.

"If I were Veneziano, they might have, but as I am not, they saw no reason to, not about that issue; they were much more concerned about the books I propose to publish, for my shipping business has paid handsomely for the state, and my printing is still under suspicion," said di Santo-Germano. "I brought my accounts to show the taxes I have been assessed have all been paid, and I reminded them I have also paid over five thousand ducats in ransoms for my ships' crews when they have been taken by corsairs, and that every man was returned safely."

"To no avail?"

"To no avail," di Santo-Germano confirmed, and a short, tense silence fell between them.

"Padre Bonnome at San Luca has offered to bless the ship again, before she departs on another voyage," said Ruggier, a bit remotely.

"Padre Bonnome is a clever man, Ruggier," said di Santo-Germano with a brief smile.

"As we have agreed in the past; a great component of the art of quid pro quo," said Ruggier. "For the *quid,* I said you would like that."

"You were right; no doubt he will inform us what the *quo* is to be," said di Santo-Germano. "If not for the ship, for the men on her. If they think their God is protecting them, they do not fear to set sail. I will make a donation, of course, to San Luca." He read through the rest of the inventory and notes. "When is the *Gilded Angel* due to set out again? Is she set for cleaning and refitting or standard patching and repair? I assume, since there is no damage assessment with this report, only standard maintenance is needed."

"That's correct. She's scheduled to go again in ten days, bound for Sicilia, Sardinia, Genova, Barcelona, then on through the Pillars of Hercules to Lisboa, to pick up English wool and Hollander lace from the *Evening Star,*" said Ruggier.

"Do you think I should hire fighting men to sail on her?" Di Santo-Germano gave the sheets of paper to Ruggier.

"Ask Captain Carazza. He'll know what will serve you best," Ruggier recommended.

"It would probably be wise to ask the other seven captains when they get back into port if they want fighting men on their ships. I want each man to be able to decide for himself rather than impose my decision upon them. It wouldn't do to have rivalries develop over protection, considering how intense their rivalries are already." Di Santo-Germano put his small, elegant hands together and stared contemplatively over his fingertips. "Nothing more from Ulrico Baradin, I understand."

"What makes you say that?" Ruggier asked in some surprise.

"Niccola said there was nothing from—"

"Niccola hadn't come on duty yet," said Ruggier. "A messenger came with his quotes for paper and ink. I left them with Giovanni, for his review."

"What manner of prices is he asking?" Di Santo-Germano looked down at the two new books. "My guess is that he has raised them."

"Of course he has. You are a continuing market now that you have produced two books, and he intends to make the most of it." Ruggier rubbed his eyes with his thumb and forefinger and yawned. "Forgive me. I have spent too long staring at sheets of uncorrected type today."

"If you want to rest, do so," said di Santo-Germano.

"Only my eyes are tired," said Ruggier, and prepared to continue.

"Then you should rest them, old friend," said di Santo-Germano, reaching out and laying his hand on Ruggier's shoulder. "There's nothing that can be done before morning, in any case, and San Luca's bells will ring at sunrise. You need not think you'll spend a slothful day—although that would not dismay me."

"As you wish, my master," said Ruggier. "I was beginning to think that I should go find Captain Carazza and bring him here for a report."

"If I know Captain Carazza, he is at Leatrice's house, and would not like being disturbed," said di Santo-Germano. "Leatrice would dislike it, as well."

"He has expensive tastes in women, if he goes to Leatrice," said Ruggier.

"So it would seem," said di Santo-Germano, faint amusement turning the corners of his mouth up. "And if that is the case, I hope he enjoys himself thoroughly."

"So we must hope," said Ruggier, not quite able to conceal the hint of a smirk that played over his lips. "And hope, as well, that he is coherent in the morning."

"That may be too much to wish for," said di Santo-Germano. "He has been at sea for many days; his first night in his home port, you cannot expect him to spend it in penitence."

"No," said Ruggier. "Although that may come."

Di Santo-Germano chuckled. "For his sake, I trust it may." He went and picked up the two new books. "Is Baradin going to come back tomorrow?"

"He said he would, sometime in midafternoon." He shook his head. "He's greedy."

"That he is," said di Santo-Germano with a thoughtful look. "Perhaps I should look elsewhere for my paper and ink. Grav Ragoczy has suppliers in Antwerp and Bruges—perhaps I could avail myself of them, as well."

Ruggier frowned. "Wouldn't that be taking a chance?"

"Why? If I say my relative, the Grav, recommended the suppliers to me—" di Santo-Germano began.

"What if your ruse is discovered? You should be more cautious than you are. If the Collegio discovers that you and the Grav are one in the same— This isn't like Karl-lo-Magne's time, when messages were few and many portions of the country were neglected for years on end," Ruggier interrupted. "Merchants exchange regular correspondence, and rulers have ministers to keep track of all manner of commerce. The Collegio would not look kindly on you having another identity in Protestant countries, particularly an identity as a publisher, for that would cast questions on all you have published here. They would shut down your press, seize your books, and confiscate the goods in your warehouse."

"If they found out. But why should they? They are unaware of my other identities—why should this one attract their attention more than any other?" di Santo-Germano asked. "I will not tell them, nor will you. Who else would know?"

"You are taking a risk," Ruggier admonished di Santo-Germano without apology.

"Of course. Living is a risk, even my sort of living. Why should I not gamble on myself? Is there a reason?" He brushed at an unseen blemish on his wide, turned-back sleeve.

"Because more than you could be harmed by what you do," said Ruggier bluntly. "I know I often urge you to be open to the possibilities in the world—"

"Hence my patronage of Pier-Ariana Salier," di Santo-Germano interjected gently.

"—but I worry when you become reckless. You have done so before, and—"

"Are you comparing Pier-Ariana to Csimenae? They have almost nothing in common." Di Santo-Germano managed to look shocked, not from genuine distress but in an effort to deflect the conversation.

Ruggier relented. "No, I am not, and you know it." He sighed. "Very well. I will say no more on this matter, at least so long as we have no cause for alarm. But if there is any indication of problems, then I will—"

"Yes," said di Santo-Germano. "I know you will. And I will thank you for it, no matter what it may seem to be now."

"Do you suppose I don't know this?" Ruggier asked.

Di Santo-Germano relented. "Of course you do. And you are gracious enough to permit me to be cow-handed about your understanding from time to time." He looked about his study. "This is certainly one of those times."

"You are tired from an evening of courtliness," said Ruggier.

"Which you, Rogerian, demonstrate superbly," said di Santo-Germano with a fleeting, rueful smile.

"But only when I choose, and only for as long as I choose," Ruggier reminded him, and went to the door. "Are you going to sleep at all tonight?"

"I may." He lifted his head at the sound of rising wind. "There will be rain again before tomorrow night."

"It's March. Of course there will be rain," said Ruggier, and let himself out of the room.

For a short while, di Santo-Germano stood by himself near the low table facing the fireplace. Then, with a small sigh, he went back to the writing table, drew up a chair for himself, selected a sheet of paper, prepared fresh ink in the standish, chose a trimmed quill, sat down, and began to write, his small, precise hand quickly filling the page with the characters of China. He wrote freely, secure in the certainty that no other man presently in Venezia could read what he was writing, except Ruggier.

❖   ❖   ❖

Text of a letter in regional German from Hagen Arndt of Ansbach to Ulrico Baradin of Venezia, carried by merchants' courier, and delivered nineteen days after it was written.

To my most industrious colleague, the distinguished ink-and-paper broker Ulrico Baradin of the Most Serene Venetian Republic, my Lutheran greetings, as the city requires, with the request that you remember me in your prayers, in case Brother Luther is wrong, after all.

Your letter came in good time, taking only two weeks to arrive. I am pleased to say that I have more than enough on hand to supply your order; I will make arrangements for it to be sent south with a well-guarded merchant-train in the next ten days, and you should receive it approximately thirty days from now. I will, myself, verify the quality of the paper and the consistency of the inks so that you will not be dissatisfied in any way with the product I deliver. Payment for your shipment will be expected in my hands within sixty days of your receipt of the order, which should allow you time to collect from the publisher ordering the ink and paper.

I was sorry to hear that Alessandro Sole lost his paper-mill on the tributary of the Po (I forget what the people call it—it flows south from the mountains, west of Udine). His disaster may be fortunate for me, but the savor of success is lessened when it is mixed with ashes. Has anyone yet found out who started the fire that burned his paper-mill? I cannot help but be uneasy while such a criminal is abroad in the land. You may say that Ansbach is a long way from that mill, but a man may walk the distance in ten days if the weather is good, and that is too close for my comfort.

You have stated in the letter accompanying your order that you may have some associates who may be interested in having their books printed in Lutheran territories rather than those of Mother Church. I will see if any of the publishers in this area are interested in such an arrangement, and will inform you of what I learn as soon as I have something to report. In the meantime, I would advise your publishers to consider leaving Venezia if their books are so controversial, for, as we know, the Church is still capable of putting dissenters in the hands of the Inquisition, another abuse of power, or so Luther says.

I anticipate hearing from you shortly, I thank you for your business, and once again, I condole with you on the death of your children. It is always hard when all are lost, no matter how young they are. Three dead in two months is a heavy burden for you to bear, particularly since you haven't yet remarried. All this, difficult as it is, would be more easily endured with the comfort of a second wife. I ask that you bear that in mind, and that the advice is given with the highest regard for you.

Hagen Arndt
printers' supplier

At Ansbach on the 10th day of March, 1530

2

To all appearances, Basilio Cuor was drunk; his broad, fleshy face was flushed, his words were slurred, and his patched leather doublet was stained with grease and wine. He lolled in the alcove near the door of the Due Bosci, an over-turned tankard of wine on the narrow plank table in front of him. As the door opened, he squinted in the sudden brilliance of the midday sun, lifting his hand to shade his eyes. "Watch what you're doing!" he roared, all joviality gone.

The man in the doorway—young, handsome, fashionably groomed, and well-dressed in a Spanish doublet of Fiorenzan velvet in a discreet dark-blue shade, his brown locks hidden by a soft velvet hat—glanced in his direction. "A little early in the day to be in your condition," said the man dismissingly, closing the door on the capricious spring weather.

"You didn't come in here to pray! Don't point to me if you're not taking your midday rest," Cuor shot back in a surly growl.

"No, I am not," said the man, and passed on into the center of the taproom, where he stood looking about expectantly. Seeing no one other than Cuor, he crossed the room to the dingy window and sat down at one of the smaller tables where he waited for someone to serve him.

At last a pale girl, no more than seven and scrawny at that, came hesitantly up to the man in the dark-blue doublet. "Signore?"

"That's Patron to you, bambina," said the man, tweaking her chin in a painful pinch. "Bring me a pot of the best that you have"—his sneer indicated he thought it would be none too good—"and a loaf of bread, if it isn't two days old or swarming with weevils."

"Our bread is clean, and our wines are from Toscana." She lifted her head.

"Very good," the man approved. "I am waiting for someone. I do not wish to be disturbed." He handed her a fiorini d'argent, saying, "This will buy me a little silence as well as food and drink."

The girl winkled the coin away, and said, "I will bring you wine and bread. Meat, if you want it, is extra."

"Their fish stew is excellent," Cuor piped up from his place in the alcove. "You will like it if you try it."

The man in dark-blue ignored this interpolation, saying to the girl, "Bring my order quickly and I will reward you."

The girl vanished as if in a conjurors' trick only to appear in less than two minutes with a tankard filled with a dark-red wine that smelled of blackberries and currants. She set this down and vanished again.

"She's the landlord's daughter, his youngest girl. In another two years, he'll be renting her out to the men with enough money to pay for her, just as he does with the mother." Cuor did not sound quite as drunk. "Oh. Yes. The Alpine flowers do not grow in Venezia."

The man in dark-blue blinked, shocked at hearing the identifying passwords from such a creature as the slovenly behemoth sprawled in the alcove. "But weeds grow everywhere," he said, cautiously offering the counter-sign.

"Drink your wine," said Cuor as he lumbered up from his table and lurched toward the newcomer. "The landlord will notice if you don't." He leaned back against the wall as if overcome with dizziness. "Go on—drink," he muttered as if running out of patience.

The landlord's daughter rushed into the taproom, a basket of fragrant bread still warm from the oven in her thin hands. "My reward?"

"Better give her something," Cuor recommended, muddling his words again.

"What would you recommend?" the man in dark-blue asked sarcastically.

"Papal coins are always welcome," said Cuor.

"More than the Doge's?"

"Occasionally," said Cuor, and tottered out of the taproom, muttering, "I'll return," as he went.

"He's gone to piss," said the child knowingly, holding out her hand.

"Given his condition, I'm not surprised. I only hope his aim isn't completely gone." The man in dark-blue put two Papal coins of darkly tarnished copper into her palm. "There you are."

She inspected them, found them satisfactory, and flounced out of the taproom, returning almost at once with a tub of fresh-churned butter. "For the bread," she said, and left again.

The man in dark-blue, somewhat perplexed, broke off the end of the bread and smeared it with butter, and took a small bite. Discovering that it was delicious, he ate the piece and was buttering a second when Cuor came back into the taproom; he regarded the unkempt man, and after almost a minute of silence, "Are you really working for the Savii agli Ordini?" he asked in hushed amazement; he found it almost impossible to believe such a slovenly drunkard was entrusted with such tasks as he was bringing to him.

At the mention of these powerful cabinet ministers, Cuor raised his hand to his lips. "Best not speak of them. I'm not the only spy in Venezia," he whispered.

"Then you are," marveled the man in dark-blue. "You are the one I have been sent to meet."

"You won't be so surprised when you've been at this a little longer," said Cuor, and motioned to the man to move over to the alcove, where he sat down again, slumping as if too inebriated to remain upright. "It is part of our work not to be noticed."

"I'm hardly a novice: I have already carried out two diplomatic missions to the Pope in Roma," said the man in dark-blue, stung at this implied doubt about his experience.

"With pomp, ceremonies, courtesy, and lies, I'm sure," said Cuor. "Since you're young, you must have powerful relatives, ones who are helping you to make something of yourself. No—don't tell me. I don't want to know." He shook his head. "That's nothing like what men like me do." As he folded his arms, he went on truculently, "You think you have managed to defend the State with your airs and graces, but that is only decoration, a distraction so that the true— Never mind." With a hard-used sigh, he leaned back. "What am I going to call you? No, don't tell me who you are: I don't want to know. I will make a name for you." He looked the younger man over with a thoroughness that was disconcerting.

"As you like," said the man in dark-blue, stiff huffy.

"I think I will call you Camilio—a good, ancient name, known but not common, something not readily remarked upon, or apt to be found everywhere." He repeated it several times, tasting it and trying it out. "Yes," he said at last. "You are Camilio. Don't forget."

The man in dark-blue shrugged. "Camilio it is," he said and went to retrieve his food and drink before he sat down to talk in earnest. He was often astonished at the unofficial servants the government had, and never more so than now. Taking his place opposite Cuor, he said, "I have been charged with bringing you new orders from . . . from our superiors."

"Yes?" Cuor seemed rather bored. "Go on."

Camilio felt nonplussed by this response, but soldiered on. "You are to undertake an observation for them."

"And what would that be?"

Without hesitation, he began, "The Greek merchant Samouel Po-lae, whose house is on the Giudecca, near the Orthodox church, like many of the Greeks: he has made many voyages to the Sultan's lands, and he is now suspected of dealing in Venezian secrets with the Ottoman court, since he prospers far beyond the merits of his trading. Half of his crews are Cypriots, and that, too, lends credibility to this concern." Now that he was dealing with his duty, Camilio felt his confidence returning, and his dissatisfaction began to fade, aided and enhanced by the excellent Toscana wine.

"I know this Samouel Polae. I have made reports on him before," said Cuor. "Has something new been discovered?"

"There is an assumption that he is an enemy of the Repubblica. What else is there to say?" Camilio had more bread and washed it down with wine.

"A great deal," said Cuor. "We have many enemies, and each has his plots against us that we must uncover." He picked up his nearly empty tankard and held it to his mouth; about half the wine spilled onto his clothes, the rest went into his mouth.

"Why do you *do* this?" Camilio cried, shoving his bench back from the table to keep the spatter off his fine garments.

Cuor chuckled, the sound as unpleasant as the rattle of arquebus-fire. "Think a moment, Camilio: how dangerous do I appear? How attentive? A man might say anything within my hearing and consider himself safe. I am clearly too far gone in drink to pay heed to whatever is said around me, or to remember it in an hour, or a day."

"And you *are* drinking. You smell like—"

"A sewer," said Cuor with a look of satisfaction.

"You disguise yourself, in fact," said Camilio.

"Naturally. I would not be useful otherwise, not given my size and shape. A spy is best invisible, which I cannot achieve. Too many men would notice me, and realize I am a formidable opponent, were I to appear capable and alert. I am easily recalled if I seem attentive—but drunk? Not even a man so large as I can be reckoned a threat if he is unable to stand without swaying." He smiled, an expression reminiscent of the perpetual smile of a jackal. "Do not make the mistake of believing the sorry character I present."

"No," said Camilio hastily. "I shall not."

"Very good," said Cuor, and leaned back, only to pull a cup and three dice from his pocket. "Put a coin on the table," he said, shaking the cup.

"Why should I?" Camilio asked. "I'm not here to gamble."

"It is best that it appears you are, so that anyone watching will think you are fleecing me," said Cuor, going on with a determined display of tutelage. "This will make your being in my company make sense. Otherwise, someone might think it odd, and regard us more closely than either would like." He slammed the leather cup onto the table, lifted it, and handed a silver coin to Camilio. "Again. And for a larger sum this time."

"But we're alone. Who will notice if I win or lose?"

"The landlord watches, don't doubt it. Moreover, the midday rest is almost ended; men will be about shortly, and we must present a tableau that seems obvious when they come to this place. So pay attention to the dice and take the coins every time."

Picking up the coin, Camilio leaned forward in the first sign of actual excitement. "Go ahead." He shoved his coin toward Cuor, putting his attention on the roll of the dice as much as on what Cuor said to him.

The dice rattled in the cup as Cuor went on, "I'll check out Polae, and I'll let you know what I discover."

"Be sure you provide as much information as you can, good and bad," Camilio instructed him.

"I am not entirely new to this work," said Cuor, an edge in his plummy voice. "Is there anything else?"

"Well, there is a second man, one to add to those you watch: the foreigner, il Conte Franzicco Ragoczy di Santo-Germano, who has a house on Campo San Luca. They say he walks to the Palazzo dei Dogei from there, preferring the streets to the canals."

"Clearly a foreigner," said Cuor. "What has he done?"

"Nothing obvious, or nothing that seems sinister, but his interests are such that this could well be a disguise, as your appearance is." This last dig made no impression on Cuor, who nodded several times. "Well?"

"I know the man. Elegant sort of man, rich but not given to extravagance. He's got ships, and a press, and the rumor is that he owns a fine collection of jewels. His house is as much a palace as anything on the Gran' Canale." He clapped the cup onto the table, lifted it, and paid Camilio again.

"You won that," said Camilio, hesitating to take the coin.

"We are not playing at dice: you're supposed to be taking advantage of me," hissed Cuor. "Claim the money."

Camilio did as he was told. "I will expect a report from you in a week. Shall we meet here again?"

"No, of course not," said Cuor. "Meet me in one week's time at sundown at San Sylvestro, near the confessionals."

"Mightn't that be a bit . . . late in the day for you?" Camilio hinted delicately. "Your disguise might be too . . . convincing."

"I will be as sober then as I am now, and I am quite in control of my faculties," said Cuor, and slammed down the cup a third time. "Rest assured, I will be there unless I am dead or taken with Plague."

Camilio went white and crossed himself. "It is wrong to say such things."

"What—that I might be killed, or taken ill?" He shook the dice-cup vigorously. "In this line of work, being killed is more likely than not, and the Plague comes from time to time, to cull the herd." The slam was loud, and brought the landlord into the taproom, only to turn away in disgust.

The nearby church of San Cassiano chimed the hour of three, marking the end of the midday rest; in a moment, all the churches of Venezia joined in the clamor until the air shook with the noise.

"It's enough to wake the dead," said Cuor, putting one hand to his ear. "Or to summon Neptune from the depths."

"I hadn't realized how loud those bells are," said Camilio. "I am usually in the Arsenal at this time of day, when I am at home in Venezia." This was a slight exaggeration, meant to impress Cuor.

"Plenty of racket there," said Cuor, and put down the dice again, handing over another coin.

"Not like this," said Camilio. He took the coin and prepared to rise. "I am expected . . . elsewhere."

"Tell your employer that the tasks will be attended to. If there is anything to discover, I will find it. If I find nothing, you may be certain there is nothing to be found." Cuor dropped the dice back in the cup and hid them away in his disheveled garments.

"No doubt, no doubt," Camilio said, trying to decide on how best to take his leave.

Cuor sensed his dilemma and waved him away. "You've had all of my money you're going to get," he complained loudly. "Away with you!"

The handsome young man obeyed with alacrity.

Left alone, Cuor let himself slump again, and began to doze—it was going to be a long night and he would need to be sharp-witted. The sunshine coming through the small, spotted windows was warm enough to ease him into sleep just as the rest of Venezia was waking up.

Camilio walked along the narrow street to the Gran' Canale and signaled for a gondola; this one had been waiting for him, and it swept up to him promptly. "Take me to Piazza San Marco, and don't dawdle," he said to the gondoliere, Iachimo, who had long been in the service of the Doge. "I have an appointment there, and I am expected."

"At once," said Iachimo, accustomed to officious young gallants. He worked his single oar expertly and soon they were passing under the partially rebuilt Rialto Bridge, threading through a complex parade of boats, gondole, and barges; the day was warm when the sun fell full on the crowd, but in shadow, the cold of winter still lingered, needling the air and sapping the warmth of the day. The Gran' Canale was a busy, clamoring place, washed by a rising tide and giving access to smaller canals along its sinuous course, fronted with warehouses and palaces intermixed, that ended in the Bacino di San Marco, where Iachimo pulled out of the stream and to the landing steps of Piazza San Marco. "Here you are, signor'. In as good time as any could have made."

Camilio alighted from the gondola and tossed a copper coin to Iachimo, then slipped through the press and confusion in the piazza toward the Palazzo dei Dogei, taking care to avoid the various officials in the gathering crowd. He looked up at the workmen on the front of the palazzo and reminded himself that eventually the city would not only be restored, it would be more beautiful than before. With that thought uppermost in his mind, he entered the palazzo and made his way through the warren of halls to the office of Christofo Sen, the senior secretary of the Savii agli Ordini; they had recently been retitled Savii da Mar, indicating that the Most Serene Republic was presently at peace, but no one used the new form, not with the Sultan's corsairs hunting Venezian merchant-ships with arrogant impunity. Camilio knocked and waited to be summoned within.

Christofo Sen was a small, angular man with prominent shoulders, knotted fingers, and a wen on his cheek; his clothes were of silk and velvet, dark-amber dogaline-and-doublet edged in gold piping and tuck-lace, his knee-length hose of glossy satin, his leggings of knitted silk. His hair was almost white, but his eyes were a deep, intense blue, and he directed his gaze to Camilio as he entered the outer room of his office. "Well, Leoncio?"

"I have done as you asked, Zio mio: I have met your man, and I will meet with Cuor again in a week. It is all arranged." Leoncio Sen coughed. "He calls me Camilio."

"Just as well," said Christofo. "It won't do to have him learn who you are." He gestured toward a wooden chair. "Sit down and tell me all."

"All?" Leoncio repeated. "To tell you all, I must tell you, Zio, that Basilio Cuor is a most . . . a most unprepossessing individual."

"I have seen him. I know how he presents himself. It would be a mistake to think that he is as incapable as he appears." Christofo Sen continued to stare at his nephew.

After a short time, Leoncio grew uncomfortable under this scrutiny, and he tugged at his narrow lace collar and coughed to conceal his growing disquiet. "I am sure he has been most useful to you. His . . . his performance is most convincing. I believed him on sight."

"You should strive for such accomplishment yourself, Nipote," said his uncle, then drew up a high-backed upholstered chair and stared at Leoncio. "And to accomplish it as cleanly as he does."

"Cleanly?" Leoncio looked astonished.

"Better than extorting money to keep secrets," said Christofo Sen.

"It spares you from having to provide me extra funds." Leoncio's voice was snide.

"Cuor is still more honorable in his calling." His uncle spat in disgust.

"Are you sure he is reliable?" Leoncio could not keep from asking.

"He has proved to be so over the years, which is in itself a sign of merit; not many men get old in his line of work. Make no mistake, Nipote: Basilio Cuor is a very able, very dangerous man."

"He implied as much," said Leoncio.

"He wasn't boasting," said Christofo. "He is subtle and deceptive. Many have been revealed as traitors because of his relentlessness."

"Mightn't he deceive you, as well as another?" Leoncio dared to ask.

"It could be possible, I suppose, but if he has done so, there is no sign of it, and in the world of secrets, such betrayals cannot long be concealed. In the time he has served me, he has proven to be loyal." He pressed his thin lips together while he contemplated Leoncio again. Finally, as if making up his mind, he said, "You have another responsibility being thrust upon you: I want you to seek out Padre Egidio Duradante."

"The courier for Pope Clemente?" Leoncio was surprised.

"Pope Clemente! Ha! That de' Medici bastard! Pope, indeed!

Lackey to the Emperor is more like!" Christofo burst out, then calmed himself. "At least Fiorenzan influence is fading at the Papal Court."

"Clemente was taken prisoner," Leoncio said, clearly thinking this a failing. "He allowed Roma to be sacked."

"The Spanish troops didn't ask his permission," said Christofo, smiling bleakly. "Find Padre Duradante and make him your friend. We need a confidant with the Pope's ear."

"Why should I be the one to speak to Padre Duradante?" Leoncio asked.

"Because he, like you, enjoys gaming, and that will provide a common interest so that your friendship will not be seen as what it is," said Christofo. "I understand that he frequents the Casetta Santa Perpetua. You must know where it is."

"I do, I do," said Leoncio, a bit awkwardly.

"And I assume you are known there?" His uncle watched him expectantly.

"Yes. They know me," Leoncio admitted, and hastened to ask, "How soon do you want me to begin with Padre Duradante?"

"Oh, as soon as possible. If this evening is not spoken for, you might venture there. Now that the weather is improving, evenings are busy again."

"Won't there be trouble? Gamblers can be imprisoned if they—" Leoncio stopped in embarrassment.

"You made the mistake of gambling during Lent, Leoncio. You mustn't be surprised that you were punished for it. You are not so minor a person that no one will report your misdeeds." He cleared his throat. "Now that Easter is past, gambling is thriving once more without hindrance, and Padre Duradante is a great exponent of that skill. You need not lose too much to him. In fact, if possible, do not lose any amount to him." This last was filled with meaning.

"I have thanked you for paying my debts, Zio, and I am serving you now in order to repay your generosity: I am cognizant of my obligations to you, you need not fear." His handsome face was wooden.

"You need not mention that. You were a foolish youth, dragged in over your head by men who prey on such impetuous young men as you were. I trust you have learned to moderate your methods, and your objectives, for if you do not, you will face a most miserable future." He shifted the subject back to the one at hand. "Find Padre Duradante, but don't be obvious about it. Fall in with him, and see what he will let slip in the excitement of the moment. Then try to promote Venezian interests with him. Do not be heavy-handed, for he is alert to such machinations, but do not forget your mission, either."

"I will do what I can, Zio," said Leoncio.

"Yes, you will," said Christofo. "You will not bungle this, you will not over-play your hand, you will not bargain your way out of any predicament you may find yourself in." He reached out and put his hand on Leoncio's wrist. "You are my brother's only son, and for that I will extend myself on your behalf to the limit of my power, and for our blood I will guard your life. But if you compromise me in any way, you will, at the very least, find yourself on a ship bound for the New World, I promise you. Your father concurs, so you need not go to him for protection or advocacy, as he will have neither to provide to you."

Leoncio sat very still. "Do the Savii know what you are doing? Have you told them what you do clandestinely?"

"Of course," said Christofo, taken aback. "Do you think I would abuse their confidence and my office in such a way as to act without their knowledge and permission?"

Brought up short by the harsh question, Leoncio shook his head. "No, Zio, I never thought such a thing. But I had to know, don't you see?"

"I see what your opinion is of me and what I do," said Christofo sharply.

But Leoncio was ready for this reaction and met it with a bland half-smile. "You may not want me to ask such things, but if I am to do your bidding, I have to understand upon what terms I do it." He sat stiffly and refused to look his uncle in the eye; he fought the urge to justify his excesses, although he knew it would be useless. To his deep annoyance, he felt as if he were twelve and not twice that age. "You were the one who taught me to be cautious in such matters, so that I would not become a pawn."

"Do you think you are one now?" Christofo demanded.

"I am afraid I might be," said Leoncio.

For several heartbeats Christofo Sen said nothing, then he made a palms-up gesture of capitulation. "You're right to question me." He got up and went to the window. "I hope for all our sakes that you do not fail in this, Nipote mio, for the Savii and the Minor Consiglio will not entrust you with another diplomatic commission if you cannot show your dependability to their satisfaction, and I will not continue to support a wastrel."

As exhilarating as it was to have the notice of such august personages as the Savii and the vastly consequential Minor Consiglio, a trickle of fear deprived Leoncio of any satisfaction. "I'll do what they expect," he promised.

"Yes. I trust you will," said Christofo, his gaze on the distant walls of the Arsenal.

"I am grateful to you for all you are doing for me," Leoncio added in a conscience-stricken voice.

"Ah, well; you're young yet. In a year or so, if you acquit yourself well, your past indiscretions will be forgotten and your reputation will be wholly restored." There was more hope than certainty in his words, but he maintained a determined optimism as he swung around to regard his nephew. "You're a smart fellow, Leoncio, and you can go far in this work, if only you can keep from succumbing to your weaknesses."

Leoncio nodded. "I understand you, Zio," he said, already planning how he would fulfill his assignment and finally be rid of the blemish that had marred his family's prestige for the last three years.

Christofo smiled at last. "I know, my boy; I know."

Text of a letter from Jaans Marijens in Antwerp to Grav Ragoczy in Venezia, written in German, carried by messenger, and delivered thirty-six days after it was written.

To his Excellency, the Grav Ragoczy of Sant-Germain, currently residing in Venezia at the Campo San Luca, the greetings of Jaans Marijens, scholar of Antwerp and author of the book Traditions and Legends among the Danes and Swedes.

Most well-reputed publisher and master of the Eclipse Press in Bruges and the Eclipse Press for Ancient Studies in Amsterdam, my most sincere good wishes to you, and my hope for the success of your publishing endeavors. It is in that capacity of publisher that I write to you, for I was very much surprised to discover that you are the master of not one but two significant presses, and therefore have far wider opportunities to offer your publications in terms of distribution throughout Europe. I have been informed that copies of your books have been found as far away as Novgorod in the east and the New World in the west, which has emboldened me to write to you.

My first work, cited above, was published in Frankfurt three years ago. With the recent upheaval in that city, many of the presses there were damaged or destroyed during the riots that have been the result of religious turmoil. I suppose you have heard about the damage done in Frankfurt and other cities, so I will not dwell upon it except to offer this as an explanation as to why I should seek another publisher for my next work which is nearly complete: Gods and Goddesses of Early Europe *in which I identify and assess the various ancient monuments found throughout Europe, particularly the avenues and circles of standing stones, and the burial barrows of ancient Kings in all parts of Europe. I have visited many regions for myself and made extensive notes on the ancient sites as well as local tales regarding them. With the current protests being lodged against established religion, I believe there is much to learn from the faiths that prevailed before Salvation was secured for Mankind.*

If you will permit me to send you the manuscript I have been preparing for consideration as a work to be included in your publication program, I would be most willing to bring it to you either in Bruges or in Amsterdam, or to receive you or your representative here in Antwerp. At this time we are still fairly safe from the Church here, and the Emperor has not acted against the printers in the region because of the Protestant presence in the cities. Yet I am reluctant to send such material into stringently Catholic territory, for, as you are doubtless aware, many books of a speculative nature, or which deal with matters not supportive to the Church, are often confiscated and added to the embers. So long as I do not expose my manuscript to such ruination, I will consider it an honor to have your consideration, and I will accord your response the highest respect, no matter what your decision may be.

Jaans Marijens
scholar

By my own hand at Antwerp on this, the 2ⁿᵈ day of April, 1530

3

Looking up from the keyboard of her virginals, Pier-Ariana Salier smiled as her patron came through the door of her music room that occupied half of the floor between the street level and the top floor of her narrow house; it was twilight, the last of sunset fading from the sky in long, glowing streamers, just visible out the narrow windows in the west wall. The gathering darkness softened her features and robbed her red-blond hair of fire, sinking her turquoise eyes in shadows and smudging the arch of her mouth. Even the blue-green of her French square-necked and puffed-sleeved robe d'Italienne was muted, and the fine linen guimpe all but invisible; only her necklace of pearls-and-aquamarines shone, and it gleamed, seizing on the last of the light and giving it form.

Di Santo-Germano returned her smile as he strolled to the chitarrone that hung from pegs on the instrument cabinet and took it down, testing its strings for pitch. "The drones are a little flat," he remarked as he worked the pegs.

"They often are," she said, playing a bit of a plaintive lament she had heard him sing from time to time. She knew the words were by Lorenzo de' Medici—the one the Fiorenzani had called il Magnifico—and that they had special meaning to di Santo-Germano; that struck her as odd, since the Fiorenzan poet-banker and uncle of the reigning Pope Clemente had been dead for nearly forty years, but there were a number of odd things about her patron, as she had come to realize, and this was one of the least perplexing of his many puzzles. She changed to a refrain she was developing for one of her own songs. "I have been trying to find a way to develop the main theme that isn't too obvious, but I haven't found it yet."

One of her four household servants came into the music room carrying a lit fuse-string; he proceeded to touch this to the wicks of the hanging oil-lamps, gradually filling the room with wavering, golden light. Then he bowed and left the two alone, heading for the kitchen and his evening meal of fish soup and bread.

When the chitarrone was in tune, di Santo-Germano began to play on it, not de' Medici's song, but something Pier-Ariana had never heard before, in a mode with which she was not familiar:

"West lies the abode of sunset,
  The place of day's end, and life's;
West lies the realm of nightfall,
Of sleeping, of darkness;
West lies the home of death
Of eternity, of immortality.
      I go westward, homeward bound."

"What a strange song," Pier-Ariana said when di Santo-Germano fell silent. "It's not Italian, is it? You translated it from another tongue, didn't you?"

"Yes; I learned it in Egypt," said di Santo-Germano, and did not add that he had first heard it during the centuries he had served in the Temple of Imhotep, tending the dying.

"Most unusual," she said, wanting to say something. She looked up at him. "You know many songs I've never heard."

"And you invent songs no one but you has ever heard before, a far more remarkable accomplishment than a feat of memory." He began to play the chitarrone again, its long neck and angled peg-box held easily against his shoulder, allowing the drone-strings to hum in sympathy to the chords he summoned from the frets. He began the *Plum Blossom Lament*, which he had learned in China a thousand years ago; its recurring three-note phrases,

"Will you, oh, will you please tell me,
  Little blossoms, where has my lover gone?"

as heartbreaking as any popular ballad of knightly romance.

"I like that. I don't know the mode, do I?" She played out the triad on her virginals.

"It is not precisely a mode. It has only five tones, each a whole step apart; it isn't often heard in the West, but it is everywhere in the East, along with others," he said, and demonstrated it on the chitarrone.

She copied it on the keyboard. "It doesn't seem very versatile," she remarked when she had played it a few times.

"The Chinese don't find it so," said di Santo-Germano. "But it is what they are accustomed to hear, as you are accustomed to modes."

Pier-Ariana's smile widened. "And you offer all you have heard, to enhance my music."

"I offer it for whatever use you may want to make of it, even if it is only to entertain you at the end of a very warm May afternoon." He returned the chitarrone to its wall-pegs and smiled down at her. He was very grand tonight, in dogaline-and-doublet in black damask silk, his dogaline sleeves turned back and fastened with ruby brooches at the shoulder to show the silver-satin lining and his dark-red silken doublet sleeves beneath artfully slashed to reveal his white camisa and its cuffs of short ruffles. On his chest, his pectoral, a black sapphire disk with raised silver wings, depended from a chain of thick silver links. His leggings were black silk, his thick-soled black shoes were ornamented with ruby rosettes, and he carried a sword and a dagger; the appearance he presented was elegantly formidable as well as undoubtedly rich.

"You do more than sing to sustain me," she said, and blushed, her fingers fumbling on the keys.

He bent down and kissed her brow. "And you give me more than music, carina."

Her blush deepened. "Di Santo-Germano . . . Patron mio . . ." She could think of nothing to say, so she ran off several fragments of melodies.

"I saw the proof pages of the book of your songs this morning, before I called upon Consiglier Arcibaldo Tedeschi." He said this as if it had no particular significance, and gave her a soft look when she uttered a squeak of excitement and shot up from her bench.

"How are they? Does it look well? Are the pages correct?" She spoke too rapidly for him to respond.

"They look well," he said as she gave a little bounce. "I saw no errors, but you must examine them yourself, and tell me if they are correct. It is your work and you deserve it to be accurate." He smoothed her hair back from her brow. "Tomorrow, if you want to go to the press, I will arrange for a matron to accompany you."

She nodded twice. "Oh, yes, thank you. I would love to see how it looks. Mille, mille grazie." She wrapped her arms around him, her head on his shoulder. "You are so good to me."

"It will take another two months before the volumes are ready to sell, even if there are only a few changes to be made," he warned her, adding lightly, "By then, you should be used to the notion of your songs being available all through the Repubblica Veneziana."

"And the Papal States?" she asked eagerly.

"If booksellers order the books, then there, or anywhere else, even the New World, in time, and from there, all around the world." He found her enthusiasm touching, and so he added, "Be tranquil. Your work is excellent, Pier-Ariana. It will be well-received."

She frowned at once. "But if it is not, what then?"

"The work speaks for itself. Anyone who dislikes it only shows he has a poor ear and pedestrian taste," said di Santo-Germano. "Do not be daunted by the opinions of others; you haven't been so far. Very few women ever attempt the sort of life you have chosen for yourself. You did not let the disapproval of others stop you before—do not do so now. You will know how well you have been received by how often you hear your songs sung."

Very slowly she nodded. "I suppose you're right," she allowed. "But if you find many who dislike my work, what will you do?"

"I will assume our opinions are different, and our tastes in music," said di Santo-Germano, kissing her lightly on the upper lip.

"You will not become . . . disenchanted?" The anxiety in her eyes wrung his heart.

"No. I may listen to the opinions of others, but I am not easily swayed. Your songs are very moving, and I put my trust in what moves me. Believe this, Pier-Ariana." He held her close until the fear faded from her countenance. "I stand by what I print."

She laughed shakily. "I'm nervous," she admitted.

"Hardly surprising," he said. "But I think there is no reason for it."

"You have to say that," she remarked, her face tense.

"It may seem so, but that isn't the case." He touched her hair again. "You mustn't succumb to doubts now, carina."

"But that is all I have now: doubts, great masses of doubts." Now that she admitted it, she very nearly collapsed. "I don't know what to say to you, di Santo-Germano. You have been stalwart in your support, and I . . . I am afraid you have misplaced your certainty."

"I would not agree, but that—"

She attempted to laugh, backing away from him. "You are truly good to me, and I know how fortunate I am. You have done everything I could possibly ask for, and more. So you mustn't think I am ungrateful, but—"

He interrupted her, keeping his voice steady and gentle so that she would not be dejected by what he said. "Spare me your gratitude. I have done nothing to deserve it. It pleases me to do this for you, and it pleases me to be allowed to publish your songs."

"In fact, you are satisfying yourself by being my patron," she said, amusement and disbelief emerging from her spate of self-castigation.

"Yes, I am," he said simply.

"Why don't you want my gratitude?" She stared at him, deeply curious.

"Because gratitude can be poisonous; it forces you to be beneath me and me to be superior instead of equals. Let us agree that I am fortunate to be rich, and that I am in a position to help you advance your work, to our mutual benefit and satisfaction, but do not be grateful. It erodes all other feelings." He held but his hand to her. "Thank me, if you must, and I will accept your thanks gladly. But do not embrace gratitude."

She stared at him. "I will try," she said.

"Very good," he approved.

"You are a strange man, di Santo-Germano, even for a foreigner. Not that I mind your being strange." She paused to remove the stopper and pour herself a cup of straw-colored wine from a tall glass bottle. "As I recall, you don't drink wine. Do you?"

"No, I do not," he said, watching her drink.

"You are like those who follow Mohammed, then?" She took a sip of the wine and looked at him.

"No, I am not." He saw the question she could not bring herself to ask. "I follow no King and serve no known gods. I have told you this when I offered my patronage."

"You also said you are an exile." She drank again, holding the base of the cup tightly.

"I am," he said. "Which is why one of the Doge's men has summoned me for later this evening."

She shook her head. "That is so sad, being an exile."

"Not sad," he corrected her gently. "I have grown used to it over the years."

"How can anyone grow used to such a state?" she asked, and finished her wine.

"One can accustom oneself to a great many things, given time and reason enough; not all of them need be onerous." He went and sat down at her virginals, starting to play a festive dance melody he had first heard two hundred years ago, before the Black Death came to Provence.

"That's a pleasant tune," said Pier-Ariana, running the tip of her finger around the rim of her cup. "Old-fashioned, but very nice."

"Being old-fashioned isn't a fault," said di Santo-Germano with a faint smile.

"Probably not," said Pier-Ariana. "But it is not a virtue, either." She listened a short while, then said, "You play very well. It is most remarkable to hear a man of rank show such skill."

"You mean men of rank do not practice, or they are too much flattered?" He continued to play, choosing now an anthem from the long-vanished days of Imperial Roma.

"That's a bit self-important. Where did you discover it?"

"It is over-blown, I agree, and self-congratulatory, but there is something charming in its bombast." He continued with the anthem: "Jupiter, the Biggest and Best," which he had first heard in Rome when Julius was Caesar. "It is a fine song, of its type."

"You haven't said where you learned it," she persisted.

"No, I did not," he said cordially. "And that should not surprise you."

She sighed in mild exasperation. "You do exhaust patience, di Santo-Germano."

"It is not my intention to do so," he told her, and finished the Roman song.

She rang for her houseman. "I want a fire built up in here, and another fire started in my bedchamber; have Gabbio attend to the latter," she told him as soon as he arrived. "You may finish your usual duties and then have until the evening cheese is served to your own use."

"Si, Signorina," said Baltassare Fentrin, bowing as if she were of noble birth.

"And ask Lilio to serve the baked fish in the dining room in an hour," Pier-Ariana said. "He said he would need half an hour to cook it."

"Va bene, Signorina," said Baltassare, and went to get the wood for the fire.

"How are they doing for you, your servants?" asked di Santo-Germano when Baltassare had gone.

"Quite well," said Pier-Ariana. "Baltassare knows his work and does it without complaint; I like Lilio's cooking, and Merula is as good a maid and 'tirewoman as any in Venezia. Gabbio is a bit slow, but very reliable for simple tasks."

"Do you need any more staff, or is what you have sufficient?" di Santo-Germano asked.

"I am well-served as I am," she said. "Better than I ever anticipated. The servants do not mock me, or defy me. Most of the time, they are not so busy that they can do nothing more than their work. But it would be useful to have the service of a copyist from time to time."

Di Santo-Germano nodded. "I will keep that in mind."

"I'm not asking for one," she said hastily. "I simply meant . . ." She looked at him, conscience-stricken. "Oh, yes, I was asking for one; if you wish to extend your goodness, do so by hiring me a copyist."

"I will, if you will tell me when you need one."

She nodded, her demeanor suddenly subdued; she took her wine-glass and filled it again. "I want to write another book of songs," she announced with as much bravery as she could muster.

"That delights me," he said, and went to her side. "If you want to do more than that, I will be pleased to see it is made available, and provide a copyist to assist you."

Finishing her wine more quickly than she had intended, she swung around and embraced him. "Oh, thank you, thank you."

He wrapped his arms around her, saying as he did, "No more gratitude, te prego, Pier-Ariana. You have given me joy with your music—"

"And more than music, as you have said," she said archly. "It is always a fine thing to have the devotion of a good man."

This time he tasted the wine in her eager kiss, and he held her as she moved close against him, deliberately pressing as much of her body to his as she was able. He could feel her desire increasing and he was eager to respond, but he held back, aware that she was doing what she thought he required, and—more mundanely—that her evening meal would shortly be ready, so he kissed her a third time and then stepped back, saying, "I am sorry that I have to leave you for a short while, but I will return later, if I would be welcome."

"I would be delighted to receive you, my good Patron," she said, reaching out to take hold of the turned-back sleeves of his dogaline, crushing the glossy silk with her fingers.

There was a hint of sadness in his dark, blue-black eyes. "Then as soon as the Doge's man releases me, I will return to you."

"Does this summons worry you? Have you done anything that would be held against you? Do you think it is possible that you will have to remain there all night?" Now she seemed afraid, as if she thought she might have to lose him to the caprice of the State.

"No; I have to make an official report on the attempt of the corsairs to seize my ship, the *Gilded Angel,* and list what was thrown overboard to divert them from their purpose." He put his hands together as if in prayer. "It is required of all ships' owners."

"Of all Venezian ship owners, perhaps, but you?" Her nervousness was increasing.

"If I refuse, I would be required to live on the Giudecca with all the other foreigners and I would not be allowed to have my press. Under those circumstances, it seems a small price to pay, since it provides me with visits to the Palazzo dei Dogei, and continued privileges granted a resident—except the chance of holding public office."

"You may believe that, but I know that Venezia is a city of illusions. All is reflection in changing water." She put her hand to her mouth and fell silent, as if afraid to say more.

"A clever observation, and one you can enlarge upon—how the water and Venezia are united," said di Santo-Germano. He reached for her hand to kiss it. "For there to be a reflection, there must first be a city."

"Yes," she exclaimed, relieved. "Yes, that is what I meant."

"Of course you did," he said. "No one would think otherwise, especially if you write a song about it." His suggestion was lightly given, but there was purpose in it.

Her face brightened. "Yes. Yes, that's what I'll do. What a good idea."

"It might be wise to begin work on the song shortly. I do not know which of your servants report, nor to whom they report within the government. But we must assume at least one of them does."

"Yet still you come to spend time with me," she said, a bit uneasily.

His smile did not last long. "Oh, men keep mistresses, as everyone knows, and you may be relied upon to keep the interests of Venezia uppermost in your mind, no matter what pleasure we share." He bent his head to kiss her palm, and although the touch of his lips was light, she felt every nuance of it.

"Is it wise to tell me so?" she asked, a catch in her throat.

"Certainly, since we both understand it. What have I said that discredits Venezia?" He released her hand. "If I come to your house much later this evening, will you be willing to receive me?"

"I will always be glad to receive you." Pier-Ariana was truly edgy now. "Though it be midnight or beyond."

"Thank you, carina. I will be delighted to return." Di Santo-Germano turned toward the door. "May you dine well."

"And you?" she asked provocatively. "How will you dine?"

He swung back toward her. "That, carina, will depend upon you."

Text of a letter from Maarten Gerben in Bruges to Grav Germain Ragoczy in care of Franzicco Ragoczy di Santo-Germano in Venezia, written in Flemish, carried by merchant-train, and delivered two months after it was written.

To the most Excellent Grav Germain Ragoczy, the greetings of the printer Mijner Gerben, and the assurance that His Excellency's ongoing program of publication is proceeding along the lines that his instructions require.

Thus far, I rejoice to inform His Excellency, there has been no more difficulty concerning the recent publication of the Reports and Assessments of the Peoples and Treasures of the New World, with Catalogues of Their Weapons and Armor. *The testimony of the Spanish Commander Miguel de Lorimondo has provided the city authorities* with information that corroborates the assertions of the author, and all legal action against him has been withdrawn, although the Church may still instigate a Process against him, making it advisable for him to avoid Catholic countries. His Excellency will need to maintain Girlando Escaltos y Quista in England for at least another two years in order to keep him safe: the author seeks to establish himself at Cambridge, which he prefers to Oxford.

The manuscript of Erneste van Amsteljaxter is in preparation for publication, and I have taken the liberty of enclosing a copy of it with this letter. I believe that the work is all His Excellency hoped it would be. It is most important that His Excellency vouchsafes his permission in a timely manner, for it is most improper for me to go to press without your authorization. I am of the opinion that her work, Lyrics and Tales of the Peasants of Brabant, will find a good reception in many northern cities, although many may disapprove of a woman going about Brabant with only her paternal aunt to protect her, even for the purpose of gathering these legends. For all her aunt is a nun, many do not approve of women traveling unescorted as they have done. Erneste van Amsteljaxter is presently in Antwerp, but has been invited to stay with the distinguished scholar Emile van Loo in Amsterdam for several months.

Ninian Paget's New Theories of the Heavens and the Nature of Clouds has gone into a second printing, and the author has asked to be permitted to amend his work should there be a third printing. I fear that the revisions Paget might make would be extensive, and it is a considerable task to alter vast amounts of text, but I will abide by His Excellency's decision.

Paper has been in short supply, as you know. It is one of the most persistent difficulties of the work we do here. I am certain that some of the trouble I have encountered in obtaining paper is due to the variety of works this press provides; if we were to print only Psalms and Testaments, I doubt we would encounter half the obstructions we have had to deal with.

I look forward to the day when I can discuss this with His Excellency face-to-face, and I hope that at such a time His Excellency will do me the honor of providing solutions to the difficulties that now beset us; it is always possible that the tenor of the times could turn

against the work we do, and the publications this press has produced
for the public.

> *In all duty and humility, I sign myself*
> *His Excellency's most*
> *Truly obedient servant to command,*
> *Mnr. Maarten Gerben*

On the 29th day of April, 1530, at Bruges

4

One of the bargemen was shouting imprecations and curses at the occupants of a private gondola; his energetic invectives carried across the water to the Ca' Fosian, where it rose among the elaborate new palaces on the south side of the Pont' Rialto; workmen labored to complete rebuilding the bridge. May had turned warm, and the brisk breeze was barely sufficient to cut through the midday heat, as penetrating as the furnaces of the glass-makers. The bargeman raised his voice again, calling on San Marco to strike the prosperous merchants in the gondola with lightning.

From his second-floor study window, Orso Fosian watched the workers and wiped his face with his sleeve, then turned to his visitor. "If May is this hot, what will July be?" He expected no answer, and went on, "I wish I could tell you that any of my ships have had any success in evading the corsairs, but they have not." He was almost fifty, still straight and imposing, although he walked slowly due to a painful back, and his face was the texture of old leather from his youth spent at sea. His dogaline-and-doublet were as fine as any in the city, of a dull-plum intertwined-leaf damask lined in a very conservative shade of pewter; the lace edging on his sleeves and collar was from Liege, and the points were accented with seed-pearls. "I have had to spend a fortune to get my sailors back, as have my brothers; the oarsmen must be considered lost to the Turks, may God punish them for their temerity." As one of the six members of the powerful Minor Consiglio, he found his loss particularly galling. He reached for the shutter and slammed it closed, shutting out the clamor and invectives from the canal below, muttering, "No more."

"A heavy burden for any man," said Franzicco Ragoczy di Santo-Germano. "Are you going to put armed men on your ships?" He, too, was handsomely dressed in a dogaline-and-doublet of black silk edged in a narrow band of silver lace and lined in deep-red satin, over a camisa of fine linen from Crete; his leggings and shoes were black, ornamented with small garters with diamond clips, at once restrained and luxurious.

"I haven't made up my mind," Fosian confessed. "It is a dreadful expense, having such guards on the ships, and most soldiers don't like duty at sea, but if they save the cargo and the crew, they are worth every ducat."

"Indeed," said di Santo-Germano.

"I have heard you have hired a company of armed men for your ships," Fosian said, a speculative lift to his thick, white eyebrows.

"For those ships traversing Ottoman waters, yes. If it proves a satisfactory arrangement, then I may put them on all the craft I own; the corsairs are broadening their hunts every month, and my captains are beginning to accept the notion of having soldiers aboard." Di Santo-Germano regarded Fosian narrowly. "What about pilferage here, at the docks and wharves?"

"It is a constant, as you must know for yourself," said Fosian. "A terrible situation, but what can anyone do?"

"Hire guards for the cargos once they're off-loaded," said di Santo-Germano at once. "Give your ships' soldiers something to do ashore beyond whoring and drinking."

"They're apt to be the most light-fingered of all," said Fosian miserably. "But you're right: cargos must be guarded, and emporia, as well, just as we guard the Arsenal. So many things must be protected." He heaved a heavy sigh. "All of which costs money."

"That it does," said di Santo-Germano, and reached into the tooled black-leather wallet that hung from his narrow belt. "Which is why I have brought this with me." He held out a small purse that jingled. "My contribution to the protection of all docks, wharves, and emporia."

Fosian took the purse and untied its knotted thongs, then turned out the contents onto his work-table; he stifled a gasp at what fell out. "Fiorini d'or," he marveled as the golden Florentine coins poured onto the wood. "So much! How many?"

"Seventy," said di Santo-Germano as if this staggering amount was nothing more than a few silver Turkish sequins; he had made the gold in his own athanor in his private laboratory, and used genuine Florentine molds and stamps to cast the precious metal.

"A princely sum," said Fosian, recovering himself enough to scoop up the gleaming trove and slip it into a small drawer in the chest under the table. "I will, naturally, inform I Savii of your contribution."

"And I thank you for that consideration," said di Santo-Germano. "This is a hard time for trading."

"So it is," said Fosian. "I can see the trouble everywhere."

The city was flourishing, and Venezia was rich beyond imagining, but di Santo-Germano knew this made her as much a target as an example to other ports. "The jealousy of rivals is the price of achievement."

Fosian held up one palm to show he was helpless to stop such envy. "This will help us; I know the Minor Consiglio will be grateful." He coughed gently. "Your taxes will not be lessened."

"I realize that," said di Santo-Germano. "That would be possible only if I were a citizen of La Serenissima."

"You could be," Fosian suggested.

"It is impractical, I regret to say," he responded with a slight, self-effacing bow. "As an exile, I fear I would not be able to sustain my obligations to Venezia—"

"—If your exile should end," Fosian finished for him. "I do understand you. And I see your point. Ah, well. If you should change your mind, I would be pleased to speak on your behalf."

Di Santo-Germano spoke quietly. "I am deeply obliged to you, Consiglier Fosian."

Fosian waved this away. "You have no reason for such obligation, not after so lavish a gift as you have provided. I would be a fool not to sponsor such a man as you."

"Nevertheless, I am obliged to you," said di Santo-Germano.

"If you insist," said Fosian, and came up to his guest to touch cheeks with him. "You are a most gracious fellow, Conte, and I thank you on behalf of the Doge and his Consiglii, and Savii."

Di Santo-Germano accepted the courtesy, saying, "I will do myself the honor of calling upon you within the next fortnight. I would like to present you with a copy of my press' latest books."

"Generous *and* perspicacious," approved Fosian. "For if I have copies of the books, how can I protest your publications?" He laughed, and started toward the door. "I am sorry you cannot join us for prandium, but as you have other business to attend to—"

"I thank you for your invitation; I am sorry I must decline. I wish you good appetite, glad companions, and a pleasant repose when the meal is done," said di Santo-Germano, preceding his host through the door. "I have been told you keep an excellent table."

"As any man in my position must, as he must dress and equip himself," said Fosian. "Well, do not trouble yourself. We will dine together another time."

"When it is appropriate," said di Santo-Germano, politely avoiding the necessity of refusing another invitation.

"As you say." They descended the broad staircase to the main floor, and the loggia that fronted on the canal. "Your gondola is here."

"Yes," said di Santo-Germano.

"You do well to keep a gondola of your own. It is safer to do so," said Fosian as he signaled for the boat to approach the loading step.

"Yes; it is," said di Santo-Germano, whose native earth provided the weight of the shallow keel he had had built into the gondola, along with certain other modifications of his own design. He stepped into the craft and bowed slightly to Fosian. "Grazie per tutti, Consiglier Fosian."

"San Marco show you favor," Fosian replied, and waved as the gondola pulled away from his palazzo.

The gondola slid in among the tangle of other gondolas, boats, and barges, the rear oar plying the waters expertly. As they reached the middle of the canal, the gondolier, Milano da Costaga, spoke up, taking care not to be overheard by any other boatmen. "Conte, there is a man following you."

Di Santo-Germano looked around, shading his eyes against the twin glint of sky and water. "Are you certain?"

"I am. I have observed him for the last three days. I believe he is a nephew of one of the Savii, or someone close to them, but I am not sure. A young foppish sort, a bit too good-looking and eager; you know the breed." Milano skillfully avoided a small rowboat filled with loaves of new bread, then swerved around another boat drawn up at the side entrance to a small palazzo.

"Tell me more," said di Santo-Germano.

"I first noticed him three days since. He was on the bridge at San Barnaba, trying to appear disinterested, but I saw him try to keep up with us as we went toward the Bacino di San Marco. Had he not started running, I would have paid no attention to him, but . . ."

When Milano said nothing more, di Santo-Germano asked, "Is that all?"

"No. I observed him outside San Luca yesterday, and this morning I saw him at the Campo San Angelo."

"Venezia is a small place," said di Santo-Germano. "Are you sure he is following me, and not simply moving in places that I move? If he is a relative of one of the Savii, he might be about any number of duties for them."

"I know a man bent on proper business, and one seeking to do harm." Milano steered toward the smaller canal that would lead to the side of di Santo-Germano's elegant house.

"I have no doubt you do," said di Santo-Germano as the gondola slipped up against the marble steps. "You must not think I doubt you, but it may not be as bad as you suspect." He tossed Milano a pair of silver coins. "Keep watch for him, but do not follow him yourself, only notice when you see him about, and in two days tell me what you find."

Milano snatched the coins out of the air. "That I will, Conte."

Di Santo-Germano got carefully out of the gondola, and stepped into the small side loggia of his house; at once Niccola came running, a sealed letter in his hand and a worried expression on his young face as he thrust the envelope forward. "Conte! Conte! This came for you."

As Milano busied himself securing the gondola to the marble pillars in its mooring spot next to the loggia steps, di Santo-Germano reached for the letter, noticing it had an impression of the Ambrogio arms in the wax sealing it. "When did this arrive?"

"Not two hours ago. A servant from the Arsenal brought it," said Niccola, impressed in spite of himself.

"Very good," said di Santo-Germano. "I'll have a look at it shortly."

Disappointed, Niccola took a step back. "Of course, Signor' Conte. But it's important."

"All the more reason to open it in private," said di Santo-Germano, and continued on through his house to the stairs, which he climbed two at a time. As soon as he reached his study, he broke the seal on the letter and read the contents, his frown deepening as he read:

To the most esteemed foreigner, Conte Franzicco Ragoczy di Santo-Germano, the greetings of Romealdo Ambrogio, merchant and clerk to the Collegio.

I am bidden to inform you that the recommendations and designs you have submitted to the Collegio for the improvement of our war-ships is under review. You will be asked to wait upon the Savii of the Collegio within the next ten days. Being that you hold no allegiance to any sovereign or any position that would compromise your situation in Venezia, your Word of Surety is all that is required of you at this time. You are asked to hold yourself in readiness, and to inform the Collegio of any travel you may be undertaking within the next year, along with sworn statements of purpose and destinations of such travel. I am certain you understand the necessity of this.

San Marco and the Adriatic preserve Venezia,
Romealdo Ambrogio

by my own hand, this day, May 10th, 1530 Anno Domini

Di Santo-Germano sat still, tapping the note on his hand. This might explain his being followed, he thought, all the while puzzling over the clerk's note. The Doge often assigned spies to those whose work was closely tied to the interests of the Venezian State, but such men usually had skill enough not to be noticed. His thoughts were interrupted as Ruggier came through the side-door that led to the stairs to di Santo-Germano's alchemical laboratory on the top floor of the house. "There you are. How is it with you, old friend?" he asked as he saw the scowl on Ruggier's face.

"I caught Euchario—"

"The under-steward?" di Santo-Germano interjected.

"The very man," said Ruggier with morose satisfaction. "He was in the stairwell there"—he pointed to the door he had just opened—"and I suspect he had been to the laboratory, although he declared he had not. He claimed he didn't know you had left the house."

"Did he give any reason for his explorations?" di Santo-Germano asked as if he were inquiring about nothing more important than the latest shipment of hides from Tana; he continued to speak in the Venezian dialect.

"He said it was to serve the State, but nothing more than that," said Ruggier in the same tongue. "I have him confined to his room, awaiting your decision about him."

"Ah." Di Santo-Germano glanced at the note he held and put it aside. "Is this the first thing he has done for the State, or has he reported my doings regularly?"

"He did not say," Ruggier told him.

"Well, we may be certain he is not the only spy in this household."

"Yes, we may," Ruggier agreed, clear disapproval on his lean face, and waited for di Santo-Germano to go on.

"Milano tells me I am being followed," di Santo-Germano said remotely. "Is it more of the same, do you think?"

"It may be."

"Did he tell you what he was after?" di Santo-Germano asked.

"I did not press him for an answer, and he volunteered only that he was serving the State, as I mentioned before; he would not say anything more, even when I told him I would demand an official inquiry, before a Judicial Tribunal," Ruggier said, clearly dissatisfied. He took a long breath. "He seems confident that his position is unassailable."

Di Santo-Germano rose and paced toward the window. "Which means it would be folly to dismiss him, for another, possibly more accomplished, would only be sent in his place."

"It is something to consider," said Ruggier.

"How long has he been kept in his quarters?" di Santo-Germano asked.

"An hour or so," said Ruggier. "I put Captain Gozzoli on guard."

"He must be annoyed," said di Santo-Germano; the Captain was his guest in appreciation for the Captain's successful completion of the Galley of Beirut without loss of cargo or crew.

"He is indignant more than annoyed, and his ire is directed at Eucharío. The Captain seems determined to talk to the Collegio to assure them of your worthiness," Ruggier said. "I told him he'd serve you better by making sure Eucharío stays in his room."

"You're probably right," said di Santo-Germano. "The Collegio might not like what they discover about Captain Gozzoli if they inquire too closely about him. The armed men he carries on the *South Wind* are as much corsairs as guards, and their Commander, Sereno Guilherme, is as eager for loot as any Ottomite."

"But Commander Guilherme and his men are *Venezian* corsairs," Ruggier reminded him.

Di Santo-Germano smiled faintly. "That does make a difference."

"The Collegio certainly thinks so," said Ruggier drily. "But Arcangelo Gozzoli would still be a poor advocate, I fear."

"No doubt you're right." Di Santo-Germano turned his back on the window. "Have all the shutters opened. There is a little breeze and it may help to cool the house."

"As you wish," said Ruggier, aware that their discussion was over.

"And tell Captain Gozzoli that I will be down shortly. I want to change into my Hungarian doublet and trunk-hose—they are less imposing than this, and cooler."

"Will you want my assistance?" Ruggier asked.

"Only as I leave my apartments," said di Santo-Germano. "I may not have everything straight."

"I will attend to that when you wish," said Ruggier.

Di Santo-Germano shook his head. "It is occasions like this that makes my lack of reflection inconvenient."

"You manage well, in spite of all," said Ruggier.

"Habit," said di Santo-Germano. "But there is no substitute for your keen eyes."

"Perhaps," Ruggier allowed, and left the study, bound for the lower parts of the house.

Di Santo-Germano set the note from Ambrogio under a leather-bound book on Mediterranean ports, then went out of his study, toward his own apartments on the east side of the house. As he walked, he reviewed what he knew of his servants, making mental notes to be more alert to their various activities. Once in his apartments, he locked the door before unfastening the two brooches that held back the sleeves of his dogaline, then he removed it, next he took off his doublet, then his short, French-style round-hose. Standing in his leggings and camisa, he went to the largest chest—a fine piece of furniture of polished oak that matched the other, smaller chests, and the upholstered chairs—and took out a broad-sleeved Hungarian doublet in black, thick cotton, and black cotton deep-pleated trunk-hose; these he donned, and then took a narrow, Polish-style ruff from an upper drawer of the chest, fixing it around his neck and securing the laces. Last, he removed the diamond clips from his garters and placed them, along with his brooches, in a small case; he carried this into the second room of his apartments, his bedroom, which was Spartan in its simplicity: a single small chest and a narrow bed set atop another chest, with only a single blanket to cover the canvas mattress. A high, narrow window provided what light there was. Di Santo-Germano put the case in the second drawer of the small chest, then left the room, unlocked the door of the outer room, and left his apartments again.

Ruggier met him at the top of the stairs. "You are impeccable," he informed di Santo-Germano after a quick look over his garments.

"Thank you," said di Santo-Germano, adding in the language of Delhi, "Best to keep to the vernacular; too many foreign words, and we become more suspect than before. You and I will have to be especially careful until we know whom among this household is spying on us."

"I understand," said Ruggier in Venezian. "It is a pity that so few still speak the tongue of your people."

"Truly," di Santo-Germano agreed. "But such is the fate of exiles." He went down the stairs behind Ruggier, saying as they neared the bottom step. "Do you remember a Roman called Telemachus Batsho?"

"A decuria, wasn't he?" Ruggier asked.

"Among other things," said di Santo-Germano. "Buckled to his work, was he not." He recalled the endless manipulations of his taxes along with the unrelenting inquiry Batsho had made into his affairs during the chaotic reign of Heliogabalus.

"I can see why he might come to mind," said Ruggier.

"I learned much from that experience," di Santo-Germano said as he stepped onto the main floor. "We will need to be meticulous in our dealings, to avoid any misinterpretations."

"Of course," said Ruggier, adding, "Speaking of dealings, I have sent another donation to Padre Bonnome, as part of your support of San Luca."

"Very good," di Santo-Germano approved, noticing that Niccola was loitering a short distance away.

Ruggier followed di Santo-Germano's gaze, remarking casually, "Will you want to order a feast for our San Mercurius the Hungarian?"

Di Santo-Germano did not so much as blink at the mention of this spurious saint, saying calmly, "You do well to remind me. Yes, indeed. It is wise to observe old traditions. We must set the cooks to planning."

"It is the last day of May, as I recall," said Ruggier.

"Yes. The last day of May," di Santo-Germano assured him, confident that Niccola would spread the news of the Feast of San Mercurius the Hungarian through the household before di Santo-Germano had finished speaking to Euchario, giving the servants something more to concern them than the fate of a single spy.

Text of a letter from James Belfountain of the Black Cross Company to Conte Franzicco Ragoczy di Santo-Germano, written in English, and delivered by courier nine days after it was dispatched.

To His Excellency, the Count Franzicco Ragoczy di Santo-Germano, presently residing at Saint Luke's Square in Venice, the greetings of the Company Commander James Belfountain of the Black Cross Company, along with the information the Count has asked the Company to provide.

The Count has said he wishes to journey to Antwerp, Bruges, and Amsterdam at the end of summer, and has asked for some indication of what the escort of the Black Cross Company would cost. There are three hundred in our Company, and although our numbers are small for war, they are more than is needed for simple escort, particularly since the Count has indicated he will have only three wagons and two dozen horses, as well as four drivers and a farrier accompanying him. For this, no more than twenty men are needed, with horses and remounts for each, and the following figures are predicated on this usage of our numbers: twenty men, forty horses, two guides, and a priest to minister to our souls.

If the weather is good and there is relatively little fighting, you should not have to pay more than twenty gold florins for each se'enight we travel, along with the cost of housing the company at such monasteries, inns, or other accommodations we may need during our travels. This journey should last roughly a fortnight and a se'enight, so your cost would be a total of sixty gold florins. If there is fighting, and we cannot go around it, then the cost would rise to forty gold florins for each se'enight, along with a fee of ten gold florins to each man wounded, and fifty to his family if a man dies.

I have had word with Commander Sereno Guilherme, who assures me that you may be relied upon to abide by your Word and the terms of our contract, so I will not require more than fifty gold florins before we depart, as a deposit on our final payment, and I will not ask that you show proof of having the total sum of our service before we depart for the Lowlands.

We will provide our own horses, tack, weapons, and guides; all other expenses are to be borne by you. If this is satisfactory, please dispatch your acceptance to us at Padua, to Marcello d'Ombrucelli at the Sign of the Blue Bear on Saint Honoria's Square. If I do not hear from you in a fortnight, I will regard that as proof of lack of interest in the terms I have proposed.

> *Your Excellency's to command,*
> *James Belfountain, Commander*
> *The Black Cross Company*

At Padua, the 3rd day of June, AD 1530. By my own hand.

5

With a long belch that sent the barmaid scurrying back toward the counter, Basilio Cuor turned to study Leoncio Sen's smug visage. "And I suppose you think you're doing well?" he asked sarcastically, though his voice was hardly more than a whisper. He looked more uncouth than usual, with large yellowish stains on his camisa from sweat and other, less savory things; his leather doublet was unfastened, its front gaping wide, and his canvas round-hose were badly in need of washing.

"Of course I'm doing well," said Leoncio. "Better than you, in any case." He touched the piping on his doublet, preening with satisfaction.

Cuor shook his head slowly. "If you think that, then you're a greater fool than I suspected, Camilio."

"You don't have to call me that," Leoncio protested. "You know whose nephew I am."

"But it's best if I don't know which nephew," said Cuor, leaning toward Leoncio. "Your uncle calls you Camilio to me."

"Why? Because you insist upon it?" Leoncio was indignant.

"Yes, I do, and you should remember the reason," said Cuor, shooting a glare at the barmaid to keep her a good distance away. "What do you think our work is? We're supposed to be invisible. So what do you do? You actually ran after di Santo-Germano's gondola, not once, or twice, but four times I have seen. And if I have seen you, so have others. You've made him suspicious by being too obvious. What were you thinking? If he hasn't noticed by now, he must be blind, and his gondolier an idiot."

"You're offensive," said Leoncio with as much hauteur as he could muster. "You are dissolute, debauched, dirty, dis—"

"I know I am. I intend to be. It is a pity you're too vain not to cultivate my slovenliness." Cuor took a deep breath. "You have almost ruined all the work I have done. Now di Santo-Germano knows he is being watched, and that makes my task far more difficult than it was. And I, unlike you, have made progress."

"You—work?" Leoncio laughed nastily.

"I have warned you not to assume anything about me," said Cuor, and raised his voice, "I'll have your money shortly; my Word on it."

"What are you doing?" Leoncio hissed.

Cuor's voice was soft again. "I am keeping the barmaid away from us. If our meeting seems ugly, we'll be left alone."

"Who'd listen to a barmaid?" Leoncio chuckled.

"Those whose work it is to listen—men like me; there are more of us than you would guess." Cuor looked directly into Leoncio's face. "Until you made such a botch of your part of our mission, I had worked up a contact with the under-steward at di Santo-Germano's house, but thanks to you, that's come to nothing; I can't get anything more out of him. The Conte has warned his staff against outsiders who are suspicious, and they have taken his warning to heart. Not even a new baker's assistant was welcome at the house this morning. And I— I—was forbidden to enter San Luca by Padre Bonnome when I asked what would usually be ignored questions about di Santo-Germano."

"Surely you don't think it is because of anything I've done?" Leoncio asked, affronted.

"I think it is precisely because of what you've done. No doubt di Santo-Germano would have become aware of something eventually, but your obvious, clumsy pursuit has alerted him much earlier in the game than I had anticipated." He shoved Leoncio's shoulders. "Camilio, you are a difficult fellow," he exclaimed loudly enough to be heard in the tavern kitchen. "Let me buy you a drink. We'll arrange things over some good wine."

"I haven't time enough to waste the day with you." He flung his hand toward the door of the ordinary-looking tavern. "I should be taking prandium with my uncle even now."

"Should you?" said Cuor. "That wasn't what he told me, this morning at Santa Maria Formosa. I met with him after he completed his morning walk along La Merceria. He said nothing about dining with you. In fact, he applauded our meeting at this time, when most of Venezia is at table."

"Do you mean you report to him directly?" Leoncio was shocked, and this time he remembered to keep his voice down.

"I do. Every ten days; oftener, if he sends for me." The shine in his eyes was not from wine, but from malicious glee. "I gather he didn't bother to tell you."

"No," said Leoncio, a cold sensation beginning to form under his belt. "He didn't."

"Well, now you know," Cuor said with satisfaction, then whistled through his teeth. "Bellissima," he called to the barmaid. "Two tankards of your best Sangue di Christi." He held up three silver coins.

From the protection of the counter, the barmaid signaled she would comply, and reached for the double-handled glass tankards that were the pride of Venezia; she reached behind her for the covered pitcher containing their wine.

"Why should I drink with you?" Leoncio muttered.

"Because we must talk, Camilio, and in a tavern, men who talk must also drink if they wish not to be noticed." He paused and looked around at the table on the far side of the room where a group of sailors were devouring large plates of prawns and scallops, drinking as much as they ate; only two other tables were occupied, and the men at both of them were more interested in their food and wine than in any of the others in the tavern. "You and I have to work in concert, not in opposition." He pointed to a table near the hearth. "That's private enough without seeming so."

"More concern for appearances," Leoncio said sullenly.

"You would do well to keep such things in mind," said Cuor as he took the seat with its back to the wall. "I can see everyone who enters, and they will notice you before me." He cleared his throat and spat. "Your uncle tells me that at the end of summer, di Santo-Germano is going to Antwerp and Bruges, or so he has informed the Collegio. He has business there, which the Collegio already knew. He is traveling overland, rather than going in one of his ships; probably afraid of corsairs. He plans to be gone a year, and has appointed Gennaro Emerenzio as his deputy in his absence. He is going to keep his house open and maintain his staff during that time, as well as his press and his patronage of Pier-Ariana Salier. It is clear that he plans to return."

"He told the Collegio all this?" Leoncio asked.

Nodding, Cuor said, "More to the point, his household and the men at his press have confirmed it. One of the Collegio's clerks is going to call up Signorina Salier to find out what she knows of his continuing patronage." He motioned for silence as the barmaid brought the glass tankards. "Mille grazie, madonna," he said as he handed over the three silver coins.

The coins vanished expertly. "My husband says that you're not to cause any trouble."

"If we do, it won't be my fault," said Cuor. "And my companion is too well-mannered to misbehave."

"Da vero?" The barmaid gave a disbelieving snort and returned to the shield of the counter.

Leoncio tasted the wine and found it fairly good. "For a canal-side tavern, this is quite good," he allowed.

"Keep your voice down, or Gezualdo will surely throw us out. He prides himself on his wines."

"Oh, very well," said Leoncio sullenly.

Cuor was not moved by Leoncio's morose demeanor. "Not that I anticipate much useful, but what have you found out about di Santo-Germano in your dogged pursuit?"

Rather than answer the question, Leoncio posed two of his own. "Why does this foreigner merit so much attention? The Collegio, the Minor Consiglio, and the Savii, all probing his every move and choice. Why not have him live on the Giudecca with the other foreigners? Then none of this would be necessary." He glowered at the cold cinders on the hearth. "I shouldn't think his being an exile makes that much difference."

"He is a successful merchant and he has a press, and he has sponsored a number of civic projects. As an exile, you must remember his allegiance cannot be called into question. Not that there aren't foreign merchants living on the Giudecca, but their situation is different," said Cuor. "For one thing, di Santo-Germano has provided the Arsenal with an improvement on the war galleys, and that makes it necessary for him to live on the main islands. It also means that he must be watched." He sighed. "I dislike northern cities, but I am ordered to follow him, and send regular reports back to the Collegio."

"Then why are we talking?" Leoncio asked. "Let the fellow go, and be thankful he's gone."

"Camilio, don't be more of a fool than God made you. The north is a hotbed of Protestantism, and that is dangerous to all who follow the True Faith. You know what has been going on in the German States and among the Swiss." He took a drink of wine and went on. "It is bad enough that the Ottomites have taken so much Christian land for their own, but now, when united faith is needed, the German States of the Holy Roman Empire and the English are coming apart from the True Church with opposition to His Holiness. A man of means, travel-seasoned and with di Santo-Germano's knowledge, would be invaluable to those turning from the Church, to say nothing of what the Ottomites would want with him."

"What nonsense you talk," said Leoncio, and took a long drink of his wine. "What do the Protestants care about Venezian ships?"

"If I talk nonsense, I learned it from your uncle, Camilio. You would do well to keep it in mind. You and I serve the same master." He folded his arms on the table. "So—you have yet to tell me what you have learned."

"His servants are unwilling to speak with me," Leoncio said reluctantly.

"Given your appearance, I should think so," said Cuor, unpleasantly amused. "Were I you, I should try the mistress."

"She won't admit me. I sent her a box of honied rose-hips, but she sent it back with a note saying that she was not a strumpet." He laughed. "As if the fidelity of mistresses were legendary."

"You were foolish to do such a thing," said Cuor.

"Why? She's like any other woman—won over with gifts and sweet words, and with more wiles than a hungry fox. You know what women of her sort are—twice as capricious as any wife. I should think she would welcome my attentions, since her patron's may not always be available to her." He smiled to show his experience in such matters.

Cuor flung up a hand in exasperation. "This isn't some light-skirted whore you're dealing with: this woman is a musician, an artist who has a book to her credit and another to—"

"Her patron has a press," Leoncio dismissed the matter. "It is another kind of gift he gives her."

"You're hopeless, Camilio," said Cuor, and drank most of the wine in his tankard, then raised his hand for more.

Offended at this dismissal, Leoncio tapped the table in irritation. "Va bene," he snapped. "What would you do?"

"Learn some of her music, and know what is thought of it, so you might speak about it intelligently," said Cuor; he had been waiting for such a question. "I would ask to hear her new works, and praise them. I would encourage her to write more."

"Appeal to her vanity," said Leoncio, nodding.

"To her artistry," Cuor corrected. "She is as serious about her tunes as any man who writes them; perhaps more so, there being so few women composing music. Make light of her talents at your peril." He added this with only a slight hope that Leoncio would heed him.

"Yes, yes," said Leoncio, nodding as the barmaid approached with two more glass tankards in her hands. "I may try what you suggest. Once di Santo-Germano leaves, I will have a better opportunity to press my suit with her. She'll be lonely, and a little novelty would likely please her."

Cuor shook his head, sighing. "You had best begin now, so that your motives will seem more genuine. She's not going to be fooled by you if you play the seducer instead of the admirer."

"An excellent idea," said Leoncio unconvincingly. "I'll consider it."

"You had better, or your use to your uncle will diminish. Your gambling priest has not brought the level of intelligence he had hoped, and your debts are mounting again."

This reminder caught Leoncio's full attention. "You know about that? How can you?"

"I must remind you again that I am employed by your uncle, as you are, and I have proven my worth many times over, earning his confidence. He knows he may rely upon my discretion so he tells me many things, and I have learned many more." He took a drink of the second tankard of Sangue di Christi. "Ah. A different bottle. This is an improvement."

"An appreciation of your custom," said Leoncio, making no apology for the slight.

"Well-earned, if true," said Cuor, refusing to be insulted. He put his hand flat on the table. "Now listen to me, Camilio: you must begin to show that you are capable of doing this work, or your uncle will not support you. For your own good, make yourself known to Pier-Ariana Salier, and do it soon, and without compromising her, for if she breaks off with di Santo-Germano, her worth to you is lost, and that would not redound to your credit."

"I will keep all you say in mind," Leoncio mumbled. He wanted to leave the tavern and join his uncle and the rest of the family for prandium, as he had planned to do, but he was increasingly wary of breaking in on the meal for fear of earning a rebuke in front of all the family.

"Do so. And remember that while I am gone, you will have another man appointed to deal with you." He drank eagerly.

"Why not simply my uncle?" Leoncio asked, peeved at this slight.

"Because he must be able to select what he knows and from what source he knows it," said Cuor with the extreme patience of one dealing with a fool. "If you tell him directly, then he must admit it."

"That is a risky game, I think," said Leoncio. "All this hidden attention on foreigners."

"The Greek merchant hasn't provided much of use, has he? He is what he presents himself to be: a merchant of the Eastern Rite, and an honorable resident of Venezia, one who is here to do business and nothing more. Have you discovered anything to the contrary, Camilio?" Cuor asked with exaggerated sympathy. "I have learned very little to Samouel Polae's discredit, and unless you have uncovered something dangerous in his dealings, I think you need only concentrate on Pier-Ariana Salier and di Santo-Germano's business arrangements while I am away."

Leoncio thought of his appointment with Padre Egidio Duradante later that afternoon at Casetta Santa Perpetua, and determined to learn something useful from the Pope's man, if only to show his uncle and this unkempt hulk that he, Leoncio Sen, was the more capable of the two of them. "I can speak to di Santo-Germano's appointed deputy; he is likely to have a great deal of information."

"No doubt. And he is also used to having men attempt to learn his employers' business," said Cuor with real dubiety.

"Gennaro Emerenzio likes games of chance as well as the next man. I have met him in one or two of the Casette where men may indulge their fancies for many things, gaming and drinking being only the most obvious pleasures." He smiled with a fine cynical air. "After wine and dice, when the blood is running high, a man sometimes guards his tongue less than he should."

"And sometimes his ears are less open than they ought to be," Cuor added. "It won't serve anyone's purpose if you cannot remember all you hear."

"I know what I have to do," Leoncio declared huffily. "You will see, reprobate that you are, that a man need not lose all his demeanor and good conduct to serve the Doge and Venezia."

"Your uncle will be pleased," said Cuor, and shoved himself to his feet. "I will speak to you again in three days, at noon at I Frari. Be sure to be there." He wagged his finger at Leoncio. "Camilio, I depend upon you," he declared, sounding a good deal more drunk than he was.

"Three days at I Frari, at noon," said Leoncio dutifully. "I will be there."

"See you bring what you owe me," Cuor persisted. "I will not countenance delays in—"

"I will, I will," Leoncio promised and saw that the barmaid was watching them with more attention than they merited. "I will not cheat you."

"You had better not," Cuor blustered, shoving out of the niche and trundling toward the door. Once in the street his stride became brisker, and he moved off through the general confusion toward La Merceria, and beyond it toward San Zaccaria and the small, neat house where Pier-Ariana Salier lived. He made his way around the side of the building and knocked on the kitchen door, calling out as he did, "Baltassare Fentrin! Baltassare Fentrin! Eccomi—Basilio Cuor come to pay you the three ducats I owe you. Open the door, Baltassare, te prego."

Just as Cuor expected, the kitchen door opened slowly and Pier-Ariana's steward poked his head out. "Oh. You."

"I said I would have your winnings to you before sundown," Cuor said as if he were used to being disbelieved.

"So you did, so you did," Baltassare said, opening the door enough to admit Cuor, but far from displaying any geniality. "You come just as we begin our prandium."

"An intentional ploy," Cuor admitted, a bit too eagerly. "I thought I would find you in, and not so busy that you would not see me." He handed three ducats to Baltassare as they made their way down the narrow corridor to the kitchen.

"You came in the hope of dining here," said Baltassare with a sigh. "I suppose we can feed you."

"Most kind," Cuor muttered.

"As you say," Baltassare responded.

"Tell me," said Cuor as if struggling to make conversation, "are you allowed much time for yourself, or is the household demanding? You said you have only a single woman to serve—does she demand much of you?"

Baltassare shrugged. "She is usually busy with her instruments and pens, so much of the day-to-day running is in our hands. We have our appointed tasks, but our mistress does not demand we do them at any particular time." He pointed to the three men and one woman gathered around the table against the wall on the far side of the kitchen; the woman sat a little apart from the others, as her status and her gender required. The men clustered at the end of the table nearest the open hearth. "Lilio, Gabbio, this is Basilio Cuor; Merula"—he nodded to the woman at the table—"Basilio Cuor."

"A pleasure," said Cuor with a forced gallantry that earned him a disbelieving chuckle.

"He owed me money," said Baltassare. "And paid it in less than a day."

"As any man should," said Merula. "It is to your credit." She indicated a place next to her. "You may sit here, if it suits you."

"I thank you profusely," said Cuor with an unsteady bow to her. "You know how to behave in a respectable house. It is apparent that you have learned from most admirable tuition."

Gabbio looked from Lilio to Baltassare as if to try to decide how he should behave. Finally he reached for a glass and filled it with trebbiano, then held it out to Cuor as if attempting to make peace.

Merula's somber face wreathed in smiles. "Indeed, yes. I had the honor of serving in the household of the Doge's son-in-law when I was trained."

Cuor, who had learned this weeks ago, pretended surprise; taking the glass from Gabbio, he said to Merula, "How fortunate for Signorina Salier, to have so worthy a personal servant as you."

Color mounted in Merula's face. "It is not for me to say."

"No; you are too gracious," said Cuor as he sat down. He looked at the others at table. "I do not mean to intrude, but it is most pleasant to pass this time in a well-ordered household instead of a tavern. I thank you most earnestly."

Merula actually simpered. "And you must have learned your manners in a higher station than we see you now."

"Alas, yes," said Cuor, allowing Lilio to bring him a bowl of sweetbreads and crab in a creamy sauce made fragrant by garlic and herbs. "My family had three ships when I was a boy, and . . . and a favorable seat in the Maggior Consiglio. Within a year two of them were taken by corsairs. That was the ruin of our fortunes; my father fled, making his disgrace complete." It was a fairly accurate story, and one most Veneziani would hear with sympathy; it would be likely to unguard the tongues of these servants.

"The Ottomites are shameless," said Lilio, passing a loaf of bread.

"That they are, and to our woe," said Cuor, accepting the bread and breaking off a hunk of it. "This is very fresh, by the smell of it."

"Made this morning," said Lilio, his stiffness beginning to fade.

"Very fine," Cuor approved as he dipped a bit of it into the thick sauce.

"Our mistress' keeper has lost ships to Ottomites," said Merula, and ignored the sharp look Baltassare shot her.

"Ah, it is ever more the case," said Cuor as he chewed.

"It isn't our place to talk about the Conte," said Baltassare with a hauteur worthy of the very highest stewards.

"I don't see why not," said Lilio. "His fortunes are our fortunes, after all. If he loses all, so does our mistress, and so do we." He put his elbows on the table. "It isn't as if we haven't talked about this."

"Among ourselves," said Baltassare sharply. "It is nothing to speak of in front of outsiders."

"He's a Venezian," said Lilio. "Hardly an outsider."

Merula put her hand on the table. "Peace, you two. This man is our guest, and it is our duty to treat him as handsomely as we may."

"Because he pays you compliments," said Baltassare. "He's a gamester and who knows what else."

"His family's misfortune haunts him," said Merula. "Who among us would not have to live precariously if anything befell our mistress?"

This sobering question silenced the discord; after a short silence, Lilio said, "It may be difficult while di Santo-Germano is in the north."

"Ah. He goes to Udine," said Cuor, having a little of his wine.

"No, much farther—to the Lowlands," said Baltassare. "For a year."

The servants exchanged single nods of significance, and Merula said, "He is returning, but he will be away for a year."

Cuor nodded. "That may be inconvenient for all of you."

"It isn't money," said Lilio quickly. "The Conte is a very wealthy man, and he has provided for this household in his absence, very handsomely. We have no concerns on that head. But there may be trouble if any of his ships are seized or he is unable to return as he planned."

Baltassare sighed. "We're told provisions are in place, but who can say?"

"He may not wish to continue as our mistress' patron," said Merula, expressing their deepest fears. "Who knows what disposition he may make, if that happens?"

The three men nodded slowly; Cuor had a little more wine. "A bad business, no matter how it ends."

"The Conte says that he wishes to publish her music, but he says it as a man who supports her and who shares her bed," said Baltassare heavily. "But if he no longer wants her flesh, what will he expect of her music?"

"He has presented her with deeds and grants," said Merula.

"Which he may rescind at any time," Baltassare reminded them all. "The Collegio will not enforce any woman's claim against her keeper."

"Can you imagine what a nest of intrigue the courts would be if the Collegio did allow such claims?" Lilio asked, and laughed harshly. "No other cases could be heard."

When the laughter had died down, Cuor said, as if it had just occurred to him, "Is there anyone else who might become her patron, or keep her?"

Merula shook her head. "I don't think so. She's not one to try such measures. I think she would make herself a nun to her music."

"A strange thing for a young woman to do," said Cuor, thinking that Camilio's task was likely to be more difficult than either of them had conjectured.

"A pity she comes from ordinary folk," said Lilio, preparing to offer second helpings of his excellent meal. "It leaves her open to so many troubles."

"Troubles may happen to any of us," said Cuor, and held out his bowl for a second helping.

Text of a letter from Atta Olivia Clemens at Nepete, north of Roma on the Via Cassia, to Franzicco Ragoczy di Santo-Germano in Venezia, written in Imperial Latin, carried by general messenger and delivered fourteen days after it was written.

To the Conte di Santo-Germano, Franzicco Ragoczy, at the Campo San Luca in Venezia, the greetings of the Roman widow, Atta Olivia Clemens, at Nepete for the summer, and perhaps into the autumn as well, unless matters in Roma improve.

Before you begin your northern journey, I thought I should send word to you of my present whereabouts, in case you should have reason to contact me in the months ahead. I am at my small stud farm here at the lake; you will remember it from your visit six centuries ago, although the house has been rebuilt twice since then. Niklos Aulirios is with me, but goes monthly to Roma to supervise my properties there, including my house in the city as well as Senza Pari, beyond the walls, and, incidentally, to keep watch over the Villa Ragoczy, which is being given a new roof, which it very much needs, even as I write this. I expect Niklos to return in four days; if he has a report for you, I will authorize him to use my messenger to carry it to you, but you may rest assured that he has taken good care of your property.

As always, I am puzzled why one of our blood would choose to live in Venezia, of all cities, amid all that water, the tides constantly in motion. It must be disconcerting at the least. But you have done so in the past, and will probably do so again, so you need not answer my question unless you have some reason I am unaware of. I find that living next to a lake, as I do here, is not nearly so uncomfortable as being near a river or on the ocean, where the water is forever moving, and rest is difficult even lying on your native earth. Certainly many of your shipping businesses require you from time to time to live in a port city, and Venezia is unquestionably that, but I cannot help but think that you must have daily inconvenience brought about by the enervation of running water, to say nothing of the sunlight.

You have said you are seeking a quiet life, and that may be, but it strikes me as odd that you are attempting to find it at Venezia, or in the turbulence of the north, for that matter, since you are bound thither when summer is gone. Not that there is much quiet anywhere, these days. Since Roma was sacked, the whole of Europe has been in a frangible state, and I doubt it will improve in the next decade, or century. Upheavals always take so much longer than anyone thinks they will—except perhaps for us and those like us, who have such long lives. I am content for now to remain here at the lake where I may tend my horses and enjoy the company of Dionigi Eso, who is a most promising young scholar to whom I have extended my protection, and who is willing to remain with me here for a year or two, exploring the past and other, more personal matters.

The horses I raise at this stud farm are beginning to flourish again; you may recall that half the herd was plundered four years ago by Spanish soldiers, the last time the house was burned. They were their own company, mercenaries, in fact, not immediately under the Crown—an excuse that has made it impossible for me to claim any damages for their theft and destruction—and so had no fear of superior authority. Carlos may be a reasonable and tolerant man in the eastern part of his empire, but he is ferocious in Spain and all Spain commands. Luckily, Eliseo, my farrier, escaped into the hills with six of my studs and a dozen of my best mares, so all was not completely lost. I have rewarded Eliseo with two foals to be his own, and the horses as well as their get to pass to his heirs, which should prove a worthwhile legacy in time.

And speaking of time, I hope you are not still morose over the True Death of Demetrice Volandrai. It is never easy to lose one who comes to your life—the Blood Bond is more than a contract, is it not?—but she admitted that she was unable to live as we must, and certainly a swift end is preferable to slow, unending starvation and madness. She has been truly dead for roughly three decades; surely you can accept the distance time imposes, for you were the one who taught me to acquiesce in the passage of time. Must I now remind you of your own lesson?

You tell me that your musician is proving an understanding mistress, which I hope is the case. Then you tell me that you have only visited her knowingly three times, and that all your other visits have been in her sleep, to mingle with her dreams. This way you seek to avoid having to bring her to our life at the end of hers, and may be an act of probity as you see it, but she may prefer to have you knowingly, and to decide for herself if she wants to come to your life; you are imposing your will on hers: why is that? You have not permitted her to make a choice, and that seems unlike you. If you are afraid of losing her, then let her know the risks of your love, so that she may make up her own mind. To do otherwise cheats both you and Pier-Ariana (you see? I do remember her name).

I have the books you sent me, and very handsome they are. I particularly liked your volume on healing herbs and roots. That will be put to good use. But the other five are not so compelling, my interests not being concerned with folk tales or travels, and my musical skills

*are limited, as you are well-aware; I leave the music to you, my most
dear friend. Still, I know these works are useful in many ways, and
when the winter comes, and Dionigi is occupied with his studies, I
may yet be glad of something to read.*

*This comes with my heartfelt concerns on your behalf, as well
as my*

> *Eternal love,*
> *Olivia*

by my own hand on the 16th day of June, 1530 Anno Domini

6

Pier-Ariana put down her psaltry and rounded on di Santo-Germano.
"What do you mean, you may have to be away *more* than a year? Are
you going to return at all?" Her small music room was glistening in
the shine of dozens of hanging oil-lamps, their soft light suffusing the
room with a pale-golden glow; the church-bells had chimed nine a
short while ago, and night was settling in over Venezia, a thin, low-
lying mist rising from the canals into the warm, damp evening.

"I am not planning to be gone so long, yet it may be that I will: it
is not what I want, carina, but it is something I must consider." He set
down the portfolio of her new motets and songs, and regarded her
steadily, his black dogaline-and-doublet making him a shadow in the
refulgent illumination. "This will be published, you need not fear.
Giovanni has the paper ordered already, and he will begin work on
the book as soon as you deliver the last of your compositions. He tells
me that the first book is doing very well, and says he believes the second will do better." His dark eyes held hers. "I gave you my Word that
you would not suffer for my absence, and as far as I am able, I will see
to it that you do not."

She hesitated, but there was no lessening of her indignation. "You
said you did not have to be away so long."

"And I assumed I did not," he responded in a practical tone. "But matters have become more complicated, and I fear I must set aside the time to deal with them. Had I been in Antwerp or Bruges and you, here in Venezia, encountered more complex difficulties than first anticipated, you would rightly expect me to allocate more time to your situation than I had at first, would you not." He held out his hand to her. "My two presses have been the subject of investigations—the one in Amsterdam may well be next—and I need to be present to disentangle the Gordian Knot that has resulted from the inquiries. I apologize for putting you in such an awkward position."

"How do you know this is true?" Pier-Ariana pursued, ignoring the last.

"I know it is true because I have received an official writ of inter-rogation this morning from certain officials in Antwerp who inform me that my presses have been singled out for full examination, not only for political lapses, but religious ones as well, for which reason they are submitting a number of questions to me that I am to answer under oath before a sworn official, and return to them as soon as pos-sible. I have spoken to one of the Doge's Savii to perform this ser-vice, so that the officials in the north cannot argue that I have defied them. If I fail to do this, my presses and all they produce will be con-fiscated and burned, and all my property seized, and my associates will become exiles, which they do not deserve." He shook his head once. "So it is out of my hands, and I must present myself in Antwerp before the end of the year. I cannot leave my pressmen and servants to answer for my policies at the risk of their lives. It would dishonor them and me if I did."

"Was that why you planned to go there in the first place—did you think something was wrong? Or did you want an excuse to be away from Venezia?" Although she had been making an effort to contain herself, she started to weep silently, tears sliding unheeded down her face.

"I was hoping to address the matter before it became—as you put it—wrong, but I seem to have miscalculated." He had to concentrate to keep from recalling the times in the past when similar errors had cost him dearly; Pier-Ariana needed his full attention.

"So you will not make any more binding plan than that you will be gone for more than a year?" She flung this at him in an emotion be-tween fury and despair. "You could be gone much longer."

"Until I understand what the actual circumstances are, I cannot pledge myself more rigidly than this: that if I must be away longer than a year, I shall inform you of it, and I will do my utmost to return as quickly as possible," he said, lightly touching her shoulder before sliding his hand down her back to her waist, supporting her without confining her. "You deserve more of me, I know, and were I better informed, I would—"

She cast herself onto his chest, her voice cracking as she gave way to crying. "Why? Why must you go? It's hard enough for me with you here; my work is thought odd, but no one disparages me, not while I have such a patron as you. No one tries to stop me from doing my work. If you are gone, what will become of me?"

"You will go on as you have—you will compose and Giovanni will take your compositions and compile them into books. You will live here with your servants, and my business factor, Gennaro Emerenzio—you know him—will tend to your expenses, just as he would do if I were here." He drew her close, making no effort to cajole her from her weeping. "Pier-Ariana, I will miss you every day I am gone."

"But it will not be enough to bring you back in less than a year," she lamented.

"I will return as soon as I may," he said, his voice dropping to a deep, mellifluous note.

"So you say now. But men are faithless creatures." She shoved herself away from him, pinching the bridge of her nose to stop the flow of her tears.

"But, as you know, I am not like other men," he said.

"You, more than most, will not remain faithful; it isn't in your nature," she accused. "I know you, and what you need. You will have other women. You must."

"But I will not compromise you," he said. Five hundred years ago he might have tried to approach her, to reassure her, but after Huegenet and Demetrice, he knew better than to attempt to persuade Pier-Ariana to change her mind; he decided to offer her the only truthful pledge he could. "My feeling for you will not lessen because I have feelings for another: believe this."

"So you tell me," she exclaimed. "Gran' Dio, I hate this! I might as well be a hapless trull, serving men's pleasure for a chance to eat." She sat down on an upholstered stool. "It isn't really like that. You're not using me unkindly; I know that. Most women would thank the Saints and Angels day and night for such a protector as you are, as I do, when I see what happens to others. And it isn't as if you've promised me anything beyond—"

"—beyond what we have now," he said calmly. "Nor did you ask it."

"And I wouldn't want it, for it would take away from my music," she said, sounding defeated. "But this is different, isn't it?"

"It is something you have not had to endure with me. I have been in Venezia for all our association." He took a step nearer to her.

"Antwerp and Bruges, and Amsterdam are all far away," she said, and sighed. "Even an urgent message, carried by private couriers, would take at least ten days to reach Venezia from there."

"There are farther places," said di Santo-Germano, thinking back to China, to Russia, to the destruction of Delhi. "I have returned from them all."

She made a mess of trying to laugh. "I should be grateful, then, that you go only as far as the Low Countries?" The shine of perspiration on her upper lip glistened in the lamp-light. "Or that you have left me so well-provided for? You say you do not want my gratitude, but you do all in your power to deserve it, in spite of your going away. You will not change your mind, will you?"

"No, but you can take some comfort that I am not cut off from you by oceans or deserts or mountains." He held out his hands to her as he had done earlier. "I will not put you at a disadvantage, carina, whether here or far away."

"But you will not put others at a disadvantage, either, will you?" Her chin came up and she glared at him through the shine in her eyes.

Di Santo-Germano took a long breath. "What sort of man would I be if I abjured my covenant with others?"

"You tell me you are not a man at all, not a living one, anyway," she said in sudden world-weariness.

He regarded her steadily. "All the more reason for me to uphold—"

"What does it matter?" She dropped her head. "You will do what you will do."

He stood still, her pain as palpable to him as a blow would be.

"They are in danger on my account. I cannot abandon them; as I would not abandon you." He spoke gently, his enigmatic gaze fixed on her.

"So you will go north," she said.

"At the end of summer. That still gives us seven weeks in which to arrange all that you require during my absence."

"Seven weeks," she said as if the words could conjure power for her. "Seven weeks."

"Yes." He dropped down on one knee beside her. "You and I will devote our time to guarding you from harm."

She bit her lower lip so that it would not tremble. "You are not going to change your mind, are you? You will go to Antwerp, won't you?"

"Yes, I will—unless there is a change in the state of affairs in the Low Countries, which hardly seems likely." He took her hand and kissed her palm to punctuate each of his promises. "But I will not forsake you. I will not be gone any longer than I must be. I will not leave you without means to live; that would be a most reprehensible imposition upon you. I will arrange matters so that you will be able to manage for yourself in my absence. I will make sure there is an official record of these provisions."

"I am most grateful," she said very deliberately, and turned her hand to enclose his. "I do not ask you to forget the others, but I do not want you to forget me, either. Without you, I have no one to turn to."

"I could not forget you, carina, not ever," he said gently, his touch as persuasive as his voice. "You are part of me."

She let go of his hand and wrapped her arms around his neck. "I wish I understood that."

"Whether or not you understand, it is true," he told her, rising and lifting her to her feet as he did. "Pier-Ariana, listen to me: you are dear to me, and will always be dear to me, from now until I am truly dead. I will not leave you to flounder, nor will I take away anything I have bestowed upon you; I have given you my Word upon it. This house is yours no matter what may happen. Giovanni will print your music as long as you care to compose it and write it down. With or without me, you will not find yourself hapless in the world." He touched her face, his fingers light and lingering. "You must not fear that you will lose anything while I am gone."

"I will lose *you*," she said, her embrace tightening. "Without you, the rest is chaff."

"You would not think so if it were taken from you," he said somberly. "I do not want you to have to accommodate other demands."

"Do you think so little of me?" She released him again. "That I seek only your support?" Before he could speak, she continued. "Of course you do. What rich man does not think such things of his mistress?"

"I do not think you accept me only for my money, or my press, and if all I wanted was a compliant female body, there are courtesans in plenty in Venezia. No, Pier-Ariana: I value you and your gifts, and I know that if you were reduced to singing in brothels, no one would remember your songs."

"Perhaps I should go on the stage, as some women have done already?" She cocked her head, being intentionally provocative.

"If that would suit you, then do as you must; it will not change my regard. It pleases me to let the world know your music." He said it bluntly, and held her while she thought out what he said. "Your songs are as dear to me as your kisses."

Pier-Ariana sighed and rested her head on his shoulder, and did her best to keep skepticism from her remark. "No doubt you're genuine in what you tell me."

"It is a matter of worth," he said, kindness making his words tender. "You have so much to offer, and I would not want to be bereft of any of it."

She tried to laugh but it caught in her throat and she began to weep again. "I apologize for—"

"For what?" he asked, and kissed her forehead.

She wiped her face with the back of her hand. "For this."

"It does not trouble me," he said. "Your talent makes you more responsive to all around you."

"I feel I am a puppet of my emotions," she muttered, her body becoming tense although she remained in his arms.

"At least you perceive these things, and you know the strength of your emotions. Most around you are equally susceptible but will not acknowledge it, or turn it to use." He waited a long moment, then added, "You have no reason to be disconcerted with me, not for this, or for anything."

"And you, are you never taken in passion?" she asked.

"*You* ask this of me?" He smiled his amusement.

"I didn't mean that." She averted her face briefly. "I meant all the rest of it."

He offered her a serious answer. "Those who seek revelation in art are creatures of passion, and display their passion in many ways."

"You accept my volatility as part of my music?" She kissed his cheek lightly. "I suppose I should be grateful for that."

"I have told you how I view gratitude," he said, and took her face in his hands, turning her head so that their eyes held. "I take you as Pier-Ariana, and all that that entails."

She studied his face. "I wish I didn't have so many uncertainties."

"And I," he admitted. "But you do, and I comprehend many of them." He stepped back as Baltassare came into the room carrying a platter of broiled sardines and a glass carafe of pale wine.

"If you would, put those down on that table." She pointed to one of two pillar-tables with round marble tops.

Baltassare did as she told him, saying, "The kitchen fires are banked for the night and all but the front door have been bolted. Do you require anything more, or will this suffice for the night?"

"You may all retire," said Pier-Ariana.

"Sta bene, Signorina," said Baltassare, and left them alone.

"He listens at doors," Pier-Ariana confided when they were alone again.

"That is not surprising," said di Santo-Germano. "I would be more troubled if he did not."

She blinked and stared at him. "What do you mean?"

"He can report nothing to your discredit if he listens at doors, not without lying," said di Santo-Germano, raising his voice enough to have it carry. "And anything put in a Lion's Mouth must be signed or it is ignored." These imposing information-boxes were posted in various places in the city, for the benefit of the Collegio and the two Consiglii.

"At least so they claim," said Pier-Ariana. "Besides, of my servants, only Baltassare reads and writes, though not very well. He could not make an accusation that anyone would regard with attention."

"You would have to do worse things than write music for either of the Consiglii to consider you a danger." Di Santo-Germano touched her arm. "The Minor Consiglio has already investigated me, so it is unlikely that they would proceed against you, no matter what your servants might say."

"I pray you are right," she said, and went to eat a few of the broiled sardines. She washed them down with a glass of the straw-colored wine. "I do not know what I would do if I had to leave Venezia."

"You have no reason to think you might have to, not on my account," said di Santo-Germano, hoping it was true. "But if it should come to that, I have ships that can take you to any port you desire."

"But I desire no other port than this one," she exclaimed. "I speak only the Venetian tongue and enough Latin to satisfy the priests. Where could I go that I would not have to . . . to sing in a brothel?" She chose his phrase carefully.

"I will make arrangements for you, if you are worried." He thought while she poured herself more wine. "I have an old associate who would probably be willing to help you. I will contact her and see what she suggests."

"When you say old what do you mean?" Pier-Ariana stared hard at him.

"I mean that she has known me for a very long time," said di Santo-Germano. "A very long time."

"Capizolo," she said in the Venetian dialect, nodding decisively.

"It is a good thing you understand," he responded. "I will tell you more once I have her answer. Then you can make arrangements that suit you, and my old friend as well." He decided to send word to Olivia in the morning; a courier could be hired to carry his letter to her estate at Nepete on the Via Cassia, and get a reply in return in twelve days.

Pier-Ariana ate another sardine and stared at the nearest oil-lamp. "I hope it will not come to that."

"I truly doubt that it will," said di Santo-Germano, and busied himself latching the shutters over the windows. "A pity to have to close up the house on such a warm night, but—"

She nodded. "But thieves are everywhere and an open window is an invitation to steal."

He looked around the room. "You would not like to lose any of your instruments."

"Or have them broken," she said, and took a step toward him. "I have been a trial tonight, haven't I? I ask your pardon for my excesses."

"You have done nothing deserving pardon, Pier-Ariana; you have expressed your affection and concern for me: what can I be but flattered?" He offered her a quick smile.

"With worries for myself larded on," she said self-effacingly. "For that alone, then, I ask your pardon."

"If you must have it, then know that you do, though there is no need," he said, and opened his arms to her, enfolding her as she reached him.

"You are so elusive, Conte. You are at once the most generous lover and the most equivocal." She turned in his arms, but only to be able to kiss his lips more easily; the remnants of sardines gave them a fishy savor. As she broke their kiss, she said a bit unsteadily, "I was afraid that you were tired of me, or had come to dislike my work."

"Why should I?" he asked, kissing the corner of her mouth.

"Because I am a turbulent woman—or so my father told me I would be," she said, fingering the narrow ruff of pleated lace along the edge of his camisa's neck.

"Fathers often worry that their daughters may not be the perfected creatures they expect, and their fears make it inevitable that their daughters will disappoint them," said di Santo-Germano, his lips lingering, feather-light, on hers.

"And how many daughters have you had, that you know this?" she teased, and then fell silent at the haunted expression that crossed his attractive, irregular features like a shadow; she wished her words unsaid, but dared not speak again.

"I've had none," he said softly. "But I have known other men's daughters." Their faces flickered through his memory, each woman distinct and precious, all but one lost to him now, through mortal death, the True Death, or deliberate estrangement. He regarded her without speaking for some little time, then lifted her into his arms as if she weighed no more than her virginals, and made for the door.

"You are very strong," she murmured. "I have noticed before."

"I trust others are less observant," he said, climbing the stairs that led to her bedchamber half a floor above the music room without any effort or lessening of speed.

A single lamp shone in the gloom of the bedchamber, just above her kneeling bench with her rosary laid across a leather-bound copy of The New Testament, illustrated with handsome wood-cuts done by Lindo Guardin, with a frontispiece in three colors. Her bed was curtained in red-and-tan bargello-work hangings, all but one of them just now closed. Two clothes-chests stood against opposite walls, both with painted scenes on their doors and panels, so that the shine of reflected water on the house-front visible out the window seemed incongruous. The walls had murals of espaliered fruit trees on rustic stone fences, so that the small benches under the windows looked as if they might be countryside amenities, and the ceiling was pale blue with clusters of blossom-like clouds gathering in the four corners.

Di Santo-Germano put her down beside her bed and pulled off his black damask silk dogaline, flinging it onto the bench under the nearest window. He touched the laces on the back of her corsage. "Shall I unfasten this for you?"

"I don't want to call Merula just now, and it can't be done without help," she said, keeping her voice low, for her 'tirewoman slept in the small apartment on the far side of the large dressing room on the other side of this bedchamber. "If you wouldn't mind?" She tugged the ends of the laces out from the top of her fine ruched-muslin gonnella.

Taking the ends of the laces in his hands, di Santo-Germano unfastened the simple knots that held the corsage closed, then loosened them until Pier-Ariana could shrug out of the upper part of her dress, revealing the sheer-linen guimpe beneath, and her corset. "How do women alone ever manage to dress themselves?" he asked the air.

"It is very difficult," said Pier-Ariana, unfastening the two dozen little bows that closed the front of her guimpe, frowning as one of the bows became a knot. "Unless one wishes to dress like a peasant, some assistance is needed. These garments need a second set of hands to be worn properly, or undone without damage." She broke the small ribbon of silk. "At least you don't try to make love while undressing."

"Why should I—since you dislike it?" He removed the fine gold chain from around her neck, and the polished aquamarine pendant that it held; these he set on the nearest chest and returned to assisting her out of her clothes.

"It's all so im*pract*ical," she complained, picking another knot of ribbon open.

While di Santo-Germano worked the ends of the broad bands holding her voluminous silk skirt and the gonnella beneath, he remarked, "A few centuries ago, noblemen wore shoes so pointed that they could not walk up and down stairs while wearing them." He dropped her skirt so she could step out of it, then started on the gonnella. "In such weather as Venezia has had, it is unfortunate that we all must wear so much to be properly dressed."

"You could do what Tiberio Tedeschi does, and dress like a Turk; he even attends meetings of the Collegio so attired," she pointed out, half-seriously. "At least he is cool in the summer."

"Tiberio Tedeschi is a man of impeccable Venezian lineage, with four Consiglieri for cousins: he could dress like a Chinese warlord and no one would say a word. But, as I am an exile, I must follow the strictures of Venezia while I am here." He held her hand while she stepped out of the pleated froth of her gonnella, then tugged at the closure of his doublet; the scent of her jasmine perfume grew stronger.

"When you are in Bruges, you will dress in their manner, I suppose?" She pressed her lips together, not wanting to remember his coming absence; she used her silence to step out of her high-soled shoes.

"Of course," he said, and started to work on the complex lacing of her corset.

"The same in London?" Her voice had gone up three notes.

"Oh, yes; and in Kiev and in Delhi, and in almost any place but Africa," he said, and bent to kiss the nape of her neck.

"Why not Africa?" She was truly curious.

"Because I cannot change my skin, and there I am clearly a foreigner, no matter how I dress. There, I am completely exposed; I cannot alter my appearance sufficiently to disguise my origins, or to present myself acceptably, as I might in China." He pulled her corset away from her body.

She turned to face him. "And you've been to China, I suppose?"

"Yes," he said. "I have."

She looked up into his eyes. "And you could go there again?"

"I might, in time. But not just now," he whispered, and bent to kiss her, following her arousal with his own. He did not move to touch her body until she took a last half-step nearer and wrapped her arms around his waist. Continuing the kiss, he slowly stroked her back, marveling in the texture of her skin and feeling the first stirrings of her arousal.

"You never remove your camisa, or your lower garments," she said as she turned a little in his arms, addressing her remarks to the top closure of his camisa.

"No, and I have already told you that I never will." He paused in his graceful caresses.

"It seems a waste," she said, attempting to pull his camisa from the waist-band of his French barrel-breeches.

He stopped her gently. "I have scars, carina—you would not like them." They extended from his rib cage to the base of his pelvis: broad swathes of porcelain-white, striated tissue which marked the disemboweling that had killed him, thirty-five centuries ago.

"So you tell me," she said as she stepped back and went to throw herself onto the bed, facedown, her bare feet sticking over the side and through the open curtains. "Just when I begin to think I am vexed with you, I realize that you have done something out of your consideration of me." She slapped the coverlet on which she lay. "I will take what you are willing to give me," she said as if conceding a game of chance. "You are a most welcome lover, no matter how you are clothed."

He went to her, stretching out beside her, where he began to touch her back and flank, making no effort to turn her on her side. His hands were adventuresome and playful, turning her body pliant. Gradually he worked his way from her shoulder to her elegant, trim waist, his kisses following the progress of his hands. Nothing he did was hurried; all his evocation waited upon her response and her pleasure. As he slid one hand around her to fondle her breasts, teasing her nipples into excitation, she gave a rapturous murmur, but remained prone, taking all his attentive exploration into herself, cherishing his magnanimity that placed her satisfaction before his own. Her breathing changed, and in a sudden movement, he pulled her on top of him to lie supine, her legs on either side of his. His camisa pressed into her back, but that hardly mattered to her as his hands went along her abdomen to the cleft between her legs, where his magical caresses continued. She was both utterly free and completely captivated by his embrace, and she felt a kind of rapture that was so wholly personal that she had no words to express it, only sensations.

Gradually she felt her body gather, and as the first of her spasms shook her, she felt his mouth touch her neck even as the fulfillment of her desire exalted her beyond the confines of her bed, her house, even her flesh, to that realm where she was deliriously enveloped in soaring melodies for what felt like hours. Finally she shifted off him, back in the world. "How do you do that?" she said at last, her breathing still a bit unsteady.

"It is your doing, carina Pier-Ariana," di Santo-Germano murmured. "I do only what you seek for me to do."

"So you say," she said, and rolled to face him so she could wrap her arms around him before she floated into sleep.

Text of a letter to Ruggier in Venezia from Bogardt van Leun in Amsterdam, written in French, carried by private courier, and delivered twelve days after it was given to the courier.

To the houseman Ruggier at the house of Franzicco Ragoczy, Conte di Santo-Germano on the Campo San Luca in Venezia, of the Serenissima Repubblica, the greetings of Bogardt van Leun, steward of the house of the Grav, Germain Ragoczy, in Amsterdam, with the assurance that all will soon be in readiness for His Excellency's arrival.

I thank you for sending us notice of the Grav's coming, and his plans to remain here for three or four months through the winter. I have followed all your instructions in regard to preparing the house, including the spreading of earth from the trunks stored in the house over the foundations, and under the floor of the Grav's room. We have also stopped all leaks from the canal that have come into the house. New paint has gone into rooms where there has been damp, and two bracing boards have been replaced on the side of the house. We have also realigned the rear door and put new paint on it as well.

We are now provisioning the house for your stay, and we have begun the inspections of all beds and bedding, and will perform those tasks you have set for us by the time you arrive. I will have taken on the required additional staff by then.

I have exchanged mail with Jaquet Saint Philemon, my counterpart

in Bruges, but have yet had no word from Simeon Roosholm in
Antwerp, which may only mean that the soldiers are delaying couriers
again, but may have more serious implications. I mention this so that
you and the Grav will be aware of what you might expect in the Lowlands. In the meantime, you may rest assured that our labors go on
apace.

    With my high regard to His Excellency and with my respects to
you,

I sign myself,
Bogardt van Leun
steward

In Amsterdam by my own hand on the 2nd day of July, 1530

7

Merveiglio Trevisan was sea-weathered and walked with a limp but
was otherwise an impressive figure: tall, richly dressed in clothing
embroidered at the slashings with lines of matched pearls. At forty-
four, he was a close friend of Alvise Mocenigo, and although he did
not trade on his alliance with the Doge, all Venezia knew of it, and
treated him accordingly. As a Consiglier of the Minor Consiglio, he
had much influence of his own. He stood in the main reception room
of di Santo-Germano's house on the Campo San Luca, a glass of excellent Toscana wine in his hand, and a genial smile revealing the
deep wrinkles in his skin. "I thank you for seeing me so promptly,
Conte," he said to his host.

    "I am delighted to have you a guest in my house," said di Santo-
Germano in perfect form; in spite of the heat his pourpoint had a
standing velvet collar and the sleeves held their exaggerated shape
with stiff taffeta ribbons reinforced with borders of silver braid and
little clusters of rubies. His camisa beneath was glossy white silk, all
unblemished, with lace at the wrist and neck; he held an orange stuck
full of cloves in one hand against the ripening odors of a sweltering

summer afternoon; the air was still and close, muffling the thunder trampling the low clouds spread over the lagoon and the hills beyond.

"I'm pleased for the occasion that brings me here. I believe the Savii and the Collegio have much to be proud of in regard to their decision; I voted for your modifications at the first and advocated for them in our debate. If the Maggior Consiglio approves your improvements, I think you may anticipate high recognition as soon as the innovations are put into effect and proven."

"Do you," said di Santo-Germano, indicating the open window. "To come out, with a storm brewing, your mission must be singularly important." He held out a round fan of painted silk. "Here. This may lessen your discomfort."

Trevisan took it and carefully studied the painting. "From China, by the look of it."

"Yes. Brought from Trebizond, along with bolts of silk, and casks of spices." He smiled. "I have also received three barrels of pepper."

At that, Trevisan put the fan to use. "Three barrels! If you were not rich already, such bounty would make your fortune."

"No doubt," di Santo-Germano agreed. "But you had something to tell me . . ." He let his rising inflection serve as an invitation.

"Oh. Yes. Your designs for modifications of the war-galleys. The Collegio and the Minor Consiglio have approved them, and this morning, so did the Doge. They all agree that although you are a foreigner, your improvements will work to our advantage, particularly raising the upper decks by three handsbreadths above the current height. Doge Mocenigo agrees that cannon-fire will carry farther from a slightly higher deck, and the new design of the keel will compensate for any possible instability the rise will require. The corvus, placed as you have recommended, will be able to inflict more damage in close battles."

"The Romans of old found the corvus useful in that position," di Santo-Germano murmured, then raised his voice, saying, "So the Maggior Consiglio is the last hurdle to clear," as if this were only a small concern.

"Yes. It will be put before them next week; I anticipate they will finish their review by the time you return from the north. It is very important that you do not remain away for longer than you have stated you will be, for the Maggior Consiglio would take your absence as an indication of intrigue. Keep in mind that they are putting great consequence on your designs. When something is that important, they act swiftly."

If di Santo-Germano found fourteen months less than swift, he did not mention it; as a body of more than a thousand men, the Maggior Consiglio often took five years to reach consensus. "If you need any more material from me to aid them in their deliberations, you have only to ask."

"You have already provided ample," said Trevisan. "I cannot imagine what more they would need from you."

"I am pleased to have given you something of worth." Di Santo-Germano paused as the thunder trundled closer. "A bad time for masts."

"True enough. Many of the ships are moored in the Bacino di San Marco, away from the docks and quays, to lessen the chance of fire. And men are posted to the Arsenal, to douse any flames that are ignited. Rain or no rain, lightning fires burn fiercely." He finished his wine and achieved a slight smile. "May the Saints be thanked that, with drinking water so scarce in Venezia, we can enjoy such good wines."

"True enough," said di Santo-Germano, a wry turn to his mouth.

"Although I see you do not drink," said Trevisan as he set his glass down.

"Alas, no; I do not drink wine. I haven't the stomach for it." He did not add that he had no stomach at all; he went to pour a second helping for his guest. "Do not let my incapacity stop you."

"It is an excellent wine," Trevisan allowed. "I thank you for your generosity."

"Someone must drink it," said di Santo-Germano at his most urbane. "If you find it so much to your taste, then it pleases me to pour it for you."

Trevisan drank, swallowing twice, then set the glass aside again. "The Collegio and the Minor Consiglio have authorized me to inform you that the Doge will hold a feast in your honor in ten days' time—well before the time you have named for your departure to the north. It is hoped that the Maggior Consiglio will pay attention to this distinction being shown to you."

Di Santo-Germano's answer was overwhelmed by a wallop of

thunder; when it had passed, he repeated, "I am honored by such an invitation, as all who live in Venezia must be." The storm was closer and there was a odor like that of heated metal on the air.

"The Doge will not be offended if you do not eat. We all know that you keep to the practice of your people, and dine in private." Trevisan coughed lightly. "It would be best if you come alone. No women will be present for the banquet, not even holy Sisters or the wives of the Savii."

"I understand," said di Santo-Germano. "And I will do as you suggest." He was about to say something more when there was a discreet tap at the door.

Trevisan waved him away. "Attend to it. Otherwise we shall have no peace, servants being what they are."

"Grazie," said di Santo-Germano, and went to the door expecting to find Niccola or Rinaldo waiting for him; instead, Ruggier stood just beyond the arch of the door, a suggestion of a frown on his usually unexpressive features. Di Santo-Germano regarded him narrowly, now alert. "What has happened, old friend? Your face is grave."

"Two ships are lost. I have only now had word from the secretary of the Savii, who provided confirmation on the report—one sank, almost everything was lost; the other was seized by Ottomites." He sighed. "Their messenger just came, in spite of the rising storm. I thought you would want to know."

"Which ships?" di Santo-Germano asked, glancing about and noticing that they were observed by Timoteo, the under-footman. "What did the message say?"

"The *Harvest Moon* and the *Golden Ladder,*" said Ruggier. "The former sank; there are a few witnesses."

"And survivors," di Santo-Germano said urgently.

"Four from the ship, and nine crates were recovered. Everything else is given up to the Adriatic." Ruggier paused for a long moment. "What if there are ransom demands from the Ottomites?"

"The ransom must be paid, of course, as soon as possible, in full," said di Santo-Germano, "and through the Sultan's Court so that there can be no reneging on the terms, and the transfer should take place on Venezian territory—Corfu, perhaps."

"We will have to make arrangements through the Collegio," Ruggier said.

"Then I shall attend to it in the next three days, or as soon as the Collegio will see me."

"You may want to consider a broad approach: you have five other ships on galleys, and there may be more unwelcome news. You may need to be prepared for more calls on your purse. Winter is coming, and storms, and more Ottomites are hunting Venezian ships."

"True enough. And while we are gone to the north, certain precautions must be made." Di Santo-Germano looked toward the reception room. "The broiled pheasant should be ready, and its accompanying dishes. Have Enrici or Rindaldo bring it up, and send Niccola to the quay to find out all he can. He's the most inquisitive of the pages. In this weather, curiosity is necessary."

"He's also the most wary," Ruggier approved.

"That he is," said di Santo-Germano. "It should stand him in good stead. He will not be tempted to do something reckless, no matter how intriguing it might be." He took a half-step backward. "It would be best if I do not keep the Consiglier waiting."

"Truly," said Ruggier, and stepped back. "I'll send Niccola out and have Enrici bring up the pheasant." He cocked his head very slightly toward Timoteo. "And I will set all the household about their duties."

"Very good of you. Oh, and make sure there is a second bottle of the Toscana with the food," said di Santo-Germano, as soon as another peal of thunder had shuddered to silence. "Keep in mind that we are being watched," he added in Chinese.

"I have done so thus far, and will continue," said Ruggier in Imperial Latin, lowering his head respectfully as di Santo-Germano returned to his guest.

Merveiglio Trevisan had finished his second glass of wine and was pouring a third. "You say this is from Toscana?"

"From the region between Fiorenza and Sienna," di Santo-Germano confirmed.

"It is quite wonderful. You are most gracious to offer it, all the more so because you are unable to enjoy it, this blood of the vines." Trevisan held up the glass, allowing the flickering lamp-light to shine in its red depths. "I thank you for it."

"You are welcome to the whole bottle, and more, if you like. I have ordered another for you delectation. You are also invited to remain here until the storm passes. This afternoon weather is inhospitable, so

I will offer you an alternative to braving the elements. Perhaps you would like to avail yourself of my music room? if not that, then my library? After your kindness in coming here, I have no wish to send you out into dangerous weather." He indicated the small, square table near the window. "If you prefer not to be exposed to the rain while you dine, I will gladly move that to the French chair." He pointed to the piece of furniture with the upholstered seat and the bent-wood arms.

"A very good precaution," approved Trevisan, wincing in spite of himself as more thunder battered the afternoon. A moment later there was another squirt of lightning, and then, hardly more than two heartbeats later, a long, rolling smash that shook the air and rattled the windowpanes and shutters and sent echoes banging along the tall buildings. When there was quiet again, the Consiglier said, "Perhaps it *would* be best if I remain here for the time being. The rain, as you surmise, must begin shortly."

"Stay as long as you like," di Santo-Germano offered, then went to secure the shutters on the windows, and to move the table to the French chair. Now only one window remained open, a small, narrow one on the north wall. "If you are not sufficiently comfortable here, I can remove us to my study."

"This is quite satisfactory," said Trevisan, taking his place in the chair. "I wish more Veneziani were as obliging as you are, Conte."

"It is kind of you to say so," di Santo-Germano said, wondering what more Consiglier Trevisan wanted of him, beyond shelter from the storm. As if to underscore his apprehension, a new clap of thunder sounded, and on its echoes came rain, pouring in cataracts from the clouds, so that the air outside was veiled in silver and all of the city looked like a blurred charcoal sketch. "Shall I shutter that window?"

Trevisan shrugged. "Not on my account. I would prefer to see what is happening out there. I always ride out storms on my decks, tied to the mast when necessary, but where I can see the fury of the waves." The sound of the rain was a loud, persistent chatter, broken with thumps of thunder. "I must say I am glad not to be at sea in this."

"I agree—wholeheartedly." Just the thought of being aboard a ship in such a storm made him slightly queasy; he had memories of tempests and floods that added to his discomfort, and was relieved when there was a tapping on the door to distract him from his recollections of Roma, of Burma, of the beach below Leosan Fortress, of Tamasra-jasi's temple, of the defile near Kiev . . . "This must be your pheasant; it has a wonderful aroma," he said to Trevisan, and went to take the tray with three covered dishes from Enrici. "Thank you for being so prompt. And you have the wine open. Excellent."

"A good day to stay in and drink wine," said Enrici, with an informality he would never use in addressing a Veneziano.

"No doubt," said di Santo-Germano. "How much rain-water do you think we will save?"

"The cistern will be half-full by nightfall, Signor' Conte," the page said, touching his forehead as he stepped back.

"Fine. Have more barrels set out. Since we are being deluged we might as well make the most of it," di Santo-Germano said, and closed the door.

"What, other than pheasant, have you here?" Trevisan asked as di Santo-Germano set the tray down.

"Aside from the wedge of cheese on the plate and the new bread, here is a risotto with crab and butter," he said as he lifted the first cover. "Pheasant"—the second cover was taken off—"and dried fruit in spirits of wine and honey. And preserved lemon rind."

"Elegant, and a touch foreign," Trevisan pronounced as he took his utensils from his wallet and began to eat.

Di Santo-Germano went to light the rest of the oil-lamps, using flint-and-steel to make a spark. While he made his way around the room, he remarked, "I have been told one of my ships was seized by the Turks—"

Trevisan washed down a large bite of cheese to say, "So that was what your man wanted."

"Sadly, yes. It would mean that I should make provision for ransom to be paid, if a ransom is demanded." This last was lower than the rest.

"By the Virgin's Tits, yes," said Trevisan. "With guarantees, so you will not pay and then lose both men and money."

"It should be paid through the Sultan's Court," said di Santo-Germano. "Otherwise, who knows what might become of it."

"So it must, so it must." He hacked off one of the pheasant's legs and bit into it. "Very tasty, and not as dry as pheasant is wont to be." He had another bit of wine and went on thoughtfully, "You want to talk to Christofo Sen about this. He'll know how it's to be handled. And he will not permit the issue to be conveniently forgot by the clerks."

"Christofo Sen?" di Santo-Germano repeated.

"You know him. Thin, rawboned, white hair, a wen on his cheek, but dresses as exquisitely as a man of his position can." He stuck his fork into the ear-shaped pasta. "Very reliable; very discreet."

"I know the man you mean." Di Santo-Germano considered this. "I'll ask to see him tomorrow."

"Tell him I sent you, if he drags his feet."

"You're most gracious," said di Santo-Germano. "I may avail myself of your offer." He stopped at the small, open window. "This rain is astonishing."

"Luckily most of the private gondole are drawn into boathouses, or they would be swamped," said Trevisan around his mouthful of pasta. "You keep a gondola and a gondolier, as I recall."

"Yes," said di Santo-Germano.

"Something of an expense, what with the taxes," Trevisan remarked as he poured himself more wine.

Di Santo-Germano lifted one shoulder slightly. "The taxes are worth the money. It is certainly convenient to have both the gondola and gondolier immediately at hand." He made no mention of his native earth in the keel that allowed him to travel over water without much discomfort.

"And a man of your position cannot be always waiting for someone to serve you, nor can you properly row your own boat," Trevisan sympathized with a wink.

"It would certainly be awkward," said di Santo-Germano, and looked again at the rain. "I doubt this will let up soon."

"Not until the Angels have wrung all the water from the clouds," said Trevisan. "Too bad about your ship, with the Doge about to fete you."

"It could be worse," said di Santo-Germano.

"True: we could have the Sweating Sickness here, as they do in so much of the north. No man would offer entertainment of any kind at such a time." Trevisan produced a grim little smile.

"I was not thinking of disease, but with politics, which can be much more dangerous," said di Santo-Germano wryly.

"And it may yet be, if the Sultan will not conduct negotiations for your men's release. Who knows what lengths you may have to go to." He smacked his lips and had more pasta; his forehead was turning ruddy and a bit moist. "A pity you have to be gone at such a delicate time."

"If it were not the Collegio and the ransom, it would be something else equally demanding," said di Santo-Germano, "and the situation in the Lowlands is truly pressing."

"You know your business best," said Trevisan. "And I have my biases as a Venezian. Still, you will want to keep in regular correspondence while you are away, in case there should be some difficulty."

"I intend to do so." His voice was quiet yet purposeful.

"Have you made arrangements for such messages?"

"There are private couriers to be hired, if there is urgency. I will leave funds for my man of business to employ such a courier from here, so that he will not have to bear the expense. Two of my ships are on the Galley of Flanders and I can entrust messages to their Captains."

"The overland courier is faster," Trevisan remarked.

"Yes, and in more danger." Di Santo-Germano strolled around the room. "With religious fighting breaking out all over, anyone crossing frontiers must be prepared to defend himself."

"They are fallen into error," said Trevisan firmly. "That monk, Luther, has much to answer for. And now the King of England is saying he will defy His Holiness and Mother Church." His choler was rising as he spoke. "Protestants! An apt name! May God save us from such heretical excesses."

Di Santo-Germano paused by a small, square table that held two branches of oil-lamps and a number of handsome objects; he picked up a carving of a jade lion with a clouded paw. "There are no wars so bitter as those fought for religion."

"When the soul is at stake, men defend it," Trevisan declared. "The Church must answer to God for every soul it forfeits to the Devil."

"That is what the Protestants claim, as well," di Santo-Germano pointed out. "And the Islamites."

"The Devil is always busy," said Trevisan, gnawing on the other leg-bone of the pheasant.

"So he might be," said di Santo-Germano. He put the lion back on the table and went to close the last open shutter. "Your pardon, but the wind is changing quarter and I would rather not have my books soaked."

"You could always move the books," Trevisan suggested with a glint of amusement in his eyes.

"Closing the shutter is easier," said di Santo-Germano. "If you want to watch the storm, I can have your chair and table carried out into the loggia, where you may enjoy it safely."

"No, this is preferable," said Trevisan. "There is more space between the lightning and the thunder, which means the worst is over." He drank the last of the wine in his glass and poured out half a glass more. "I don't want a muzzy head in the morning."

"Would you like a tankard of hot ale?" di Santo-Germano inquired.

"I would prefer lemon juice and honey in hot water," said Trevisan. "I have a fondness for it."

"Then you shall have it," said di Santo-Germano, and rang a small brass bell to summon a page.

Rinaldo answered this call, and repeated the particulars of what di Santo-Germano wanted for his guest before he hurried off to the kitchen.

"You are truly a most accommodating host," said Trevisan. "I wonder: would you give me the pleasure of one of your pages if I asked for it?"

"That would depend upon the page," said di Santo-Germano, unflustered by this forthright question. "They are in my care, not my possessions. If it suited one to oblige you, that would be between the two of you."

"You are most tolerant of your household, to allow a servant such a choice for himself," said Trevisan, a bit dubiously. "To allow a servant to have charge over his preferences could soon lead to insolence."

"I have learned over time that servants treated well mean a smooth-running household, and where there is resentment, there is also slovenliness and disloyalty," Adroitly he shifted the subject. "Have you noticed how the Ottomites organize their households?"

"That I have," said Trevisan. "I was once in Beirut and was asked to the home of a prosperous merchant there. He was a good man, genial and educated after the manner of his kind, a man of fortune and excellent connections; it pleased him to entertain Christians, to show them how Allah had enriched him far beyond anything God had done for us." He drank the last of his wine. "His Allah, he says, will always favor his family."

"Did you agree?" di Santo-Germano asked, drawing up a Fiorenzan chair and setting it at right angles to Trevisan's.

For the rest of the long, wet afternoon, Trevisan offered garrulous accounts of his various adventures, and di Santo-Germano listened as if all he heard was new to him.

Text of a letter from Prescott Greystone, bookseller of London, to the Count of Saint-Germain at Eclipse Press in Venice, written in English, and delivered seven weeks after it was dispatched.

To the Most Excellent, the Count of Saint-Germain, resident in Venice on the Field of Saint Luke, and publisher of Eclipse Press,

Your Excellency:

I am in receipt of the twenty volumes I ordered from your Press in February, and I am pleased to tell you that all are in good order. I am enclosing a draught for ten guineas, nine pence, four farthings. It is a pity that the late King Henry VII seized all the funds in the London branch of the Medici Bank, for that would make my business with the Continent run much more smoothly.

Also, I have been in communication with the Antwerp and Bruges Presses you were kind enough to bring to my attention. If their quality is equal to what you produce in Venice, then I shall soon be placing an order with that Press as well. In any event, I am pleased to know of them.

Let me thank you for the promptness of your delivery of my order—less than four months after it was placed, I have the volumes in hand, a most commendable dispatch in your dealings, my Lord, and one that encourages me to continue this association. May this letter have as swift a journey to you as your books did to me, as a sign of our mutual benefits.

With every good wish for your continued prosperity, good health, and fine reputation,

> *I am, my Lord Count,*
>   *Most faithfully yours to command,*
>   *Prescott Greystone*

No. 4, Cotter Lane, London, England, the 11ᵗʰ day of July, 1530

8

"Then you must sign this, and impress your seal on the wax," said Gennaro Emerenzio, spreading the parchment open to its fullest extent and holding it firmly while di Santo-Germano signed his name and reached for the small dish of heated sealing wax. "Just fix it there." He tapped the place provided for the seal with one finger, watching critically as the dollop of hot, dark-red wax settled on the page. A speck of wax stuck on the pleated lace at the cuff of his long, dark-plum pourpoint, and he hissed at his own clumsiness.

"This should satisfy everyone, even the Church," said di Santo-Germano as he pressed his seal into the hot wax, leaving the impression of his device: a disk with raised, displayed wings. "This gives you access to my funds for eighteen months or until my return. You have my schedule of payments and my usual household expenses, and the authorization to meet them. All my servants are allowed three weeks each year to visit their families, and an allowance for their travels; it is stipulated in the material I have brought to you." He laid his hand on the small, bound account book. "I also am leaving jewels with you to cover any unanticipated expenses. In this purse"—he held up a black-leather pouch—"are six rubies, nine sapphires, four diamonds, seven emeralds, twelve moonstones, ten opals, eight yellow topazes, and five blue ones. The largest jewel is the size of a hen's egg—a ruby; the smallest—an opal—is about as large as a pea. Most are about the size of the end of my thumb."

As he listened to this impressive list, Emerenzio's eyes grew large. "That is . . . that is a sizeable fortune, Signor' Conte."

"They are provided to cover very high expenses, such as ransoms for my ships and crews, repairs on my house, and any untoward expenses that come about on the press. Giovanni Boromeo will inform you if the gold I have advanced him is insufficient." He smoothed the front of his pleated black doublet, and twitched the French cuff-ruffles of his white-silk camisa.

"If your generosity to him is anything approaching what you are entrusting to me, he must consider himself the most fortunate printer in all Venezia." This fulsome praise was sincere but overly flattering, so Emerenzio, who knew di Santo-Germano disliked excessive plaudits, did his best to modify them. "You are a very wealthy man, of course, and that enables you to be a truly generous master and patron; you set an example many Veneziani would be well-advised to follow."

Di Santo-Germano held up his hand. "Do not continue this adulation, prego."

"It is richly deserved," said Emerenzio, unable to stop himself. "You are—"

"I am," di Santo-Germano interrupted firmly, "an exile who knows how much his well-being depends upon the good-will of those around him."

"So you say," Emerenzio attempted a smile and managed only an obsequious grin. "If that is your understanding, I will say no more about it."

"Thank all the forgotten gods for that," di Santo-Germano remarked with another of his elusive smiles.

"Regarding your patronage, you are more generous with your musician than you need to be. No woman requires the kind of life you have given her. You provide too much temptation, and you know how women are: she will take advantage of it, I warn you." He coughed. "I do not speak against her, but you know what women are when they are indulged."

"But I do not consider Signorina Salier to be indulged; she has an ability, and in order to explore it to its fullest, she does not need to be burdened with the worries and demands of everyday life. I am in a position to make this possible for her." His dark eyes held Emerenzio's hazel ones. "It is the least I can do."

"Of course, of course," said Emerenzio hastily. "I only hope that you do not live to regret your kindness to her."

"You need not fret," said di Santo-Germano with a faint, enigmatic glint of amusement in his dark eyes. "I have lived long enough to regret many things, but I doubt it would be possible to regret easing Signorina Salier's life."

"But it is— You are unlike so many others." He gathered his thoughts and rushed on, "I have dealt with many of the fine merchants in Venezia, and I know many of them to be pinch-purses, unwilling to part with a single ducat unless they can realize two from it."

"How unfortunate that they are unwilling to enjoy their success," said di Santo-Germano levelly.

"Gaining more gold *is* their enjoyment, spending it causes them distress," said Emerenzio. He tested the sealing wax to be sure it was cool, then rolled up the parchment, circled it twice with a silk ribbon, reached for the dish of hot wax and dropped it on the ribbon and the parchment, then pressed his personal seal on it. "There. I will see it is recorded at the Collegio."

"Thank you," said di Santo-Germano. "I trust you will see to the administration of the various funds I have left for my absence?"

"As we have agreed. Living money and household expenses to Pier-Ariana Salier, publishing money to Giovanni Boromeo, household money to your palazzo in addition to the servants' wages, anonymous household and living money to Claudio Cinquanni while he prepares his work on the movements of the stars, anonymous household and living money to Gianni Parenti to allow him to devote his time to the collection and study of herbs. You have a grant for Fra Zacco at San Pietro di Castello for his repair on the old organ there. Also you will continue to provide living expenses to any and all Captains of your merchant-ships while they remain here in Venezia, and equal shares of ten percent of the profits of the sale of cargo to the crews on all merchant-ships arriving during your absence, just as you have done since your arrival in this city." His expression was increasingly exasperated. "Your magnanimity occasionally borders on absurdity."

"Nonetheless, it is my wish and you will see the conditions fulfilled, I am confident," di Santo-Germano said, and went to the window to look out on the busy morning as boats and barges bustled about with the first deliveries of the day. He felt the weight of the angled sunlight and was keenly aware that he would need to reline the soles of his shoes with his native earth very shortly, for the heat that bit into him was not from the August day alone, but from the sapping power of the sun itself. He recalled the time, ten centuries ago, when there had been a darkening of the sun, and he had found much less discomfort in direct exposure to its rays. He turned away from the window. "Do you require anything more of me today?"

"Only that you present your household inventories, so that I may tend to keeping you properly supplied." He removed his soft velvet cap and rubbed at his thinning, russet-colored hair. "I must think of some place to secure this purse," he said, as much to himself as to di Santo-Germano. "It isn't safe to let it be exposed. Servants get into everything."

Di Santo-Germano regarded Emerenzio steadily. "Do you have the brass tiger I gave you? the one with the emerald eyes?"

"I keep it in my strong-room, with all the official papers I handle. It is locked day and night, and I alone have the key." He straightened up, not wanting to seem unmindful of the value of such a gift. "I could put the pouch in a strongbox and secure it with a heavy lock."

"And announce to anyone who sees it that something of value is contained therein," said di Santo-Germano. "I think not. Let the tiger guard the purse." He saw the startled look Emerenzio was quick to conceal. "The figure is hollow, and there is a clever slide-door in its belly. I have the key to open it—it is very small, and you will have to find a place where it will not be lost." He held up an elaborate brass key no longer than his little finger; it was beautifully ornamented, with patterns of leaves entwined from the tiny, circular bow-grip to the little spine of irregular cuts that ran most of its blade. "This was made in India, as was the tiger," he explained. "You do not insert and turn it, you fit the shaft into the pattern on the belly that matches it, and then you press and slide, and the compartment will open."

Emerenzio stared, fascinated. "What a clever invention," he said as he reached for the key.

"This key, if lost, cannot be replaced." Di Santo-Germano handed it to him. "Keep it on a cord around your neck during my absence," he recommended. "That way you are unlikely to lose it."

Emerenzio held the key carefully. "It's exquisite," he said. "I will do as you suggest. I can imagine that this key could easily be lost if it isn't handled carefully."

"Yes. There are only two keys. I have the other one, and it is always within my reach," said di Santo-Germano.

"On a cord around your neck?" asked Emerenzio.

"No; in a place much safer than that," said di Santo-Germano, and offered nothing more.

"Just so," said Emerenzio after a short, awkward silence. "Is there anything else, Conte?"

"I will send my manservant with the inventories for you after the midday rest," said di Santo-Germano, offering a single nod. "I will take my leave of you."

A sudden burst of shouting rose from the meeting of the canals on the east, the yelling echoing off the tall, marble fronts of the buildings, and bringing angry cries for answers.

"I can think of nothing more at present, not with that din raging." He reached up and closed the shutter, reducing the noise to a muffled drone. "If I remember something, you still have a month before you leave, and doubtless, we will meet again several times before your departure. Surely that will be enough time to complete anything left undone today." Emerenzio inclined his head respectfully. "Thank you, Conte, for all you have done."

Di Santo-Germano made his way toward the door; the shouting had died down to occasional outbursts and a few trenchant oaths. "It is I who should thank you for your diligence in attending to my business affairs."

"That is most gracious of you, Conte," Emerenzio said, keeping half a step behind him. He paused in the small, square loggia of his house and glanced toward the narrow Rivi San Pantalon which connected two slightly larger canals. "I see your gondolier is waiting for you, in spite of the ruction."

"I should hope so," said di Santo-Germano, the tap of his heels on the marble floor echoing in the loggia.

"I imagine you want the same for him as you do all your servants?" Emerenzio asked as he hastened after di Santo-Germano.

"He is in my employ," said di Santo-Germano as if his expectation were obvious.

"Yes, yes; you are very even-handed with your servants," said Emerenzio, nodding emphatically.

"Such methods avoid carping and jealousy among them," said di Santo-Germano, almost as if he were offering an apology for his fairness.

"So you have said." As Emerenzio reached the steps down to the water, he paused, holding out his arm, as courtesy demanded, to assist di Santo-Germano into the waiting gondola.

"Grazie," said di Santo-Germano, accepting his help. "Have a care with that key."

"I will," he promised, and stepped back onto the next tread; he glanced toward the canal ahead and saw it was clear of traffic. "Good day to you, then; may God give you prosperity and good health."

"And to you," said di Santo-Germano, and signaled Milano to shove off from the steps. He felt the annealing presence of his native earth in the keel of the boat permeate him, restoring his energy and lightening his mood. "Any news, Milano?"

"Nothing to mention," said Milano, working his long oar expertly.

"Ah. Then there is something."

Milano was occupied with turning the gondola in the narrow confines of the intersection of the two canals, and so said nothing until they were gliding under the Frari-Santa Margherita Bridge. "Three nights ago, while I waited for you near Signorina Salier's house, I happened to see that young man I have mentioned before: the one who was following you."

"And you suspect he was following me again?"

"I think he may have been, yes," said Milano, checking the speed of his gondola as they slid past a narrow barge piled high with apples and lemons; they approached the Gran' Canale with no increase in celerity, for there was a great deal of traffic maneuvering along its broad, sinuous curve. "He is not easy to miss, skulking like a mummer!"

"Is this the only time you have seen the fellow?" di Santo-Germano asked as Milano found his place in the stream of water-craft.

"Since I first brought him to your attention? No. I have seen him once with the Papal courier, Padre Duradante, at the Casetta Belle Donne." He waited for anything di Santo-Germano might say about his visiting such an establishment; when there was no response, he continued. "I believe the grand little puppy lost a considerable amount to Padre Duradante that evening."

"Did you happen to find out his name?" Di Santo-Germano winced as the morning sun struck the side of his face as Milano prepared to turn once more.

"I understand he is related to one of the Savii's secretaries, or so the porter boasted," said Milano. "Signora Giuletta does not allow her wealthy patrons to mingle with humble workers—with the exception of her women, of course."

"Of course," said di Santo-Germano.

Milano leaned on his oar and the gondola turned toward the narrow canal that passed the side of Campo San Luca. "They are cleaning one of the canals near the Arsenal, and so there are many delays there."

"They blocked the section of the canal two days ago, as I recall. When they set up the barriers and pumped the water out, they found a dead body, or so I have been told," di Santo-Germano remarked as the gondola slipped into the entrance of the smaller canal.

"That they did. I talked to one of the cleaners that night, he was still rattled by it. The man was not identifiable, but there is some speculation that it was a sailor from another country, because among the bits of clothing left on him, there was a bronze ring marked with Greek letters, and he had a Greek medal around his neck on a chain. The cleaner said that the body will be sent to the Greek church on the Giudecca for rites and burial." Milano pulled heavily on his oar, then performed a complicated feathering, and the gondola went easily into the space between the marble pillars in front of di Santo-Germano's house. "The Greek priests came and took the body yesterday. All the workers were glad to have it gone."

"It's always better if the unknown dead are foreigners of humble birth," di Santo-Germano observed sardonically.

"And this one was so humble, he left no name, and no means of being certain where he came from," Milano observed as he waited for di Santo-Germano to step out of the boat.

"Truly," said di Santo-Germano, stepping up into the loggia. "Go have your cumuo. You have earned it." This Venetian drink was a combination of wine, honey, and cream, heated, and then cooled, and considered a treat. "Tell Pompeo that I will do myself the pleasure of visiting the kitchens after prandium."

"That I will," said Milano. "You know, for a new fellow, Pompeo is working better than I'd hoped."

Di Santo-Germano laughed. "In a Venetian household, everything depends on the cook, does it not?" He waved Milano away and strolled across the loggia, a preoccupied stare in his eyes. Then he heard one of the pages call him, and his full attention was on the youngster. "Yes, Enrici?"

"There is a letter for you. Ruggier has it in your study." The youth, whose eyes were far more worldly than the other two pages' were, gave di Santo-Germano a calculating look.

"Indeed?" Di Santo-Germano waited for Enrici to say more.

"It was brought by a courier. From the Lowlands; at least that's where the courier came from." His face showed nothing but a kind of reckless anticipation.

"Did he," said di Santo-Germano, and handed the lad a brass coin. "For your trouble," he said as he turned toward the stairs to the upper floor.

"Rinaldo's pretending to be sick today," Enrici called after him. When he was certain that di Santo-Germano was listening, he added, "He says he can't work."

Di Santo-Germano paused on the third step of the flight upward. "Are you certain he is truly well? that this is only sham?"

"He claims his guts ache, but no one else has such a malady," said Enrici in a tone that bordered on smug. He hesitated. "He is pale and sweaty, but we all sweat in such weather. Rinaldo! You know how much he coddles himself. When it is hot, he is exhausted, and he has a cough from October to April."

"Where is he?" di Santo-Germano asked as he came down the stairs again.

"In his bed, of course. He doesn't want to get up." It was easy for Enrici to express his contempt; his lip curled and he rocked back on his heels.

"I shall deal with him at once," said di Santo-Germano, striding purposefully across the loggia toward the servants' corridor. "Tell Ruggier that I will be with him in a little while."

Enrici bowed. "I will, Signor' Conte."

Di Santo-Germano continued on, paying no attention to this minor concession that Enrici had made; he was reminded of the many times in the desert that he had seen men laid low by heat and lack of water. Venice was no desert, but fresh water was rare here, and from time to time men suffered from want of it. Di Santo-Germano hoped he would not find such a condition in his youngest page.

Text of a letter from Onfroi van Amsteljaxter in Bohemia to Grav Germain Ragoczy of Saint-Germain in care of Conte di Santo-Germano at Campo San Luca in Venezia, written in Latin, and delivered by messenger eighteen days after it was dispatched.

To the most respected and well-reputed Germain Ragoczy, Grav Saint-Germain, in care of the Conte di Santo-Germano residing at the Campo San Luca in Venezia, capital of the Most Serene Republic of Venezia, the greetings of Onfroi van Amsteljaxter, currently teaching in the household of the Landsmacht Dieter Flugelshund von Grussenwald,

Your Excellency, I write at the instigation of my sister, Erneste van Amsteljaxter, who has assured me you would not be adverse to having communication from me at this difficult time. She says she has written you in regard to the predicament in which I find myself, and that she has broached this matter on my behalf. I have seen her book, Lyrics and Tales of the Peasants of Brabant, *which you were kind enough to publish, and so I have some reason to hope that her convictions regarding your goodwill are not wholly without foundation.*

That said, I must ask that you keep what I tell you in confidence. My circumstances are precarious and may become dangerous in the near future, if there is no change here in Tabor—although I must stipulate that I am at Grussenwald, the Landsmacht's estate, three leagues from Tabor itself, which has proven fortunate in the last months. This region has been subjected to religious turmoil of late, and the most recent upheaval has come from the Hussites, who follow the preaching of Jan Hus: he may have been burned at the stake more than a century ago, but his presence in this area is still growing, and there are frequent clashes among his adherents, those who are committed to the teaching of John Calvin, and those who remain faithful to the Roman Catholic Church.

Two years ago I made the mistake of publishing a tract on the inconsistency inherent in killing in the name of Jesus, the Christ, Who deplored all aggression in His flock. This document was seized upon by various preachers and priests and denounced as heretical by all the factions currently in dispute. Until last Easter, the Landsmacht was willing to support me, but he has recently been taken by the zeal of Martin Luther, and has therefore given me a year to find other employment, which I am more than willing to do, but I cannot safely leave the protection of Grussenwald, for then nothing could stop the clergy of the region—Catholic and Protestant alike—from condemning me for apostasy of one sort or another. He is making himself ready for the End of Days.

I write to you in the hope that you will secure some degree of present immunity from persecution for me. I have no wish to be imprisoned, which I fear I must be if I remain where I am, yet I can find no place where I might avoid the hazards of religious struggles; everywhere I turn, I see men in arms over faith, and I despair. This may be a more accepting region than some, but that acceptance can vanish in an instant, and zeal take its place. If you have any recommendations to make, I will give them my whole attention, with the pledge that I will be prepared to go a great distance in order to secure the peace and indemnity my studies demand.

Let me extend my gratitude to you in advance of any action you may take on my behalf, for I have been much disappointed in the obdurate rejection I have encountered from many in the last several months. I pray you are all that my sister has told me you are, and that you will comprehend my present difficulties. If my supplication is not repugnant to you, I ask that you respond to my inquiry as soon as it is convenient for you to do so. I am daily made aware of the Landsmacht's increasing rancor with me; I begin to fear that he regrets his generosity, and will dismiss me out-of-hand, which must expose me to every kind of peril.

If you are minded to aid me, anything you offer would be most gratefully accepted, and sooner rather than later, for I am becoming desperate. For my sister's sake, I implore you not to dismiss my plight.

> *In hope and with my highest regard,*
> *I am, Your Excellency,*
> *Wholly at your service,*
> *Onfroi van Amsteljaxter*

By my own hand at Grussenwald, nr. Tabor, on the border of Bohemia and Moravia, on this, the 20th day of July, 1530 A.D.

9

Pier-Ariana was still trying to hold back tears, but her efforts were no longer successful; she clutched her long, deep-green cloak wrapped tightly about her, and peered up at the moon, in its shrinking third quarter, hanging above Venezia, casting a feeble luminescence over the sleeping city. A slow, calm wind out of the southeast ruffled her loosely braided hair and toyed with the hem of her cloak. "I wish you would wait until dawn," she said with a wobbly smile. "I wish . . . Oh, Conte, I cannot help but wish that . . ." She could not let herself go on.

"I know," he said, so gently that her tears increased. Although it was dark, his elegant black dogaline-and-doublet caught the torchlight, the silver threads in the exposed lining of the dogaline and the heavy links of his pectoral collar shining more than the moon.

"If you could wait a while—until everyone goes in for prandium," she appealed to him. Her eyes shone like opals where the torchlight struck her gathering tears. "It's not so long. You could do that, couldn't you—wait until prandium?"

"That would mean crossing the lagoon at midday. You know running water and tides in full sunlight can be difficult for me," di Santo-Germano said, leaning forward to kiss her cheek. His pectoral device swung with the movement, one of the raised, silver wings brushing her hand. "You have nothing to fear in my absence; you will want for nothing."

"But for you," she said, and stuffed her knuckles into her mouth to keep from crying in earnest.

"My master," Ruggier called softly from the stairs to the narrow canal; three dark shapes waited in the channel, piled with chests and crates and luggage. "The barges are filled and ready; Milano has his boatmen in position to take us across the lagoon." There were four squat boats in a line, each with its nose shoved against a barge, each boat with four oarsmen and a steersman—large, strong men, all of them, hired to propel the barges that were so essential to Venezia's survival.

"A moment, old friend," di Santo-Germano answered. "I fear Signorina Salier is dismayed; she is in need of comfort." As he spoke, he realized that any comfort Pier-Ariana might have could not come from him. "Is there someone you would want with you now? You told me you preferred to remain alone, but if you have changed your mind, I will arrange for—"

"Oh, go," she exclaimed abruptly, exasperation and misery vying for the uppermost of her emotions. "Do not prolong your leaving—it only makes it worse. I don't want you to go, and I'm trying to postpone the moment until you cannot leave at all." She pressed her lips together to stop them trembling, then hurried on, "Don't send for anyone—not my cousins, not my aunt, nor my step-brother, who would not leave his family on my account, or welcome me into his. None of them are you, di Santo-Germano. No one can take your place." She hissed through her clenched teeth. "I hate this."

"Cara donna," said di Santo-Germano, reaching for her hands, and bending to kiss her palms, knowing he could not ease her sorrow. "Perhaps I should not have asked you to come to see me off."

She gazed at him. "No, you were right to let me wish you a safe journey. That's not it." Her eyes filled again. "Why must it be the Lowlands? Why not some harsher place? Maestro Willaert has made the Lowlands seem such a captivating country, full of handsome men and beautiful women."

"Maestro Willaert is an exile, carissima, and he imbues his city of origin with the best of his memories," said di Santo-Germano. "He has made Venezia his home now, and it shows in his music."

"You are also an exile, and you do not say such things of your former country," she reminded him, as if catching him in a fault.

"Ah, but Pier-Ariana, I have been gone longer," he said with light, ironic amusement; he had been gone for thirty-three centuries. "You cannot compare our circumstances."

"My master," Ruggier prompted.

"A moment," di Santo-Germano said. "Until I am sure that Signorina Salier is willing to let me go."

"Oh, no. I will not be willing, Conte, not ever. But I will become resigned." She tried to pull her hands from him, then gave a sob and flung herself into his arms. "Promise you will return to me. Promise!"

"I have given you my Word, carissima. Unless a catastrophe intervenes, I will fulfill my bond. You will not be wholly without good friends. Giovanni Boromeo will stand by you, and Consiglier Fosian."

"As a favor to you," she said. "Who would be my friend if not for you?" She was appalled at the suggestion of a whine that had crept into her voice, and she stared past him. "I should not be so paltry."

As if he had not heard the last, di Santo-Germano said, "Anyone who loves fine music would befriend you, Pier-Ariana, and count himself honored." He kissed her eyes, finding the taste of her tears vexing, for they punctuated her distress at his departure. "I have no wish to sadden you."

"Then remain here; do not go to the Lowlands at all," she pleaded even as she pushed herself out of his embrace. "I know; I know you can't stay," she went on, stifling her weeping with a visible effort. "But I wish with all my heart that you would."

"I am truly sorry I must disappoint you," he said, sensing Ruggier's growing urgency as the eastern sky began to pale.

"Yes, I know. But you must. And you told me this would come. You have done all that you may to prepare me." She took another step back from him. "You said you would send me letters while you're away."

"I will," he vowed.

"If you fail me—" She stopped. "You have always been straightforward and honorable with me, and so I trust you will be so while you are gone."

Di Santo-Germano met her gaze steadily. "Gennaro Emerenzio has my instructions, and so does Orso Fosian. If you have complaint of anyone, you have only to speak with one of them and they shall address it, or explain to the Collegio why they do not. Both men will see that you are—"

"—looked after. Yes, I know," she said again in undisguised aggravation. "I have no reason for complaint, but—" She put her hands to her face as she began to cry again. "Devil take this horrible weakness," she muttered unsteadily.

"Pier-Ariana," he began, starting toward her.

"Oh, go. Go. Go!" She wrenched herself around so that she could not look at him. "I will not embarrass either of us any longer." Saying that, she swept across the loggia toward the reception room; in a moment Niccola was stumbling after her, half-asleep and uncertain where his duty lay.

"We should be under way," Ruggier said quietly. "Dawn is advancing, and the Black Cross Company will be waiting."

"I know," said di Santo-Germano as he glanced toward the reception-room door in time to see it swing closed. He shook his head once, a minute motion that was intended for his own understanding and none other's.

Ruggier pointed to a small chest on the longest barge. "I think you will find that most tolerable for our short voyage."

Di Santo-Germano pressed his lips together, then went to sit on the chest Ruggier had indicated, one of several that contained his native earth. "I hope the instrument-maker delivers her four-octave-and-five hammered dulcimer this afternoon; he is supposed to do so. I trust she will find consolation in the music she makes upon it."

"Do you suppose she will want to play even so remarkable an instrument as that? All things considered?" Ruggier asked, his voice hardly more than a whisper as the boats pushing the barges shoved away from the steps of di Santo-Germano's house.

"She is a gifted musician; playing will mitigate her unhappiness," said di Santo-Germano, a flicker of discomfort crossing his attractive, irregular features as the impact of the water took him. "It grieves me to cause her distress, but if I spare her, I put others at risk on my account, and as I cannot abandon her, so I cannot abandon them, either." He spoke in the language of Visigothic Spain as he glanced over his shoulder at the receding front of his landing steps.

"You have mentioned that before," said Ruggier, his accent slightly better than di Santo-Germano's.

"And you have been kind enough to listen," said di Santo-Germano, his dark eyes unreadable in the fading night. "I apologize."

"There is no reason you should," said Ruggier. "I would be more troubled if you did not have to wrestle with yourself." He stepped toward the front of the barge and lifted his lantern, the better to see the narrow canal as they slid along the dark passage.

The barges emerged into the Gran' Canale, the boats pushing them taking full advantage of the light traffic on the water to make an easy sweep; they turned eastward toward the Pont' Rialto. Once clear of the islands, they would head across the lagoon to Mestre where James Belfountain and his men would meet them. The Gran' Canale bowed around to the north and then turned westerly, bringing them beyond the Rialto Islands and into the lagoon, where they bore northward, the boats pushing the barges making slow but steady progress toward the shore as the eastern sky filled with the glow of an August sunrise heralded by a consort of gulls' cries. Slowly the shape of the distant hills emerged from the early morning haze.

The Mestre docks were busy already, the long shadows of dawn shimmering pink-gold where the new light touched them. At the jumble of piers, moorings, and docks, many barges were being loaded to carry the daily provender across the lagoon; others were picking up barrels of water and of wine, casks of oil, wooden tubs of butter, wheels of cheese, sacks of flour, firewood, as well as cages of live animals bound for the slaughterhouses beyond San Nicolo dei Mendicoli. The shouts and whistles drowned out the screech of the gulls that flocked to snap up bits of vegetables that had fallen from their barges. A few coasting traders were tied up in the deeper water of the harbor, waiting for this first flurry of the day to take on the cargo they would carry southward to Fusina and Chioggia, to Comacchio and Ravenna, Cervia and Rimini, or eastward to Caorle, Grado, and Trieste.

Milano guided di Santo-Germano's barges to a fairly quiet dock, and shouted for the porters waiting there to lend a hand, adding as incentive, "A fiorin d'argent for each man who works at the transfer. A ducat to share among you if you finish unloading before Mass is complete at Santa Maria del Mare!" He flicked his hand in the direction of the old church just beyond the docks and warehouses, then he turned back to the barges. "When the barges are secured, you may all find a tavern for something to refresh you; Milano has the funds to cover the cost of a good meal for each of you."

On the docks, five men scrambled toward the barges, a few of them calling to comrades, one shouting, "Where do you want these chests and crates taken?"

Di Santo-Germano steadied himself, and called out, "There should be a wagon-maker in the street that fronts the docks. The man is called Ideo Albergo: he will have wagons with him—four wagons, and two spare teams of horses. These chests and crates and boxes go into those wagons."

"We saw him," one of the porters shouted, and spat as he pointed behind him. "By the inn. With a group of English fighting men."

"That will be the very man," di Santo-Germano said as he flipped a couple copper coins to the porters, and then picked his way across the gangplank to the relative safety of the docks where he stood a long moment to wait until his vertigo passed. Pulling several fiori d'argent from his wallet, he knew he had the full attention of the porters. "Do you see the man in the dove-gray wool livery? on the largest barge?" He pointed to Ruggier. "Take your orders from him. I am going to summon the wagon-maker and the soldiers to move the wagons nearer, so you will not have to drag the crates and chests very far."

This brought affronted grunts from the porters, but they took the proffered coins and made for the gangplank, calling out for instructions.

Di Santo-Germano went off toward the street, feeling stronger with each step as he put the water behind him and once again trod the earth. He was adjusting his soft silken hat as he came around the end of the dock's warehouse onto the cobbles of the street and caught sight of a group of men in cuirasses, all holding horses while they drank their morning wine in front of a small tavern. Just beyond them, a nervous man with big shoulders in loose linen sleeves shoving out the arms of a much-marked leather cote sat on the box of a new wagon, three more lined up behind him. Di Santo-Germano took his eclipse-pectoral and held it aloft. "You there!" His voice carried well without becoming harsh.

A few of the armed men turned at the sound of his voice, and the wagon-maker was almost comically relieved; it was he who shouted, "Conte! Is that you?"

"It is," said di Santo-Germano, moving more swiftly without apparently lengthening his stride. He looked about, asking in English, "Who among you is Belfountain?"

A man of medium height with an ugly, uneven scar running across his forehead and over the bridge of his nose stepped forward. "I'm James Belfountain," he said in an accent that put his home in the middle of the island. "You're Saint-Germain?"

"Or di Santo-Germano, whichever you prefer," he answered. "I am pleased to meet you. These are your men?"

"Most of them. There's three still at the tavern, breaking their fast," said Belfountain, hitching his thumb in the direction of the three-story building in the shade of Santa Maria del Mare. "I can summon them at once, if you like."

"Let them eat. The wagons have yet to be loaded." He took a black-leather purse that hung from his belt and handed it to Belfountain. "As we agreed."

Without apology, Belfountain began to count the gold coins the purse contained. "Fifty gold florins?"

"You will find there are fifty-five—against unanticipated expenses," said di Santo-Germano, and continued toward the wagon-maker, addressing him in the Venetian dialect. "Signor' Ideo Albergo?"

"Oho," said Belfountain with a sudden brightening of his expression as he continued his count. "Good enough."

"Conte," said Albergo, sinking back against the high back of his seat. "You come in a fine hour."

"The soldiers will not hurt you," said di Santo-Germano. "If they have harmed you in any way, they will answer for it."

"No, no, they haven't," said Albergo, looking about nervously. "I was worried that they might seize my wagons if you failed to come." He tugged on a rein, and one of the four flaxen-maned, liver-chestnuts raised his head, mouthing the bit. "They'd certainly want the horses."

Di Santo-Germano kept his thoughts to himself as he said, "Yes. No doubt. Most knights find dray horses make good mounts, and these teams look to be fine animals."

"I had the tack from Porphirio Dandin, as you ordered. He said this is the best he has. There are ten sacks of grain in the fourth wagon, along with leather for patching, and two spare sets of reins.

Also an anvil and ten horseshoes." Albergo cleared his throat. "I arrived before dawn, and I have been waiting. The English soldiers make matters very bad."

"Why is that?" di Santo-Germano asked.

"They have been strutting, playing at fighting, and they threatened to bugger my youngest apprentice, on the third wagon. The only thing that stopped them was that their leader said you would not pay them if they did." He looked toward the spire of the church when it poked over the inn. "But you weren't here."

"Perhaps not when you first arrived, yet as you see, I am here now." He spoke with quiet authority, hoping to ease the wagon-maker's evident anxiety. "I trust they will not misbehave now."

"Truly," said Albergo, patting his brow with the sleeve of his smock. "My apprentices are driving the other wagons you ordered." He glanced over his shoulder as if to assure himself that the young men had not vanished. "Just as you stipulated. Three wagons, six teams." His nervousness was communicating itself to the horses; they began to fret, tossing their heads and stamping.

"And you had the teams from what breeder?" Di Santo-Germano looked at the first team, making note of their size and condition.

"All from Maffeo da Castello Sassosso; I presented your authorization, and he brought the horses," said Albergo. "They all are from his stable, none older than six, including the riding horses, at the rear of the fourth wagon. Your arrangements have been most carefully made." He cleared his throat. "The sum of all this is sixty-eight ducats, including the wagons, the horses, and the delivery."

Di Santo-Germano realized that the price was high, and he suspected that Albergo was adding to the price to cover his morning trials, but he opened his purse and handed over the money without cavil. "If you will move the wagons to the end of the dock there, so they may be more handily loaded?"

"Of course. As you say." He nodded repeatedly. "We'll attend to it at once." Swinging around on the driving-seat, he called out, "Decio! Timoteo! Fiober! Move up to the docks!"

The horses responded to the tap of the reins as if pleased to be active again. They trundled off toward the docks, their new tack creaking as much as the wagons clattered. The extra riding horses ponied behind the third and fourth wagons along with the two spare teams.

"Captain Belfountain," said di Santo-Germano, turning back toward the Englishman.

"Yes, Count," said Belfountain.

"How soon will your men be ready?" He looked toward the church, hearing the *Credo* chanted within.

"They could be ready in half an hour," said Belfountain.

"Does that include saddled and mounted?" di Santo-Germano asked, aware of the extent of preparations the soldiers still had to make.

"All right: an hour." Belfountain frowned at his hand as if he had never seen the knot of scar tissue at the base of his thumb.

"Very good," said di Santo-Germano. "An hour then, and we may depart."

"I should think so." Belfountain shrugged. "I'd best go warn them." He took a few steps, then stopped. "We have men to drive our wagons, but what of yours?"

Di Santo-Germano shaded his eyes against the brilliant sunlight. "I work with a paper dealer named Ulrico Baradin; he has agreed to send two of his best drayers to me."

"And where are they?" Belfountain asked suspiciously.

"They will be here shortly," said di Santo-Germano, hoping he was right; Baradin had promised him his most reliable men, and had accepted payment for their services. "They were told to meet us at Santa Maria del Mare." He glanced toward the church. "They may be at Mass."

"They may. With or without them, when the hour is up, we will go," said Belfountain, and strolled back toward the tavern, whistling as he went.

A short while later Milano came up to di Santo-Germano, saying, "Your cases are all off the barges, Conte."

"Thank you, Milano," said di Santo-Germano, handing him half a dozen coins. "For your men and for you."

"You are always generous, Signor' Conte." He slipped the coins into a pocket inside his canvas doublet. "You will inform me when to expect your return."

"Of course." Di Santo-Germano looked away from the water. "A year goes very quickly."

Milano hitched his shoulders in noncommitment, saying only, "So long as we have boats and barges empty here, I'm going to see what we can carry back to Venezia; we'll pick up a few more coins doing that." He ducked his head. "God give you a safe journey, Conte. May no enemy, or plague, or misfortune visit you in your travels."

"And to you, Milano," said di Santo-Germano as he noticed Ruggier approaching him, a sheaf of papers in one hand and a ruler in the other; with a small sigh of relief and regret, di Santo-Germano put Venezia behind him and went to attend to the final lading of wagons.

Text of a letter from Leoncio Sen to Padre Egidio Duradante, delivered by Christofo Sen's page the evening of the day it was written.

To the most revered Papal Courier, Padre Egidio Duradante, presently at the Casetta Leatrice, the greetings of Leoncio Sen, nephew to Christofo Sen, and citizen of the Serenissima:

I write to inform you that, lamentably, I must ask you to be patient for another day; like yours, my fortunes are ebbing at present. I have yet to collect the ninety-six ducats I have won from Gennaro Emerenzio, and until I do, I am unable to pay you the fifty I owe you. I do realize this is a considerable sum, and it is pressing the limits of friendship to disappoint you in this way, but I fear I must do so. Emerenzio has assured me that he can have the money he owes me in my hands by this time tomorrow. As soon as I have it, I will do myself the honor of waiting upon you at Casetta Leatrice, and I will discharge the debt in full.

I know this is a debt of honor, and that it must be paid. You need not doubt me, for I have always paid my obligations in full, have I not? And Emerenzio is not some reckless sailor, bent on carousing while he is ashore, and knowing he can escape to sea if he overextends himself. No. Emerenzio is a man-of-business for several merchants in this city, with a reputation for fair-dealing and responsible actions. Therefore I am much more confident in asking you for this slight extension, since with such connections as he has, Emerenzio is unlikely to be unable to put his hands on sufficient funds to compensate his debtors in full.

Of course I will be delighted to join you this evening for the private entertainment you mentioned. I know that Casetta Leatrice is known for the masques and theatricals produced there. As I have never before been present at such a performance, I will look forward to this most keenly.

> *With sincere devotion,*
> *Leoncio Sen*

By my own hand at Ca'Sen on the 11th day of September, 1530 Anno Domini

PART II

ERNESTE VAN AMSTELJAXTER

*T*ext of a letter from Atta Olivia Clemens, en route from the Papal States to Orleans in France, to Ragoczy Sanct' Germain Franciscus, in care of Andre Pesselent, printer, in Bruges; written in Imperial Latin, carried by private courier and delivered nine days after it was dispatched.

To my constant friend, Ragoczy Sanct' Germain Franciscus, currently Grav Saint-Germain, Conte di San-Germano, and whatever other names you may be using at the moment, the greetings of Atta Olivia Clemens, Roman widow, currently traveling into France, and for that reason, this letter must be brief, for I find writing in a moving vehicle, a most trying exercise, and for that reason I ask you to excuse any infelicities of style or execution. When we stop this evening, I will engage a courier to carry this to you, in care of your printer in Bruges, and hope you will have it in good time.

Yes, in spite of my earlier intentions, I have realized that it is prudent for me to be away from the Papal States just now, what with Charles and Clemente still locked in conflict, so I am returning to my horse farm near Orleans, in the hope that I may avoid some of the less pleasant developments in the current upheaval among the Christians, who cannot decide how best to deal with their faith, and are therefore killing one another over their doubts. Magna Mater! how I miss the days of my breathing life, when such concerns weighed little on the people of Roma. No one bothered then about what others believed so long as it was no imposition upon anyone.

I am sorry to say that my companion, Dionigi Eso, has been taken in charge by the Church to be examined for possible heresy. Something he wrote in one of his scholarly works has drawn the criticism of a Dominican, who read it and decided it was subversive, although I cannot see how his explication on the possible improvements in accuracy in navigation could be heretical. Sadly, at present I have only one real ally in the Papal Court, and I am wary about seeking his support at this time, for he, himself, is under scrutiny. On the advice of Cardinal della Rovere, I have arranged to place my estate in the care of my manager, and he has promised to send me regular reports about Sanza Pari, which should be enough to alert me if any mishap requires my presence and attention. He has also pledged to learn as much as he can about Dionigi Eso's fate. I am afraid things will not go well for him.

I apologize for the blot in the previous line; this nib is giving out, and the coach is rocking heavily.

Niklos Aulirios is remaining at Nepete until I send for him. He will set up the care of your Roman estate as well as mine, and he will prepare a full report for you before he leaves Roma to come into France. I am certain that Niklos will be most careful in his arrangements—he has always been so in the past. I have allocated funds for him to use, and I have drawn on the monies you left with me so that Villa Ragoczy may be kept properly, as you would wish.

I do not yet know how long I will stay in France, but you may be sure that I will inform you when I have made up my mind on that point. If the Spanish continue to war on all Protestants, then I may seek another part of the world entirely. You know how to direct your messenger to find me at my horse farm, as I know how to reach you through your printer. I ask you to keep me informed of your travels. I would prefer to know where you are rather than send four letters toward the cardinal points of the compass in the hope that you may receive one. With that in mind, I bid you a safe and rapid journey north, and a swift resolution to the problems that have beset you.

> *With my continual love,*
> *Olivia*

By my own hand en route to France, on this, the 21st day of September, 1530

1

"I think rain is coming," James Belfountain said to Grav Saint-Germain as they pulled to the side of the road that led up into the mountains, allowing the horses to rest before beginning the next leg of this day's journey. "The sky has the look of it. God's Teeth! to have rain at the most difficult stage of the journey."

"May steep roads be the worst we encounter," said Saint-Germain from his place on the box of the lead wagon.

"You will say otherwise if we must climb in mud," Belfountain warned. "I'd rather brave outlaws than mud."

Saint-Germain looked up, his hand raised to shade his eyes. "I doubt the rain will come before sunset," he remarked. "But I agree that there will be rain." He settled back on the driving-seat. "What lies ahead on this road?"

"Two more long climbs. There is a stretch of forest, a second ascent, and then a high meadow," said Belfountain. "The last rise is more than ten leagues ahead. The men will have to travel light for the rest of the day, I fear: only grieves and cuirasses. Nothing on the horses above tack—they'll tire and overheat if they have to carry much more than a rider."

"A sensible precaution," Saint-Germain approved.

"But we're in no condition to fight, if we're set upon," said Belfountain, his frown revealing his worry.

"Best to keep all the men on alert, then. The forest is more risky than the meadow, I would think," Saint-Germain remarked mildly.

"True enough," said Belfountain. "And this climb has already taken a toll on the horses. I must send a rider back to the remuda, in case one of the men needs a fresh horse for the climb, and be sure our wagon's team is still sound." He stretched his arms and rubbed at his face as if to remove the dust that had accumulated there.

"If you would like, you can move your priest into my second wagon; then you can put all your spare weapons into it, and keep them dry," Saint-Germain offered, and before Belfountain answered, went on, "Your wagon is fairly crowded with two men in it along with your food and equipment." He patted the arm of his black, padded-silk doublet, noticing how much dust had accumulated in the fabric. His knee-length pantaloons were smirched, and his high boots were coated in it. He wore only a signet ring, and it was concealed by gloves; he had learned long ago not to display his jewelry while traveling, knowing how great a temptation jewels could be.

"Won't your manservant mind?" Belfountain asked.

"No. He might enjoy the company, as I suspect your priest would, too," Saint-Germain answered, knowing Ruthger would once again prevent the priest from looking through the books they were carrying north, some of which the priest would find objectionable.

"Good of you, Count. I'll let him know." He whistled through his teeth and one of the flanking riders came over to him; after listening to a number of sotto voce instructions, the rider headed to the rear of the company. "We will reach an inn, about four leagues from here. It would be sensible to stop there for the night; the inn has a pasture and a spring. The horses could rest before we reach the last long climb." Belfountain indicated the spread of trees farther up the slope. "Now that we are entering Hapsburg territory, you will need to be more alert. There are brigands in the wood, and Protestants in the towns, and here we are more subject to local rules than would be the case in Venezian territory."

"A difficult combination, brigands and Protestants," Saint-Germain agreed. "I would prefer not to have to fight off either robbers or zealots. You are twenty armed men, but all of you could not hold off an outraged rabble, or a band of thieves." He had done both many times before and had no wish to engage in such conflicts again.

"It is prudent to avoid fights on the road, in any case," said Belfountain. "You must have learned this, traveling as you do."

"As I do," Saint-Germain agreed.

"About our lodging," Belfountain resumed. "Do you mind seeking out the inn I mentioned?"

"If you are satisfied that it is reasonably safe and has room for us all, then why should I protest." Saint-Germain removed his gloves and rubbed his hands together, bending his tired fingers before donning the gloves again. "I trust we will not be charged double or triple because of our numbers, or that your men will not be required to hunt their own supper."

"No, you will get fair value. I know the innkeeper and have patronized his inn before. The beds are lumpy and the food is plain, but the place is safe, there are chambers enough for this company, and the innkeeper knows how to hold his tongue." Belfountain laughed curtly. "His extra charges are not too outrageous, and he does not allow any whores but his own to service the travelers, so not many men are robbed."

"I am pleased to hear it," said Saint-Germain ironically, resting his elbows on his knees to ease the strain on his arms.

"Then we will go there." Belfountain rose in his stirrups and swung his sword to get his men moving again. "To the Hawk and Hare."

A few of his men shouted their approval of this plan, and urged their horses into a stretchy walk so that they would make the most speed possible without out-distancing the wagons.

"How long will it take to reach this inn?"

"Four leagues, most of it uphill? Three hours, I would guess. Plenty of time before nightfall," said Belfountain, pushing the truth a little. He paused. "I wouldn't want to make camp in the open in such a night as this one will be."

"Well enough," said Saint-Germain, deciding that he would have to inspect the wagons, particularly the wheels, in case the long climb had loosened one, or damaged a spoke or a rim.

For the next hour they kept steadily on, stopping once to let the horses drink from a bouncing stream that cavorted among the rocks on its way down into the narrow valley below, and once to pick the last of the sweet, dark berries growing wild at the edge of the woods. Once inside the forest and under the trees, Belfountain arranged his men in a more protective order, setting nine of them in flanking positions, putting two of them ahead as scouts, six around the horses of the remuda, and two at the rear to guard against sneak attacks; Belfountain's farrier drove their wagon with the remuda ponying after, somewhat behind Saint-Germain's three. They covered the next two leagues in as much silence as they could maintain so that they might hear anyone approaching them; then they caught sight of smoke rising through distant trees, a sullen black smudge against the wisps of clouds.

"Fire!" the soldier named Bartholomew shouted, pointing at the smudge above the green in obvious dismay.

Belfountain ordered his men to hold. "The smoke is dark; more than wood and pitch are burning," he said as he scrutinized it. "And it isn't spreading."

"It smells of burning flesh," said Saint-Germain quietly.

"Are you sure?" Belfountain rounded on him, his hard face more imposing than usual, his hand on the pommel of his sword.

"It is not easily forgotten, that smell," said Saint-Germain, no flicker of emotion in his eyes though he had a stab of recollection of Roma, thirteen hundred years ago, when the burning flesh was his own, and thirty years ago in Fiorenze, when Estasia had given herself up to the flames.

"A farm, then? A barn going up?" Belfountain ventured as his men started to fret. "Or—"

"Or a small village," said Saint-Germain. "There are many of them in these mountains."

"Let us hope," said Belfountain, "that this is nothing more than a local celebration, then, and the smoke is from a pig or a goat, and not from an excess perpetrated by highwaymen or mercenaries or clergy." If he was aware of any irony in his remark, he gave no indication of it. "Our road does not lead eastward, so we need not concern ourselves with them. We will put it behind us in half a league."

"Let us hope," Saint-Germain echoed, for he knew the smoke was from no goat or pig; something far more sinister was burning in that remote village, and he wanted to be away from it.

"Claudell, Haskins!" Belfountain shouted to his scouts up ahead. "Hold a moment until we can see you. We want to take no chances here."

"You may want your men behind to close up, as well, closer to the remuda and your wagon," Saint-Germain suggested.

"A good notion," Belfountain approved, and signaled to another of his men. "Have Wainsford and van Doost close up the distance behind. Tell them to keep careful watch: I don't want anyone to be snagged from the rear." The man touched his steel visor and swung his horse around; Belfountain watched him go, then gave his attention forward. "We must move a little more quickly. The rain will be upon us shortly."

"So it will," said Saint-Germain, glad his driving-seat was filled with his native earth to protect against the enervation rain inevitably caused; much as he disliked being out in it, he hoped the rain would quench the fire to the east of them.

"There is another steep part of the road ahead. Once we're up that, the inn will not be far ahead." Belfountain signaled his men to move on at a fast walk. "Don't exhaust your horses," he warned.

The wagons creaked and groaned, their harnesses jingled and squeaked, the wheels trundled, the horses blew and their hooves thumped on the soft, leaf-strewn earth. Saint-Germain held his team to a steady pace, feeling the four liver-sorrels lean into their collars, their flaxen manes flying from the increasing gusts as the road turned upward again toward the top of the ridge. Their afternoon light diminished and the wind picked up more steadily, strumming the trees so they bent and purred like favored cats, the boom of the wind heralding the storm gathering to the west of them.

Belfountain pulled his big, thick-necked Hungarian destrier up close to Saint-Germain's wagon. "We'll need to move a little faster once we're past the slope. This climb is taking too long. The rain will be here before we reach the inn."

"So I think," Saint-Germain agreed, not looking forward to enduring more running water.

"We will have to be careful not to be mired in mud," said Belfountain, voicing his apprehensions.

"Yes, I know," said Saint-Germain, then added, "Do you think it would be wise to send a rider ahead to the inn to secure rooms for us, and to bring aid if we take over-long to arrive?"

"Not yet," said Belfountain. "Once we crest the incline, I may do that, especially if the wind is stronger."

"As you wish," said Saint-Germain, and sat forward on his driving-box, readying himself for the next acclivity.

By the time they reached the top of the double-switchback the first stinging drops were slanting in on the wind. The horses, already tired, were growing fretful, and driving them in the thickening rain proved a demanding task. The road was soon slick with mud, and rather than go faster, they had to slow their progress. Belfountain dispatched one of his men to ride ahead to the Hawk and Hare, telling him to bring help if the rest of them had not arrived one hour after sunset.

"How reliable is he?" Saint-Germain asked as the young mercenary went trotting off, his armor noisy enough to announce his passage for half a league around.

"Haskins? He's the best of the youngsters," said Belfountain. "Comes from a long line of soldiers. His oldest brother is part of Essex's company. If Haskins hadn't four older brothers to require a place in the world, he would have ducal colors of his own. As it is, he must take employment where he can find it."

"Then I will assume there will be no reason to trouble myself on his account," said Saint-Germain, lifting the hood of his cloak forward to provide more protection to his face.

"Trouble yourself rather on ours," said Belfountain, swinging his horse around and reaching for his sword as a group of peasants came rushing out of the trees, some holding axes, some grasping pitchforks. "To me!" he shouted to his men, and prepared to block the peasants' advancement.

Saint-Germain reached under his driving-seat and pulled out his treasured katana, given to him more than three centuries ago by Saito Masashige; he prepared to draw it from its scabbard as he stopped his team and secured the reins around the brake-handle, then rose to his feet, ready to fight.

Belfountain moved a little ahead of the closed line of his men. "Halt! All of you!" he shouted, first in Venezian Italian, then in Alpine Austrian. "What do you want here?"

This was answered by frantic, angry shouts and bellows.

"Be quiet!" Belfountain shouted in Austrian and then in Venezian. "Choose one among you to speak, that we may understand you."

The men gathered together, and finally one angular fellow stepped forward. "Be you Catholics, Orthodox, Islamites, or Protestants? Which teaching do you follow, and what Crown do you support?" His dialect was an odd mix of Venezian and Austrian with a bit of Croatian included.

"What manner of business is it of yours?" Belfountain asked brusquely.

"We will make the demands here!" the angular fellow shouted, his voice high and stridulous.

"Men! At the ready!" Belfountain barked in English, and his company drew their weapons and leveled them at the group of peasants, who huddled together, their improvised weapons seeming inadequate in the face of the soldiers. Belfountain spoke in the Austrian dialect. "You will not attempt to detain us. Our business is no concern of yours."

"Armed men are killing folk in this region, by order of Huldrych Zwingli, for the new Emperor favors the Pope, who crowned him! Everyone knows it!" the angular man shrieked, lifting his baling hooks high above his head, then lunged forward and dug the long hooks deep into the flank and rump of Claudell's horse; the gelding screamed, kicked and bucked, nearly unseating his rider, and managing to clip the furious peasant on the side of the head with his hoof as his rear legs buckled and he sank heavily onto his on-side stifle. The man staggered back, keening in agony, blood welling from his cheek.

The peasants began to mill together, horrified at what their companion had done; it was one thing to threaten armed men, and quite another to attack them in earnest. Two of them lifted their weapons pugnaciously, and took a step forward, all the while looking from their injured comrade to Belfountain's men, three of whom were preparing to move in on them.

"Hold!" Saint-Germain ordered; his voice, although not strained or loud, carried to every man.

Belfountain glared at Saint-Germain, pointing to Claudell, who was dismounting as best he could without further injuring his gelding. "We're going to lose a good horse, thanks to these fools! One of you men, bring a pistol and put him out of his misery!"

Mondroit came from the front right flank, dismounted, and began to charge his pistol. Everyone had gone silent.

"There is no sense in courting more losses," said Saint-Germain as he slipped his katana back into its scabbard and climbed down from the wagon, going to the injured man as Mondroit prepared to shoot the gelding. "I want to see what happened to your face," he said to the peasant, who had sunk to his knees, now whimpering with pain.

"You will kill me," the man accused, barely understandable.

"No, I will not," said Saint-Germain. "Believe this." He stood beside the peasant, noticing that the man was beginning to shiver. "Ruthger, bring a blanket," he called out.

The peasants were muttering amongst themselves, casting infuriated glances at the armed men and the black-clad man. One of them raised his woodsman's axe and took a tentative step forward just as Mondroit fired a single ball into the middle of the gelding's brain; the horse jerked, then collapsed.

Belfountain's men moved closer to the peasants, ready to attack, anxious for Belfountain's signal to set upon the ill-armed rabble.

The injured peasant wailed and fell onto his side; Saint-Germain knelt beside him.

Going about Saint-Germain's request as if nothing were amiss, Ruthger climbed down from the second wagon, a folded blanket of two-colored wool in his hands. He paid no attention to the soldiers or the peasants, but went directly to Saint-Germain. "Is there anything else you would like?"

Saint-Germain had been studying the peasant, and realized that he was badly injured. "I think a carry-bed will be needed, and my medicament in the dark-blue glass vial." He spoke in Imperial Latin, keeping his voice low. "We'll need a second blanket, as well, or a canvass roll."

"Are you certain?" Ruthger's somber face betrayed nothing of his concern. "He is conscious and not confused."

"That will not last," said Saint-Germain with regretful certainty as he carefully draped the blanket around the man's shoulders, and pulling it close around his hunched body. "He will soon begin to babble and to drift into a stupor. Once that happens, he is as good as dead."

Ruthger looked down at the peasant, who was shaking in earnest now. "Are you sure he cannot be cured? Surely you know something—"

"I am," said Saint-Germain. "His skull is cracked in at least two places. See how his face sags under the eye and the blood coming from his ear? He will not recover no matter what I do, so he might as well die as easily as possible. It's syrup of poppies or agony."

"I'll fetch another blanket, and the vial," said Ruthger, and went off to do those things.

Claudell and Mondroit were struggling to remove the tack from the dead horse, tugging at the saddle to pull the girth from under the body.

Belfountain rode a little closer to Saint-Germain. "What about this fellow? Do we leave him? What do you think the others will do?"

Saint-Germain shook his head. "I cannot say. But I know what we should do, to ease this bad situation: make a carrying-bed for this man, and help the others to ready him to travel."

"Why should we bother? We can push our way through," said Belfountain.

"Not without risk of further injuries," said Saint-Germain, "and that could delay us still more."

Sighing through his teeth, Belfountain took a long moment to consider his response, then said, "Very well." He raised his voice. "Help these men make a travel-bed. Their companion will need it. You! Cathcart! You take charge!"

Cathcart muttered something pithy as he dismounted and handed his reins to Belfountain. His Venetian Italian was far from expert, and his accent was harshly English, but he made his intentions plain, and finally one of the peasants lowered his pitchfork and came forward. "Thank God," Cathcart said in English, and then switched back to his version of the northern dialect. "We have a roll of canvass. If you can bring two poles, we can fashion a carry-bed for your fellow there."

One of the peasants hefted his long-handled hoe. "Will this do?" he offered, avoiding the condemning glance of two others among his companions. "We have an orchard-hook, too. It has a substantial, long handle."

Ruthger came back to Saint-Germain, a long roll of linen in one hand, and a small vial of dark-blue glass in the other; a second blanket was tucked under his arm. He held these out to him, the blanket providing support for the bandages and vial. "What more should I do, my master?"

"Since you had the good sense to bring a bandage, you can help me to wrap his head so the broken bones won't shift any more than they must; once the syrup has taken hold, we will bind his head," said Saint-Germain, dropping down on one knee beside the stricken man. Doing his best to use the local speech, he said, "I have medicine for you; it will ease your pain and let you rest while your friends take you back to your home."

The man moaned and his eyes fluttered, and he wheezed more than he had before.

"First I need to see your face," Saint-Germain continued. "If you will lower your hands for me?"

Behind the three of them, Cathcart had finally enlisted the aid of three of the peasants, and was now unrolling canvass and trying to explain how it was to be attached to the handles of hoes, hooks, and swineherd's weighted staff.

The peasant shuddered and lowered his hands a short way from his face, his fingers tense as talons. His color was ashen and a thin line of blood ran from his nose. He shuddered and his left hand spasmed.

"You will have to swallow this," said Saint-Germain, holding the unstoppered vial to his mouth and preparing to tip the liquid in.

The carry-bed was almost finished, and the peasants began to talk among themselves as to who should be bearers, all the while watching the soldiers uneasily and making gestures of protection.

Now a light spattering of rain pattered down, hardly more than a suggestion of damp, but both Belfountain and Saint-Germain looked up as Belfountain burst out, "Mary's Tits! We'll have mud for sure!"

Saint-Germain continued to concentrate on the peasant, who was coughing with the effort to get some of the syrup down. "Steady, good fellow. Steady," he encouraged as he managed to get the last half of the vial's contents into him.

"How much longer?" Cathcart asked Saint-Germain. "These men are getting restless."

"I cannot blame them for that," said Saint-Germain, rather remotely; his attention was still fixed on the injured man. "We want to wrap his head, and then you may take him," he said to the peasants in a fairly good version of their dialect.

The rainfall grew a bit heavier and the wind-gusts returned, shoving at the mountain as if to move it. The peasants huddled together, resentment mixing with chagrin as they watched Saint-Germain deliberately secure the long strip of linen around the man's head; by the time he was finished with his task, the peasant was barely conscious.

Cathcart helped load the peasant onto the carry-bed, and stood back so that his companions could lift the carry-bed and head off toward their village, some of the men already worried about the storm.

"What do you want to wager they don't abandon him a league from here?" Belfountain said to Saint-Germain.

"It will depend upon the weather," said Saint-Germain.

"And how bad his wound is," added Belfountain, a note of curiosity in his observation.

"It is a very bad wound," said Saint-Germain, looking up as Ruthger approached holding a shining lanthorn. "Very good, old friend. We will need light very soon."

"So we will," said Belfountain. He motioned to his men. "Get your lanthorns, all of you!"

As his men hurried to do as he ordered, Saint-Germain climbed back onto the driving-box of his wagon and hung the lanthorn on its bracket at the edge of the driving-box so that the way ahead would be illuminated, for although the dark did not impede his vision, he knew that Belfountain and his men would be wary and perplexed if only they had to take the precaution to light the road ahead. Picking up the reins, he resigned himself to an hour of rain.

Text of a letter from Joseph-Marie Derricot of Liege to Christofo Sen in Venice, written in Latin and carried by private courier; delivered fourteen days after it was dispatched.

To the most esteemed Secretary to the Venezian Savii, the respectful greetings of Joseph-Marie Derricot, abiding at Liege in the Inn of the Shuttle and Loom, and, in accordance with your instructions, informing you of the arrival and departure of persons of interest to the Savii.

You had informed me, some weeks since, that an eminent foreigner, known in Venezia as Franzicco Ragoczy, il Conte di Santo-Germano, might be expected to pass through this city, for such were his plans as filed with the Minor Consiglio. From your description, he had hired armed escort and was bound for Antwerp, Amsterdam, and Bruges. I wish to report that last night there arrived from the south, a foreigner calling himself Ferenz Ragoczy, Grav Saint-Germain, who was accompanied by armed men, a manservant, and the priest and farrier of the soldiers. He wore a signet ring I have briefly seen: it is a disk with raised displayed wings, black on silver, which he presented to establish his identity when he first entered the city. This would be consistent with what you have said regarding this man; coupled with the similarities of name—which can be accounted for in terms of regional language—I am almost completely convinced that I have seen your man, and that he is truly bound for the Lowlands, as you supposed.

This Grav Saint-Germain is presently at the Old Mill, an inn of good size, able to take in all his armed men, provide them food, bed, and drink for a fairly substantial amount, but not exorbitant, as is charged at the Starry Crown. He has paid for three nights there, and so I must suppose he will be here at least that amount of time.

I was told that he had received a courier from Antwerp, apparently something about a house there, but I have no details to offer you. Suffice it to say that his presence in Liege is not a secret, nor is it intended to be, and that Saint-Germain has already offered bona fides to the leaders of the city and its Guilds. I am persuaded that he is engaged in nothing nefarious, that he is not planning to abscond with money or other treasure, and that he is planning to return to Venezia within the year, for the soldiers have said that they are engaged to escort him south-by-east come June, and that their leader, an Englishman named Belfountain, has already established the terms of their journey.

I shall inform you of any developments not already set forth here, such as any detention here or deviation from the stated plans of this Grav. The state of the city is such that there is some risk that the present leaders may have more inquiry to make of the Grav, since he has shown proof that he owns presses in various places. Books can be hazardous in these precarious times.

Be certain that your ducats will be put to good use,

> *And that I remain*
> *Your most humble servant to command,*
> *Joseph-Marie Darricot*

At Liege, by my own hand, on this, the 8th day of October, 1530 Anno Domini

2

Bruges was blustery, with sharp winds off the North Sea cutting along the streets and shrieking down chimneys, sapping the last of autumn's warmth and replacing it with the promise of an early winter. Occasional patches of blue shone through the racing clouds, lending an evanescent cheer to the waning day.

Coming through the door on a shove of the northwesterly wind, Ruthger nodded to Jaquet Saint Philemon, who had hurried to answer the knock on the door, saying, "I'd wish you good afternoon, Saint Philemon, but it certainly isn't, if the weather is any test of the matter." He swung his knee-length, fur-trimmed, mulberry-colored chamarre off his shoulders, revealing a short, old-fashioned huque in double-woven English wool of russet-brown over knee-length pin-tucked barrel-hose in dull satin of raw ocher; his leggings were dark-gold and his high-topped shoes were made of Cordovan leather. He handed the chamarre to the steward, going on, "Maarten Gerben will be here within the hour to see my master. I trust I may find him in his study?"

"Yes," said Saint Philemon, giving his cuff-bands a fussy twist. "He left his apartment about two hours ago, and went to his study as soon as he had been given the cards left for him."

"Thank you." Ruthger started toward the stairs to the second floor, then stopped. "The tailor is coming around later today, shortly before sunset, delivering two new suits of clothes—one for my master and one for me, and taking measurements for others."

Saint Philemon had a short, fierce, inner debate, then remarked, "That will be of benefit; aside from your chamarre, your garments are not in the current mode, except for your Venezian clothing, and such is not appropriate here. You will be glad of what the tailor brings you."

Ruthger came close to laughing. "Just so."

"You will want to be notified when he arrives, I would suppose," said Saint Philemon, setting the door-latch with care; it would not do to have the wind blow it open.

"Yes, and when Gerben arrives," said Ruthger.

"I'll attend to it," said Saint Philemon, going to fetch a footman to keep watch on the door.

Ruthger climbed the stairs to the second floor; they were not so steep as the stairs in the house on Campo San Luca, but they made up for this in their narrowness. As Ruthger continued upward, he decided that another oil-lamp in the stairwell would relieve its constant gloom, and determined to instruct Saint Philemon to secure one to the wall at the first small square step that served as a landing. At the top of the second flight, Ruthger took the corridor leading southeast and tapped on the double doors at its end.

"Come in, old friend," called the voice from inside.

Ruthger turned the latch and stepped through the double doors: Saint-Germain's study was the largest room in the house, set at the back of the building, over the kitchens. There were two trestle-tables, a book-stand, two tall stools, and three closed cabinets, along with two chairs, and an upholstered bench facing the hearth where this afternoon a small fire burned. Saint-Germain himself was perched on one of the stools at the larger of the two tables, a small beam-scale suspended from his hand, the greatest portion of his attention fixed on the two objects he was weighing, one a brass spool, the other a haphazard knob of gold. He wore an English doublet in black-silk twill, piped in silver, with a narrow ruff of exquisite point-lace. His barrel-hose were a bit shorter than Ruthger's, made of polished satin, and leggings of black silk; although he was a decade out of the current fashion, he had lost none of his elegance. "Well enough for a first effort," he said as much to himself as to Ruthger as he tossed the gold into the air and caught it. "The athanor will need some minor repairs."

Ruthger waited until Saint-Germain set the scale down, then said, "Gerben is coming today. I persuaded him that he would do better, speaking with you directly, than continuing this endless exchange of messages. There is going to be confusion or an interception if you continue as you have."

"Excellent," Saint-Germain approved. "I will be glad to receive him at last."

"He asked me to warn you that he is being watched," Ruthger added.

"As are most printers in Bruges," Saint-Germain observed, taking care to speak the local dialect in case any of his household might be listening.

"That they are," said Ruthger. "But that does not mean we should be unmindful of it."

Saint-Germain swung around on the stool to face Ruthger. "You have the right of it, of course. We do not want to add . . . ah . . . fuel to the fire." His sardonic witticism held a grim reminder of the printers and book-makers whose businesses had been burned to the ground during the last two years by various outraged mobs rampaging through the city.

"By no means," said Ruthger with a trace of acerbic amusement on his features.

"Is Gerben concerned for his bindery?" Saint-Germain asked. "Or is it the press itself that he worries for?"

"What printer in the Low Countries would not be concerned for both?" Ruthger countered, and went on in Venezian Italian, "He did his utmost to present the appearance of confidence and composure, but his eyes flickered often and he jumped at sudden sounds. His clothes are loose on his frame, so I must suppose he has recently lost weight, yet he doesn't appear to be ill, only troubled."

"I see," said Saint-Germain thoughtfully in the same tongue. "What more did you notice?"

"His shop is short handed," Ruthger reminded him, "and he has only two apprentices now: last year—"

"—he had four," Saint-Germain finished for him. "That is discouraging, at least for him."

"At least," Ruthger seconded. "He lost one apprentice to high fever and putrid bowels, but the other left for Mass one day and never returned."

"Kidnapped, does he think?" Saint-Germain asked.

"Not kidnapped: he fears the lad was taken by the Secular Arm of the Church, and is being held in one of the monastery prisons," Ruthger said, his emotions carefully banked. "It's that, or he fled the country."

"Had he done anything to merit such attention?" Saint-Germain inquired, an edge in his voice as he tossed the gold again, and caught it, then set it on the table.

"Gerben didn't say, but he thought that the youth had been working with some comrades to print up broadsheets—you know, the kind that are posted on walls throughout the city, most inflammatory in their rhetoric, inciting disputes and conflict among the various local religious factions." Ruthger paused. "Until they are white-washed over or torn down."

Saint-Germain gave a single nod. "It is not something about which Gerben may safely make inquiries, if that is the case. Neither the civil nor the religious authorities take well to those who spread dissension among the people, and small wonder. Gerben's oppugns on the apprentice's behalf could lead to his interrogation for making inquiry."

"Assuming, if he were not detained, he would be told anything at all," added Ruthger.

"Yes; assuming that," said Saint-Germain, getting down from his stool and pacing the length of his study. "It is getting worse, is it not?" he asked from the far end of the room.

Ruthger had been with Saint-Germain long enough to know that he meant the tension between religious groups. "Yes, and it will not soon be better."

"No, I fear not," said Saint-Germain, picking up the gold and holding it to the light. "Seven ounces, English weight. I was hoping for ten."

"Seven ounces is not a small amount," Ruthger remarked as he took the lump of gold Saint-Germain had made in the athanor.

"If matters were more settled, then I would agree," Saint-Germain said.

"But you're worried," said Ruthger.

"That I am," said Saint-Germain in the dialect of Bruges. "This city is like a pot on the simmer. It could soon boil over, and that could mean more hardship than most citizens now endure. Spain is proving a hard master for their Netherlands, and Clemente is unlikely to rein in any Hapsburg, not since the Spanish sacked Roma."

"Do you think the Church will try to bring the city to heel?" Ruthger sighed.

"Spain would doubtless like to make such an attempt, and the Church might permit it, but the Holy Roman Emperor would not countenance so oppressive a course, or so it appears." Saint-Germain glanced toward the door, aware of a soft sound beyond it. He signaled to Ruthger, and then went on, "Protestants are more tolerated by the Austrian Hapsburgs than the Spanish Hapsburgs, though they are all ruled by the same man."

"Does that lessen or increase the instability, do you think?" Ruthger moved a few steps nearer the door.

"It is too soon to say," said Saint-Germain. "If the Spanish have their way, there will be blood in the streets and then the chance for negotiated resolution will be lost. You know how these confrontations escalate: we have seen it before."

Ruthger put his hand lightly on the door-latch. "How many more times will this happen?"

"Pitting faith against faith?" Saint-Germain came back down the chamber. "As long as the gods are a mystery, or so I fear."

At his signal, Ruthger opened the door, to find Oton Marchand, the senior footman, standing close to it. "So!" Ruthger said. "You carry a message?"

Oton colored to the roots of his fair hair. "I . . . I . . . that is . . . No message." This admission ended on a brusque sigh.

"So you were listening." No one moved as Saint-Germain regarded Oton steadily for a short while. Then, apparently satisfied, he said, "Well, you are come in good time. I have an errand for you."

"Certainly," said Oton in a rush of an emotion that might have been gratitude. "Whatever you require."

Saint-Germain saw the flick of Ruthger's eye, but continued on as if he had not. "Have a plate of sausage and cheese made ready, and bring a pitcher of beer and a tankard, if you will."

"Certainly," said Oton, and started away from Saint-Germain, his features twisted in dismay. "Your pardon, Grav; I should not have—"

"You will need another tub of wood if you want to keep your fire going," Ruthger pointed out.

Saint-Germain offered a rueful smile. "Thank you for noticing. Yes, by all means, have a tub of wood sent up, Oton. It would not do for me to receive Gerben in a cold room."

Ruthger nodded as Oton hastened away, "I wonder to whom he reports?" He did not expect an answer. "I'll go to the kitchen to get your tray, and leave you to prepare your dispatch to Gennaro Emerenzio; the courier will be here in an hour."

"You are good to remind me," said Saint-Germain, ducking his head as if chagrined by his lapse in memory; he reached into a drawer under the table and pulled out a sealed envelope, which he handed to Ruthger. "This should be sufficient. The courier is one of Belfountain's, or one we have hired here?"

"Yes; one of Belfountain's. As part of the retaining contract I struck with him on your behalf." He slipped the envelope inside his doublet, frowning a bit, then said, "If anyone should inquire, am I at liberty to reveal the terms of your agreement with Belfountain?"

Saint-Germain's glint of a smile told Ruthger that he had been right: Saint-Germain wanted any household spies to know about his arrangements with private couriers. "Certainly, if they have good reason to ask for it."

With a slight nod, Ruthger left the room, securing the latch before going back down the narrow stairs to the main floor, and from there along the corridor to the kitchen.

Wenzel Horner, the chief cook, was a man of moderate height, but with shoulders and forearms like a blacksmith. Just now he busy cutting up cabbage for the pork stew cooking in the large pot hung over the coals in the maw of the fireplace. He looked up as Ruthger came in. "It's you, is it? What am I to do for the Grav?"

"He would like a tray sent up for his visitor—when the visitor arrives," said Ruthger. "Sausage, cheese, and beer."

"I have a barrel we have just tapped; it is better than many barrels have been of late." Wenzel yawned. "Is that all the Grav needs me to do?"

"Don't feel unappreciated," said Ruthger. "My master's privacy in his dining is the custom among his people. Do not feel offended that he does not avail himself of your excellent cooking."

Wenzel sniffed. "One would think he has no consequence at all— he never has guests to dine, and he, himself, keeps his own company for his meals, whatever they may be."

"It is the way of those of his blood," said Ruthger in a tone that deflected any further pursuit on the cook's part.

Wenzel scraped the chopped cabbage into a bowl. "I have apple-bread in the warming ovens, or does that tempt you?"

"Alas," said Ruthger, and then said, "But I am sure my master's visitor would like to have it with his sausage and cheese."

"I will see he has a slice or two," Wenzel said magnanimously.

Knowing that the cook's pique had been mollified, Ruthger left the kitchen, bound for the steward's quarters, where he spent a short while in reviewing the household accounts with Saint Philemon. By the time he returned to the kitchen, he had handed off the envelope to Belfountain's courier and received a note from the butcher, saying that there were fresh lambs in the market. As he approached Wenzel to arrange about shopping, he was informed word had come from Oton that the printer Gerben had arrived and was waiting in the vestibule. Making a rapid decision, Ruthger said, "Have Oton escort Gerben to the Grav's study. I will bring the refreshments up to them."

The page who rushed to do this was a lad of eleven called Joris who often spent his afternoons with Wenzel in the kitchen, learning the secrets of cooking, and playing solitary games with ladles and forks. He was an ambitious, eager boy, all elbows and knees and restless energy, whose only living relative was an uncle serving aboard a merchant-ship.

"That boy has a very high opinion of you," said Ruthger, a hint of warning in his voice.

"He's clever enough; in a year or two, I may make him my apprentice, if his interest hasn't waned," said Wenzel, trundling over to the cast-iron oven and taking out one of four loaves of bread, holding it with the tips of his fingers to avoid being burned; he went to the chopping board beside the tray on which sat a plate of sausages fresh from the oven, next to two large wedges of cheese, one white, one dull-gold.

"No doubt he will be a credit to you, if you don't abuse his esteem for you," said Ruthger. "Lonely boys can credit those they value with virtues no one man can possess."

"You have some experience in this?" Wenzel said as he took a knife and began to slice the loaf.

"Yes. Years ago," he said, not adding that it had been over thirteen centuries since Marius' devotion to him had brought about the youngster's death in the terrible riots that had inflamed Roma at the end of the reign of Heliogabalus.

"I wouldn't have thought you were a man to be influenced by the adulation of a child." Wenzel set the sliced bread in a small basket and covered it with a square of linen.

"I believe I was missing my son," said Ruthger, and added, "He died—many, many years ago."

Wenel's laugh was short and sarcastic. "You had a son?"

"I had," said Ruthger, and volunteered nothing more as he picked up the tray Wenzel had finished loading. "The beer?"

With a snap of his fingers, Wenzel hurried to the outer pantry, disappeared only to return almost immediately with a large stoneware pitcher filled with dark, fragrant beer. "There." He held it out and then reached for a tankard to put on the tray. "May the printer have a good appetite."

"Amen," said Ruthger, and started toward the backstairs, bound for Saint-Germain's study.

Maarten Gerben was seated facing the fire, his big hands extended to the fire, revealing permanent ink-stains on his nails and knuckles. He was in his late twenties, thick-bodied and round-faced, in somber-but-prosperous clothing in dark-gray English wool. Although his features were clearly often cheerful, his expression now was reticent and fretful. He stopped speaking as Ruthger came into the room, giving a quick, anxious glance at Saint-Germain.

Saint-Germain was standing behind the second chair, leaning easily on the high back of it. He signaled Ruthger to set the tray down within Gerben's reach. "You may say what you like in front of Ruthger," he told Gerben calmly. "He has my complete confidence. You may rely utterly on his discretion."

"I am sure you may do so," said Gerben with a slight emphasis on *you.*

"And you, as well," said Saint-Germain, indicating the tray.

"After your examination by the Archbishop's Council, you can still put such trust in the man?" Gerben marveled.

"I am not in prison, and they questioned Ruthger as well as several others in the household. And you," said Saint-Germain. "He said nothing to my discredit then, nor would he now."

Gerben hunched his shoulders. "Other men have misplaced their trust."

"So they have, and I have been one of them, upon occasion," Saint-Germain agreed, sensing this was as much a ploy as a complaint. "Help yourself to anything you like."

"Will you not join me?" Gerben asked, looking hungrily at the plump, hot sausages.

"Thank you, no." He came around the chair to sit down. "If you will, tell me more about the problems you've been having."

Gerben rubbed his hands together. "It is just the same for printers throughout Bruges, and the rest of the Low Countries under the heel of Spain." He reached to pour himself a tankard of beer, but stopped, as if worried about being overheard.

"That is becoming more apparent with every passing day," said Saint-Germain.

"You have the right of it," said Gerben, reaching for the fork to prong one of the sausages; as the tines penetrated the casing, three little spurts of grease gushed out. "Oh, excellent," he approved as he lifted the sausage to bite the end off.

"I will tell the cook," Ruthger said solemnly.

"Yes; do," said Gerben, chewing steadily, the first signs of pleasure softening the hard lines in his face.

Ruthger nodded and stepped back. "Is there anything more?" he asked Saint-Germain.

"Not at present, no, thank you." He glanced toward the door. "Perhaps you will return in half an hour?"

Understanding that this meant he was not to go far, Ruthger bowed slightly. "That I will."

As soon as the door closed behind Ruthger, the satisfaction vanished from Gerben's countenance. "You must be careful. Even trusted servants have been known to trade their masters for freedom. Keep all secrets to yourself, and no one can reveal them to your disadvantage."

"I have no such worry on Ruthger's part, but I will be careful of the rest," said Saint-Germain, aware that the printer had good reason for such a warning.

"You must," said Gerben urgently. "In the last month two of my friends—men with presses of their own—have had their books seized, and they themselves have been put in prison for seditious activities. Their authors have left the country. And, for that matter, so have most of mine." He scowled ferociously. "One of my remaining apprentices has said he is going to sign on a ship bound for the New World. There are fortunes waiting for men with talent, he tells me, and he will not have to feel the Church looking over his shoulder all the time."

"Is he planning to be a printer in the New World?" Saint-Germain asked tranquilly.

"I don't think so," Gerben said, and finished his sausage. "He says a man who can read and write can become a copyist or a notary, and in time, an advocate, and they will need such men as the New World becomes civilized." The recitation of these optimistic plans made him more morose; he speared a second sausage.

"Have you found a replacement for him?" Saint-Germain guessed this was the reason for Gerben's despondency.

"I thought I had," said Gerben. "But the boy's father has changed his mind since the recent detentions. He's apprenticed the lad to an apothecary." This time his bite was emphatic, an outward manifestation of his inner demoralization.

"Always a useful profession," Saint-Germain murmured.

"But it points the way, don't you see?" Gerben pleaded. "It shows that anyone printing any books may be held accountable for what they say, or what they are deemed to say, and the Church imposes many things on those who try to present any material that does not—" He stopped and took a long drink of beer. "I apologize, Grav. I have been so . . . so . . ."

"Distraught?" Saint-Germain suggested. "I can see that."

Gerben took another long drink. "I have cause for my concern, wouldn't you agree?"

"Yes, I would," said Saint-Germain, sensing that Gerben was trying to come to the point of his visit.

"Yes." He took a deep breath. "I wish to ask you, keeping all these things in mind—" He stopped suddenly. "I mean, if you would only consider my situation. I wish to continue in this work, more than anything else, but I am afraid that it may lead me into trouble—trouble that would prevent me doing anything more of use, either as a printer, or as a man." He sagged in his chair, as if what he had said had deflated him.

"I gather you would like to move your press to another city," said Saint-Germain.

Staring at Saint-Germain as if astonished that he had achieved so much in that hectic outburst, he said, "Yes. I would."

"Have you a locale in mind?" Saint-Germain asked.

"I do," said Gerben. "I have written to a merchant who has warehouses on the Channel Islands. He has said that in return for my keeping records and inventories of his cargos stored there, he will permit me to set up my press in the smallest of his warehouses."

"The Channel Islands," Saint-Germain repeated slowly. "Have you chosen the one you prefer?"

"Jersey," said Gerben, so quickly that Saint-Germain suspected he had made up his mind just now. "King Henry—who is Duke there—may be having his difficulties with Rome and the Pope, but I doubt those conflicts will touch the Channel Islands."

"If Henry Tudor prevails, I think you may be right," said Saint-Germain. "I gather you want my permission to do this, and my support."

Now Gerben looked sheepish. "Well, yes, Grav, for if I lose your patronage, I cannot make this move, or any move."

"Ah," said Saint-Germain, and leaned forward in his chair. "I do not expect you to put your work and your life at risk for my sake. If you have found that it is too dangerous to do your work here in Bruges, then, by all means, find a safer place to go, and with my good wishes, if you need them. I will continue my support of your press for as long as you continue to publish."

Gerben's chuckle was weak from this assuagement. "I was prepared to have to do much more than this," he admitted before he emptied his tankard and hurriedly refilled it.

Saint-Germain regarded the printer in silence for a short while, then said, "As soon as you have made your arrangements, notify me, and you will be provided the funds you need for your move." He wondered why the merchant with the warehouses had not extended his beneficence to sponsorship as well, but decided not to add to Gerben's distress; he listened attentively while Gerben expounded on his plans for his press, so that when Ruthger returned, as he had said he would, he discovered Gerben talking animatedly, his food half-eaten, and Saint-Germain giving him his full attention, a slight, contemplative smile the only indication of his thoughts.

Text of an accounting from Giules d'Attigny, tailor of Bruges, to Grav Saint-Germain.

Most excellent Grav,

I hereby submit my bill, with an accounting for the clothes I have made for you in the last three weeks, with added amounts for putting other work aside in order to finish your garments before your departure for Antwerp. I have already deducted the generous initial payment you made, and ask for a prompt remittance of the balance, as you assured me you would provide prior to your departure Monday week.

I have, as you requested, reckoned the amount in ducats.

Three chamarre, one of satin, two of fine wool   3dt

five chamise, two of linen, three of silk as provided by
  the Grav   2dt
two pair of barrel-hose, one in damask, one in wool   3dt
three pair of knee-hose for riding   3dt
six pair of leggings   1dt
two Flemish doublets, lined in silk   2dt
one Flemish dogaline, lined in damask silver silk   3dt
one French doublet-and-dogaline in brocaded silk,
  as provided by the Grav   5dt
      Less deposit of   10dt
      Owing   12dt
Presented on this, the 2nd day of December, 1530, by

Your most obedient,
Giules d'Attigny
tailor of Bruges

The accounts for your manservant are appended below, and come to the amount of 11 ducats.

3

"Shall I draw the curtains again?" Ruthger asked in the wan, watery light of Christmas morning that shone through into this, the uppermost floor of Saint-Germain's Antwerp house; it was set near the outskirts of the town, on a slight rise, inside a tall, wrought-iron fence, amid a cluster of newer buildings that had grown up around the four-hundred-year-old Old Mercers' Center where cloth of all sorts was still displayed for sale, but now that venerable building also housed jewel merchants and traders bringing cargo from the Spanish holdings in the New World.

Saint-Germain shook his head and sat up again on his ascetical bed, answering in the same Imperial Latin as Ruthger had used to address him. "No. Not while the noise goes on, certainly." He nodded in the direction of the single window in his bedchamber, that gave a view of neighbors' roofs and chimney-pots. "It should stop in an hour or so."

Bells sounded from the spires of the churches of Antwerp; the ringing to welcome Christmas was countered by a somber crowd of Protestants, walking through the city along the major streets, singing the hymns of Martin Luther and exhorting those late to Mass to throw off the oppression of the Church of Rome and embrace the reforms of Luther.

"If we are fortunate, there will be snow by midday; everyone will be driven indoors, so the holiday will not be marred by bloodshed," said Saint-Germain as he reached to draw on the Persian caftan of heavy black silk that served him as a chamber-robe. "I take it this household is up?"

"Indeed it is," said Ruthger. "All but three are gone to worship."

"That is . . . most interesting," said Saint-Germain with a sardonic lift to the corners of his mouth that some might mistake for a smile.

"The three who remain are the stableman and his two children," said Ruthger at his most bland.

"He is a follower of one of the more extreme teachers, is he not? one inclined to pious simplicity and private enclaves?"

"Among other things, yes: he is a Hutterite," said Ruthger. "Hutter's followers have been expelled—"

Saint-Germain rose. "—from almost everywhere, as I recall," he said, stretching. "Just as well, then, that he and his children stay off the streets. There is trouble enough with regular Protestant factions and Catholics abroad today. I trust the staff will not do anything to spite them."

"Factions. Why call them after Roman racing corporations?" Ruthger wondered aloud.

"Because they are much the same in style: loyal to the point of obsession, unthinking in their endorsements, and determined to support their group in front of all opposition, even if it causes themselves damage to do so." Saint-Germain shook his head, and went on slowly. "The Church is much in need of change, but riots and burning will not bring improvement, it will only increase the Church's obduracy, which will push those protesting to more extreme positions, and soon both parts of the debate will be working to the destruction of the other side, as the Reds attempted to do to the Greens during

Traianus' reign, and the Blues did when Constantine held his last Roman games."

"The Cathars and the followers of Pier Waldo fared badly, and they only defied, not opposed the Church," Ruthger reminded him.

"Yes, their manner might have been successful had Innocent III not been in a frame of mind to Crusade: he had to make an example of any hint of apostasy. In those times, news moved slowly, and that helped those groups who held together within their own regions. But the Pope was not then as he is now, and could not afford even passive opposition, not in 1208, while you and I were in China and had to rely on Olivia for all our news of the West. He put England under interdict in the same year, and Henry Tudor is making England's response at last, three centuries later, when news travels much faster, and information is available to many more people," said Saint-Germain with a solitary shake of his head. "In the thirteenth century, the Church needed the revenues from its holdings in the south of France. Corruption did not vanish from the Church because the Cathars or Waldensian heretics identified it, and paid dearly for their temerity, nor will it now, in spite of each new Protestant divine. Now the Church does not want to lose its revenues from northern Europe, so Luther and his like must be suppressed."

"Do you think the Church will succeed?" Ruthger turned as an especially loud peal echoed over the city.

Saint-Germain thought a bit, and answered slowly. "That is still uncertain. The Church has more than Protestants to contend with, which adds to the complications. If the Church can stem the tide from the Ottomans, then perhaps it will prevail, but in the meantime, the strategy it has chosen serves to entrench opposition, not to unite the faith, to deal with the Spanish power that has influenced so much of the Italian peninsula. And by tightening its hold, the Church drives more and more of its flock away. This time, the conflict could do worse than start a Crusade, it could sunder whole nations. You remember how often Roman politics mixed with the Great Games, using the sporting alliances to influence political issues. This is much the same; this morning there are Protestants marching in the streets, daring the Church to stop them, just as the racing factions used to do in Rome, but with more dire consequences facing them."

"They are willing to accept the consequences, or so they claim. They would tell you that their dispute is over faith and God, and the failure of the Church, not winning teams of horses," said Ruthger, watching the movements in the streets below.

"That would not change the damage they do, except to make it more bitter," said Saint-Germain.

"We will hope for snow," said Ruthger, going to adjust the coverlet and sheets on Saint-Germain's narrow bed.

"Yes; we will," said Saint-Germain, stepping into thick-soled slippers; their lining of his native earth counteracted the enervation of the sunlight. He rubbed his chin, remarking as he did, "I believe it is time I was shaved, and my hair trimmed. I begin to feel a bit scruffy."

"So I have thought since we arrived here, four days ago," said Ruthger. "You are receiving three of the authors whose books you have published, through your various presses in the Lowlands, this afternoon. You will want to make a good appearance, I think."

"How diplomatically done, old friend. You are right: I should present myself well—not only to impress them, but to show that I am in a position to provide them support, should they need it. So, if you would, plan to bring your razor and your scissors as soon as I finish my bath." Saint-Germain considered a long moment. "I'll want the Flemish doublet Giules d'Attigny made, the woollen barrel-hose, and the chamarre in red-black wool. One white chamise, a silk one, and my black-sapphire pectoral on the silver-link collar. And the Flemish buckled shoes; the earth lining has been replaced, I trust." He glanced at the window. "Do you remember how d'Attigny looked when Karl-lo-Magne ruled here? —Or what this region was like?"

"It was a wild place—but then, so was all Franksland," said Ruthger. "This portion of the land was all forest and open fields, leading to salt marshes, with a few small villages and fishing towns."

Saint-Germain steepled his fingers, only the tips touching, and made a circuit of the room, the hem of his caftan whispering along the planks of the floor as he walked. "I was much taken with this region, then; and later, during the Black Plague, I—" He stopped. "And now, another burden is imposed on this district, and its people."

"Of their own making," Ruthger remarked, a suggestion of disapproval in his tone of voice.

"At the instigation of zealots, each purveying his own state of grace," Saint-Germain amended. "I had hoped that the rancor would diminish, but it seems unlikely now; that saddens me."

"I fear you are right," said Ruthger, and changed the subject. "You have asked the authors to dine with you, haven't you?"

"Actually, I believe the invitation said I offered them a Christmas meal, which I intend to do; I spoke with Harcourt day before yesterday, so he could prepare," he said carefully.

"He said he had purchased two geese for the occasion," Ruthger informed him. "And last night he had a fish delivered from the market still flopping in the basket."

"Very good," said Saint-Germain. "Harcourt seems a capable cook."

Ruthger chuckled. "You have sampled his cuisine, my master?"

"Because I do not eat does not mean I cannot smell," Saint-Germain said, and went on crisply, "I will want to bathe around midday, but until then, I have a few matters to attend to in my laboratory." He gestured to the large room beyond this one, where he had installed his athanor and other equipment.

"Is there anything you will need me to do for you?" Ruthger asked.

"Make sure there is extra wood for all the fires, old friend. Today this house must be warm everywhere." He regarded Ruthger, an expression between amusement and determination on his attractive, irregular features. "I wish to provide the household every incentive to remain indoors today."

"Out of harm's way," Ruthger agreed; Saint-Germain inclined his head in agreement. "I concur. I will see that the fires are built up. Will you need me until midday?"

"I doubt it; do as you wish with the time," said Saint-Germain.

"I will have my meal in peace in the kitchen, while most of the household is gone; no one will remark that I eat my meat raw, which I believe will serve us all in good stead. The less strange you and I appear, the less likely we are to attract unwanted attention," Ruthger announced. "This time I have a very fine, plump partridge and a pheasant. I put the birds into wine as soon as I killed and dressed them."

"I can but imagine," said Saint-Germain, waiting until Ruthger left the room to venture into his laboratory, where a handsome, new clock kept fairly reliable time on the wall above his work-table. As he sat down, the hands indicated it was almost nine; the next time he looked up, the hands read 12:31. Saint-Germain set his work aside and left the laboratory, bound for his bathroom on the floor below. The household bustled around him as he watched Ruthger supervise the filling of his tub from buckets of hot water fresh from the stove, and as he sank into the bath, he could smell the aroma of geese stuffed with chestnuts rising from the hearth two floors below.

Shortly after two, Saint-Germain appeared in the reception hall, all rigged out in his finery, his hair trimmed, his jaw newly shaved, and the silver links of his collar gleaming against the red-black of his chamarre and black doublet. On his small, beautiful hands, fine rings shone and winked. Nine of his servants found excuses to come to the main floor to have a glimpse of him as he put three elegant Venezian glasses in order on a tray of antique Chinese brass. He then took down an ornate bottle of liqueur and set it next to the glasses.

"Is everything satisfactory, Grav?" asked Simeon Roosholm, the steward, as he came into the reception room.

"In this chamber, most certainly. I trust the dining hall is ready?" He turned in the direction of the door leading to the dining hall. "And Harcourt's staff is prepared?"

"Yes, to both," said Roosholm, a man of twenty-five whose bearing and demeanor suggested complete steadiness. Half a head taller than Saint-Germain, and lean on a large, square frame, he wore a long doublet in dark-blue over a lawn chamise, with a sprig of holly pinned near the collar as a token of the season. The only possible flaw in his appearance were his ears, which were round and red and stuck out from his face like two half-saucers, but this was his affliction to endure, and he did that as he did everything else—stolidly.

"And provision was made for the staff to dine well," said Saint-Germain, watching Roosholm narrowly.

"Yes. My wife has devoted the day to making preparations in the servants' hall, and provided the tokens for all, as you have told her to do. I am sure all is to your satisfaction, Grav." He rocked back on his heels in a show of pride for his wife, who was responsible for all the hangings, curtains, draperies, bed linens, and napery in the household. "You may be certain that she has done her utmost."

"You have a most worthy spouse," said Saint-Germain.

"I thank God for her every day," said Roosholm with feeling.

"And never more so than on Christmas Day, I should imagine," said Saint-Germain, walking around the reception room and making note of the decorations: holly over the doors, gilded acorns in a bowl on the central table, and fir branches hung on the expanse of the chimney. He had ordered that there be nothing to dismay either Protestant or Catholic, and found himself pleased with what Roosholm and his wife had achieved. "I take it the dining hall is as well-decorated as this room."

Roosholm nodded in the direction of the arched doorway that led to the dining hall. "If you would care to look? All is in readiness."

Saint-Germain surprised his steward by opening the door himself; he paused to take in the cavernous chamber, noting that there were sprays of evergreens over all the windows, although the curtains were drawn, and a wreath of holly over the fireplace. "This is most satisfactory, Roosholm."

"So long as it is to your liking," said Roosholm.

"That it is. I hope you will have a feast reflective of my pleasure," said Saint-Germain.

"We are having a roast suckling pig, as you permitted, stuffed with apples and leeks," said Roosholm, a bit of hesitancy in his remark, as if, now that the meal was being cooked, he had over-stepped his mark.

"Excellent," Saint-Germain approved. "A keg of beer is set aside, I hope, for your celebration."

"It is," said Roosholm, increasingly uncertain.

"Very good. It is fitting that you should keep merry on this night." He began to smile slowly. "Do not bother about my guests. I will attend to them, and I will see that the dining hall is not neglected."

Roosholm winced: "It isn't right that you should be a servant, not when you have a staff to attend to your guests."

"For any festival but this one, I would agree. But tonight, it is fitting that the lowly be raised up and the high practice humility." He had thought of this explanation during the morning in his laboratory, and realized he had guessed correctly. "Let me have this honor, Roosholm, and you will have no reason to feel slighted or compromised."

"Since you are determined upon this course, I can but comply, with the thanks of all your staff." The stiffness of his speech belied the smile in his eyes.

"Then make your last examination, and go join the rest," said Saint-Germain. He favored Roosholm with a suggestion of a nod.

"You are most gracious, Grav," said the steward. "Doubtless your humility will be well-received in Heaven."

"So long as my guests are satisfied, I will be, as well," said Saint-Germain.

"Do you plan to admit them to the house as well?" Roosholm asked.

"Ruthger will do that for me. It is quite appropriate, under the circumstances," said Saint-Germain. "I will not bring any discredit upon you, Roosholm. It would reflect badly on us both if I did."

Roosholm coughed once. "I will inform your staff of your decision, and we will drink your health for the coming year."

"For which I thank you," said Saint-Germain, and indicated the door leading to the servants' part of the house. "Once the dinner dishes are brought to the dining hall, all of you will be released from your duties until tomorrow morning. Harcourt may choose which of the pages will carry the platters into the dining hall, and then they, too, will be at liberty. Tomorrow you may supervise the distribution of food to the poor."

"As you wish, Grav," said Roosholm, fretting but unwilling to challenge Saint-Germain's specific instructions. He bowed rigidly, turned, and left the dining hall.

Saint-Germain went to the fireplace and laid another log on the fire, watching closely until it began to burn. He was about to light the candles in the standing chandelier in the center of the table when the knocker sounded. Leaving the dining hall and closing the door, he took up his position in the reception room, choosing a place to stand that would welcome his guests without causing them to be too put off by his obvious high station, or too rebuffed by what might appear a lack of consequence. He could hear steps approaching, and then a light scratch on the door. "Enter," he called to Ruthger.

The four guests accompanying Ruthger crossed the threshold,

then paused, taking in Saint-Germain as well as waiting to be announced.

"Grav Saint-Germain," said Ruthger in very good Flemish, "allow me to present Seur Evangeline, the aunt of Erneste van Amsteljaxter; and Deme Erneste van Amsteljaxter."

The nun, in the simple habit of a Sister of the Assumption, curtsied moderately, her eyes averted. "May God bless you, Grav, and give you long life," she said quietly; she did not extend her hand, but held apart from him and the rest with the studied composure.

"Thank you, Seur; I have been fortunate in my longevity," said Saint-Germain, and gave his attention to Erneste van Amsteljaxter. "It is a pleasure to meet you, Deme; I admire the fine work you have done."

Dressed in a slate-colored silken, triangular-sleeved saya and a closed skirt without embroidery over a very moderate farthingale, only a small, lace ruff to set off her face and provide cuffs for her inner sleeves, her pale-brown hair pulled back and covered by a cap similar to those worn by scholars, Erneste strove to appear as unfemale as the strictures of fashion would allow. She curtsied slightly, daring to look Saint-Germain directly in the face as she did. "I must thank you for considering my work, Grav, and for allowing me to have my book printed. Many another press-owner would not so extend himself."

"More fools they," said Saint-Germain, and indicated the chairs near the hearth. "If you and your aunt would care to sit down?"

"I am Hildebrandt van der Horst," said the next guest, a man nearing forty, with graying hair and worn face, in a long, deeply pleated scholar's robe. His manner was as severe as his style. "You printed my work on—"

"*Diseases Afflicting Cattle, Goats, and Sheep, with Treatments and Palliative Methods for Such Maladies,*" Saint-Germain told him. "An excellent compendium, and one I think must be welcomed everywhere."

Van der Horst was almost struck silent. "Most gracious," he mumbled.

Ruthger stood next to the last man, who wore a ribbed doublet and padded short-hose in the style favored in England. "This is the Honorable Bradleigh Milestone, recently come from Oxford."

"My lord Grav," said Milestone in poor Flemish.

"I take it your father is a knight, Signor' Milestone," said Saint-Germain in English, offering a little bow.

"Sir Laughton Milestone, yes," he said with every sign of relief. "Your Amsterdam press published my treatise on the political implications of—"

"International mercantilism," Saint-Germain finished for him. "Yes. A most innovative premise, and an intriguing conclusion."

Milestone nodded, less surprised than van der Horst had been. "I am afraid it has not been as well-received in the institutions of government as I had hoped it would be."

"Thus your visit to Antwerp," Saint-Germain ventured, and went on in the stilted Latin of scholarship. "You are all welcome to my house; you honor me in coming here." To emphasize this, he went and filled the three glasses with the savory liqueur he had put out for that purpose. As he carried these back to his guests, he went on, "This is a cordial of ancient lineage. I trust you will enjoy it, and consider it my pledge of friendship and continuing support for your work." He offered the tray first to Erneste, who took the glass, holding it up to the light of the dense cluster of tall wax candles standing in front of a mirror of Venezian glass, providing light and concealing the lack of reflection of his hand.

"The color," she said. "It appears changeable."

"It is a pale, clear green," said Saint-Germain, nodding to her as he presented the tray to van der Horst, who took the glass as if he feared it might break.

"Most . . . intriguing," van der Horst said as he sniffed the contents of his glass.

"You are having none?" Milestone asked as he took the third glass.

Rather than answer directly, Saint-Germain said, "I am your servant this evening, in recognition of the importance of the day. I will not eat or drink with you; instead I will do as the great men of Fiorenze have done in times past, and I will wait upon you." Thinking back to the last Christmas feast he had taken with il Magnifico, he looked directly at Milestone. "You have nothing to fear, Signor'. You will come to no harm at my hands."

"You gave no glass to the nun," van der Horst challenged.

"No; I have been informed that she takes only sacramental wine and will not touch strong spirits." Saint-Germain ignored van der Horst's snide tone. "I respect her wishes."

"Then she must be pleased that you have not put her to the embarrassment of refusal," said Milestone, also in scholars' Latin.

Seur Evangeline looked down at her hands, remarking as if to the forest of tapers in front of the mirror, "It is not for me to be embarrassed by another's deeds."

A moment of awkward silence fell, only to be broken by Ruthger's return, announcing, "Your meal will be presented shortly. If you will please enter the dining hall?" He opened the door and stood aside while Saint-Germain's strange assortment of guests trooped into the room, their expressions alert without being completely genial.

"Comity may be hard-won, my master," Ruthger said to Saint-Germain in an under-voice as he stepped back, closing the doors again, and shutting himself out of the dining hall.

Text of a letter from Capitan Ferrando de los Cerros to Bishop Varne Govert of Antwerp, written in Church Latin, and delivered by Frey Rafael.

To the most esteemed Bishop, Varne Govert, Capitan Ferrando de los Cerros sends his greetings on this, the 19th day of January, 1531 Anno Domini, to report on the origins of recent events of disruption and heresy which have plagued Antwerp of late.

Of those who profaned the holy day of Christmas with their marches and their Lutheran hymns, we have detained fifteen of the leaders, nine of whom are prominent men, and have applied to the courts for relief from their incarceration. I fear that when they have pleaded their case, they will be released to cause more mischief. I apply to you for your recommendation on how best to deal with these men. Were it for me to decide, I would cut out their tongues and blind them so that they could preach no more disobedience to Holy Church, nor could they pollute their souls with heretical texts. But it is not my office to do such things without your order, and so I apply to you for that, or to enforce whatever sentence you are moved to impose.

In addition, I have ordered the destruction of nine presses, for they have published works that do not meet with the approval of the Church, and so must be eliminated from this city, so that they can work no more mischief in the world. As you must already know, publishing of profane books has become unfortunately common in this part of the world, and so it is incumbent upon us to stop all presses not engaged in printing holy texts. Let these secular publishers seek some otherwhere to practice their apostasy; until the Church has lost its sway if they wish to pollute Christendom with works that turn men's eyes from the Glory of God to those mundane concerns that interfere with the teachings of the Church in regard to the workings of this world, they must accept the consequences of their impiety.

Let us rejoice that the King and Emperor Charles has vowed that his son will be raised and educated in Spain, so that we will have a King who is truly one of us, not an Austrian advanced by marriage to the leadership of the richest nation on earth, and who will know that heretics are not to be permitted to sully the faith of God. May that happy day come before we are overwhelmed with Protestants and worse.

I have enclosed with this copies of the reports of the men working for various publishers regarding the works they are presently making available. Those with the most suspect lists are presented first, those with the least are presented second, and those with the lists with the least consistency in point of view are presented last. Many of those in the third grouping have tended to address issues of what may be called science, that is, the study of things in nature. These works are the most subtle, for although they may have no superficial religious implications, their cumulative perspective may serve to undermine the faith of many by attempting to remove from God's Law such things as the nature of the world, the importance of animals, domestic and wild, in God's Plan, and the measurements of the earth and heavens, beyond those already set forth in Holy Writ. Of particularly dangerous content are those works based on the discoveries in the New World, for all such compilations can bring into question what other matters God may not have imparted to us, and thereby undermine the faith of those who deal with such matters.

I await your decisions in regard to these reports, and I will act promptly to carry out your will as soon as you have stated it.

Yours in the Name of Christ,
Ferrando de los Cerros, Capitan

in Antwerp, by my own hand

4

Erneste van Amsteljaxter stared around Saint-Germain's study, her eyes wide. "So many books," she exclaimed softly, almost reverently. "There must be four hundred of them." She was dressed much the same way she had been when he had first seen her: in an unornamented dull-purple vaya with triangular sleeves, a very moderate farthingale under her simple skirt, and the merest touch of lace at her neck and sleeves. Today she was somewhat less reserved than she had been on their first meeting, and she smiled without seeming to compromise her dignity. "You must have taken years and years to collect and read them all." She seemed mildly preoccupied, and not entirely due to the books on the shelves; the pelucid northern light from the window made her face as luminous as that of the haloed Magdelene in the local church.

"Fortunately, Deme van Amsteljaxter, I have had years and years," he said, watching her more closely than she knew; Ruthger had admitted her to the study a few minutes earlier and Saint-Germain was keenly aware of her acute discomfort from being alone in his company, so he devoted himself to easing her edginess.

"Because you have wealth," she said, a suggestion of wistfulness in her remark. She looked down at her hands.

"Among other things," he said, and indicated a leather-bound volume closed with iron hinges. "That book may be beyond price." He had bought it for a goodly amount some years ago, after the Black Plague had swept through Europe, from the heirs of a nobleman who had purchased it from a companyless Crusader four centuries before that. It had been old when the heirs had sold it, and now it was ancient enough to be a treasure.

She squinted at the spine, a bit too relieved to have her attention directed to the tome. *"The Roman Art of Crystal-Grinding,"* she translated slowly, puzzlement marking her features. "My father would have been fascinated, I suspect. Crystal-grinding? Why should Romans want to grind crystals?"

"For the same reason it is done now: to make spectacles to improve eyesight," said Saint-Germain. "The Romans of old had very real skills in making such things." He had an instant of recall, watching Nero at the Circus Maximus, wearing his wire-rimmed, green-crystal spectacles, a tribute to his racing corporation and the intense Roman sun.

"They built fine bridges, and wonderful buildings," she allowed. "But they had many faults."

"Yes, they did, to both observations," said Saint-Germain, remembering how he had watched the construction of the Flavian Circus during one of his stays in Roma; it was now called the Colosseum and was partially in ruin, but it still had the power to impress.

"I was not aware of their ability to grind crystals," said Erneste. "I wonder if there are any left to study." She went to the fireplace and held out her hands to warm them over the merry flames.

"There are very few still intact," said Saint-Germain, who had a dozen of them hidden under the floor of the second atrium at his Roman villa.

"For what reason are there so few?" She set the book aside, her fingers lingering on the hinges.

"Perhaps because crystals are more fragile than bridges, and their virtues are less obvious," Saint-Germain suggested, recalling the centuries of supremacy of unlettered barbarians whose arrival had marked Roma's fall; he went on a bit more briskly. "I am delighted to welcome you to my house, Erneste van Amsteljaxter, and to my study, since you are fond of books, but I wonder why you have come this morning, especially in such blustery weather, and rain coming before nightfall." He hoped he had not been too forward in putting this question to her.

"Do I intrude?" she asked quickly, uncertainty showing in every aspect of her demeanor. "Would you prefer that I leave?"

"No; I am curious—one of my failings." His swift smile vanished as soon as it appeared. "Your aunt Evangeline is with you, Deme van Amsteljaxter—Ruthger informed me—so you are clearly upholding the proprieties." Her aunt, as he knew, was in the main withdrawing room, doing needlework.

She stopped still, her face flushing. "I fear I am being most importunate in coming here, and were it not for the mortification I feel, I should not have bothered you," she admitted. "But I have only recently discovered that three months ago my brother had written to you to ask for your help." She put one hand to her flaming cheek, not daring to look at him. "I am dreadfully chagrined that he would do such a thing—you, a stranger with no ties to him any stronger than that you have published my book. I came to apologize on his behalf."

"His circumstances seemed a bit precarious," said Saint-Germain. "He had good reason to seek help somewhere."

"That they were—his situation's precarious. And may well be still." She turned away from him and went toward the fireplace, staring into the flames as if to banish other visions from her thoughts. "I have written to him four times since Christmas, and I have had no word from him in return. I only know that he had written to you because I received a letter from the Landsmacht's secretary, saying that my letters had arrived but that my brother has been unable to answer."

Saint-Germain studied her thoughtfully. "It is winter," he reminded her as kindly as he could. "Messages travel erratically in winter. It would seem, from the note you have received from the secretary, that his messages—or yours—have probably been delayed."

"That is possible," she said, her words measured and her manner controlled. "But couriers have twice arrived with letters from Bohemia and Moravia since Christmas, and they have affirmed that the letters carried there have been delivered, at least most of them, so they must be in the Landsmacht's hands; why he should have them I hardly dare to imagine. Tabor is not so small a place that the couriers would not go there to collect letters, and Grussenwald is not so very far from Tabor." She coughed. "I know my brother was troubled by the Landsmacht's growing religiosity, and feared that his employment would end before the promised time—"

"So he said in his letter to me." Saint-Germain motioned her to a chair. "I was given to understand you had encouraged him to write to me."

"Not encouraged," she protested as she sat down. "I only ventured to say that you might be able to advise him if he were dismissed out of hand, as I fear he may have been. The secretary only said that my brother could not answer any letters."

"You were not in error to make such a recommendation, if that is what he wishes; I will do what I can for him," he said, and waited for her to go on. "Is it? his wish."

"I don't know," she said, unwilling to look at him. "He has told me so little since he warned me of his difficulties, and I am left to worry, and speculate, neither of which brings me any solace. There are stories every day of men and women—and children—put to torture and death for speaking against—"

"Why is that, do you think—that he has provided no other information to you?" The question was enough to stop her increasing dismay; Saint-Germain went to the heavy shelving and took down a small book of elegant love songs, composed more than three hundred years before. "Is he likely to fail to inform you of any difficulties he may have encountered? You know his character—would he inform you with his problems, or would he seek not to burden you with them?" He read hesitation in her restless gaze. "Let me put it another way—would he expect you to shoulder his difficulties if he is in a precarious situation? Have you done it before? Or do you fear he has been made a prisoner or become repentant, and that is the reason you have heard nothing?" Looking at the four-line staves with the odd, square nones, he heard the plaintive melody of the third song sound in his head while he waited for Erneste to form her reply.

"I am troubled that he has not—" She faltered, her voice becoming unsteady. "I thought he would have sent me a letter, you see, no matter what state of mind he may be in. He always has in the past. I inquired after his health, but learned nothing about it. And the secretary said he could not answer, not that he had not received the letters."

"But there was nothing from your brother himself." Saint-Germain said nothing more, waiting for her to speak.

"No. Nothing from him, and that is what causes me the most

distress, and why I am afraid for him." She put her hands together almost as if in prayer, and studied the walls around her.

"And since he has not sent any word to you, you would like me to use my influence to find out if any mishap has befallen him, or anything that would account for his silence," Saint-Germain supplied for her, marking his place in the song-book with one finger and closing the book around it.

She shook her head. "I am not so forgetful of my place that I would do such a thing," she protested. "I am beholden to you already, deeply so, and I would rather not increase my indebtedness."

"You have no reason to be—what I may or may not do for your brother does not devolve upon you in any way: believe this," he said gently.

But she continued on as if she had not heard him. "I am troubled about my brother's silence, but I cannot ask you to discover what has become of him. I have nothing to offer you in thanks for what aid you may extend to him."

"Why do you think that it would be your obligation, Deme? You are asking on his behalf, not your own, are you not?" Saint-Germain asked.

"I . . . I was hoping you might advise me. Now that I have heard from the secretary, I am at a loss how to proceed. I would like to make inquiries on my own, but not if they would be dangerous for Onfroi." She looked about the room as if it were new to her. "You have no reason to help us."

"I have no reason not to, either," he said.

She rubbed her hands together more forcefully. "No. That wasn't my purpose in coming here. I wanted you to know that I would not trespass on our association in so improper a way. You must see that. Yet, though I know it is reprehensible, I hope I may prevail upon you to write to the Landsmacht to find out what has become of . . . Onfroi. He is more apt to send you information than he is to vouchsafe it to me. I don't ask you to prevaricate or—" She laced her fingers together, then unlaced them again. "And if this would mean another debt—"

"What can I do to convince you I do not think concern for your brother is improper, nor an occasion to be taken advantage of—but you are anxious, are you not?" He watched her struggle with contrary impulses, but held his tongue while she debated with herself.

Finally she sighed. "I admit I hope you will undertake to discover what has become of him, not simply because I ask it, but to know what might endanger the books your company produces."

"I have such interests, I agree," he said, letting her take this in. "No doubt your brother could provide me with a great deal of useful information."

"Yes. I think so, too," she said, relieved, then frowned again. "But he might not have sufficient to justify your—"

"What is it?" he asked, guessing the answer.

"I know that if you should lend him assistance on my behalf, you might have expectations of me that I may not desire to meet, no matter how grateful I may be— So for that reason alone, I would prefer not to be so greatly obligated to you. If you will tell me what I may do, then I will not impose upon you any longer." This last admission was made hurriedly, somewhat angrily, and with renewed confusion. "You must think me very naive."

"Hardly that," said Saint-Germain, pulling his finger out of the song-book and returning it to the shelves only to take down a copy of Erneste's book. "This is a most intriguing volume: *Lyrics and Tales of the Peasants of Brabant*. I was particularly struck by the story of 'How Valeria Was Wooed by the Night Demon.'"

"Because the hero is a priest?" she asked just above a whisper. "There are versions in which he is a knight."

"He is a most unlikely hero, I agree," said Saint-Germain smoothly, "but no; that is not what impressed me—I was struck by Valeria using a mirror to discover whether or not her suitor was a demon. That device is unusual, and for that reason, also distinctive."

"Because you thought the mirror should have shown the demon as terrible as he was?" Erneste asked, doing her best to steady herself through this discussion.

"No—because the mirror showed nothing at all," said Saint-Germain, a wistful note in his voice.

Erneste sat a bit straighter. "Isn't that the most horrible thing that could happen: that the demon had no shape, that he took his appearance from her desires?"

"Is that what happened?" Saint-Germain opened the book and thumbed to the page he sought. "Here it is: '*Alas, when she held up*

the priceless mirror, Valeria saw that there was no image on the sur-
face of the glass. She knew then that the priest had spoken truth, and
she made the Sign of the Cross, whereupon her lover shrieked blas-
phemously and vanished with an appalling oath in a gout of flames.
His accursed vow remained after he had gone: that nothing could
save her from joining him in Hell. She went to the priest who had
helped her, and he accepted her repentance and forgave her sins.'"

"It is a vivid story," she said when he closed the book; she seemed
half-apologetic and half-proud of her work. "If it weren't so remarkable, I wouldn't have included it, for it may cause distress to some
who read it."

"You say that you heard the story from an old woman, who had
heard it from her grandmother, who was said to have learned it as a
child," Saint-Germain observed. "If two such venerable women were
not too distraught by its themes to tell it, then why should you hesitate."

"Yes, Grav. The old woman was proud of all the tales she knew,
for most of the people of her village didn't know half so many as she,"
Erneste declared. "Her name was Kundarie, and her family had once
lived farther east, near to Luxembourg."

"Most . . . interesting," said Saint-Germain, ironic amusement
lending his countenance a somewhat more angular cast, as he had a
brief, intense memory of Heugenet, who had come to his life two
centuries ago, only to die the True Death at her own hands a quarter
century later. She had known him for what he was, and had embraced
what he offered, however briefly. Her memory was easier to bear than
that of Demetrice.

"I found many tales had diverse versions, and those versions were
so remarkable that I could not record each variation, or I would have
been forced to limit the book to a single tale." She studied the spines
of the books on the shelves with a kind of longing. "Even you might
weary of such a volume, as much as you love books."

"Variations on a single tale?" he asked.

"Yes," she said as if admitting to a flaw in her character.

"I might, but I doubt it. That might prove most interesting, such a
focused comparison," said Saint-Germain, studying her more openly.
"Which of these stories would you choose, if you were to prepare such
a volume?"

Erneste touched her modified kettle headdress, attempting to conceal a bit more of her face. "I haven't given such a notion much thought," she admitted slowly. "But perhaps the story of the sons or daughters turned into birds or animals of different kinds through sorcery or other evil and then back through virtue would be the most divergent example I can think of just now. And one that would not be seen to encourage tergiversation in anyone."

"That is a very ancient story, Deme van Amsteljaxter," said Saint-Germain who had first heard a version of it almost three thousand years ago, while he had been serving in the Temple of Imhotep.

"So the priest in Saint-Etienne des Argenielles said when he had heard his mother tell me the version she knew," said Erneste with a returning confidence. She managed a suggestion of a smile. "Is that something you would like to publish, if I should undertake such research? A book of many versions of the same story? Would that interest you?"

"It might," said Saint-Germain.

She shook her head. "That is discouraging."

He looked a bit startled. "It shouldn't be," he said in a kind voice. "It is not lack of faith in your work that makes me hesitate, it is the scrutiny to which my publications are subjected—to which all publications are subjected just now. You are right, such a compilation as you envision would probably be approved by Church authorities."

"You say probably," she pointed out.

"As I must. The Spanish arm of the Church favors a very stringent, doctrinal interpretation of all works, including those not directly and favorably bearing on the Church, and the standards they put forth are somewhat . . . shall we say . . . arbitrary." He studied her face, aware that she was debating within herself. "Deme Amsteljaxter?"

Finally she looked toward him. "Grav, I cannot venture to ask you anything, not now. There are so many aspects to your . . . participation. Let me have some time for reflection; then I will know what I think best to do."

"As you wish. But do not fear to ask me to make official inquiries— so far as I, a foreigner, may do so—if your methods do not succeed," he said, making a point of keeping his distance.

"What do you—" She stopped herself. "I apologize, Grav. I think it best that I leave now."

"To avoid any possible appearance of impropriety," said Saint-Germain smoothly. "I do understand."

She rose and curtsied to him, her face averted so as not to imply any hint of invitation. "You have been very good to receive me," she said with a fine show of courtesy. "I thank you."

"You have no reason to do so; not yet," he said to her. "I look forward to speaking with you again, when you have reached a decision."

She studied him for almost a minute, her silence as intense as a volley of rifle-fire. "If I cannot reach Onfroi, then yes, I will speak with you again. But I warn you, I will make no bargains then that I have not made with you already."

"I did not doubt that," Saint-Germain murmured, and kissed the air immediately above her extended fingers. "For your sake, I hope you have direct contact with your brother as soon as possible."

"Most kind," she said, and started toward the door. "I'll think about the book."

"If another notion strikes you as better, do, please, let me know of it," he said, keeping his distance for her comfort. "Ruthger will arrange for a messenger for you, if this will suit you."

"A messenger? That is a very expensive luxury for my aunt and me to bear." Color rose in her cheeks.

"Consider it part of my costs of publishing. It is necessary that I think ahead, so that I may produce books on a schedule that coincides with the voyages of my merchant-ships. Books gain few readers if they sit in warehouses, waiting to be sent to market." He spoke easily, as if this were a common arrangement that any sensible maker of books would expect to bear. "I think your current book is being well-enough received to incline me to want a second book from you. Providing you a messenger will simplify our dealings. I will have journeys to make, and it would be prudent to have some means to remain in communication with you."

Erneste went pale. "Of course," she said, trying to make up for what she supposed had to be the gaffe of a new author.

"Very good," he approved, with a slight bow. "Ruthger will inform you within two days the name of your messenger, and when he will call upon you."

"Thank you." She spoke only a bit above a whisper, then went—a bit too hastily—to the door to let herself out.

Saint-Germain stood alone in the study, his head lowered in thought. He was so preoccupied that he hardly heard the soft knock that came roughly ten minutes later. Shaking his head as if to waken himself, he called in Imperial Latin, "Come in, old friend."

Ruthger slipped into the room, his face set in severe lines. "She was willing to have a messenger?"

"When I implied it would be unauthor-like of her to refuse, she was willing," said Saint-Germain, a slight, sad amusement in his dark eyes.

"So I gathered," said Ruthger.

"I can tell she is worried about compromising her honor," Saint-Germain went on, his manner superbly neutral.

"The Spanish are very rigorous about such matters," Ruthger reminded him. "She is already exposed to criticism, being a literate woman."

"And not a nun," Saint-Germain added. "Her aunt has some protection."

"Precisely," said Ruthger, and went to light the oil-lamps with the flint-and-steel he carried in the wallet on his belt.

"I'll be careful, for her sake."

Ruthger loosened the rope holding the main lantern up near the ceiling, lowered it, and began to light its various individual lamps. "Do you plan to visit her?"

"No," said Saint-Germain. "Neither sleeping nor waking. She is much too frightened to accept a lover in any guise, let alone one such as I am—a foreigner of dubious status in the town, and one who sells books. I am already something a bit unnatural in her mind. If I attempt even sleeping contact, it would be enough to turn her against me, though I merely kissed her mouth."

"That's unfortunate," said Ruthger, making sure all six lamps were burning properly.

"But necessary, I fear," said Saint-Germain. "No, while I am here I will have to confine myself to visiting sleeping women in the outer parts of the city, where the Spanish patrols are infrequent." He coughed once, delicately.

"Yes; necessary; the Spanish would be glad of an excuse to confine you in a cell," said Ruthger, preparing to pull the lantern aloft again. "Incidentally, the under-cook found someone at the kitchen door today."

Saint-Germain regarded Ruthger levelly. "I must suppose that is not unusual, so why mention this person?"

"The fellow told me it was a large man, in stained clothing, seeming to be drunk, although it was early in the day," said Ruthger, securing the rope to the wall-cleat once more.

"Again, this is nothing remarkable," Saint-Germain pointed out, and waited for a response.

"The under-cook said the man spoke in Italian." He looked directly at Saint-Germain. "We may have been followed."

After a brief moment of consideration, Saint-Germain nodded once. "So we may," he agreed.

Text of a letter from Gennaro Emerenzio to Deodato Chiuventan, of La Fortunata, Campo San Jaccopo, Venezia.

To the most worthy Deodato Chiuventan of La Fortunata, the greetings of Gennaro Emerenzio, business factor, accompanied by the sum of two hundred thirty-six ducats in full and complete discharging of my debt to your establishment, and an additional one hundred twenty ducats to ensure my continuing welcome at your establishment.

I am enclosing copies of letters of payment to all those players to whom I am also indebted, showing that the sums have been paid in total, and that I have no further debts to discharge to any patrons of your most excellent gaming house. The full amount is over six hundred ducats—a considerable amount, I will agree—which each man will inform you they have their share in hand.

I am certain I will not encounter another such run of bad luck, and if the Saints do not favor my endeavors, I will pledge to remain more current in my debts than has been the case for the last four months. I have access to a fairly large sum of money at present that should tide me over any more disappointing periods.

I am thankful to you for keeping my name from being enrolled with the debtors of the city, for that would surely end my business as factor and agent for many merchants, which would, in turn, necessitate my absence from the city for at least ten years, to vacate the debt. Other misfortunes would attend on such a calamity. My property would be seized and all my goods sold, and that would not have allowed me to repay one-tenth of what I owed, for as a man of business,

I have pledged to put the interests of my clients above my own, and this surety would be meaningless were I shown to be unable to fulfill the office with which I have been entrusted. This way, I remain of good character, my business may continue, and my patrons will be able to collect the sums I have held in trust within a reasonable length of time, for I assume that most of them, being absent from La Serenissima, will not all of them demand a full accounting at one and the same time.

If you will be good enough to sign or mark with witness the acknowledgment of receipt of the monies as described above, and give that receipt to my courier, I will express my thanks to you in person at your tables within the week. I thank you for your patience, and it pleases me that you can benefit because of it.

In the certainty that you will honor our prior arrangements,

I sign myself,
   Your most devoted and grateful
   Gennaro Emerenzio

in Venezia, on the 3rd day of March, 1531

5

Ink darkened the lines of the hand, his nails, and his cuticles that he held out to Saint-Germain. He was perhaps forty years old, with a noticeable limp due to an unflexing ankle; his clothes were of good quality, but worn. His collar had been turned at least once, and the edges of his lace cuffs were frayed. "Mercutius Christermann," he said, adding, "printer by trade, and seeking employment." He looked around the vestibule in Saint-Germain's Amsterdam house, still filled with covered furniture and unopened boxes. "I've been told that you're new to the city, and that you are the owner of Eclipse Press for Ancient Studies, or some such name."

"I have not been here in some while, but my press has done its work without me," said Saint-Germain, making a gesture of dismissal to Ruthger, who had admitted the stranger to the house. He contemplated this unexpected arrival, thinking back to what the supervisor of his press had told him since his arrival two days ago. "I will not remain here long, myself. I have business in Antwerp to which I must return. Willelme Klasse supervises the press here, as I suppose you know. Perhaps you should speak with him."

"Does that mean I am wasting my time, then?" Christermann asked. "Without an endorsement from you, it is unlikely that he would take me on."

"To do what? As I have not yet heard what you are seeking, I am in no position to recommend you to anyone," said Saint-Germain, nodding in the direction of the front parlor. "Tell me what you are seeking, and I may be of use to you—and you to me. If you do not mind the drapes, I will ask you to sit down."

Christermann considered the shrouded settees and shrugged. "If there are no insects . . ."

"None that I am aware of, but I have only been here a few days, and not all my property has caught up with me, nor has my household been able to attend to opening the house completely." He looked about the room. "I have as much as is here because this house has long been owned by those of my blood, and I did not have to fully refurnish it."

"And there are more people arriving from Lisbon every day, seeking refuge from their ruined city," said Christermann.

"That there are," Saint-Germain agreed. "If the earthquake was only half as bad as the stories make it seem, it was dreadful."

"There will be books written about it," said Christermann, tapping the side of his nose with his forefinger to show his perspicacity.

"And you intend to be part of it," said Saint-Germain.

"As you must, as well, or why are you refurbishing your house?"

"Hardly refurbishing, merely making comfortable. The chairs are old-fashioned, but sufficiently comfortable for our purposes—or they were." He chose a high-backed, shallow-seated chair, plucked the muslin drape off it, and inspected the chair beneath. "New upholstery would be wise," he said to himself.

Christermann laughed, and dropped down on a settee, not bothering to remove the drape. "Not when one has ink everywhere," he declared.

"No doubt," said Saint-Germain. He waited and watched his visitor closely.

"I'll be direct," said Christermann when his host made not further comment. "I should expect you know that I am seeking work."

"So I surmised," said Saint-Germain, an air of polite curiosity about him.

"I am from Amsterdam, and only recently have I returned here, and that return was not wholly my choosing. Still, it is good that I'm home." He paused a moment as if to recruit his strength, then went firmly on. "Until a year ago I was employed in Liege, and all was going well in my work, but then the publisher brought out a pair of books, one that was said to be from ancient texts, disputing certain biblical accounts and events, which was bad enough—the Church and the Protestants denounced it—but not content with that, he prepared a text on various contemporary theories that run counter to the tenets of Christian faith, regarding the nature of the heavens, and that raised such an uproar that all in his employ had to flee or answer to the courts." He coughed. "I, as supervising pressman, was one among a dozen who were facing a Process, and so, before that could begin, I departed with little more than the clothes on my back, and a dozen coins in my wallet."

"Have you a family?" Saint-Germain asked. "Are they safe?"

"I have a brother and two sisters; one of the sisters lives here in Amsterdam with a husband who will not receive me—that is because he fears the Holy Office more than my sister's wrath. My other sister is married to a merchant and living just at present in Hamburgh; that is where I may go, if I have to leave Amsterdam, as I fear I soon must if I find no employment, as I have no wish to be a beggar, not in these hard times. My brother is a strict observance Cistercian monk, and that means that he has left the world; he has taken a vow of silence, along with all the rest. My wife and children died during the summer fevers, three years ago, in Liege. In the space of six weeks, they all died." His genial features grew sad and he looked toward the curtained window. "I had a son and a daughter, and my wife was pregnant. That was a great loss, my family."

"For whom you still grieve," said Saint-Germain gently.

The printer hardly seemed to hear him. "You know how those plagues spread: the weavers took the fever first—that was a bad blow to Liege—and then the vendors of foods and goods, and from them to the city's tradesmen. At least the Lisbon earthquake was swift, not measured as the Plague is. My wife was stricken first in our family, becoming ill two days before I did. She insisted on nursing our children until she collapsed. Three days later she was dead. The older child did not outlive her by a week."

"Do you hold yourself accountable for their loss?" Saint-Germain asked, no trace of censure in his voice.

"That I do," he admitted. He lapsed into silence again. Finally he cleared his throat and went on, "I would like to think that you are willing to consider giving me work; I know how to run any press you may have. That is no idle boast, and I will prove it to your satisfaction if you like. I am told that you aren't much influenced by the Church, or its policies."

"Not when I can afford not to be," said Saint-Germain.

"Oh, a clever one," said Christermann. "That speaks well of you. Certainly you are wise to be cautious. Who knows? I may be a spy for the Church, come to find out if you are helping the causes of the Godless."

Saint-Germain smiled briefly. "Not with such hands as those. Whatever else you are, you are most certainly a printer. What you believe is for you to settle with your own conscience."

Christermann held up his hands. "I take your meaning, Grav; these hands are the work of years. You are right: I have been a printer for over two decades." He lowered his hands, continuing doggedly. "Whatever else I may be, as you said, you may be sure that I am seeking work, and with a publisher who is not in danger of being closed by order of the Bishop or the Spanish."

"So far, I remain unscathed," said Saint-Germain, regarding Christermann with increased speculation. "However I must tell you that my company is under scrutiny, and my situation may change abruptly. If such uncertainty is unacceptable to you, then I would advise you to look elsewhere."

"That scrutiny is extended to all makers of books wherever the Church has influence," said Christermann with a tremendous sigh.

"So I am informed," Saint-Germain remarked. "I may be more closely than some, because I am a foreigner."

"And a rich one, from what I have been told, as well as one who supports Guilds; you have the good opinion of many who print books," said Christermann with a bluntness that surprised Saint-German. Apparently Christermann noticed this for he went on, "If you will pardon me for my candor, I would be grateful for your graciousness, and were I in a position to do so, I would not have imposed upon you in this way. But as I've told you, I am in urgent need of work, or I will have to leave the Lowlands—leave or starve at menial employment—and I would rather not have to give up the little I have left. That, and I would prefer to remain in Amsterdam, if I am able to earn a living; Amsterdam is my home, and since I have only this place to hold me now that my family is dead . . . The Guild will accept me, and I need not learn a new language at this point in my life."

"I can understand your desires," said Saint-Germain. "I know how compelling native earth can be."

Christermann uttered a single chuckle. "A nice turn of phrase, that. I must remember it."

"You are most kind," said Saint-Germain, reaching for a little brass bell to summon Ruthger. "If you will permit me to offer you some food and drink, we can discuss this further. I am inclined to hear you out."

The shine in Christermann's eyes made it clear that he was hungry, and although he was unused to receiving such flattering invitations from anyone—let alone a foreign nobleman—he was too famished to consider the impropriety of accepting. "I . . . I hope that I'm not inflicting—"

"It is hardly that if you and I are discussing what work you have done." He glanced toward the door as Ruthger tapped on it, then opened it just enough to provide room for himself.

"My master?" He stood very straight, his reserved manner making a favorable impression on Christermann, who often judged nobles by the hauteur of their servants.

"This printer is Mercutius Christermann, quite experienced, as you may see by his hands. If you will have the cook prepare some pork and turnips with onions, and bring cheese and beer, I would appreciate it." Saint-Germain paused. "Is there bread ready yet?" He saw Ruthger's nod. "Very good: bread and fresh butter to start, I think."

"Of course. And perhaps a little fried fish, to go with the bread?" Ruthger suggested.

"An excellent notion," Saint-Germain approved. "As you see, the man is hungry."

"Then I will tell the cooks to hasten," said Ruthger, then hurried away.

Christermann studied Saint-Germain. "You are being most hospitable. That's unusual."

"I am not responsible for others' lack of courtesy," said Saint-Germain in a tone that did not invite inquiry.

"That wasn't what I meant," said Christermann quickly, worried that he had over-stepped himself more than he had done already.

Saint-Germain held up his hand. "I am not offended: believe this."

Nodding emphatically, Christermann said, "I will." He stared around the room. "Your house has a broad front."

"And several steps, all of which I can afford," said Saint-Germain, his dark eyes showing a glint of amusement. "It was built to my . . . great-uncle's specifications almost eighty years ago."

"Did the city tax on building width and the number of steps then, or has it happened since the house was built?" Christermann asked.

"I do not believe my great-uncle bothered himself with such matters," Saint-Germain replied, managing to sound completely disinterested.

"If such things do not concern you, then you must be wealthier than rumors say you are, and that is—"

"—a matter for gossip, to be revised and improved in the telling." Saint-Germain made a gesture of dismissal. "Suffice it to say, I can afford to pay another printer without putting myself at a disadvantage, and without asking you to work for apprentice's wages." He achieved a look of great indifference. "You have many years of printing to your credit, and that must command respect. If you will, I would like to know something of what you have done, and for whom, and the names of those with whom you have worked." For an instant he hesitated, then went on, "If you would also tell me how you made yourself bold enough to approach me personally, I would consider that a sign of good intent."

Christermann's face darkened, and he glanced toward the window in confusion. "If you would . . . My situation is . . . Matters are despera—That is, I don't . . ." Finally he went silent.

Saint-Germain moved to a chair near the window, so that the shine of day was behind him, casting his face into shadow. "Suppose you start again?" he suggested gently. "I can see you are a printer, and I know from the condition of your clothing that you need money, but there are many reasons to account for that, and I would like to know the whole of it."

"I have told you the truth," said Christermann, his shoulders hunching in spite of himself.

"Some of it," Saint-Germain corrected cordially. "It is the rest that interests me—what you have omitted from your account."

"I have told you—" Christermann began, only to stop himself.

"You have told me as much as you believe you must; I am more interested in what you have left out," said Saint-Germain with easy patience. "Your family died three years ago, you said? And you were in Liege until last year? You were working for a printer of suspect books?"

"Yes. My brother-in-law," said Christermann as if confessing to a crime.

"He kept you on after his sister died?" Saint-Germain asked.

"He did, albeit grudgingly. He held me responsible for her death, and our children's, but I was the best printer that he had ever had working his press, the Guild supported me, and he kept me working for him as long as he was able. When he let me go, it was because he was in trouble."

"Because the Church became dissatisfied with the books he produced," said Saint-Germain.

"That is what happened." Christermann was becoming defensive.

"I am certain of it," said Saint-Germain. "I know Gilpin Purviance, at least by reputation; he is known to be reliable and intelligent. I was pleased to hear that he had got out of Liege, but sorry that he has had to go so far to be secure. Still, he is free, which many another printer is not."

For several minutes Christermann said nothing; then, "Gilpin Purviance is my brother-in-law, it is true." At last he looked at Saint-Germain, but could not make out his expression, for the light behind him obscured his features. "What more do you know?"

"I know you agreed to sign an admission of wrong-doing before you fled, and that in Liege there is a price on your life, as there is on Purviance's, since you did not, as it turns out, actually sign the admission. I know you were considered an audacious fellow for turning against your wife's brother, and that the Guildmaster was advised to sanction you, but did not. Officially the Spanish and the Church may pronounce the *Anathema* on you without any protest from the Guild, although they did not expel you. With the Holy Office seeking you, finding work must be extremely difficult." Saint-Germain let Christermann reflect on this before going on. "I did not recognize you at first, if that is what you think, but I knew enough of what happened in Liege to be able to deduce who you must be when you had told me about your work. Printing and book-making is a very small community, for all the leagues it covers, and little goes on in it that all the publishing world does not know of it."

Christermann sighed. "Then you will not engage me."

"Have I said so?" Saint-Germain rose as Ruthger returned with a well-laden tray in his hands. "First, eat. Then we must talk. But you must not withhold information, for that makes both of us vulnerable."

"The pork-and-turnips is cooking," Ruthger said as he put the tray down. "The dish will be ready shortly."

Christermann seized the wire cheese-slicer and set to work, sectioning off three irregular slices with a speed that demonstrated his hunger.

"I am pleased to hear it," said Saint-Germain, then added, "Will you send the steward on an errand for me?"

"Bogardt van Leun is just now setting up the wine-cellar," said Ruthger. "Would you want him to complete that task before—"

"I am sure the cook can supervise the servants," Saint-Germain replied. "I want information from the Printers' Guild."

"So!" Ruthger exclaimed. "I see why you want an Amsterdamer to go."

"It is hardly surprising, given how insular this city can be," said Saint-Germain, a flicker of amusement in his dark eyes, and added, "The Guild has provided me only the most minimal information."

"What is van Leun to do there?"

"Inquire about the standing of this Mercutius Christermann," said Saint-Germain, his eyes snapping in the direction of the middle-aged man who was starting to devour a slab of new bread thickly buttered with a small wooden paddle, and a wedge of cheese.

"Is there anything you want to know beyond the usual information?" Ruthger inquired.

"No; unless there is something the Guild wishes to pass on to me, something that may have bearing on Christermann's standing in the Guild. Otherwise I know enough of his history to have a good notion of what dangers he may present." He motioned Ruthger away, adding, "Tell van Leun sooner is better than later."

"Certainly, my master," said Ruthger with a slight shift in expression that might have been a smile.

"You understand me too well, old friend," Saint-Germain murmured as Ruthger withdrew and closed the door. He stood still for a moment, then returned to the chair with its back to the window.

"This is very good," Christermann said as he wolfed down another thick slice of bread.

"I should trust so," said Saint-Germain, watching Christermann eat, aware that the man was now a little flushed.

When he had finished a second wedge of cheese and drank down half the pale, shining beer, Christermann wiped his mouth with the long strip of linen provided. "A foreign touch, this cloth; some of the French use them in Liege. Most of us use our cuffs." He studied the black smudges his hands left on the linen. "I apologize for that, but it can't be helped."

"It is the badge of your trade, and one I am inclined to honor," said Saint-Germain. "Now tell me: have you ever printed music books before, or are you limited to texts? You need not explain the difference to me; I am familiar with them. I want only to know your experience."

Christermann accepted this readily, answering as if reciting from memory. "I have done a music book only once, and it was a very difficult process, that I will say, through no fault of the music. It's amazing that the book ever was finished, what with the composer changing his mind every few days and demanding that whole lines of notes be reset. We altered more than twenty-six pages to his order, and even then he wasn't satisfied." He cut another slice of cheese, taking care to peel off the rind before biting energetically into it. Chewing, he said, "I know how the pages are set for music, but I prefer that I stay with words."

"There are always hazards," said Saint-Germain. "You are fortunate if setting new pages is the worst of them."

"*Anathema,* for instance? or prison?" Christermann looked away. "Hazards: you call them that?"

"Why, yes, as I would call a severe storm, or a bad winter, or a famine, or a plague a hazard," Saint-Germain said with hard-won tranquility as his long memories roiled.

"What of war and slaughter?" Christermann challenged. "For surely such are coming."

"I fear you are right," said Saint-Germain. "They are hazards, too, and the more unfortunate because many of them are avoidable."

Christermann laughed out loud, with a total disregard for proper social conduct. "You are a foreigner, and from what I have heard, an exile, and you can still say that?"

"I most of all," Saint-Germain responded quietly.

Giving a shrug, Christermann shifted on the settee and reached for the glass-sided tankard of beer. "Then you are a more reasonable man than I am." With that, he drank all that was left in three large gulps. "Most men in your position would not be so . . . reasonable."

"I am somewhat more experienced than most, perhaps," said Saint-Germain with a deferential nod.

Christermann leaned back. "Will you employ me?"

"That is a very blunt question for a man in your position," said Saint-Germain at his most genial, refusing to be pressured.

"It is my position that makes me blunt," said Christermann, studying the contents of the tray as if trying to determine what he ought to do about the remaining food. Deciding, he took the last of the cheese and bit into it, pursing his lips as he chewed.

"Do not worry," said Saint-Germain. "You will not go hungry here."

Caught off-guard, Christermann managed a chagrined-but-muffled chuckle. "No doubt you have the right of it; you have been most generous so far." He swallowed hard and added, "Don't think I am unaware of the courtesy you are showing me."

"It is the least I can do for you," Saint-Germain said, noticing how cautious Christermann was under his air of bonhomie.

"Out of hospitality," said Christermann.

"At the least," Saint-Germain agreed.

The silence that settled between them was only superficially comfortable, and could not long be sustained. "I am willing to work, Grav, and I will be loyal," said Christermann.

"I have no doubt that you have excellent intentions," said Saint-Germain, not adding his own reservations as to what those intentions might be.

"Then why do you—" He stopped as Ruthger again came into the parlor, this time carrying another, heavier tray with a covered dish upon it, and a larger pitcher of beer.

"The rest of the meal," said Ruthger, setting this down and removing the first tray with a proficiency that seemed almost magical.

"Very good. And when you have a chance, bring a pot of China tea and a jug of fresh milk." Saint-Germain nodded toward Christermann. "I hope this is to your liking."

Christermann had reached for the deep spoon set on the tray and then pulled a knife from his wallet, using the latter to cut the pork. "Very tender," he approved. "And very moist. Pork so often dries in the cooking." As if to make a point, he jabbed the point of the knife into the largest of his slices and held it up, juices running down the blade and onto his fingers.

"Enjoy your meal," Saint-Germain said, then gestured Ruthger to come to his side. "While you are out, I have a second errand for you."

"Tell me what it is," said Ruthger, in Byzantine Greek.

"Call at the house by Holy Trinity Church. You know the one I mean," Saint-Germain said, still speaking the Amsterdam dialect. "Ask the man there if he will call here tomorrow."

Ruthger bowed slightly. "As you wish, my master," he said, still in the Constantinopolitan tongue.

"Thank you; let me know as soon as you have returned." He dismissed Ruthger, then looked back at Christermann. "When you are finished, we will conclude our business."

Christermann managed to grin as he chewed. "I am at your disposal, Grav."

"That is very good of you," said Saint-Germain, wondering if Christermann would be so sanguine if he were aware that the house where Ruthger would call after he spoke to the Guildmaster of the Printers, following van Leun's introduction, belonged to the most formidable advocate in all of Amsterdam—the house of Rudolph Eschen.

Text of a letter from Basilio Cuor in Amsterdam to Christofo Sen in Venice, written in secular Latin, carried by private courier, and delivered ten days after it was written.

To the highly esteemed and most puissant secretary of the Savii agli Ordini in la Serenissima Repubblica Veneziana, Christofo Sen, the greetings of your most devoted servant, Basilio Cuor, from the dismal city of Amsterdam, from Het Bouw Tavern hard by Saint Stephen's Church.

Say what they will about the canals, this place is no more like Venezia than it is like the distant ports of Araby—perhaps less, for here it is cold, and the merchants are like clergymen in appearance and manner. Never would Tiberio Tedeschi be permitted to wear his gaudy silk robes here, and the good burghers are not the sort of men to ceremonially marry the North Sea as the Doge does the Adriatic. But it is a city built on trade, they have that much in common with Venezia, and at the canal-side taverns you may hear languages from across the world spoken. Last night I had a bottle of Alsatian wine with two sailors from Poland, and a white-haired devil from Denmark. Sailors are much like sailors the world over, I would guess. From China to the barbarians of the New World, sailors face the same perils for the same purpose, and that makes them more similar than dissimilar. They all told stories about the Lisbon earthquake, saying that more than ten thousand are dead from it, and each trying to best the last with tales of more horrors.

Franzicco di Santo-Germano is indeed here in Amsterdam. He has two trading companies I am certain of, and a publishing business called Eclipse Press. He calls many of his businesses Eclipse for his heraldic device. From what I have learned, he is prosperous, and although they call him Grav and not Conte, and Saint-Germain instead of Santo-Germano, he is clearly the same man, and he has the same manservant he kept with him in Venezia. I know di Santo-Germano has been to Bruges and Antwerp, and apparently is returning to Antwerp shortly.

I have been able to intercept five letters from Venezia sent to di Santo-Germano, three from his mistress. I am pleased to tell you that he knows nothing of her present plight, and with a little ingenuity, I should be able to continue my efforts for another month or so. At present, with di Santo-Germano so much a foreigner here, I am able to pass myself off as one of his household, at least to the satisfaction of the various couriers who come here, since they keep very regular hours, which makes my tasks much easier.

Nothing di Santo-Germano has done so far has made me believe he is doing anything contrary to Venezian interests. His most outrageous activity is book-making, and that is known to local authorities as well the Spaniards who serve here on behalf of the King of Spain, and the Catholic Church. There are rumors that his press may be seized, but so far, nothing of that sort has happened to him; however, one of his pressmen has been summoned to the local tribunal to answer some questions. I am going to drink with the soldiers from Spain tonight, and I will try to learn more when I do.

I hope your nephew's scheme to drive di Santo-Germano's business agent into ruin will succeed. Relying on gambling as a means of fortune, good or ill, is undertaking more risk than I would advise, and your nephew would not appear to have the resolve to keep to his intentions. I am not there to help you, and so far, your nephew has been unable to compromise Pier-Ariana Salier, as well as drive Emerenzio to the kind of desperation you require. Perhaps if La Salier could be proven a harlot, then Emerenzio would not have to resort to embezzlement to gain control of di Santo-Germano's fortune. A pity the Conte will have to lose his lady and his money, but what can an exile expect?

May the Carnival bring you joy and the deliverance of Easter fill you with the love of Christ, for the glory of our faith.

With my pledge to continue to inform you,

> *In singular dedication to you, the Savii agli Ordini, the Minor Consiglio, the Maggior Consiglio, and the Repubblica Veneziana,*
> *Basilio Cuor*

By his own hand in Amsterdam, the 26ᵗʰ day of March, 1531

6

With a laugh that sounded like an unrosined bow dragged over old strings, Leoncio Sen reached out audaciously to take hold of Pier-Ariana. "Your fidelity is misplaced, ninotta, believe me. Your Conte has left you, and no one will think the less of you for taking anoth—"

"How dare you!" She rounded on him, her eyes shining with fury.

Leoncio offered his best placating smile. "I mean you no disrespect, ninotta, only the assurance that you need not suffer if you would prefer not—"

Pier-Ariana shrieked to shut out the words she dreaded might be true, and reached for a small vase of red-and-gold glass, preparing to throw it at her most unwelcome visitor. "You have said as much as I have any desire to hear: now I want you out! Leave!"

"I am not ready to go," he said smoothly, confidently. "We have much to discuss, you and I."

"*Go!* Or I will summon help."

"Which of your two remaining servants do you expect will escort me?" Leoncio taunted, reveling in his power over her. "The old woman or the—"

The vase shattered on the wall a handsbreadth from his head, and Pier-Ariana, her face distorted in fury, rushed toward the door, shouting, "Lilio! Lilio! *Lilio!* And bring a cleaver when you come!" She could not keep from weeping; she felt her face blotch with red and she wanted more than ever to get this velvet-clad interloper out of her house. "Out of my house!" she shrieked, trembling with the force of her rage. "*Out!*"

Leoncio took a step away from her. "You're overwrought. Small wonder, to be treated so shabbily. If di Santo-Germano were a Veneziano, you might have some recourse against him. As it is, you are entirely dependent upon his provisions for you, and that has not been . . . all you expected, has it? Only your 'tirewoman and your cook are left, and I understand they are owed money. They won't be able to stay with you forever, no matter how much they may wish to.

With the Conte away, how can you keep this house? You must soon be out on—"

"I have a deed of occupancy; the only thing I cannot do is sell this house—otherwise it is mine; I will manage my affairs as seems wisest," she was goaded into saying as she tried to wipe the tears off her face with her inner sleeves. "The deed is fixed; it was ratified for fifty years before di Santo-Germano left." She could see the craftiness in Leoncio's eyes and regretted having said so much.

"How very generous of him, to give you the gift but then not provide the means to keep it." His sneer made his features ugly; he forced himself to offer a more concerned look. "Still, it may not be his fault: he may have come to some misfortune. We don't know what the disaster in Lisbon may have done to his holdings there. He may have lost ships and warehouses, as has happened to many another. He may have forfeited contracts along with his losses."

"He may," she said, somewhat uncertainly, tears still shining on her face.

"And you are showing him respect by not abandoning him, which is to your credit." Leoncio nodded. "I have spoken with his business agent—Gennaro Emerenzio; you must know him?—and he has said that the Conte's accounts are all seriously depleted."

"I don't believe him!" Pier-Ariana burst out.

Leoncio regarded her slyly. "Because you have better information? Have you a secret that will provide for you?"

"Even if I had such a secret, I wouldn't need it." She tossed her head. "Because I know that di Santo-Germano has many business interests, and bad as the Lisbon tragedy was, his losses there did not represent the whole of his wealth."

"He boasted and you believed him," said Leoncio, shaking his head.

Pier-Ariana closed her eyes, nauseated by the spurious kindness Leoncio conveyed with his mendacious interest. "Signor' Sen, I have nothing more to tell you; please leave my house," she said in as calm a voice as she could summon.

"If you insist, I will," he said. "But I ask you to keep my offer in mind: I would gladly take on your maintenance rather than see you on the street or in debtors' prison, which must happen if the Conte does not provide relief for you soon."

"It will not come to that," she said, marshaling her dignity.

"Madama?" Lilio said from the door. He held his cleaver in his hand, but not raised to strike. "You called me?"

"Yes, Lilio, I did. Signor' Sen is just leaving. If you would be good enough to escort him out?"

"Certainly, if that is your wish," said the cook, his manner less confident than his words.

"It is," she said, moving aside so Leoncio could depart without getting any nearer to her. Her shoes crunched on the broken vase; she did her best to ignore it.

As he reached the door, Leoncio lowered his head politely. "I go for now, but will return, ninotta; never fear." Satisfied with his mission, he left her alone in her house, strolling away into the peach-tinged afternoon light made sparkling by a faint gauze of fog in the city. He was very well-pleased with what he had accomplished during his visit to Pier-Ariana. He had suspected that di Santo-Germano might have left a secret cache of funds with her, but that seemed not to be the case, unless Pier-Ariana were cleverer than she seemed, and therefore Emerenzio would soon be reduced to ruin and would become his creature or end up working a galley oar. Given Emerenzio's age and position, Leoncio was reasonably certain that the business agent would prefer to have to serve him privately than face public humiliation, to say nothing of the consequences of his sleight-of-hand with other men's money. This would mean that he—Leoncio Sen, the wastrel, the gambler, the feckless, the man everyone said was incapable of doing serious work—could finally demonstrate his usefulness to the Savii, and earn the good opinion of his uncle. At last he would be a man of position, respected and powerful, not a lackey to Christofo, not an unprofitable expense, not an embarrassment, not a family obligation, but a family vindication. The family would be proud of him, and no one would speak ill of him again. He began to whistle as he walked, paying little attention to the crowd around him, and in a short while he reached the handsome Casetta Santa Perpetua, where he was admitted and shown to the larger of the gamblers' parlors, escorted by a page displaying so much deference that those watching might suppose Leoncio to be the scion of a wealthy merchant.

From his place at the dice-table, Padre Egidio Duradante looked up, and motioned to Leoncio to join him, his smile a smug one. "I warn you, Signor' Sen, the Saints have been touching my dice today. I have already won over a hundred ducats, and hope to gain more." He was wearing standard priestly garb, but his lucchino was made of rich, dark-gray silk over a camisa of fine, bleached linen, all of which made him look more like an advocate than a priest.

"That's because you have the Pope's confidence residing in you— not even the dice dare to oppose you," said Leoncio as he perched on a stool across the table from Padre Duradante, and next to a brocade-clad trader from France; from his glum demeanor, he had been losing to Padre Duradante for a while.

"How can you bother with talking?" the Frenchman demanded in dreadful Italian.

"It is pleasant to talk," said Padre Duradante in excellent French, making no effort to diminish his gloating or to offer simulated sympathy for his success. "It makes losing money much more enjoyable."

"You're not losing," said the Frenchman, and shoved another three ducats onto the painted table.

Padre Duradante smiled and shook the dice in their leather cup, tossing them almost negligently onto the table, watching them roll with an avidity that showed his nonchalance to be sham.

"Tell me," said the Frenchman as the dice settled with a two, a three, and a six showing, "do you know the dice are proper?"

"Are you saying they have loaded dice at this casetta?" Padre Duradante was affronted now, and he stood up very straight. "Sanson! Sanson!" he called out, indignation raising his voice by four notes.

Sanson Micheletta sauntered over to the table, his dissolute features now a mask of good-will. "Padre—you have a problem?"

"No. Had I a problem, I would not continue to come through your door. This man has one, however," he said, pointing to the Frenchman. "Because he is losing, he thinks the dice are inaccurate."

"Does he?" The owner of the casetta reached down and picked up the dice one by one. "They are carved from ivory, as you see, and the faces are painted. All the edges are beveled to the same degree. How could these be weighted?" He held them out to the Frenchman. "You may want to examine them for yourself."

The man took them and rolled them experimentally between his flattened palms, testing their weight and shape. Reluctantly he handed them back to Sanson Micheletta. "They seem true enough," he conceded.

"But perhaps you would prefer a new trio to play with? One that has never been used before?" Sanson asked, and snapped his fingers; instantly a page appeared at his side. "A new trio of dice for this table. See these are put aside. Signor' Hautecrete is not pleased with them."

The page took the dice and vanished, and in a very short while, new dice were brought to the table by a lovely young woman with fine Greek features and an enchanting accent, rigged out in clinging silks from Antioch, the lengthened bodice of the new fashions showing off her slender waist. "For Signor' Hautecrete," she said, offering him a unimpaired view of her elevated breasts framed by a corsage of golden lace studded with pearls.

Guillaume Hautecrete took the dice and did his best to ignore Apollonia, who was leaning into his arm. "Padre, you had best hope that France does not go the way of England, and others, as well. You cannot forget that Ferdinand is Charles' brother, and a Hapsburg before he is anything else."

Padre Durandante recognized this ploy for what it was, and offered a sour smile. "If Frenchmen will give up their salvation as readily as the English have, and all for a King's harlot, then perhaps God is preparing for Judgment Day, after all, and no one will emerge unscathed, let the Holy Roman Emperor do as he will. Not that a roll of the dice will change either England or France or any German state." He took the dice from Hautecrete, and remarked quietly, "I would like to resume play—would you?"

"I suppose I will," said Hautecrete, and moved another two ducats from his depleted pile onto a painted oblong on the table. "There."

Matching the amount, Padre Duradante shook his dice and threw them. This time only two of the dice were winning, and so Hautecrete received one of his ducats back, seizing it and hanging on to it as if he feared it would escape through his fingers. He laughed harshly and looked from Padre Duradante to Leoncio Sen. "If you play with him, know you are dealing with the Devil."

"I have suspected as much," Leoncio rejoined with a smirk. He set down his bet and waited for Padre Duradante to roll the dice again.

"This is too rich for me," said Hautecrete, who gathered up his few remaining coins and stalked out of the parlor, bound for the tavern at the rear of the casetta. After a moment, Apollonia followed after him.

"Safer to gamble," said Padre Duradante as he watched her go.

"At least dice will not give you the pox," agreed Leoncio.

"But if one must have pox, she would make the infection memorable," said Padre Duradante; he tossed the dice and smiled as he won again. "I apologize for any hardship I may impose upon you."

"Your forgiveness, Padre, but I doubt it," said Leoncio, handing over his money. "You like to win too much."

"You are quite ingenious, Signor' Sen; you say just enough," Padre Duradante told him, accepting his slight for a compliment, as he gathered up the dice for another throw.

Over the next hour, the trio of dice went back and forth between Padre Duradante and Leoncio Sen, and their stacks of ducats rose and fell on a swift tide of fortune, with neither pulling so far ahead of the other that they were forced to stop their game, or their play turned rancorous. Finally Padre Duradante dropped the dice back in their cup and announced, "I'm hungry, and I can smell aromas from the kitchen. Let us go to the dining room."

"Of course," said Leoncio, scooping up his bounty and shoving it into his wallet; all in all he was down about twelve ducats on the night—not a vast sum as gaming went, but enough that his uncle would complain of it when he heard.

"This is a very elegant casetta, this Santa Perpetua," Padre Duradante remarked as he led the way toward the dining room. "I hope it continues successful, though in times like these, relying on chance is precarious."

"No doubt Sanson shares your feelings," said Leoncio, smiling at his own wit. "He is a very canny man, is Sanson."

"So I have heard, and from many sources," Padre Duradante said as they passed through the doors opened for them by Moorish slaves.

A waiter came up to them, bowing and asking, "What would you like to eat, Signori?"

"I am told you have a fish cooked in a bread that is said to be excellent tonight," said Padre Duradante. "Some of that, I think, and then, perhaps, a duck in red wine would be good. Not too tough, or fishy—if the duck is from the land, so much the better."

"The Padre has a fine palate," the waiter approved obsequiously, and clapped his hands to summon a page to seat them at one of the small round tables. "Our ducks come in from Padova twice a week, and those we cook now arrived this morning. If that is satisfactory?"

"Are they brought by barge, alive, in cages, to be killed here?" Padre Duradante pursued.

"Yes. We killed and hung half the order this morning. The rest we'll do over the next two days." The waiter pursed his lips.

"We'll chance it, then," said the Padre as the waiter left them in the care of the young African page.

"You could order pigs' feet and cured cabbage and he'd fawn just as much," Leoncio observed as the waiter vanished through the kitchen door.

"But why should I have an inferior meal because the waiter is supercilious?" Padre Duradante asked,

Leoncio laughed aloud. "No reason." He pulled a chair out for the Padre and then took one himself.

"Perhaps you will tell me what has you so gratified," Padre Duradante asked as another waiter approached their table.

"What wine may I bring you, Padre?" asked the waiter.

"The Toscan Montecello, and fine glasses for such a wine," said Padre Duradante with an air of satisfaction. As the waiter went away, he studied Leoncio for a short while. "So, if you will, tell me what has happened to give you that unctuous air."

"I had a bit of luck earlier today—not with dice or cards, but in another matter." He smiled. "I believe I have the key to gaining two things I seek with a single stroke."

"A most fortunate turn," said Padre Duradante. "I should hope that you are not trading on that stroke quite yet."

"Why should I not? The matter is all but settled." Leoncio refused to frown, although the Padre's warning robbed him of some of his satisfaction.

"*All but* is still subject to the fluctuations of fortune." Padre Duradante contemplated Leoncio for a short while, then said, "I assume part of your plan includes that unscrupulous Signor' Emerenzio. I also assume you must know he is purloining funds from the accounts he holds in trust in order to pay his gambling debts?"

Leoncio frowned. "Yes, that is a part of my—"

"—scheme?" Padre Duradante finished for him. "I thought as much. You want to suborn him, don't you? Bind him to your service so unequivocally that any deviation from your intentions may expose him to calumny and worse."

"Hardly calumny, considering what he has done: rather it would bring him to justice," said Leoncio firmly.

"As you say," the Padre remarked with a shrug. "It would make him reluctant to oppose you in any way."

"Yes. And a man in his position can reveal much useful information with the proper persuasion."

"But whipped dogs bite more cruelly than well-treated ones," Padre Duradante reminded him.

"A strange observation for the Pope's man to make, if you will excuse my saying so," Leoncio observed.

"Matters of faith are different than worldly considerations; a whipped dog is not a soul in danger of dogmatic equivocation," said Padre Duradante. "To chastize in the Name of God is nothing like mundane coercion—it is the duty entrusted to us as the servants of God, and the means by which we secure our salvation." He smiled as the waiter returned with a bottle of wine. "Very good," he said as the cork was withdrawn from the neck and the first, rich aroma of the wine emerged like a demon from a jewel-case.

The waiter brought glasses for the two men and poured the deep-red liquid. "Is there anything else?"

"Not just now," said Padre Duradante, waving the waiter away. "I think you'll like this vintage," he said in a tone that indicated serious conversation was at an end for the duration of their meal.

Leoncio raised his glass. "May God send you good health, Padre."

"And good fortune," Padre Duradante added, a cynical amusement in his eyes.

For the duration of their meal they exchanged gossip and engaged in the kind of verbal jousting that both men enjoyed. When they finished with their fish, Sanson sent two of his most beautiful women to join them—one blond, one dark—although he knew neither Padre Duradante nor Leoncio would be particularly interested in their talents; most serious gamblers were not readily distracted.

"Not tonight," said Padre Duradante, stroking the exposed arm of the fair-haired woman beside him.

"Perhaps another time, then?" she purred.

"Perhaps," he agreed, and kissed his fingers at her as she and her companion went away, remarking to Leoncio as a bowl of sweetbreads and crab in cream with garlic was brought to them, "With such women as those, Sanson must know every secret in Venezia. Who could hold anything back from one of them?"

Leoncio laughed because it was expected of him.

It was almost two hours later when they rose from their table and returned to the dice-room where they found a heavy-eyed Gennaro Emerenzio at the central table, his camisa deeply wrinkled, the inner, turned-back sleeves of his dogaline stained with sweat, the dice-cup in his hands, a determined expression on his face. He glanced up as he saw Padre Duradante and Leoncio Sen approaching, and his eyes darted away from them.

"Buona sera," said Leoncio with spurious geniality. "I thought you might be here, Signor' Emerenzio."

"I came to try my luck, just as you have," said Emerenzio, as if the words were pulled out of him.

"Yes; my point exactly," said Leoncio, reaching into his wallet for a dozen ducats. "You won't mind if I join the game, will you?"

.Short of insulting Leoncio, Emerenzio could not deny him the right to a game, so he hitched his shoulders and said, "It would be my pleasure."

"Very sporting of you," said Padre Duradante, drawing up a stool and putting down ten ducats. "A small amount to begin, in case the Saints have put their sights elsewhere."

"But you are—"

"—needed at Il Redentor? Not until the *Angelus,* which gives me an hour or so for our entertainment." The Padre braced his elbows on the table. "You were going to throw against the house, were you not? Well, now you will have a better chance of winning something."

Emerenzio sighed and drooped like a windless sail. Then he visibly restored his resolve, improved his attitude, setting the seal on his fate by shaking the leather cup. "Why not?" He looked at the two men flanking him. "Put down your money, Signori," he said, preparing to toss.

Padre Duradante was quick to comply, Leoncio marginally less so, but prompt enough to have three ducats down by the time the dice left the cup. "Dio mio," the priest muttered as one die bounced and rolled off the end of the table.

With a burst of loud laughter, Emerenzio gathered up the other two and went to retrieve the third. "I'll have to roll again."

Leoncio put his hand on Emerenzio's upper arm. "Let me have a look at the dice, if you would, Gennaro."

Emerenzio held out the leather cup, his indifference at this challenge obviously forced. "Go ahead and look. You'll find nothing amiss."

"No, probably not; even you are not such a fool as to foist false dice onto a gaming house," said Padre Duradante, taking the cup and rolling the dice between his hands. "But you cannot know if the fall damaged the bevel." He closed his eyes, concentrating on the three ivory cubes. Finally he opened his eyes. "They seem right enough, but, do you know, I think we would all play more happily with a fresh trio."

Emerenzio nodded, his face blank. "As you say, Padre Duradante."

Padre Duradante's smile was as wide as it was false. "I know we shall all be more comfortable with the results." He clapped his hands for a page, and handed over the dice. "One fell, and may have lost true."

"Very good, Padre," said the page, and bore the dice away.

"There. You see?" Padre Duradante said consolingly, "Now none of us can have reason to be suspicious."

This reassurance was clearly cold comfort to Emerenzio, who shook his head and declared that he could not imagine why such an exchange was necessary. "But, as you say, there can be no suspicions this way."

Leoncio bowed to the table-top. "Your field of honor awaits. Shall you enter the lists? We're waiting." To make his point, he put four ducats on one of the painted squares and watched as Padre Duradante placed his bet, thinking as he did that Padre Duradante had the coffers of the Church to draw upon if play went against him, while he had to appeal to his uncle.

"I have done all I can," said the priest with an air of saintliness that absolved him of all disappointments.

Emerenzio stared at the new dice, reaching for them as if he feared they were red-hot, dropped them into the cup, rattled them well, and tossed, letting out a stifled yelp as the dice came to rest.

"You will do better next throw," said Leoncio, claiming his ducats and the dice-cup from Emerenzio before placing his next bet. This, he told himself, was going to be a wonderful night.

Text of a letter from Onfroi van Amsteljaxter in Heidelberg to his sister Erneste van Amsteljaxter in Amsterdam, carried by academic courier and delivered nineteen days after it was written.

To my dear sister Erneste, the affectionate greetings of your brother Onfroi, presently in Heidelberg, at the Inn of the Six Red Feathers, where many scholars stay during their brief time here. Until I know what my situation may be, you will be able to reach me here.

Yes, I am safe, and for the moment my resources are such that I need not draw upon you for my living, but I have found that the Landsmacht—you know of whom I speak—has written to the university here, complaining of my Godlessness and advising against my employment, so I may once again be cast upon the world without means to make a living, or the safety of being permitted to teach. For the time being, I am tutoring a Bohemian scholar in reading Frankish Latin in exchange for meals, and I have earned a few small commissions writing letters for merchants and other travelers, and translating those they have received. I never thought our peripatetic existence in youth would prove valuable now, but so it is: my knowledge of Latin, Austrian, Bohemian, Bavarian, Venezian, Fiorenzen, Provencal, French, Spanish, Gascon, and Flemish may not be profound, but it is workable enough to earn my keep. I have also begun to read broadsheets to the foreign scholars here at the Six Red Feathers, and they often buy me tankards of beer and wine for my trouble; thus I am able to keep my room paid for, at least for now.

I am pleased to hear that your little book has been doing well— quite an unexpected development, I should say. No doubt this eases your concern for me, as it gives me hope that my need will not cast you into penury: perhaps it will also make it possible for you and our aunt to remain in Amsterdam, so you may avoid the present unrest in Antwerp. I hope that, as you say, your publisher may consider doing another text for you. That would be a most excellent development for you, and for me, should I have to impose upon you. At present I am in need of little more than four or five ducats to last until August, for my summer earnings will be less while many of the students are away.

I am deliberating about speaking to an advocate to limit the damage that the Landsmacht can do to me. It is unfortunate that I do not yet have funds enough to pay for the services I would need, and that has made me loath to mention this to you, but that the sooner I may be honestly employed, the sooner you will not have to burden yourself with my cares; if you could add five ducats to retain an advocate, then I know you will be rewarded later for your generosity.

I realize, my dear sister, that this is a burden on you, and one you may not be able to accept, given your circumstances. Let me impose upon you, then, to the extent that upon your recommendation, your patron, the Grav, might see his way to considering publishing my work, The Promise of the New World, Its Peoples and Resources. I realize my work is based upon reports, not first-hand knowledge, but it is as thorough a compendium as your publisher is likely to find anywhere, and more varied, in that I have spoken to soldiers and sailors as well as captains and priests. I have even interviewed a Spaniard but lately returned from Peru, who claims to have seen the apparent King of the natives, a man who was besting his brother in war, the Royal Priest At-U-Alpa. His story was most compelling, but it may not have been true. Still, I intend to include it in my work, so that all will know what is being said of the people of that distant, mountainous land. It seems to me that in years to come, knowledge of the New World could prove useful to scholars and travelers alike.

For myself, I would like to be able to teach here in Heidelberg, not only because of the superiority of the university, but because I am certain my studies may prove useful to many of the scholars working here. If not in this place, I will have to consider more distant institutions, such as Fiorenze and Oxford, as the current turmoil around me has made seeking a chair nearer to Amsterdam a potentially dangerous move. There may be other applications for my skills: much of my work could be of the practical kind, such as assisting in translations and in securing and cataloguing new information as it arrives here. I am predicating my assumption on the hope that I will be vindicated of all wrong-thinking, and my reputation made uncontroversial. If that cannot be accomplished, and I am forced to leave Heidelberg,

then I would like to establish myself at some fine school, one with op-
portunities for me as well as good standing in the world of learning to
build upon.

But one thing at a time: first I must emerge from the cloud of con-
testation that the Landsmacht has set upon me, or all else may be lost.
Once that is done, I will be delighted to pursue my academic goals
with full rigor and determination. With your help, I know I will
emerge from this present embarrassment with my standing improved,
at which time I will be able to do as a brother should, and provide you
some portion of the support you have accorded me.

Extend my good wishes to our aunt, and continue to keep yourself
as carefully as you have done until now. I pray for you, dear Erneste,
and hope that we will meet again in this world as well as the one to
come.

Your most affectionate brother,
Onfroi van Amsteljaxter

By my own hand at Heidelberg, on the 2ⁿᵈ day of May, 1531

7

Eleazaro Justo San Martin y Sobrano stood in the middle of the
printing room of Eclipse Press, his arms folded, his sword swinging at
his side. His doublet was of black suede piped in gold, his hose were
mid-thigh length, of studded, stiffened black-painted linen, his leggings were gunmetal-gray, his shoes were black and buckled in gold.
"You claim that you have not broken the law, Señor?"

Saint-Germain achieved a partial smile, addressing him in Castil-
lian Spanish. "I am properly addressed as Grav, Capitan, and I am
certain I have not broken the law; not any law in Amsterdam, in any
case, which, I recall, you do not control." He, too, was in black, but his
clothing—today in the Venezian style to emphasize his foreignness—
gave an impression of elegance instead of threat. Rather than his
silver-linked collar with its pendant eclipse in silver and black

sapphire, he had fixed a single, square ruby at the base of his soft Italian ruff; the left hand was gloved, the right bore only his signet ring on his Mercury finger.

"Not specifically, no, but we do control Antwerp, where you have another press, and that one has suspended publication while their works—*your* works, Grav—are investigated, and your men questioned about your practices," said Capitan Sobrano. He nodded toward the window and the east-southeast, in the general direction of Antwerp. The high window was open to let in the timid warmth of the day, and to provide a fair quantity of limpid northern light; the tools and equipment were all clean and in order and the stacks of paper near the press were so luminous they seemed to glow from within.

"Yes; so I was informed by private courier yesterday morning. And to think the Antwerp press has only just released *The Life of Frederick the Wise, Elector of Saxony;* the first copies went on sale six days ago. Come now: the Church could hardly object to the life of a man who so admirably upheld his faith, since his namesake is about to rule there." Saint-Germain inclined his head slightly, as if to respect the late ruler. "Frederick the Wise deserved his cognomen."

"He also supported Luther and other Protestants," the Spanish officer observed. "If you intend to promulgate tolerance for heresy it is hardly surprising that you have no one—"

"I have no such intention, although I do admire Frederick's permissiveness, for he would have had war with his own subjects had he been more strict, a prudential stance Charles' brother would do well to emulate," Saint-Germain said, glancing around his printing room and turning his palms up to show he had nothing to do or say about the lack of industry there.

"Better for his soul had he stamped out the heresy before it took root. As it is, his people may be lost to the Protestants." The Capitan's pointed beard angled outward to emphasize his intention.

"I fear most of your censure stems from a misunderstanding of Eclipse Press," said Saint-Germain, doing his best not to stray into matters of dogma. "If my printers and binders were here, they could confirm the plans I have for the future; they certainly know which books we are preparing for sale, and which are planned to be prepared during the next year—assuming we can find sufficient paper for our needs. The warehouse that burned last week had just received eleven bales of paper—but I suppose you know that?"

"A great misfortune," said the Capitan, gloating.

Saint-Germain let this pass. "You may take my future plans from what I have done in the past: if you would look about you, you would see that I have no titles more outrageous than a collection of variations on folk tales, which is planned for this spring, and which contains nothing more offensive than the stories peasants tell. After that, I am considering a book of maps of the Papal States and the Two Sicilies." He did not add that he had drafted the maps himself.

"Yes," said Capitan Sobrano with a faint, unpleasant laugh. "If they were here."

"This amuses you?" Saint-Germain's self-composure concealed his alarm.

"It must, for, as you say, it bears so directly on your plans." He actually laughed aloud. He walked down the length of the printing room, touching the press as he passed. "You see, on the authority of the Emperor and the Pope, your men have been detained: pressmen, binders, typesetters, compositors, leather-workers, embossers, goldsmiths and gilders, the lot of them. For the sake of public security, they will be subjected to examination, and if we are satisfied that they have not contributed to civil unrest or to religious error, they will be released."

Saint-Germain kept his temper in check, knowing this man wanted to goad him into ill-considered remarks. "I am surprised that you were allowed to do so."

"Why should that be? The Church is strong here, and there are so many Protestants that they are at one anothers' throats: Calvin's adherents, disciples of Luther, Anabaptists, and even a few followers of Hutter—all of them competing to corrupt the most souls. God and the Pope must be rejoicing to see such folly, for surely these heresies will end through mutual antagonism. Our garrison is here in support of the Church, sparing the city's officials the need to endorse what we do." He stopped next to the bindery tables and picked up an awl. "There are some ignorant men who might mistake this for a weapon."

"They would have to be very ignorant indeed," said Saint-Germain, able to remain affable in spite of his increasing dismay.

"A man like you has the wherewithal not to have to remain here.

Your printers and binders and the rest will probably be released, but who knows what accusations they may lay at your door, Senor Grav, in exchange for their liberty and the liberty of their families? There is always work for an honest tradesman, but the activities you have undertaken may cast doubts upon them, and they will not want that, for themselves, their families, their Guilds, and their city." He set the awl down again, not bothering to align it with the other tools. "If you close this business and leave, no smirch would stick to your character, for, as you say, the Crown has compromised authority here."

"Except such flight would sting me mercilessly—worse than anything you might persuade the courts to do to me. I would deplore my lack of integrity, and that would cause me great anguish, so I fear I must remain here until I am satisfied none of my workers will face punishment on my account," said Saint-Germain. "Your warning is much appreciated, as is your intent, but I fear I must remain, to see that no injustice is visited upon those who work for me; I have no wish for anyone to suffer on my account." He indicated the door that led out into the small shop at the front of the printing room. "I thank you for your concern, Capitan. I will take all you say into consideration, and I will be at pains to see that those in my employ are afforded the full protection of the law."

This had not been the Capitan's purpose at all, but he did his best to reclaim what he could of his offensive. "You might want to tend to your own situation first: these men may not be worthy of your support."

"I will not know until I support them, will I." Saint-Germain began to draw on his fine Italian glove, the black leather supple and glossy. "You have acted on your purpose, and I have listened to what you wished to tell me. Unless you have something more to say, our business is concluded. Now all that remains is for each of us to proceed as we think best." He held the door for the Capitan—an almost unheard-of courtesy—adding, "I will send a note to your superiors, commending you for coming to me."

Capitan Sobrano glowered. "There is no need for you to do that, Senor Grav."

"That, I believe, is for me to decide," said Saint-Germain, making a gesture to indicate the cramped shelves of the shop. "While you're here, if you wish to make an inventory of what I offer for sale, I will be willing to wait while you do; if you would prefer to attend to this another time, you must pardon me, but I had best be about the task of finding other printers and binders. I have a schedule to maintain." He had gone to the front door to close the shutters on the front windows.

"You may find that a more difficult task than it was before, given the state of publishing in Amsterdam, and the desires of Emperor Charles and the Church. As to the inventory, I will attend to that later; one of the clerks will come to inspect your shelves; I haven't the time for such tasks," said Capitan Sobrano, his gaze flicking contemptuously about the room; Saint-Germain realized that the Capitan was very nearly illiterate for he made no attempt to read any of the titles in front of him, not even the two in Spanish.

"Then I will detain you no longer," said Saint-Germain, opening the door to the street.

The Capitan stepped onto the narrow street fronting the canal. "You have given me much to think about."

"As you have given me," said Saint-Germain, fixing the lock on the door-latch before turning away from the Spaniard and striding along in order to conceal the vertigo the nearness of the canal caused him, and the general disorientation he suffered surrounded by so much running water. He was aware that the Capitan was watching him, looking for any weakness he might report; this was more than Saint-Germain was willing to concede, and so he kept on steadily, taking advantage of the first corner to go left, down the alley along the flank of the new little church dedicated to the Holy Trinity. Once certain that the Capitan was not behind him, he slowed down to a strolling pace and began to review the short discussion in his thoughts; why had the Capitan visited him, beyond the desire to gloat? Why had his workmen been detained, and what help could he provide them without increasing their danger? Who had reported his press to the Church, or had the Church been watching him as a matter of course, as it had many others? So preoccupied was he that he nearly walked into a tall, portly man in a stained and patched leather doublet and Italian-style hose. "Pardon," he said in Dutch, and then in French. He could not make out the man's features, which were partially obscured by the wide brim of his leathern hat and the general disorder of his hair.

The big man seemed nonplussed. "E niente," he said—it's nothing—in a Venezian accent, backing up as if to get away from him.

Saint-Germain was startled to hear that tongue spoken in this place, and began to apologize for not using his language. "I have offended you; I ask your pardon for it. I should have noticed your shoes—only Veneziani wear such shoes, or has that—"

"The Grav is mistaken," the man muttered brusquely in dreadful Flemish.

"Let me assure you that I meant no insult," Saint-Germain persisted, wondering suddenly how this stranger knew his rank and now determined to learn more. "I'll stand you a drink for—"

But the man faded back into the shadows of the alley, slipping away in a silence that was unnerving in such a large fellow.

Saint-Germain watched him go, his night-seeing eyes less hampered by the darkness than most living men's; he saw the big man enter the church by the narrow door usually reserved for clergy. "Strange," he whispered in his native language. Little as he wanted to admit it, he was as much disquieted by the discovery of this Veneziano as he was by the threats of Capitan Sobrano. He resumed his walk homeward, arriving there five minutes later, feeling slightly queasy from crossing three bridges on his way. Ordinarily he would have taken a slightly longer route that would have spared him one of the bridges, but today speed seemed more essential than comfort.

He entered the house using his key without bothering to raise the knocker. Stepping into the vestibule and then into the long corridor, he found his steward, Bogardt van Leun, bringing a tray with fresh hand-rolls, butter, and a large cup of ale to the front parlor. "Van Leun," said Saint-Germain, startled to see his steward on this errand.

"Grav," said van Leun, almost equally startled. "I beg your pardon. I didn't hear you knock."

"Because there was no knock to hear. I used my key," said Saint-Germain, then indicated the tray van Leun was carrying. "I gather from this bounty that there is company?"

"Yes; an advocate has called. He says that you have retained his services," said van Leun.

"Rudolph Eschen," said Saint-Germain. "I had not expected to see him so soon."

"So he told me," said van Leun. "Your man Ruthger instructed me to admit him and get him some refreshment, and then he left to go to your—"

"To Eclipse Press," Saint-Germain finished for him.

"I should have thought you would have encountered him on your way," said van Leun.

"I came by different streets than I usually do," said Saint-Germain, nodding to the parlor door that was slightly ajar. "Let us not keep Advocate Eschen waiting."

"As you say, Grav," van Leun responded, using his elbow to open the door. "Grav Saint-Germain," he announced as he stepped through the door.

Rudolph Eschen was an imposing man: tall, broad-shouldered, crag-faced, with keen, clever eyes the color of Chinese turquoise. He was well-dressed in somber dark-brown; the broad collar of his chamarre was of marten-fur, but lacked any fripperies of fashion that would detract from his dignity. At thirty-seven, he was at the height of his powers, and he knew it. Rising to his feet, he offered Saint-Germain the suggestion of a bow. "Grav. I am relieved to see you."

"If you mean that some of my employees have been detained by Church officials, I share your relief." He gestured to his steward to put down the tray, then said, "Thank you, van Leun."

Van Leun obeyed the implicit dismissal, and withdrew from the parlor.

"Please." Saint-Germain indicated the tray. "I am not presently hungry."

"Very kind of you," said Eschen, sitting once again on the straight-backed settee. "I heard about the detention not an hour ago, and as soon as I was at liberty, I came here, to offer my services." His eyes crinkled. "I have accepted your payment, so it is fitting that you avail yourself of my talents."

"Very true," said Saint-Germain. "I am worried for the safety of those in my employ—all of them, not just those working at the press, for it seems to me that everyone is at risk, no matter how exemplary their lives. I know how these inquiries tend to spread, and how insinuation transforms into known fact as the questioning continues to expand."

"I have already filed a petition on behalf of your workers that they not be turned over to the Secular Arm without a hearing," said

Eschen. "It is just a beginning, but it puts the Church authorities on notice that they must do their work in public view, which is to our advantage."

"Providential," Saint-Germain approved with an ironic twist to his lips. "I thank you for your efforts."

Eschen did not quite laugh, but there was a trace of amusement in his hewn visage that indicated he appreciated Saint-Germain's wit. "No court in Amsterdam will approve of handing anyone over to the Church for torture. Not even the Catholics would want such a thing to happen, certainly not here, in public view. There's too much unrest in the city as it is; if there is any incident, no matter now minor, that touches off the people, there will be riots and worse."

"Unfortunately, I concur," said Saint-Germain, his expression settling into grim lines. "I am concerned for the writers whose works I publish: they could well be caught in this lunacy."

"So they might." Eschen took a sip of the ale. "I will have my clerks prepare letters for any you stipulate, and I will send them instructions on how to proceed if they are asked to present themselves to Church authorities. If they are taken without notification, then I will act as soon as I receive word from you to proceed on their behalf. I will put this petition before the judges by the middle of June; I doubt they will hear the matter sooner. You may want to appoint a member of your household to be your messenger to me; one of the lesser servants would be best, as they're the least likely to be detained themselves." He reached for a hand-roll. "The Guilds are already in an uproar over the various Catholic and Protestant efforts to make the Guilds include oaths of faith as part of their membership conditions." He broke the roll in half and paddled a helping of butter onto the soft white bread. "The Master of the Joiners' Guild has said that a hammer is a hammer and it strikes the same, whether a Catholic or a Protestant or a New World native wields it."

"If he works as precisely as he speaks, he is most deserving of his position," said Saint-Germain.

"The Spanish may hold it against him," said Eschen. "And the Emperor cannot deny the Spanish some satisfaction, being their King."

"Unrest leads to difficult situations at the best of times," said Saint-Germain, memories of Lo-Yang and Thebes, Roma and Fiorenze,

Avignon and Delhi, and places with names long forgotten, simmering in his thoughts.

"Truly." Eschen began to eat, nodding his approval of the hand-roll. "This is really delicious. Aren't you going to have some?"

"Alas, no," said Saint-Germain. "Those of my blood tend to require a very limited diet."

"Then I hope you won't mind if I take my fill?" Eschen smiled as he bit into the other half of the hand-roll.

"Please do," said Saint-Germain, leaning back on the mantel of the fireplace, his shoulders touching the enameled wood. He watched the advocate eat, saying nothing until the ale was almost gone and Eschen's attention was once again directed toward him. "Regarding your concerns about the temperament of the city, there is a spice merchant in Calais, a cousin of Hendrik van der Meer, whose ships anchor in this port: he—the cousin—has written to van der Meer that the danger of travel now includes risk of being taken as a heretic, or set upon by rebellious peasants, not in Germany or Spanish territory alone. Does it seem so to you?"

"There are examples of such things reported everywhere," said Eschen, wiping his mouth with the linen strip provided for him. "You are hardly the only man in Amsterdam to be under scrutiny just now."

"I did not assume I was," said Saint-Germain, nonetheless feeling relieved that he had nothing more to deal with than any other publisher in the city. "Have you any idea why their attentions should light upon me, beyond the bounds of chance?"

"Not specifically, no; or not any I might suppose would bring about such examination. But I did discover one thing: it appears that a widow, the Widow Rukveldt, living near Saint Bartholome's Church, reported to her Confessor that she had had impious dreams of you, and wished to repent of her dreams, and of the sins you and she committed in her sleep. Do you know her?"

"If she is the young woman with the very light hair and greenish eyes whose husband was a silversmith, then I have met her on perhaps six occasions; at fetes and processions and the like—much as I have met any number of women whose houses front the canals of this quarter. A handsome woman in her way, and of strong character." There had been more private meetings and greater revelations, but they occurred while the Widow Rukveldt slept, and he kept that to himself. "What has she said about her dreams?"

"Only that they cause her many sins of the flesh. It distresses her that you are in them," said Eschen. "Or so the secretary of the court told me. As a follower of Luther, he is opposed to acting upon unsubstantiated complaints."

"How, in the name of good sense, could they substantiate her claims? These are modern times, not two centuries ago, when men could be imprisoned for their dreams, and termites could be sued for eating part of a church." Saint-Germain shook his head.

"They need some more information regarding you and your habits, to see if there is anything in your nature that could account for her accusations. I am of the opinion that your foreignness and your wealth are sufficient explanation, but the courts may not agree. That is why all your staff has been taken in charge of the judges—at the order of the Church. Despite Protestant objections, the men lack the wherewithal to pay the bond the judges have set for their release—"

Saint-Germain was pleased that he had taken the precaution of making gold and silver in his athanor during April, for he was certain he now had a sufficient supply of the precious metals to provide the bond required. "Where have they taken my workers? Are they in prison, and if they are, whose prison are they in—the Church's, the Protestant's, or the city's?"

"They have been detained in one of the larger Catholic churches, I believe. I'll find out which by noon tomorrow." Eschen faltered, clearing his throat. "So far, as I understand it, they have not been harmed. The Church clerks are questioning your men to see if the widow is a tool of the Devil, offering lies to the ruin of good Christians, or if she has been bewitched, and if she has, by whom." He regarded Saint-Germain narrowly. "Have we anything to fear in such context?"

Saint-Germain opened his hands. "Nothing that I can think of," while he inwardly cursed himself for visiting the woman in her dreams four times. "Is she in any danger?"

"If she is lying, or if they decide she's lying, of course she is." Eschen drank the very last of his ale. "And if she has any claim to witchcraft, she may well be burned. Does that change what you told me?"

"No, not as such; I have no reason to suppose she is a witch," said Saint-Germain, wincing at a sudden, sharp recollection of the Piazza della Signoria in Fiorenze, where Suor Estasia walked into one of the pyres to burn, and Dukkai with her throat cut; he coughed. "But it troubles me that she could suffer because of what she has said, and about dreams. All living men and women dream. That does not mean she has committed diabolic acts, because she dreams. Whatever else she is, she is not a witch," he reiterated emphatically.

"How can you be sure of that?" Eschen challenged.

"Because she is a mother and she would not be likely to expose her children to the dangers of witchcraft, not with her husband dead and no relatives in Amsterdam who would take them in," said Saint-Germain, choosing the most common argument offered in defense of accused widows.

"There are those who would say that her widowhood is what has inclined her to witchcraft, to protect her family, however damnably," said Eschen, the habits of advocacy inclining him to put himself at cross-purposes to Saint-Germain for the sake of anticipating arguments.

"They would be wrong in this woman's case," said Saint-Germain.

Eschen held up both his hands. "Grav, let us extricate you from this coil before we turn too much attention to the one who caused it."

"Very well, but she is not to be abandoned," Saint-Germain told him.

"I will do what I can to be sure she comes to no harm, but I cannot promise to protect her to your disadvantage. I am pledged to uphold your best interests first and foremost." He leaned back on the settee. "I have a notion that we would do well to go voluntarily to the public courts and offer a statement under oath that will proclaim you to be a man of rectitude and morality. They are summoning that woman whose book you have published—"

"Erneste van Amsteljaxter?" Saint-Germain ventured, although he knew it could be no other; he managed to keep the alarm out of his voice.

"That's she," said Eschen. "If we give a—"

"But what can they suspect her of doing?" Saint-Germain interrupted.

"What else: seduction and corruption," said Eschen.

"They believe that I seduced her?" This seemed impossible, especially after all the care he had taken to be sure the proprieties were observed.

"No; of course not. They think that *she* has seduced and corrupted *you*," said Eschen, and stared as Saint-Germain burst into rare laughter. "Why do you find that amusing?"

"Because it is—very," he answered. "Her aunt Evangeline, who is an Assumptionist nun, has always accompanied her as a chaperone, and I have been at pains to avoid the least hint of indecorum. Or do the good clerics think one of their own has encouraged her niece to debauchery?"

Eschen considered this and nodded slowly. "I hope this is true, for if it is, such precautions as you have taken may stand you in good stead. Though some of the Assumptionists have been aiding the women who are adding to the city's unrest, and that may count against her."

"That trouble with the wool-workers?" Saint-Germain asked.

"Yes: not that it should concern us now." Eschen made a quick motion with his hand and sat forward to indicate they had other matters to discuss. "You said you were chaperoned while the woman was here. Can you tell me who can verify your claim? Not your manservant, since he's as much a foreigner as you are, but someone familiar with this city."

"My steward—who is from Amsterdam—can vouch for both of us." Saint-Germain pondered what Eschen had said. "Would you like to talk with him while you are here?"

"Yes, but not just yet; there are more immediate matters for us to discuss."

"Hardly surprising," said Saint-Germain, his expression taking on a wry cast.

"You may well find this amusing, Grav," Eschen warned him. "But do not assume it cannot touch you, or cause you damage. This is something much more mercurial than it looks, and that is where the danger lies. Depending upon which way the public sentiment turns, your circumstances may be advantageous or disastrous, and there is no way to determine how it will go, or how quickly. I will work with as much haste as I can, but you must remember that most of what is going to happen is out of my hands. I'll do what I can to check the damage, but the law puts limitations on my efforts, and on yours." He put his elbows on his knees and looked up at Saint-Germain. "You will need to be prepared."

"For what?" Saint-Germain inquired, thinking back to other times and other places to similarly volatile times.

Eschen nodded twice, signaling his satisfaction with the question. "That, my dear Grav, is what we must attempt to sort out."

Text of a letter from Giovanni Boromeo in Venezia to his patron, Franzicco Ragoczy, Conte di Santo-Germano, in care of Germain Ragoczy, Grav Saint-Germain, in Antwerp, written in the Venezian dialect, delivered by courier eleven days after it was written, and carried by private messenger four days later to the Eclipse Trading and Mercantile Company warehouse in Amsterdam.

To the most esteemed foreigner, Franzicco Ragoczy, Conte di Santo-Germano, through the good offices of your kinsman in Antwerp, the urgent greetings of Giovanni Boromeo, printer of Venezia, who beseeches Your Excellency to reply as quickly as possible, and with full answers to the questions I put to you, for even if the information is troublesome, it is preferable to the continued silence I have had from you in regard to my last six letters.

I have taken in your page Niccola, and one of your footmen, but with the falling revenues of this press, I fear I cannot extend myself any further than I already have, although I have attempted to find other situations for all but four of your servants. I wish this were not necessary, that there was some way to keep the household intact, but such is not sustainable any longer, and unless you have reserves unknown here, your house in Campo San Luca may well have to be sold before the end of the year. As it is, I am using my own savings to keep our publishing work on-going. I cannot continue in this fashion for more than five months, and then I will have to resort to the same kind of economies that have overtaken Pier-Ariana Salier, which would mean curtailing our publishing schedule still more stringently than I have done already.

Even though your fortune was lost in the Lisbon earthquake, as your business factor tells us, the least you could do is to inform those of us still in your employ what likelihood there is of you making a recovery, and when. I am willing to do all within my power to maintain our publication program, but if I am to do this, I must have some money or none of my printers will work for me, as their wages would be uncertain. I know you left a certain amount of money on deposit with the Savii, but that it is to be used for taxes, and so I can only point to it as proof of past earnings. So far, all reports from Gennaro Emerenzio are discouraging at best, and he can give us no assurance that you are ever going to regain even a portion of the wealth you once had.

The news from the Spanish Netherlands is hardly more heartening than the news from Lisbon. It is as if all the world has run mad, with the full consent of the Kings of the earth and the Pope. Perhaps there is a devilish contagion from the New World that has entered into the people of Europe and made them all crazed, for surely the situation among the Catholics and Protestants has become dire. Emerenzio has informed us that he has had no direct communication from you for months, and that he fears you may have become a victim of the fighting that we are told rages in many northern cities. He has pledged to try to discover if this is the case, or if you have been made a prisoner by the Protestants, and to do what he may to secure your release, if you are being held on charges.

I pray this reaches you, and that you will finally provide an answer to all these questions that have mounted up so troublingly. I hope that you may yet deliver your press from ruin, and regain the elegance of living that you possessed but a year ago. I trust that as your ships return from their voyages their cargos may serve to restore your fortunes and lead to greater wealth for you. May God grant you a return to good fortune, and to Venezia, where you are sorely needed.

In all duty and respect,
Giovanni Boromeo
master-printer

At Campo San Proccopio, Venezia, this 1ˢᵗ day of June, 1531

Erneste van Amsteljaxter pushed past Ruthger, almost stumbling as she entered Saint-Germain's study. "You must come, Grav! You must come!" she exclaimed, then clapped her hands to her mouth, looking abashed at her outburst.

"She says it's urgent," Ruthger said somewhat unnecessarily as he held the door open.

Saint-Germain glanced up from his close perusal of the binding on the latest book from Eclipse Press: *The History of European Trading Ports from Ancient to Modern Times.* The shutters were still open, the evening being only slightly cool, and the oil-lamps and candles flickered in the slow breeze, scented with the salt water, tar, and the city. "She? Who has come—" Then he recognized the woman. "Deme van Amsteljaxter. Welcome." It was an automatic greeting, but seeing how distressed this visitor was, he got to his feet as he set the book aside. "What is the trouble, Deme van Amsteljaxter?"

For an instant she looked dazed; she stopped, undecided, in the center of the room, her face briefly limned by the light: her skin was unusually pale and her eyes were sunken in deep livid shadows. "Grav," she said suddenly, as if awakening from heavy sleep. "Oh, Grav, I . . . You must help. Please. No one else would have us."

"Of course I will help, if it is in my power to do so," he said, and took a step toward her.

For once she did not retreat: she held out her hand and rested it lightly on his arm. "I hope you may; I hope someone may," she sighed, and her head drooped.

"Deme van Amsteljaxter," Saint-Germain exclaimed as he reach to support her with his arm. "What is wrong?" He glanced up at Ruthger. "Bring Deme van Amsteljaxter a cup of hot wine."

"Hot?" Ruthger asked, a little taken aback by such instruction; the June dusk was hardly chilly.

"She is pale and her hands are cold," said Saint-Germain in the tongue of Kiev. "She is in need of revival."

"I understand," said Ruthger, and hurried away toward the stairs.

Using his arm across her back to guide her, Saint-Germain moved Erneste to the broad, leather-upholstered settee in the study, and helped her to sink onto it. Once she was settled, he crouched down beside the settee, took one of her hands between his, and said, "Tell me what has happened, Deme." He would have preferred to use her name rather than her title, but he could not be certain that they were not being watched by one of the servants, and so he maintained a strict propriety with her.

Erneste pinched the bridge of her nose, and untied her English-style, angular coif; there were small spots of blood along the edge of the stiffened linen, and a faint smear on her cheek. She loosened the ribbands holding the under-cap and finally pulled it off, revealing a coil of putty-colored braids. "Oh, God help me." Without the linen and buckram framing her face, she looked much younger, and more vulnerable than she did with the coif on.

"Do what, Deme?" He said it lightly enough, but there was an underlying purpose to what he asked. "What can I do for you, in God's stead?" He picked up the headdress and held it inattentively in one hand.

She finally looked at him, and blinked slowly. "I . . . I'm sorry; I shouldn't be here. I shouldn't be here," she said like a child found filching sweets; she straightened up. "I thank you for admitting me, Grav, but I realize I have made an error in coming here. I will not trespass on your hospitality. I'm sorry for intruding. Doubtless you have many other matters to attend to than this foolish woman's megrims."

"Yes, I do have other concerns, but not just at present." He looked up into her face. "What has happened to make you come here?"

"A misfortune—you need not be concerned about it." She was about to get to her feet when Saint-Germain said, "You came here for a purpose; I am curious to know what that was, and why you have changed your mind."

She stared up at him, then forced herself to direct her gaze elsewhere. "Oh, dear." Erneste took the slate-blue edge of the triangular outer sleeve of her vaya and began to pleat the fine-woven sayette between her fingers, pressing hard at the fabric while she strove to regain her composure, and extricate herself from the awkwardness into which she now realized she had plunged herself. With her concentration on her fingers, she said distantly, "It's my aunt."

"Aunt Evangeline?" he asked to be certain. "Has anything happened to her?"

She gave a single, tiny nod. "She's . . . she's unwell. I'm worried about her. She needs a physician, you see, and—" Impatiently she wiped her eyes. "I apologize for this most unseemly—"

"Her condition must be serious indeed for you to come here on her behalf, risking gossip," Saint-Germain interrupted softly, the last of his statement ending on an upward note.

"I fear she may die, she is so lethargic and disoriented," said Erneste softly, and began to cry, not loudly but with such poignance that he was astonished.

"Deme, Deme, do not—"

"I know she will die. I cannot doubt it," she said quickly, dropping the sleeve and leaning heavily on the upholstered arm of the settee. "I hoped that she would be well, with good physicians and nursing, but they will not take her in at Saint Anne's Church, where her cloisters are: they won't take any of them in." She wiped her face with trembling fingers. "I asked the Mother Superior to reconsider, for mercy and charity's sake, but she said she could not, that her hands were tied."

"And why should they be?" Saint-Germain asked, wondering if Erneste's association with him might account for such a refusal.

"You recall, sixteen days ago, there was an uprising, mostly of women?" Erneste did not go on.

"The riot about a wool-house in a churchyard?"

Erneste nodded. "Yes; my aunt was with the wool-workers, the women who sought to keep the wool-house. She has encouraged the women in the past, and when needed, she has worked with them, carding and spinning. The women were to have a wool-house of their own: the Guild had given provisional agreement, but then there was trouble, and fighting broke out. During the second assault, my aunt was struck by a cudgel on the head and shoulder and in the body, and she was forced to leave the confrontation. She could not go to any physician, for the Church would not permit physicians to offer their services to an insurrectionist—those who did risked heavy fines."

"A difficult situation for anyone hurt, I should think," said Saint-Germain.

She sighed abruptly. "I took her into my rooms, against the wishes of the householder; I paid him extra, and I set about nursing her as best I could, although I am not very adept at such things."

"I should think you would give excellent care," said Saint-Germain, and saw her attempt a wobbly smile.

"Thank you, Grav." She glanced toward the nearest tree of oil-lamps, then back at him. "The night before last, the householder said we must leave, and had all our goods loaded into a cart; he said he would have to pay a fine if we remained under his roof. When I asked him where we were to go, he said it wasn't his concern, and that so long as we were gone from his house, he would be satisfied."

"Why did you not send me word of this?" Saint-Germain asked, anticipating the answer.

"I have already imposed too much upon you. Were I not desperate, I would not be here now, but I could think of no one else." She dabbed the hem of her sleeve at her eyes. "I'm sorry to be so wanting in—"

"Your weeping does not affront me; I am more disturbed that you did not come to me last night," he said. "Where did you go?"

This time Erneste took four deep breaths before she answered. "There is an inn of sorts near the major warehouses, called The Grey Tern, and it is a place that takes in all comers, if they have money to pay." She swallowed hard. "I procured a room with a parlor on the third floor for a week—I paid the porters to carry our belongings and my aunt up to the rooms, and bought a special meal for her, so that she would not have to bestir herself."

"Did you have to leave any belongings behind?" Saint-Germain inquired.

"The householder said he would relinquish them to me when I found suitable housing," she said, a bit startled by the question.

"Perhaps he will reconsider, and release them to my care, on your behalf," said Saint-Germain genially enough, but with a purposeful note in his voice. He softened his next query. "How did your aunt fare in this new setting?"

Erneste's face grew more somber. "For most of yesterday, she seemed to improve. Her fever lessened and her color brightened, and she could walk on her own, if slowly. But by evening, she began vomiting, and the substance of it was brown and thick and ropey." She put her hand to her mouth as if to stop her own words. "She has lost her balance on three occasions and her thoughts are jumbled and unsteady. When I offered her the medicine I had purchased for her relief, she accused me of trying . . . to poison her. She struck my hand away, and then she fell on the floor, and refused to get up. I went to Saint Anne's again on her behalf, and they would do nothing, having been forbidden by the Church to assist any of the rebellious women—that is what they are calling the women now: rebels—and to report any woman with suspicious wounds to the authorities. There are hundreds of such women in the city, denied succor and shelter because of their stand." She put a hand to her cheek. "Oh, Lord. God forgive me. I shouldn't have come here. Grav, I apologize for bringing this to you. I didn't think: you may be accused of giving comfort to the rebel women, and there are fines being imposed for doing that." As she said this last her weeping grew more extreme. "I don't know what to do, Grav. I haven't thought of anything I might do to—"

Ruthger's tap on the half-open door shocked them both. Saint-Germain rose and turned. "Do come in. I trust you have the wine?"

"I do," said Ruthger, and added in the dialect of Yang-Chau, "I took the liberty of adding a few drops of your composing tincture. I doubt she'll taste it." He handed over the tankard on a small tray, while he continued in Dutch, "The staff are worried. Is there anything you want to tell them?"

"Tell them only that Deme van Amsteljaxter has come to request aid for her aunt, who is badly hurt."

"That should suffice," said Ruthger.

Saint-Germain regarded Ruthger thoughtfully. "I think it may be wise to put together a case of medicaments for me. If you will?"

"Certainly. What do you want in the case?" Ruthger watched Saint-Germain hand the tankard to Erneste, then added, "Whom are you treating, and for what malady?"

"I believe Seur Evangeline has sustained inward injuries and is suffering from a severe blow to the head as well. So my sovereign remedy should be included, and tinctures of pansy and of willow, along with a vial of milk-thistle infusion, ground Angelica-root for a tea, and a cup of syrup of poppies in spirits of wine. That should do for a start." He frowned as he reviewed this in his mind, adding, "Anodyne unguents as well, and a roll of linen bandages."

Erneste had taken a generous sip of the wine, but she turned to stare in dismay at Saint-Germain's remark. "Bandages? You are going to bleed her? Because I bled her yesterday, and she seems not to have made a full recovery from it, though she said it did her good."

"No," said Saint-Germain, "I will not bleed her, Deme; I doubt it would benefit her to be bled a second time. But her head has been bludgeoned, and her skull may need the protection a bandage may provide. When a head has been struck, often the bones need to be shielded from other hurts." He disliked having to be less than candid with Erneste, but he knew that at this time candor would be an unkindness and serve no useful purpose.

Erneste sighed. "Oh. Yes. I hadn't thought of that." She took a longer draught of the heated wine, saying, "You have put cloves in it. It's very good."

Saint-Germain gave a quick, one-sided smile, knowing that Ruthger had found a way to completely disguise the taste of the composer. "I trust it is to your taste, Deme?"

"Oh, yes," said Erneste, taking another sip to demonstrate her approval; a faint trace of color appeared on her lips.

Ruthger gave a crisp little bow. "Thank you, Deme van Amsteljaxter." He glanced at Saint-Germain. "Is there anything else, my master, or shall I go to prepare your case?"

"You may go," said Saint-Germain; Ruthger left the room, taking care to set the door ajar, aware of the implications a closed door would create. "If you have no objections, I will accompany you to see your aunt—after you finish the wine. I hope I may have something among my medicaments that will relieve her suffering."

"Would you treat her? I know she needs more expert care than mine, and you have some experience of treating wounds, haven't you?" she asked, her eyes once again filling with tears. She shook her head as if to rid herself of her weeping. "I'm so sorry."

"You have no reason to be," Saint-Germain assured her, reaching out to steady the wine-tankard in her hand.

She was silent for a long moment. "If I had thought this through, I wouldn't have come here. I beg your pardon for—"

"You have nothing for which to apologize, Deme van Amsteljaxter."

He saw that this repeated assurance had not convinced her, so he continued. "In fact I might well have been offended if you had sought out anyone else during this difficult time. I take this as a token of trust, and I thank you for it."

"Are you telling me this as a means to ease me, or do you truly mean it?" she asked, staring up at him.

"Certainly I meant it. Did you not want help from me?" His question was gently posed, and he did not press her for an answer while she drank again. "Erneste?"

A little more color brightened her cheeks at the use of her name. "I do want your help, Grav, but I hope you will not be—"

He spoke without indignation or choler, but with a calm sadness. "What must you think I am, to suppose I would impose my desires upon you as a condition of caring for your aunt."

"Oh, no," she said, flustered. "That isn't what I meant—"

"Is it not." He studied her for a long moment, no censure in his gaze.

She schooled herself to better behavior. "I intended no discourtesy. But you see, Grav, I have nothing to pay for your care, whatever it may be." She hesitated. "You have been generous in the shares you have given me in publishing my book, but with all that has happened, and my brother needing money, I have very little left, and I will have nothing to provide us shelter and food if you must be paid." She looked him directly in the eyes. "But I cannot ask you to work without recompense, and so I must find something to offer you in exchange for your—"

"Impose no qualifications upon your pledges that you cannot fulfill," Saint-Germain advised her, his voice low and tranquil.

"But it is unfair to expect—"

"Perhaps it is, but it is my decision to make, not yours. And it is my decision to help your aunt—you have not coerced me, or cozened me." He lifted one of her hands and brushed his lips over the knuckles. "What others may or may not do is not your responsibility, and so you have no reason to take that on yourself."

She stared at him, shaken by what he had said. "I can understand how a man of your position might decide such a thing, but I have not your good fortune, and I must answer for the welfare of others in this world. My aunt depends upon me now, and my brother. I cannot refuse them." She finished her wine in a manner of one concluding a debate.

"Then I fear you will bring yourself much needless grief," he told her kindly as he held out his hand to assist her to rise.

"Such is the legacy of all women," said Erneste with a fatalism she would not have displayed had she been less fatigued and had not drunk such a generous portion of wine. She put her hand into his and allowed him to assist her to rise. Then she bit her underlip. "I . . . I fear The Grey Tern may not be the sort of hostelry you are accustomed to."

"I have, in my time, spent the night in caves and in hovels, and on many occasions I have slept in barns and under hayricks," he said, an ironic light at the back of his dark eyes as he recalled some of the less savory places he had taken shelter during his long years of life, places that he did not mention to Erneste. "A dockside inn will not offend my sensibilities. I hope you will not trouble yourself over such things."

Erneste made another attempt at a real smile. "Thank you; I should have realized you would be gracious."

Centuries earlier he would have been tempted to give a jocular answer, but over the long decades—now numbering over twelve thousand decades—he had learned not to mock those who were suffering, so he only said, "If you will tell me how we are to find the place—"

"It will be fastest to travel by canal, if you have a boat we may use?"

Saint-Germain sighed at the prospect of having to travel over running water, and resigned himself to the vertigo it would cause even with the lining of his native earth in the boat. "I have the services of a boatman and his craft. I will send Ruthger to summon Piet to meet us as soon as he can bring his craft. I trust you will be able to guide him?"

"Oh, yes. Then we should reach her before the end of the hour." Erneste rubbed her hands on her inner sleeves. "Oh, thank you, thank you, Grav. I pray you may not have cause to regret this decision."

Saint-Germain crossed the room to close the shutters, his demeanor composed as he fixed the latches. "I may, but not nearly so much as I would regret doing nothing." He returned to her side and knelt to pick up her coif. "You may want to put this on again. Or I have a hooded cloak you could borrow, if you like."

She took the coif and stared at it, noticing the blood for the first time. "My aunt's," she said as if astonished to see it; she turned to Saint-Germain. "If you don't mind, I would like to borrow the cloak. I didn't realize that—" She held up the coif so that Saint-Germain could see the blood.

"Certainly," said Saint-Germain. "If you will stay here, I will fetch it along with my case of medicaments."

Confusion almost overcame her again. "Oh, no, Grav. I didn't mean . . . You shouldn't have to—"

"Deme, I have some instructions to issue to this household, a few provisions to make. I will return as quickly as I am able. If you like, you may choose something to read in my absence." He offered her a slight bow and before she could speak again, he stepped back into the corridor, and went off to his laboratory, where he found Ruthger standing in front of his ancient red-lacquer chest, placing the last of the rolls of bandages in his small leather case.

Without turning, Ruthger said, "I have sent for Piet."

Saint-Germain smiled quickly. "Thank you, old friend: you anticipate my every need."

"Then allow me another expectancy, and order rooms prepared for Deme van Amsteljaxter and her Aunt Evangeline." He closed the case and buckled it, then moved back and closed the red-lacquer chest. "I have this ready."

"After all these years I should not be astonished, but I am," said Saint-Germain as he took the case from Ruthger.

A suggestion of amusement shone in Ruthger's faded-blue eyes. "No, my master, you should not be."

"Then I will rest assured that all will be prepared when I return later this evening, although I cannot yet tell you what hour that is apt to happen." He nodded once and was about to depart when something more occurred to him. "If it is possible, there should be a supper ready for the women—soup, perhaps—something that can simmer for some time."

"I will attend to it." Ruthger was still for an instant, then reached inside his doublet and brought out a letter. "This was brought by Kees at the warehouse a short while ago. He said it was carried by a special messenger from Antwerp."

Saint-Germain took it, studying the handwriting on the address. "I will read it later this evening." As he went out of the laboratory he wondered allowed, "What can Giovanni Boromeo want that is so urgent?"

Text of a letter from James Belfountain in Antwerp to Grav Saint-Germain in Amsterdam, written in English, carried by three of his men and delivered three days after it was written.

To the Grav Saint-Germain presently in Amsterdam, the greetings of James Belfountain presently at The Two Gold Lambs in Antwerp, on this, the 21st day of June, 1531.

My esteemed Grav, I have received the sum of seventy ducats and your letter from your messenger in partial payment for the escort by me and four of my men for you and your manservant from this city to Mestre in the Most Serene Republic, to be accomplished at as great a speed as horses and circumstances will allow. Your proposal of payment of twenty ducats a day for the journey, not including food and lodging, is acceptable, and will count against the monies I have in hand from you. I also accept your offer of a bonus of twenty ducats apiece if the journey can be made in less than ten days, barring acts of God, or of His followers.

We will provide a limited remuda, with a single remount for each of the group. I and my men will provide arms for the journey, which will be included in the daily hire, except if we should have to engage any armed opponents: in that case, the daily hire will double for that day, and you will pay for the replacement of any arms, armor, horses, or other equipment lost in such conflict.

You will carry sufficient money to permit us to procure remounts on the road as needed. Needs of shelter and food are to be my concern, and I will dispatch men at once to make suitable arrangements along the road, whose services as scouts will be included in their pay; a reckoning of these totals will be rendered upon our reaching Mestre.

Your letter informs me that your presence is required in Venice immediately. You may depend upon me and my men to do our utmost to enable you to arrive as quickly as can be possible. In demonstration of that intention, I will hand this to my men at once, and send them on their way to Amsterdam.

I look forward to the opportunity of serving you again, my Lord, and I thank you for your patronage.

> Believe me to be
> Yours to command,
> James Belfountain

PART III

FRANZICCO RAGOCZY, CONTE DI SANTO-GERMANO

*T*ext of a letter from Rudolph Eschen in Amsterdam to Germain Ragoczy, Grav Saint-Germain, in care of his steward Simeon Roosholm in Antwerp, with instructions to forward it to Saint-Germain at his present location, delivered to Roosholm by private courier four days after it was written.

To the Grav the most honorable Germain Ragoczy of Saint-Germain, this from the advocate Rudolph Eschen, on this, the 2ⁿᵈ day of July, 1531, from Amsterdam.

Grav: I have in hand all the deeds, trusts, and transfers you brought to me three days since, along with your instructions in their regard, hard upon your departure from this city, and I am writing now to confirm those instructions so that you may review and modify them according to your wishes before I proceed with enacting them.

Item: to give full and unqualified support to Mercutius Christermann so that he may continue to keep Eclipse Press in operation as long as the city laws and the Church will allow it; for the running of the press, you allocate the sum of ten ducats a month, for supplies and similar expenses, another five ducats, to be paid from your account at the van Wech Trading Trust, and from the Foreign Merchants Depository. For Christermann himself, you authorize five ducats a month, to allow him to live in reasonable comfort. To those pressmen and others who have elected to leave your employ, you have instructed me to provide a month's wages as part of their release: this is another example of your admirable character but I would be remiss in my duty if I did not tell you that I am not in favor of such munificence.

Regarding the continuing publications from Eclipse Press, you expect Christermann to produce at least four books in a year, and if he undertakes a more ambitious program, to adjust his funds accordingly. You have arranged for your books to be carried on your ships for sales abroad, the numbers and titles to be recorded here and where sales take place. I have executed the final copy of the contract you made with Christermann, permitting him to hire such men as he needs to produce the books scheduled and in preparation, with your admonition that he is to use his best judgment where your previous workers are concerned.

I must tell you again, Grav, as your advocate, that I believe you are being too generous to those men who allowed themselves to be bullied into leaving your company. I repeat my previous advice—give them nothing, not even a recommendation, as they have done nothing to deserve your assistance. Also, as this Christermann is untested on his own, I would advise giving him a less free-handed amount of money until he has proven he is capable of fulfilling his tasks. I can think of few businessmen who would not second my admonition.

Item: to Erneste van Amsteljaxter, unconditional life tenancy of your house, for herself and such companions as she may wish to have receive her hospitality, with such funds as are needed to maintain the building and the household, to hire such new servants as may be needed, and to make such changes in the house as may be prudent. In addition, you offer her the right to use the house in any way that suits her, as long as it is in accord with the law. You permit her to house those four women who were wounded in the so-called Women's Revolt at the end of May for as long as it suits her, with no restrictions put upon her because of what many may see as an endorsement of an illegal act. In spite of this imprudent support of rebellious wool-workers, you have given her autonomy over the property for the duration of her life, as well as the use of your town carriage and your coachman, and your barge and bargeman, for which you will pay wages and maintenance. You also provide her with an annual grant of one hundred ducats so that she may be free to write and study as she wishes. You also wish to provide the funds for erecting a headstone for her Aunt Evangeline, of which I shall inform Deme van Amsteljaxter within the week.

Item: for Bogardt van Leun, an annual stipend of twenty ducats beyond his usual salary, and the promise that he and his wife will have employment in your Amsterdam household for as long as they so desire, with the use of the cottage you own to the southeast of the city when he reaches the age of forty-five, when he will be eligible to retire from your service without loss of pay either to himself or his wife. You also propose to pay for the education of any children, male or female, they may have.

Item: to Dries Altermaat, the authority to conduct business in your name as official factor for Eclipse Trading and Mercantile Company, with such sums as are needed to keep the company ships in good repair, ditto the warehouses, to provide reasonable sums for such demands of business may require, and sixty ducats per year for his work: this on condition that the trading accounts of Eclipse Trading and Mercantile Company be scrutinized and verified semi-annually, with penalties for any irregularity beyond the amount of ten ducats. He is to work in regular consultation with your dispatcher and warehouse supervisors, and to provide monthly reports on those matters, along with inventories, to my office for my perusal, and my promise that any dispute in facts and figures will be addressed promptly.

This last is, in my opinion, a very sensible provision, and I am pleased to see you have decided to include this element of restraint in your unusual magnanimity; few businessmen in Amsterdam are either so wealthy as you, or so willing to spend with your unselfishness. I will not refuse to follow your orders, but I would not be fulfilling my responsibilities to you if I did not remark on my reservations, especially in regard to your fortune, considerable though it may be. You may say that it is your practice, because of your long absences, not to restrict those in your employ by not allowing for unforeseen events; while that is all very well, you will permit me to observe that what you deem advisable I can only see as extravagant and possibly reckless, for your very largesse invites those in your employ to take advantage of you. With that for a caveat, I will carry out your instructions in every particular.

Item: for any in your household or business brought before either civil or religious tribunals in this city, I have in hand one hundred fifty ducats to provide for the defense of any requiring it, and the bond that the court may require on their behalf, with the added assurance that should such a detention occur, I will notify you by private courier at once, with an account of the charges and the likely progress of the case, insofar as it is possible for me to determine such. You guarantee me an additional three hundred ducats if so great a sum is needed.

As agreed, I will tender you quarterly reports regarding your businesses and property in this city, as well as any actions, requests, *or changes from your household, your press, and your trading company. I will use the courier you have paid for, and I will act within three days on any crucial development to apprise you of each and every significant change in regard to those actions and accusations. Insofar as my acts are in accord with the law, I will assure you that I will honor my fiduciary responsibilities as laid out above.*

With every wish for your continued good health and prosperity,

> *I am*
>> *always at your service,*
>> *Rudolph Eschen*
>> *Advocate-at-law*

By my own hand: a witnessed copy of this letter is included among my records of our association.

1

At Antwerp, James Belfountain joined with the rest of Saint-Germain's escort which now numbered five; they traveled light, with only two pack-horses for their goods, and a single remount for each man in their remuda. Four leagues outside Antwerp, they turned south along the merchants' road to Cologne, through the sodden summer heat, and the persistent dust-cloud that marked their progress. On the road there had been delays—two the result of over-turned wagons, one caused by villagers throwing rocks at all who approached their gates, one caused by a fire in a field and grove of elms and oaks—putting them almost half a day behind what they had planned.

"Do we press on?" Belfountain asked as they approached the outskirts of Cologne. "It is three hours until sundown."

"The horses are weary," said Saint-Germain. "And the evening is not going to be much cooler than the day."

"Then we remount shortly and pony them in the remuda, all no faster than a trot," said Belfountain, patting the sweaty neck of his blood-bay. "We won't make up all the time we've lost, but we won't be even farther behind." He wiped his face with the hem of his light fustian summer cloak, worn more to keep off the dust than to provide unwanted warmth; he left a gritty smear across his forehead. "I would advise that we go on, if you want to reach Venezia within ten or eleven days."

Ruthger shaded his eyes and studied the clouds forming to the southwest. "We may yet have a thunderstorm before midnight."

"That we may," Saint-Germain agreed. "I should think we would not want to be in the open if a storm begins."

"There is the rain itself, and the risk of fire," Ruthger said. "Lightning can set a wood ablaze in an instant."

"It can also strike a house, or an inn, or a barn," Belfountain said. "If there is a thunderstorm, everywhere is dangerous."

Jacques Oralle, a seasoned soldier at twenty-two who was from

Bensancon, ahead on their way south, said, "Even if it rains, I don't think we'll get caught in the mud, not if we keep to the main road."

"Why not cut across the open country?" Timothy Mercer, a young English soldier, interjected. "We could save time, and spare ourselves unpleasantness."

Oralle held up his hand. "No; we would lose time, not save it, at least not in this region. Without the merchants' roads and market roads, the fens would be unpassable, but the merchants' roads, in particular, are well-drained, and among the last to mire. The market roads, a little less so, but this summer has not proven to be too wet in spite of all the storms."

The wind sprang up suddenly, shifting around to the southeast, and as it whipped past the small group of mounted men, it bore to them the cloying, metallic odor of decaying flesh; as fast as it had shifted, the wind moved again back to the west. Belfountain and Saint-Germain exchanged quick glances, and Saint-Germain said, "All may not be well in Cologne."

"Not with the charnel house on the wind; I know that much," said Maddox Yeoville, who had only recently joined Belfountain's company, and had come—amid ambiguous reports—from the household cavalry of Henry VIII.

"If it is fever, then it will spread, and we must get beyond the miasma or we, too, will sicken," said Belfountain.

"If it is the charnel house, and not the gibbet," said Saint-Germain, aware from the smell that no disease had killed the bodies that carried that stench. "In either case, it may be easier to enter Cologne than to leave."

"It is often better not to do than to have to undo," Ruthger pointed out.

"It is probably best if we don't enter the city, not while there are secondary market roads we may travel. We have had to detour twice already; another such will not disaccommodate us, although it may delay us by another day." Belfountain looked at Saint-Germain, his brow rising inquiringly. "If we create delays, our pay can be held back, so moving on is to our benefit, isn't it, Grav?" he reminded them all. He leaned forward to ease his back a little, his brow touching the crest of his blood-bay's neck. "I think we could go along as far as Beau Roison before nightfall. We should reach there in two hours if there are no problems; that will allow us an opportunity to rest the horses and have our dinner before everything is soaked. And departing in the morning could be swifter than it would be from Cologne."

"If the rain is heavy, it could slow us tomorrow," Ruthger observed, noticing as he did that Saint-Germain was listening intently. He regarded Saint-Germain carefully. "What is it you hear, my master?"

"Bells, and not ringing changes, but sounding the alarum," said Saint-Germain, his tone slightly distant, his attention on the city ahead. "I think it would be best if we use the market road, not the merchants' roads, and keep on. When we near Beau Roison, then we can consider what to do."

Belfountain raised his hand to signal his men. "Then we will move on, away from the gates and on to the south market road. We'll leave the merchants' roads to larger trains than ours."

"And to the Spanish patrols; they keep to the merchants' roads, and pay not a copper for their doing so," said Mercer, made uneasy by his own remark.

"Most of the Hapsburg lands here are under the control of the Austrian branch of the family, and much less inclined to worry about heresy than the Spanish," said Saint-Germain. "We will shortly be out of reach of Spain and across the frontiers of Charles' Lorraine territories."

"A Hapsburg is a Hapsburg, and they are all treacherous," said Yeoville.

Saint-Germain glanced over at the young man. "While I may agree with you in many regards, I think Charles is a capable administrator, although his brother appears to like the minutiae of government more than Charles does."

"They all like killing honest Protestants," said Yeoville, and looked away, his face set, his manner guarded.

"Not all: another thing in Charles' favor: he dislikes having to kill his subjects over unanswerable questions," Saint-Germain remarked. "Given the Holy Roman Empire's present fracturing, Charles' policies have maintained it better than many another has." He remembered his first glimpse, not quite six hundred years before, of Otto the Great, who had not been content with Karl-lo-Magne's old title of Emperor of the Franks and Longobards and Imperial Governor of all the Romans in the West but had embraced the extended distinction of Holy Roman Emperor, the title the Frankish nobility had used unofficially since Haganrich the Fowler ruled; he dreaded what that tenth-century warlord would have done in the circumstances now confronting Charles V. He tried to shut out the recollection of cities sacked and put to the torch, of peasants rounded up to serve as slaves in the Emperor's household, of broken bodies cast into common graves, of children spitted on swords. "At least," he murmured in the tongue of Saxony six hundred years ago, "we have not come to that."

"Grav?" Belfountain asked.

Realizing something of his recollections must have shown in his face, he was able to summon up a half-smile. "I ask your pardon," he said quietly. "I was lost in thought—how politics and religion make for dangerous partners, as we see all around us."

"All the more reason for you to return to Venezia," said Mercer, nodding as if he had made an original point.

"Oh?" Ruthger interjected before Saint-Germain could speak. "You assume politics and religion are separate in Venezia?"

"No," said Mercer, affronted. "But it isn't as confusing as what is happening in the north, is it?"

"Not in the way that such matters are in upheaval, certainly; Venezia has a different style in dealing with dissidents," said Ruthger.

"That is exactly why Venezia will never have such disarray as they have in the Netherlands and the German States," Giulio delle Fonde said, speaking up for the first time; he was in charge of the pack-horses and the remuda, a position he found useful for staying out of any discussion of politics, claiming that the horses demanded all his attention.

"Or so we hope, and that is all we can do at present—hope, and that will change nothing but our own minds," said Belfountain as he nudged his blood-bay to the position slightly ahead of Saint-Germain. "The market roads are toll-roads, Grav. You will have to pay to use them."

"I have money in my glove," Saint-Germain said as he started his gray gelding moving again. The brief respite had not been sufficient to restore the horses, so they began at a walk, giving both men and animals a little easier time of it.

"We will change horses just before going through the gate; most toll-houses have a shelter-stall for such purposes." Oralle rose in the stirrups and looked back. "That group of men with their families and carts is still on the road, about half a league behind us now."

"Poor devils," said Belfountain. "To be uprooted from their homes and cast off on the world because they do not trust the Pope."

"Who does trust the Pope? De' Medici or not, Clemente is a pawn of the Spanish, or he would have to be a martyr," said Oralle, ready to press on, and fretting at their slow pace. "For all of us, it will be ten copper Fredericks."

Saint-Germain had only silver coins in his glove, but he knew what the men of his escort expected to hear. "Even secondary roads are becoming more expensive every day."

"So they are," said Belfountain, moving his open hand in a circle above his head to indicate to his men that they should follow him to the right at the next turn. "And with groups such as the one behind us using the roads, it is small wonder that the cost of them increases. In May I saw a much larger group of families from the Swiss Cantons bound for Calais, of all places. Their town—near Zurich—had come under Huldrych Zwingli's influence, and they would not renounce their Catholic faith, so were cast out on the world, like Cain."

"More's the pity," said Yeoville.

"If we avoid these groups, the armies patrolling the merchants' roads will pay less attention to us, or they have in the past," Belfountain declared. "It will not serve us to be detained by any of them."

"Do you assume that they suppose you're giving the wanderers protection?" Ruthger asked.

"That's their excuse—whether they believe it, who can tell," said Belfountain. "I'm surprised we have only come upon this one company. We will have to be careful if we encounter others."

"Who will scout?" Saint-Germain asked. "Oralle?"

"He comes from this region, and should know the by-ways, if such knowledge is necessary," said Belfountain, signaling to that young man to move ahead of them, adding in his English-accented French, "If anything seems amiss, inform us at once."

"I will," Oralle called back as he urged his spotted horse forward to a point about fifty yards ahead of the other six.

"These warm, close nights always seem hard to bear," said Mercer. "The horses fret, and no one sleeps well."

"True enough," Belfountain agreed. "You don't see many nights like this one back in England, as I remember."

"No; not too many," Mercer said, and gave his attention to the road ahead.

They traveled on through the fading afternoon, making no sound but the steady thud of their horses' hooves. At the toll station, they changed mounts, taking their evening horses from the remuda-line and returning their day horses to it. In half an hour they were saddled again and ready to continue; Saint-Germain paid their toll and a bit more for the use of the shelter-stall, and they continued on at the jog-trot into the clinging warmth of the evening as the declining sun left a glistening wake leading into low-lying clouds on the western horizon. They passed broad fields where cowherds and shepherds were driving their charges back toward farmsteads that seemed little more than hummocks and berms in the deepening twilight.

"That's Beau Roison," Oralle called from a bend ahead on the road.

"Where?" Belfountain responded, his voice unexpectedly loud.

"Perhaps forty yards ahead; just beyond where the road dips." Oralle had stopped on the road, waiting for the other six riders to catch up with him. "There." He pointed to a cluster of about fifty buildings, the remnants of an old stone wall encircling thirty of these, a monument to the age of the place. Five streets twisted through the buildings, most connecting to market-squares or ancient gates in the old wall. Spires of three churches poked into the violet sky, rising over the thatched roofs of the other buildings. "They say the Romans of old founded the town, because there is an old ruined building that legend says was a bath."

Saint-Germain realized he had been in this place during his travels with Gaius Julius Caesar during his conquest of Gaul; then this had been a rest-camp for wounded soldiers where he had spent time working with the wounded, and then recovering himself, in Aumtehoutep's care: the bath had been the only permanent building in the settlement. "A charming legend," he said.

"Legends won't help us now," Belfountain muttered, and spat to ward off the evil omen as an owl sailed over them on silent wings.

"Not many lights showing," Mercer observed as he peered through the dusk, and pointed out a few windows with a shine of golden-snouted lamps in them.

"No," said Belfountain thoughtfully, rousing himself to assess the surround so he might know best how to approach the town; he contemplated the road ahead, then turned to Saint-Germain. "Well, Grav, what do you think?"

Saint-Germain's dark eyes were not as hampered by night as were the eyes of living men, but he was careful not to give away too much of what he saw. "I would suppose that there is a travelers' inn on the edge of the town; that is the usual pattern in these isolated places. It might be best if we go there, rather than into the town."

"They'll have word at such an inn about what lies ahead," said delle Fonde; his voice was hoarse and his remark ended on a cough. "It's the dust," he explained.

"Cover your face with your neck-cloth, as I do," Yeoville suggested.

"He'd look like a highwayman," Mercer said testily.

"Then suffer and cough," said Yeoville, shrugging to emphasize his indifference.

"My men are tired," Belfountain said as much to stop the carping as to explain the resentment around him.

"Not surprising," said Ruthger.

"Do we go onward?" Belfountain asked, pointing toward the town. "At least as far as the travelers' inn?" He expected no answer and got none. "Where is the inn, Oralle? Do you know?"

"On the southeast side of the town," Oralle told him. "I should think they will have a lantern lit."

"Excellent," Belfountain approved, and decided to order the small party to move on; their progress toward the town was marked by a chorus of barks from farmers' dogs, although no farmer or other peasant came to greet them. "Not a good sign."

"Let us hope they have not armed themselves to keep us away," said Saint-Germain, who had often experienced such reception in the past.

"Do you think that likely?" Yeoville asked, reaching for his sword.

"No; I think that if they wanted to scare us off, they would have done so before the dogs started barking," said Saint-Germain, and saw Belfountain nod. "They may want us to ride on; that would account for their silence."

There was a brief silence, then Oralle said, "There may be smugglers in this region. The town would make a point of taking no notice of them."

"What would they be smuggling?" Ruthger asked.

"Beer, wine, jewels, weapons," said Oralle. "Some are even bringing masks and ornaments from the New World."

"Smugglers or no, the travelers' inn will welcome us," said Belfountain with conviction. "If we pay enough."

"That is no concern for any of you," said Saint-Germain, who knew it was expected of him. "I can offer a handsome sum for our stay."

Far to the west the piled clouds winked with lightning, but no grumble of thunder followed.

"Rain is coming," said delle Fonde. "And because of the rain, our horses will do better in a stall tonight."

"Then let us go on to the inn," said Belfountain, starting his horse walking again. "The southeast side of the town, you say?"

"As I recall it, it was," said Oralle. "It was thus four years ago. I will know the place when I see it."

"Good enough," said Belfountain, and chose a narrow track that appeared to circle around the town. "This should take us to what we want."

The path was a bit damp in places where the river that grazed Beau Roison's flank spread out to create a marsh, but other than that the way was as unimpeded as the merchants' road to Avignon. Finally a three-story building loomed up ahead; there was a courtyard surrounded by a stockade, and a barn that gave onto a good-sized pasture. There were the sounds of a dulcimer and shawm coming from the building, and a few voices lifted in song.

"That is where we are bound, it seems," said Belfountain, starting forward.

Mercer held back. "What if they are not—"

"This is a little town; I doubt we'll find a company of Spaniards in the taproom, or any men with illicit cargo in their packs. This is too obvious a place for such things, and there is too much gossip in travelers' inns," said Belfountain abruptly.

"I was thinking highwaymen, perhaps," said Mercer. "They're not as obvious as smugglers."

"Highwaymen," Yeoville repeated. "Why should there be highwaymen in this place more than another?"

"Because no one from the town has challenged us," said Mercer.

This simple statement was enough to make Belfountain rein in. "You mean that all this could be a trap for unwary travelers."

"I fear it may be; yes." Mercer glanced around at the others; delle Fonde shook his head, Oralle stared at the stockade as if determined to pierce through it by the intensity of his stare alone.

"Belfountain," said Saint-Germain, "I will go to the tavern, on my own. Either I will return to you, or I will ring the kitchen bell; if I do that, assume it is safe to come inside. If I summon you in any other manner, then leave this place and wait for me in Bensancon. If I fail to come in five days, Ruthger will pay your fee and he will depart for Venezia."

"But Grav," Belfountain exclaimed in amazement, "it is you we are bound to protect. You are the man who has bought his safety from us. You cannot put yourself in harm's way to save us—our obligation is to risk our lives to preserve yours."

"Then think of this as a kind of game I seek to play for my own amusement," said Saint-Germain.

"It is no game, my master," said Ruthger in Byzantine Greek.

Saint-Germain dismounted from his gray and looked up at Ruthger. "I know."

"Then why must you—?"

"We are all tired and hungry, and we must rest if we are to keep on at this pace. And we need to know what lies ahead." He had changed from Greek to French. "Better to risk one than lose all."

"I cannot argue that," said Belfountain. "But it should be one of us."

"Belfountain, think a moment. You are clearly a soldier: equally clearly I am not. Which of us do you think would be more welcome in the taproom if the inn is an honest one?" Saint-Germain gave Belfountain a short while to consider his answer, then said, "I will attend to this, make whatever arrangements I can, and will provide you the agreed signal."

Belfountain was uneasy with this approach, but could not come up with anything to offer instead. As Saint-Germain began to walk toward the inn, he said, "Have a care as you go. They may have men posted outside."

"If they do, I will trust that I will see them first," said Saint-Germain.

"But if they should capture you—" Belfountain persisted.

"Then we will all be at a disadvantage," said Saint-Germain, and continued on as if he had nothing more on his mind than the gathering storm and avoiding getting his fine silver-buckled boots smirched by the wallow that extended beyond the line of pigsties.

Text of a letter from Atta Olivia Clemens, from Orleans, to Sanct-Germain Franciscus, in care of Eclipse Trading Company in Amsterdam, written in Imperial Latin, carried by private courier, and delivered thirteen days after it was written.

To my most dear, most aggravating, most mystifying friend, in the present guise of Grav Saint-Germain, the affectionate greetings of Olivia, from my horse farm near Orleans on this, the 19th day of July, 1531, in great concern for your well-being.

So I have your note of the 5th day of July, saying you must return to Venezia in a short time. I am sending this to you in Amsterdam in the hope that it will arrive before you depart, but with the confidence that your factor will send it on to you if you have departed by the time this reaches the Lowlands. Your note tells me that you fear some irregularity in your finances may have put your associates in Venezia at an unintended disadvantage, and you must hasten to set the whole matter to rights. I wonder if those who have not been worthy of your trust have any idea what they will reap for their perfidy? You must forgive my delight in the confrontation I am imagining. For all the centuries and centuries I have been one of your blood, I have never known you to slack in the redress of wrongs, nor to mistake vengeance for rectitude. Though you say it is easier for you to pardon desperate acts because time does not weigh upon you as heavily as it does on the living, I know you will not expose yourself or others to injustice, and tolerant as you are, you do not give countenance to criminality.

In your determination to help those who have borne hardship because of you, do not, I pray you, decide to give over all you have in compensation to them. I know you, my most dear Sanct' Germain, and I know you can be generous to a fault; I laud your impulse to rectify all unjust misery that is caused by association with you, and I wish I had the greatness of heart to emulate you, but my nature is not as forbearing as yours, so I caution you that excessive recompense may create expectations that neither you nor anyone alive can fulfill, and that will prove a burden that will only increase, never diminish. Think of how Clodotius battened on you, greedy as a leech, with the intention of using all your kindness to sink his hooks still deeper into you. For one who has lived the millennia you have, to be taken in by so venal a man astonishes me, yet I am worried that you might fall into the same estimable error. For my sake, if not your own, stand firm for the sake of those to whose defense you are rising.

You still have that property near Attigny, do you not? You might find it serves your purpose to go there while the various courts address the treachery you have described. I realize that may put you in the path of various rural outrages undertaken to vindicate multifarious religious views, but where in Europe is this not so? South of the Alps there is the Church, but that does not spare you, for the Spanish seek to impose their will on the Pope at every occasion. In Attigny, you would be able to speed messages from the north or the south without having to be present yourself, and thus you would not have to expose yourself to detention and worse. I say this only because the upheavals among the peoples here have become increasingly violent, and if such violence should turn on you, it might be more than you are able to recover from: they are burning heretics, you know, and breaking others on the wheel, to be an example to those who do not accept the salvation they offer. My most-dear friend, I would rather you off in the remotest reaches of Asia or the Americas than broken on the wheel and cast into a pit of lye. I cannot bear the thought of you risking the True Death to correct some mistakes in arithmetic.

Here in France there are constant rumors about the excesses of the Protestants in the north and northeast. To hear the gossip, we are to expect legions of outraged Protestant Saxons and Hessians armed with staves and pitchforks to march across the fair land of France, destroying everything they encounter, and burning all those good Catholics who do not immediately renounce their faith in favor of Protestant teachings. The Abbe in the village has said that he is certain that there are peasants here who would welcome such an invasion, *and I cannot wholly dismiss his concerns, which is why I have mounted a watch on my lands and buildings. It is bad enough that I am foreign, but I am a woman, and that makes me more subject to scrutiny than any foreign man, and so I am being as circumspect as I can in my search for a lover, as well as in my dealings with the Abbe and the townsfolk.*

To inform you of more pleasant things, I have now four fine studs at this horse farm, and the prices they can command for covering the mares of others has kept this place expanding for the last quarter-century. One of the stallions may interest you, for almost all his get are gray, and I know your preference for grays. Shall I put three of my mares in foal to him for you, so that you have the foals to look forward to? I would count it a privilege to supply your stable.

With the hope that you do not have to pay too high a price—in gold or in things more precious—upon your return to Venezia, and with the warranty that my deep affection and my wholehearted love remains unswervingly yours, from now until I am dust,

> *In saeculi saeculorum, as the Abbe puts it,*
> *Olivia*

By my own hand, given to Niklos Aulirios to carry to Orleans where he is to entrust it to a professional messenger.

2

"Mestre tomorrow, no later than midafternoon," said Belfountain as he squatted next to the campfire contained in a ring of stones; three rabbits turned on spits over the flames, lending the odor of cooking meat mixed with wild thyme and garlic to the smoke rising from the fires. Mercer and delle Fonde shared the task of working the cranks, paying far more attention to their meal preparations than to what their leader was saying.

"How many figs are left?" Mercer asked delle Fonde, trying to pat the saddlebag on the ground between them.

"A dozen or so; probably two apiece. Here. Let me deal with the cheese." Delle Fonde moved aside so Mercer could work the three spits himself while he cut up the last of the cheese into thick wedges and dropped them into a cooking pot with a handle; he took a jar from his saddlebag and opened it, then poured the contents into the pot and began to stir it with a wooden spoon.

Belfountain reached down and put another dry branch on the fire. "Sixteen days. Only three days more than I reckoned we would need to reach Venezia—under the circumstances, an excellent passage. No fighting to speak of, at least not of our concern, and no theft beyond a little pilferage at the Terlingen posting house. Forty miles covered yesterday, according to the stones, and thirty-eight today. All in all, a successful escort mission." It was a fine night, the sky overhead so shiny with stars that it seemed as if the darkness had been buffed to a brilliant gloss; getting to his feet Belfountain looked up and nodded his approval. "A cheerful evening for the last of our journey, though we spend it in the open. It is all to the good."

"Better than that storm two nights ago, at the pass," said Mercer. "It has been a wet summer." It being the last night of their mission the men were more at ease, gathered around the campfire for light more than warmth on this pleasant summer night, already anticipating their promised three days at liberty that would begin as soon as they reached Mestre.

"Thank God for it, or there would have been more killing, especially among the peasants," said Oralle.

"And more delays for us," said Mercer.

"Peasants and Protestants are rebelling everywhere this summer," said Yeoville, and went back to mending the scabbard that held his heaviest sword.

"And there are other workers taking up arms, as well," Oralle remarked. "Wool-workers, weavers, all demanding justice for—"

"We were lucky to get around the worst of them," said delle Fonde.

"Rebellion, uprisings, revolts—they're all just excuses for defying the Church," said Mercer.

"We're past the worst enclaves of the Calvinists and Lutherans—that's reason to be glad," said Oralle.

"You hope," said delle Fonde, who was stirring up a mixture of melted white cheese, sour wine, and thick chunks of stale bread.

"He's right: Protestants are everywhere. At least there are enough of them that they can stand against the Church. Not all heretics are so fortunate."

"Stands to reason the Protestants are behind us; Venezia is a Catholic republic," Oralle declared.

"Jews and Eastern Rite Christians are allowed to worship in Venezia without risk, so the Veneziani can make the most of their trading with the men from the east," said delle Fonde, a note of disapproval in his voice. "There is even a chapel for the Ottoman merchants to worship their Allah, on the Giudecca. I have seen its tower."

"The Minor Consiglio has familiars to keep watch on those places," said Oralle, dismissing the matter. "Those who go to those places are known."

"There are spies all over," Mercer observed. "Even in the confessional."

"Have a care what you say in Confession, then," said delle Fonde.

"Or buy an indulgence and avoid Confession entirely," said Yeoville with a merry, cynical laugh. "I don't know about any of you, but I'd never tell a priest half of what I've done. If I must have an indulgence to expiate my sins, then so be it."

Belfountain shook his head. "It's more than indulgences that Protestants object to—Yeoville is right: priests are known to gossip, and many honest sinners are compromised because of it. That's what many Protestant Christians believe."

"Others have before them, and paid for their faith in blood," said delle Fonde, his expression hard.

"Are Protestant Christians any more virtuous?" Oralle directed this to Mercer. "Or do they only think they are?"

"The Church is saying that because of the Protestants, devils will be released upon the world, deceiving men," said Mercer. "Without the Church to guide men, all will go astray into the hands of Satan."

"There are peculiar doings in the world, no doubt," Yeoville said as if glad of such a development.

"It is a dangerous time," said Mercer.

"All the more work for us," said Belfountain. "So long as our faith is the faith of the man who pays us."

"We can be sure of steady work, putting the fear of God into anyone who won't pay us," said delle Fonde with bitter bravado.

"You mean sack a town for the Glory of God?" Mercer asked. "Why not?"

"What would God achieve for a sacking?" Delle Fonde spoke so softly that almost no one heard him.

"Which God?" Oralle guffawed and clapped his hands.

"Any God, so long as we can keep the spoils," said Mercer.

"And are paid in advance," said Belfountain.

"I wonder what would happen if Calvin and Luther were locked in a cell together?" Yeoville asked suddenly, and answered his own question. "I think they would tear one another to pieces."

"In the name of a just and merciful God," said Mercer, shaking his head. All but delle Fonde chuckled as Mercer intended they should, but because of delle Fonde's silence the chuckles faded quickly.

"All right, man: what is it?" Belfountain asked.

"I . . . I'd rather not—" delle Fonde said apologetically. "It is nothing that should concern you."

"Now that we are in Venezian territory?" ventured Oralle. "Is it the Catholic Church that keeps you silent? Or are you defending Protestants by saying nothing of what you know?"

Delle Fonde became more reticent still. "That isn't the issue."

"Oho," said Mercer, smiling again, but without a trace of good-fellowship. "What is the matter, Giulio? Is there something you're hiding from us—your comrades-in-arms?"

"Secrets are worse than ferrets," said Yeoville, quoting the old Italian-Swiss proverb in order to goad delle Fonde into revealing more.

"Leave him alone," said Belfountain. "It has nothing to do with us. Every one of you has secrets, as is your right: no man in my Company has to tell more of his past than he wishes, and that goes for all of you. You may keep the faith you have or have none, as it pleases you. But see you do not fight about what you do not know about one another."

"Yes. We may not know but we can guess, and our guesses are probably worse than the truth, but if he wants to risk that . . ." said Oralle, and suddenly yawned. "If only we had a little wine left."

"Or some beer," said Mercer. "A jug of it apiece."

"Wine is better in this part of the world," Oralle said, hoping for a sharp reaction.

"Tomorrow you may swill until you cannot stand upright," said Belfountain. "Tonight we have no wine left."

"A pity," said Oralle.

These complaints diverted the others from questioning delle Fonde, the men carping to one another that they longed for wine or beer, anything to relieve their thirst, and that it was unfair that they had nothing to drink.

"There is a stream not very far away," Ruggier pointed out.

"There is," said Belfountain. "But its waters are not wholesome. Those who drink from it often suffer from the bloody flux."

"Ah," said di Santo-Germano as he came into the glow of the fire-light from where his few cases and chests had been piled and covered for the night; his black clothing made his appearance unnerving for the Company, and two of the men crossed themselves. "So that's the problem: a good thing to know. Bloody flux is to be avoided." At another time he would have offered these men a tincture to rid the water of its contamination, but he had not brought any of that preparation with him on this hurried journey. "Then best not to drink of the stream—the animals should be kept from it, as well. I will find a spring for them while you sleep, so they will be able to slake their thirst in the morning."

"Wine and beer are safe, and they warm the heart," said delle Fonde, a forlorn note in his statement. "Do you not agree, Conte?"

Di Santo-Germano looked over at delle Fonde, a bit startled by the question. "If the choice is wine, beer, or unwholesome water, then wine and beer are preferable, at least for men. Not all creatures are as susceptible to the flux as humans are." It was a safe enough answer, and it allowed the men to debate which was better—wine or beer; no conclusion was reached, but none was expected, and it ended shortly before the rabbits were ready to eat; the men took out their knives in preparation for their meal. Excusing himself, di Santo-Germano walked away from the campfire toward the remuda to groom the horses, as he had done every evening they had camped on the road.

"An odd one, the Conte," said Mercer. Since they had crossed the borders of the Venezian Empire, the men of the escort had taken to using di Santo-Germano instead of Saint-Germain, and Conte instead of Grav, and they had stopped calling his manservant Ruthger and now referred to him as Ruggier. "I don't think I've seen him touch wine or beer. Or water, for that matter." He glanced in Ruggier's direction, clearly seeking a comment.

"My master dines and drinks in private. It is the custom of those of his blood." Ruggier nodded toward the pot of cheese-and-bread. "That will burn if you hold it too close to the fire."

Delle Fonde drew his pot back from the flames, and looked about sheepishly. "I ask your pardon, comrades," he said pointedly to the hungry men sitting around the campfire while he stirred the pot more energetically.

Mercer pointed to Ruggier. "I have also noticed that you eat in private—each of you; alone."

"It is a habit I have picked up from my master over my years of service, for he often travels—as exiles must—and it is easier to live by his habits than to constantly learn new ones; in many places, we have had to stay apart from others, as custom requires, so it is not unreasonable for me to dine alone," said Ruggier calmly but not quite truthfully; he knew that his diet of raw meat would seem repellant to these men. "I have provided fowl and game for us to eat, and you know I always take my share."

"From that, we must suppose that your master hunts only for himself as well as dines alone. And he, like most men of high station, does not share." Yeoville made this a challenge, lifting his chin and raising his voice.

Ruggier remained unflustered. "You would be correct." There was a brief, awkward silence among those gathered around the campfire; it ended as delle Fonde took one of the spits and began to cut portions of rabbit for the men, who seized their shares in their hands and knives, and began eagerly to eat. Ruggier got to his feet, saying as he did, "May you make a fine meal. I will be on guard from midnight until dawn?"

"You will," said Belfountain. "Yeoville will be with you."

"Very good; at midnight, then, and on until dawn," Ruggier said with a half-nod in Yeoville's direction, adding, "I am going to assist my master with grooming the horses."

"Of course you are," said Belfountain, his attention fixed on the second spit that Oralle was removing from its place over the flames; the meat sizzled where the flames had blackened it, and the small thyme leaves fell off like little cinders. "Tell him that we will be under way at first light."

"Gladly," said Ruggier, and continued on toward the remuda line, where he found di Santo-Germano brushing the mouse-colored gelding he had been riding earlier.

"Belfountain's blood-bay has a bad bruise on the offside fore-pastern," said di Santo-Germano as Ruggier came up to him; he spoke in the language of Persia. "It probably happened when we were coming down from that defile, through the brush. I'm surprised he is not lame."

"Belfountain will want to find a remount tomorrow, then," said Ruggier in the same tongue.

"I'll treat the bruise tonight; that should help," said di Santo-Germano. He finished brushing the gelding's coat and set his brush aside in favor of a long-toothed comb for the mane and tail. "Those men—they're noticing too much about us, are they not."

"They are, and they're beginning to ask questions," said Ruggier. "I think they will be pleased to see the last of you, and of me."

The sound of laughter drifted to them from the bright ring of the campfire.

"Small wonder," said di Santo-Germano; he busied himself easing a burr out of the horse's mane. "Last night, while I feigned sleeping, I kept breathing so that the guard would not become aware that I do not have to breathe but to speak. I should do the same tonight—as should you."

"I know," said Ruggier. "I think Yeoville is determined to find something amiss with us."

"That's the last fig!" Oralle bellowed, and was answered with a scuffle.

"Yes; I think so as well. It is his nature to be suspicious, and the rest follow his example. That is why I have confined my feeding to game, and only game, on this journey; I cannot risk discovery, particularly from men such as these, who are touchy of their honor." Di Santo-Germano worked the comb steadily as he went on. "Tonight I will stand the early watch with Belfountain and—it will be delle Fonde, I suppose."

"It is his turn," said Ruggier. "I will have Yeoville with me on duty."

Di Santo-Germano moved to the rear of the horse and took the tail in his hands to begin combing. "I am inclined to keep this gelding. He's steady-tempered and he has more stamina than the others in this remuda."

Ruggier's long experience with di Santo-Germano allowed him to recognize that his master was bringing himself to a point indirectly, so he waited patiently, saying, "I am sure that will be possible."

Combing carefully, di Santo-Germano sighed. "How well you understand me, old friend." He finished his task and set the comb aside with the brush. "I have been expecting something of this sort. These men have traveled too closely with us for them not to have noticed that we are something more than merely foreigners, and that is troubling to me."

"Because of all we have encountered of late," Ruggier said.

"Yes, that and the hard lessons learned over the centuries. Little as the Catholics may like Protestants of any sort, and all manner of Protestants dislike Catholics with a poisonous intensity, all of them would turn their fear and fury upon such a creature as I am, or you are, and justify their actions in the name of both religions. As much as the rival Christians despise one another, they loathe anyone deemed unnatural far more." He stared off into the night, seeing farther than the starry darkness. "At least they will move on tomorrow, after we reach Mestre."

"They may speculate—" Ruggier began.

"So they may, and they are welcome to do so, once they are out of the Venezian Empire; to whom can they confide their misgivings but one another, and how can that endanger you or me?" said di Santo-Germano. "It would probably be best if I help them to have good reason to depart, what do you say: a generous bonus for them to return promptly to Antwerp, perhaps?"

Ruggier answered in the Venezian dialect. "I say it is a prudent thing to do, and that you will do what you decide is best."

"Da ver'," di Santo-Germano agreed, and raised his voice as he heard delle Fonde approaching. "You come in good time: what am I to do for you, Signor' delle Fonde?"

Delle Fonde halted at the edge of the remuda; behind him the men of the Company brayed and hooted derisively, sounds which delle Fonde made a point of ignoring. "I am about to begin my guard duty."

"And you come to summon me to my task; thank you," said di Santo-Germano. He glanced over at Ruggier. "There are only the dun and that new horse—the liver-chestnut—yet to groom."

"I will attend to them," Ruggier assured him. "I'll let you know when I've finished."

"Very good," said di Santo-Germano, and went over to delle Fonde. "I am at your service."

The mercenary laughed once. "No, you're not," he said, and pointed back toward the others who were finishing their meal. "We are all at your service, careful as you are not to remind us. But it is more than that—you take risks for us, and you pay for more than you agreed to, and you never ask any of us to do more than you would, and you tend to chores to spare us. So: I have seen how you take pains not to dwell on our differences."

They were a short distance from the remuda now, going toward the first in a crescent of simple tents. "What would be the purpose of such distinction? We are all traveling the same roads, and for the same reason."

"Say what you will," delle Fonde remarked, emboldened by their coming separation, and less inclined to observe the proprieties than he would have been earlier in their journey, "you and your manservant are unlike others we have escorted. In larger groups, I would not have noticed as much, but with so few of us, and traveling so fast . . ." He glanced uneasily over his shoulder. "I thank you for not entering into our disputes."

"Why should I?" di Santo-Germano asked. "I am not one of Belfountain's Company, I am the man who engaged your services. I have no place in those disputes, unless they concern me directly."

Delle Fonde considered this. "Surely you must have convictions, expectations, and—"

"I do, but I have learned, over time, to keep most of them to myself," said di Santo-Germano as they passed the second tent.

"Yes; though you share our work and our dangers, you hold aloof from us, not just in your dining privately, or in your refusing to drink with us. I cannot help but wonder why."

Di Santo-Germano regarded delle Fonde for a long moment, then said, "Let us agree that, in these times and these places, it is safer for you not to know. I have no desire to put you or your comrades at risk for my sake, beyond the risk you have as my escort."

"So you have secrets, too," said delle Fonde.

"Anyone does, who has lived as long as I have," said di Santo-Germano, lengthening his stride; delle Fonde, who was much the same height as di Santo-Germano, had to move faster to keep up with the foreigner.

"Life gives many secrets, soon or late," delle Fonde agreed, adding quietly, "All of the Company has secrets."

"And yours weighs heavily upon you," said di Santo-Germano.

Delle Fonde shrugged. "No more than many other men's do." He stopped as he heard the bushes rustle. "But I hate to be mocked."

"A wild goat," said di Santo-Germano.

"Are you certain? There are wild boar in this region, and bear."

"I am certain," said di Santo-Germano, who could see the animal at the edge of a thicket.

The men around the campfire got into a scuffle which Belfountain broke up by knocking Mercer's and Oralle's heads together.

"It's the promise of liberty that makes them fractious," said delle Fonde. "They are inclined to pull at their bridles."

"Then better for them to rest well tonight," said di Santo-Germano, and they completed their next two rounds of the campsite in silence, watching as the men banked the campfire and went off to their tents, a few of them continuing desultory conversations for a short while, all aware that morning came too quickly to allow them the luxury of midnight discussions. Soon only Ruggier remained awake with delle Fonde and di Santo-Germano tending the horses and cleaning tack in anticipation of the morning ride.

As they reached the tent farthest from the fire, delle Fonde stopped still, listening to the soft drone of insects and the first snores from his comrades asleep in their tents. "I don't think I will be staying with Belfountain after this. I am going to claim my prize-money and return home."

Di Santo-Germano cocked his head. "Is this a recent decision?"

"No," said delle Fonde. "Not really. I have been gone more than nine years, and I know my parents are getting old; they may even be dead, as could anyone. I would like to see them again, if they live, and my two brothers, and my three sisters. I want to know if they are all well. If I could read and write, perhaps I would know something, but—"

"And where do they live?" asked di Santo-Germano.

"In the mountains of Savoia," said delle Fonde, and continued as if compelled to speak. "I thought I would not miss them: we parted badly." He coughed. "They had arranged a marriage for me—a good marriage in many ways—but the affianced bride and I . . ."

"You were not suited to each other," di Santo-Germano suggested.

"That was the heart of it. She came from a Catholic family, and I did not." He held his breath at this revelation. When di Santo-Germano said nothing, delle Fonde scowled, and began to speak again, reciting a story he had known since childhood. "Back in the days of the Crusades, when all the Jews were expelled from France, there was, as a result, a derth of goldsmiths and silversmiths in that country, and so a number of Roman goldsmiths and silversmiths were offered work there. My many-times-great-grandfather had been making molds for coins in Roma—which is how we got our name—"

"Of the stamps, or molds," di Santo-Germano translated from a Roman dialect earlier than the one spoken there now.

"Yes." Delle Fonde stared into the darkness at the middle distance, and went on, still somewhat enveloped in the hazy dream the tea imparted. "Sabinus—my ancestor—accepted employment and brought our family to Lyon, where he was authorized to mint coins for the Crown and the city, as he had done in Roma. After many years, he became a convert to the teaching of Piere Waldo, and for that, his sons were arrested and imprisoned, and he was branded on the forehead and told to go to the Holy Land to pray for forgiveness at Jerusalem; when he did not return, all the family was excommunicated and threw in their lot with Waldo's followers and settled in Savoia, remaining close to our religion—Christian but not Catholic—down the generations. Many of my family have been executed for being heretics because we have remained faithful to the Waldensian Creed."

"But not so faithful that they would not wed you to a Catholic," di Santo-Germano pointed out.

"You understand," said delle Fonde with visible relief.

"I grasp the problem," said di Santo-Germano, taking up delle

Fonde's account. "So you left, and gradually, you have come to value what you left behind. It is not an uncommon experience." He recalled the many times he had seen such forces working in someone's life, and felt the familiar pang that accompanied his own recognition of how far he was from his own family, his people, his breathing days, his gods who had made him one of them. "You have a feeling of interrupted circumstance, of lost continuity."

"Just so," said delle Fonde with a little sigh as he began to walk the camp perimeter again.

"You would like to have that familiarity again, before it is lost," said di Santo-Germano, walking beside delle Fonde.

"Yes! You," delle Fonde dared to say, "must know the same—being an exile. You must miss them as you would a severed arm."

"True enough, but I cannot return to them," said di Santo-Germano, making no other remark about his past. "However, if you visit your family, do not be astonished if what you are seeking is difficult to find—you have had years apart, and you have had experiences that none of your family will share with you."

"Do you fear that for yourself?" delle Fonde asked impulsively.

It took di Santo-Germano a moment to frame his answer. "It is difficult to be without context; it is a burden that does not lessen with time."

Delle Fonde made a face of chagrin. "I should not have—"

"Clearly you wish to speak to someone, and of this group, I or my manservant are the least likely to use this information against you," said di Santo-Germano.

Now delle Fonde made a gesture of regret. "It was wrong for me to speak to you, Conte. If you will forgive my impertinence?"

Di Santo-Germano held up his hand. "No. You have said nothing for which you should ask pardon. If anything, it is I who should ask pardon of you, for permitting you to say so much." He saw delle Fonde take a step back, shocked. "I could easily have silenced you when you began to speak, but I did not; I brought your questions on myself."

Delle Fonde smiled uneasily. "But I imposed upon you, Conte."

"Hardly imposed. Rather let us say that you and I have taken advantage of our parting to come to comment upon matters that cannot be shared with closer associates."

"Like those we meet in taverns," said delle Fonde, "to whom we impart secrets without worry."

Di Santo-Germano nodded in what could be considered agreement. "You may rest assured I will keep your confidence, and by tomorrow you and I will part company in any case. Whom could I tell of your family's religion, and why should I speak of it at all?"

"Yes," said delle Fonde. "Why should either of us say anything?"

As they continued on their rounds, neither spoke again until they were relieved at midnight by Ruggier and Yeoville.

Text of a letter from Basilio Cuor in Amsterdam, to Christofo Sen in Venezia, carried by private courier, and delivered fourteen days after it was written.

To the most estimable Christofo Sen, secretary to the Minor Consiglio, in Venezia, the greetings of Basilio Cuor in Amsterdam on this, the 23rd day of July, 1531;

I am confirming my note of ten days ago: Saint-Germain, or di Santo-Germano, if you prefer, is gone from Amsterdam, and from Antwerp. I presented myself at his houses in both cities, and was misdirected—deliberately, I believe—back to Amsterdam, which lost me precious days in following him.

It is my belief, based upon what I learned from the woman occupying his house in this city, that di Santo-Germano has returned to Venezia, and may even now be in his house on Campo San Luca; she was careful to tell me very little, but I mentioned that I had business with his trading company which would prove profitable for him, and she suggested that I speak to his advocate to learn to whom I could broach this matter, for the advocate has di Santo-Germano's direction in Venezia and other places. Proceeding on this information, I made inquiries of one of the clerks of his advocate, but the man is as tight-lipped as a clam, and would tell me nothing useful, but the assistant to the factor Altermaat confirmed that di Santo-Germano is bound for La Serenissima, and so I am confident in expressing my certainty that he is once again in the city.

I have arranged to accompany a group of merchants bound to the south, and I will stay with them until a faster-traveling band will admit me to their number. I anticipate arriving in about three weeks—sooner if it is possible—when I will present myself to you to make a complete report as regards this Saint-Germain or di Santo-Germano. I do not think I should commit such information to paper, for fear it may fall into the wrong hands.

> *Until I present myself to you,*
> *I remain your most truly devoted servant,*
> *Basilio Cuor*

3

All the windows in Giovanni Boromeo's print-shop were open, but the heat of high summer lingered, pungent from the canals, and undisturbed by breezes. The water had a harsh, brazen shine, and the sky glared down with the full weight of midday. Four apprentices struggled to align paper in the main press while another two busied themselves in preparing the type for the next page. Boromeo himself, his giaquetta set aside and his camisa pulled out from his hose, red-faced with effort, wrestled a pallet of paper nearer the press itself.

"Feel the grain!" Boromeo ordered the pressmen. "Follow the paper, don't force it!"

The sound of an opening door from the side of the print-shop that faced the Campo San Proccopio provided all the sweaty, aggravated men the opportunity to stop working, at least long enough to see who had arrived.

"Gran' Dio e tutt' santi!" Boromeo exclaimed as he swung around to face the dark figure outlined in the hazy brilliance. "What do you want?"

"I am here in answer to your summons," said di Santo-Germano, coming through the door and into the print-shop. He was superbly dressed in a black-silk doublet piped in silver, with silver lace at throat and wrists; the dogaline that topped this was also silk: fine black satin lined in silver taffeta. His hose were black, slashed and studded in more silver, and his leggings were black, as were his low, thick-heeled boots. He wore a sword, but had not bothered with a hat, and in spite of the heat, there was no trace of moisture on his face or clothes.

Boromeo stood very still, as if disbelieving his senses; all around him work ceased and the men stared, the only sounds in the room drifting in from the canal just beyond the open door. Slowly Boromeo took a step toward the man in black-and-silver. "Conte?"

"Eccomi," said di Santo-Germano, bowing slightly, sounding more Fiorenzano than Veneziano.

"Thank merciful Heaven," said Boromeo as the noise in his print-shop resumed.

"I came as quickly as I could," said di Santo-Germano. "Your letter dismayed me."

"At last!" Boromeo exclaimed. "I had feared you had been thrust into a Protestant prison—or worse—a Spanish one."

"Fortunately neither. Yet I find that I might as well have been, for all the information I have been provided."

"But I have been telling you for months how badly we were faring here," said Boromeo. "I prepared my report every month, and put it into Emerenzio's hands to be copied and sent on to you. I even provided him paper for his clerk." His face darkened, as if this were the ultimate betrayal.

"I have had only superficial reports from Emerenzio," said di Santo-Germano. "Nothing from you until you sent one to me on your own."

"Only superficial reports," Boromeo repeated. "Nothing about the precarious state of your business? from anyone?"

"No. Emerezio assured me he was sending me all information entrusted to him. He claimed that the earthquake in Lisbon had caused a delay in some of my profits, and that he needed time to prepare an accurate assessment of how much would be needed to restore the trading company there, and in the meantime, those of my ships bound for the New World would be setting sail from Oporto, and a new wharf and warehouse would have to be built there." Di Santo-Germano held up his hand. "I have spoken to one of my ships' captains already, and he informs me that no such building is taking place."

"I am astonished to hear it," said Boromeo with heavy sarcasm. "If you were not informed of how matters stood here, then why should the state of affairs elsewhere be any different? I understood that you had been informed by Emerenzio of what your circumstances were here and in Lisbon—that you knew of the severity of your losses."

"Alas, no," said di Santo-Germano. "Had I heard earlier, I would have taken steps to correct matters."

"Delfino, do not bother yourself with our discussion," Boromeo snapped suddenly, rounding on one of his apprentices; when the youth turned away, Boromeo gave his attention to di Santo-Germano again. "You certainly acted swiftly when I contacted you, and I am grateful to you for such swift response: I had the funds you sent from the north six days ago; the courier came directly here, requiring only twelve days to make the journey—a punishing pace, to be sure. Apparently he took your instructions to make haste to heart. As you see, I have put the money to good use." He gestured to indicate that his shop was busy. "That paper was delivered this morning."

"Excellent," approved di Santo-Germano. "If you haven't sufficient money to complete your projects, you have only to inform me of that fact, and I will see you have what you need." He glanced around the print-shop. "I do not see Niccola here, or Mascuccio."

"Niccola is carrying messages for me; I suppose you'll want him back again? Mascuccio has gone to work at the Casetta Santa Perpetua; he left when my funds could not continue to cover his wages." Boromeo coughed delicately. "He was given a reference by Gennaro Emerenzio—he said he regretted he could do so little for your former servants."

"No doubt," said di Santo-Germano sardonically. "I have called at Signor' Emerenzio's place of business, without being permitted to speak with him."

Boromeo stared, shocked. "Conte?" He glanced around his print-shop again, aware that the men were listening.

"That was after I went to my house on Campo San Luca and found only a single footman left there with an under-cook, and half the household furnishings gone," said di Santo-Germano. "I have left my manservant there to make inventories of what is missing."

"You say there has been theft at your house? On top of all the rest?" Boromeo exclaimed.

"No; I say that many things are missing—I have not yet determined the reason, although theft is likely." He paused. "I also went to

Pier-Ariana's house and found a merchant from Pisa in it. What do you know of this?"

Boromeo was about to answer when he realized that what was being overheard would provide fodder for gossip. He straightened up and waved vigorously. "All of you: take your prandium now, and return after your midday rest. The Conte and I have much to discuss."

Reluctantly the men gathered up their wallets and straggled to the door leading out of the side of the shop, onto the Campo San Proccopio, and the small cluster of hastily erected canvas-sided stalls where food was being prepared to supply the many craftsmen who worked in the immediate district.

"A good precaution," di Santo-Germano approved.

"By nightfall there will be dozens of versions of our conversation circulating in the city," said Boromeo as if he were acknowledging a fault.

"That will suit me very well," di Santo-Germano declared, and went on as he saw confusion in Boromeo's face. "How else am I to rout out Emerenzio if not through questions from his fellow Veneziani?"

Boromeo blinked. "You want my workers to talk?"

"Oh, yes. And to spread as many rumors as possible, without too much invention in their telling; let it be known that I have returned and that I am making inquiries into the state of my businesses. If Emerenzio wants to hide from me, so be it. But he shall not be allowed to do so without scrutiny." Di Santo-Germano walked to the center of the shop, out of the blocks of light from the open windows and doors. "Tell me all that you can."

"About Emerenzio?" Boromeo speculated. "Or would you like me to cast a wider net?"

"At heart I want to know about Emerenzio, yes, but include all that his acts have entailed."

"That may take some time," said Boromeo, going to shut the quay-side door. "And you will have many false accounts to sort through."

"More than you suppose: today I have as much time as you need; tell me as much as you know," said di Santo-Germano, and leaned back against the tall rack of type-trays, prepared to listen, asking only a few questions as Giovanni Boromeo told him of all that had transpired here in Venezia over the past year. The midday rest ended, and the men and apprentices returned to their work, but Boromeo took another hour to finish his account. At last he thanked Boromeo, saying, "You have given me much to deliberate; I must take my next steps after heedful consideration."

"For your own sake, and others," said Boromeo. "All of us could be at risk if Emerenzio has the chance to oppose you."

"Yes; that is clear. But what puts you in danger is also dangerous to him, for he has overstepped himself," di Santo-Germano said with calm purpose. "He might have managed if he had only stolen from an absent foreigner, but from good Veneziani—that is another matter entirely."

"If Emerenzio had played you so foul, then he will be a desperate enemy," Boromeo warned.

"No doubt like a cornered crocodile," said di Santo-Germano in grim whimsy, and went on in a more detached voice, "When the *White Gull* arrives from Amsterdam, she'll be carrying books from the press I have there. I have ordered them delivered directly to you. You may sell them yourself, or arrange with a dealer to handle them. All I ask from you is a full record of—"

Boromeo interrupted. "—of all our transactions, and the amounts paid. Of course. I will copy all that I have on hand and bring it to you myself, tomorrow. After what Emerenzio has done, it is the wisest course to have as much proof of his crimes as you can obtain. You will need to gather your proofs circumspectly if you are not to lose more to Emerenzio's avarice." He folded his big arms and studied di Santo-Germano. "Will you permit me to help you in your dealing with Emerenzio?"

"I may, depending upon how this all falls out," said di Santo-Germano. "You have been damaged by his actions, so you should share in his comeuppance." Di Santo-Germano straightened up. "I am going to return to my house now, and see what my manservant has found out. Then I will try to find Pier-Ariana." He lifted his brows. "Would you have any information on where she has gone?"

"I don't know. She brought a manuscript of songs to me at the start of summer, but I haven't seen her since then," said Boromeo uncomfortably. "The book has yet to be set, so I have had no reason to speak with her. Had I known she was bearing so onerous a burden—" He stared at the press and the men working it. "Perhaps I should have done something, but I knew you had secured her that house, so . . ." He finished with a bunglesome shrug.

"I understand," said di Santo-Germano, aware of the many difficulties Emerenzio had caused. "I will return again, not long from now; if you need to send me a message, direct it to the Campo San Luca house. I will be staying there."

"And Niccola?" asked Boromeo. "What is to become of him?"

Di Santo-Germano considered. "If he wishes to return to my service, I will be glad to have him; if he desires to stay here, then he shall."

"You are most generous, Conte, most generous," said Boromeo.

But di Santo-Germano met this praise with a self-effacing turn of his hands. "No, I am not. What man is well-served by a reluctant page? And who wants to train a recalcitrant apprentice?" He inclined his head. "I thank you again, Signor' Boromeo."

"You have no reason to thank me, Conte," said Boromeo as he bowed di Santo-Germano out of his print-shop to the canal. "Shall I summon a gondola for you?"

"No, it is not necessary. I still have my own," said di Santo-Germano, and raised his hand to signal to Milano da Costaga to bring his craft up to the steps that led down to the water.

"Signor' Conte?" asked Milano as he helped his employer into the special, earth-lined boat.

"Back to San Luca, Milano," said di Santo-Germano, offering a single wave to Boromeo.

"More trouble?" Milano guessed as he swung toward the Gran' Canale. "Or more of the same?"

"I fear more of the same," said di Santo-Germano, then lapsed into a thoughtful silence as the sun bore down on him and shone off the water. Finally, as the gondolier turned his craft into the Rivi San Luca, di Santo-Germano spoke again. "It seems my factor here has been using my money as his own."

"So I assumed from what Raffaele told me," said Milano, mentioning the lone footman left at the di Santo-Germano's Venezian house. "In June, I heard him explaining to Padre Bonnome why he could not provide money to San Luca this summer, and when I asked him what was wrong, he told me."

"Ah, Venezia," said di Santo-Germano as he got out of the gondola and went up the two freshly scrubbed marble steps into his house, saying over his shoulder as he did, "I may need you later this evening."

"Then I will be at your service." Milano touched his oar and the gondola slipped away into the shadows cast by the tall houses on either side of the canal.

Raffaele, the footman, had been sorting through a carton of newly arrived glass goblets that would replace those taken from the household. Rising slowly so as not to overset any of the beautiful goblets standing around him on the floor, he pressed his lips together and said, "There is too much to do, now you are returned; I will need more help, Signor' Conte."

"Of course you will. You may recommend to Ruggier anyone you like, and he will engage them if they prove satisfactory," said di Santo-Germano.

"I would prefer to begin with a cook and a few more footmen," said Raffaele. "And you will need a houseman or a steward—I haven't the training for such work."

"Whatever suits you best," said di Santo-Germano as he climbed the stairs and went toward his study. On this floor there had been very little taken, and di Santo-Germano touched the familiar objects as if to make certain that they were still in place. Going through the study door, he found Ruggier with three sheets of paper spread before him, most covered with notes in his archaic hand. "Have you determined yet how much is gone?"

Ruggier showed no surprise at di Santo-Germano's question. "For the main floor, yes; the inventory is still being conducted on this floor, and the one above. It isn't as bad as we feared at first; the furniture that has been sold is mostly the kind found in all households: the dining tables and chairs, the clothes-press, the two Turkish couches, the crockery and goblets and the chest to hold them, the two upholstered benches, the work-desk, most of the bed linens, the painted basins, the silk draperies from the—"

"In other words, at Emerenzio's instigation, the whole of the house has been turned into a source of money for him." Di Santo-Germano stared down at the floor, a suggestion of a frown between his brows. "I have lost more goods than I can think of, over the centuries, some of

254 *Chelsea Quinn Yarbro*

them valuable beyond measure, but that was through exigencies of circumstances, and although the losses were sad or bitter, they were not inherently repugnant. This willful confiscation—and for so demeaning a purpose—is different, and it offends me to the soul."

"This is not the same," Ruggier agreed.

"No, it is not," said di Santo-Germano, ending the matter. "When the inventory is—"

"I will put it into your hands," said Ruggier.

"I am maladroit, old friend," said di Santo-Germano with a quick, rueful smile. "I have no reason to urge you on, for you are already doing all that you may, and I appreciate all your efforts." He sighed. "At least I still have the athanor and the rest of my laboratory equipment. I shall have to make another four packets of gold to compensate for Emerenzio's depredations."

"You will work tonight?" Ruggier asked.

"In the late watches, I will, and the next few nights as well. After I have made another sally through the city." Di Santo-Germano began to pace. "Padre Bonnome tells me, as of this morning, that Pier-Ariana may not be still in Venezia, but he has not found out where she is living. He may be wily and political, but he is glad to have my annual donation once again, and he will help me if he can get more: the roof of San Luca is in need of repair."

Ruggier waited patiently. "Is there anything you would like me to do for now? Is there someone you would like me to enlist in the search?"

Di Santo-Germano shook his head. "If she had shared her blood with me another two times it would be much easier to find her: the Blood Bond would guide me. As it is, I have only a vague sense of her presence." He stopped. "I will have to go about the city, looking for her, and I may not discover anything useful. It is exasperating. She is in need because of me, and I am having difficulty providing her remedy."

"Milano may help, if you enlist him," said Ruggier. "He has been constant in your absence."

"Because his salary was paid through Merveiglio Trevisan, with a report to Emerenzio; he would have had to find other patronage had Emerenzio had control of Milano's salary." Again di Santo-Germano took a turn about the room, asking the air, "What does he *do* with the money he has stolen?"

"The rumor is he gambles," said Ruggier, remaining unflustered.

"Yes; yes." He touched his hands together. "But if that is the case, he has gambled away enough to build and outfit fifty ships. Such losses must occasion some notice, and in a man such as Emerenzio, who is not known to be wealthy, such profligacy should be all the more distinguished since it is so disproportionate to his means."

"Gamblers may lose and then win," said Ruggier.

"Apparently not Emerenzio," was di Santo-Germano's wry rejoinder. "He seems predisposed to lose."

"And that is lamentable: what is reprehensible is that he loses money not his own," said Ruggier.

"Certainly an unfortunate habit," said di Santo-Germano. "But I will shore up my accounts over the next few days; I will have gold in plenty in three days—well beyond what is required to rectify the defaults Emerenzio has occasioned. Once I have brought my various taxes up-to-date I will be allowed to file a complaint about Emerenzio's conduct. I am only sorry that I cannot demand restitution personally and directly, rather than through the Maggior Consiglio."

"Can't you challenge Emerenzio face-to-face to produce his accounts?" Ruggier asked.

"If I were a Venezian, I could. But I am a foreigner, and I must have the permission of the Maggior Consiglio before I take action against a Venezian, no matter how blatant the Venezian's trespass might be." Di Santo-Germano shook his head twice.

"Sic semper Venezia," said Ruggier, coming as close to humor as he ever did.

"Sic; truly," said di Santo-Germano, and went to open one of the shutters, only to notice that the glass in the narrow side-windows had been shattered. He touched the remaining shards warily. "Now, who . . ."

"There are nine broken windows on the ground floor," said Ruggier, a suggestion of perplexity in his remark. "None of the shutters are damaged, so the windows must have been broken to some purpose during the day, or from the inside; at least one shutter would show breakage were that not the case."

"True enough," said di Santo-Germano. "Has Raffaele anything to say about the windows?"

"Only that he has no notion who did it, or why," said Ruggier in a tone that suggested he was not completely persuaded.

"So," said di Santo-Germano, to indicate he agreed with Ruggier. "And the under-cook? What has he to say?"

"Vulpio has told me nothing, but I think he is afraid of Raffaele," said Ruggier. "It may be that to get a candid answer from Vulpio you will have to dismiss Raffaele, or engage a steward to supervise them both."

"No doubt you are right, and I shall seek your advice—but after I have made another attempt to find Pier-Ariana and have made up more gold. I have two small caches of gold I can use for now—until I have made enough to fill my coffers. For now, there are more immediate requirements being visited upon me, and on the gold Emerenzio knows nothing about." Di Santo-Germano patted the black-leather wallet hanging from his narrow, embossed belt of silver links.

"Shall I tell Padre Bonnome that you will donate the money to repair the church roof?"

Di Santo-Germano answered readily. "Why not? It will help to restore my reputation, as well."

"He will be thankful for your gift, I am sure," said Ruggier, his demeanor contained to the point of inscrutability.

"I will take what comfort I can in that knowledge," said di Santo-Germano, an ironic light in his dark eyes. "Money and faith, money and faith—what wonders they promise and what havoc they wreak."

"They do," said Ruggier in superb neutrality.

With a single, sad laugh, di Santo-Germano opened a concealed drawer in the side-panel of the writing-desk and removed a black-leather pouch roughly the size of his hand; the pouch was secured with broad bands of thick Turkish silk, and it clinked as di Santo-Germano tied it to his belt next to the wallet. "But money has its uses: for now I am going out to see if it can lead me to Pier-Ariana."

Text of a letter from Onfroi van Amsteljaxter in Nuremberg to his sister, Erneste van Amsteljaxter in Amsterdam, written in German, carried by regular postal courier, and delivered nineteen days after it was written.

To my most dear sister, presently in Amsterdam at the house of Grav Saint-Germain, my greetings on this, the 10th day of August, 1531, from Nuremberg, where I have come with my good friend, Constans Dykenweld, to investigate the current ructions in this old city. Your reply will find us at the Red Cock near the Cistercian church.

I have in hand the pouch you sent me, and the nine ducats it contains will do much to make my stay here more tolerable than it has been. You answered me most promptly, and in such a generous way that I am more deeply obliged to you than ever. How fortunate that you have an open-handed patron to support you, one who does not mind that you have occasionally to assist your younger brother in his moments of travail.

This place has been in such turmoil as you cannot imagine. Only a few days since we witnessed a flogging of obdurate Catholics by agents of the Protestants in the city, followed two days later by a burning of witches, watched over by monks and priests. The Protestants did not challenge the right of the Catholic clergy to do this, but instead tacitly admitted that in such matters, the Roman Church is more expert than they. It was a shocking thing to see the women, only in plain shifts, being devoured by the fire, their bodies jigging like monkeys as they blackened. One man, who had repented of his witchcraft, was hanged while the women who had served him burned. Surely if the Devil is truly abroad in the land, he is rejoicing in all this cruelty.

I have had no word yet from your publisher, this Grav Saint-Germain you have spoken of so enthusiastically, and you have made it clear that you will not speak up on my behalf to him, regarding the publication of my work. How am I to make my way in the world if you will not extend this very minor support while I seek the same degree of success you have attained for myself? You must understand that, without the endorsement of my former employer, I cannot hope to be engaged as a tutor unless I have some other accomplishment to mitigate my lack of recommendation. Why will you not do your utmost to secure me such an advantage? You cannot want to continue to advance me monies against my eventual engagement, can you? Then why not speak to your Grav and request his consideration of my work?

But I will not hector you, Erneste. You have had much to deal with in the last few months, and although we must always disagree, you and I, as to the wisdom of your actions, we must also respect that both of us have to honor our own consciences, which we have done. If *you will take in abandoned wives and hapless widows, that must be between you and the Grav, in whose house you live. If he has no grounds for complaint, then how can I have any?*

I will remain here for another three months, unless the policies of the town become so stringent that all foreigners are excluded, in which case I will return to Heidelberg, and to my tutoring and letter-writing; I would not like to have to eke out a living in that manner one instant longer than I must, so if you are aware of any opportunities of which I might avail myself, I beseech you to inform me of them at once. I can only hope that some worthy occupation within my scope will present itself, for I will then be able to present myself to the world in a manner appropriate to my station and education. Unlike you, I cannot forget that our mother was the youngest daughter of a landed official of the Emperor, who had the misfortune to fall in love with her brothers' tutor. If our grandfather had lived, I know you and I would not be in our present predicament, but if you will not approach our aunts and uncles, then I will follow your lead, and remain aloof from them, as well. You will have to forgive me if I urge you to reconsider your position from time to time.

At least you are able to maintain yourself fairly well, which is to your credit. I do agree that having other women in your household would make it inappropriate for me to reside with you, for their sake, if not for mine. It would be harmful to me to have it seem I have ambitions that could include being a whoremaster, for no matter how chaste your companions may be, an unmarried man among them makes it impossible to escape calumny, which could stain my character beyond remedy.

I am off now to see a trial of a coachman on a charge of kidnapping. This case is exciting much attention, for the missing man is a follower of Hus, and therefore at odds with both Catholics and most Protestants in Nuremberg, whose disappearance is fortuitous. The rumor is that his kidnapping was arranged by one of the rival clerics, and that the coachman is meant to be a scapegoat for these men, no matter who they may be.

With highest regard and many thanks,
Your devoted brother,
Onfroi van Amsteljaxter

4

"Merveiglio Trevisan was here this morning, with di Santo-Germano, asking how our inquiry into Gennaro Emerenzio's affairs is progressing," said Christofo Sen to his nephew as he closed his office door. He had loosened his stiff collar-ruff, for although the day was blustery, it was hot, and the wind carried the odor of charring on it from fires in the woods between Padova and Stra. "When a Conte—even one from who-knows-where—comes to me in the company of a man of Trevisan's position, what can I do but give them the whole of my attention, and the benefit of what I know?"

"And you told them—?" Leoncio asked. He did his best to look at ease, but he was shamming; he felt as if his careful planning had failed and that he was facing the kind of exposure that could only bring disgrace upon him—something he knew his uncle would not tolerate.

"I told them that I was awaiting a report: which I am." He glared at the handsome young man. "What am I going to tell them, Nipote?"

"You are going to tell them the truth, Zio: that I am doing my utmost to find the missing man. It is no easy thing to find someone who is determined to remain hidden." This was a half-truth, for he had found Gennaro Emerenzio three nights since, and had warned him to go to ground, at least until the furor was over, and the pressure was off both of them.

"Are you?" Christofo asked.

"Am I what?" Leoncio countered, buying a little time to better frame his explanation.

"Are you doing your utmost?" Christofo demanded. "Or are you continuing to visit gaming establishments and spend hours trying to locate that woman you want to make your mistress?"

"I am doing what you have asked me to do," Leoncio responded, stung at such a scathing suggestion.

"You are putting my requests ahead of your pleasures?" Christofo asked as if to drive his point home.

"Of course I am," said Leoncio, standing a little straighter and schooling his features to a demeanor of rectitude.

"Then you must have an idea of how much longer you will require to bring this man to court. You must have eliminated many bolt-holes from your roster—haven't you?" Impatience made him brusque. "Venezia is not so vast that you need weeks and weeks to search its dens of vice."

"The dens are many and hidden, Zio," said Leoncio in as self-effacing a manner as he could summon up. "I have ruled out several possibilities, but too many questions yet remain for me to tell you where this man is to be found. I don't want to give you inadequate information."

Christofo leveled a long, knobby forefinger at Leoncio. "But I am depending upon you to bring Emerenzio to justice, and not in the distant future, but within the month—another twelve days, at most. You know him—you know his habits: you will find him, and you will do it before the week is out, or you will seek other protection than mine." He paused to take a steadying breath. "Do you understand me, Nipote?"

Leoncio hated to be called *nephew* in that demeaning tone, but he stopped himself from making a sharp reply: this was not the time. "Yes, and I will do my—"

"Do not say *utmost* again, Leoncio, unless that is what you actually intend to do," his uncle warned.

"I will make my best effort, Zio mio," Leoncio amended hastily, thinking that Emerenzio should have paid him more to remain silent. "But I don't—"

"You had best do so, for he has a great deal to answer for," said Christofo. "The longer he eludes the courts, the—"

"How do you mean, a great deal?" Leoncio asked, forcing himself to behave more self-assuredly than he actually felt.

"There is, to begin with, a misappropriation of private property, but that is not the worst of it: it appears that this Emerenzio has embezzled more than four thousand ducats from di Santo-Germano alone." Christofo saw the astonishment in Leoncio's eyes. "Yes. More than four thousand ducats. So you see, this is not some petty crime, but a great deal of money, to say nothing of the household goods he seized and sold." He sat down. "I had not realized that di Santo-Germano had

such a great fortune at his command, but clearly, he did, and Emerenzio must answer for its reduction."

"More than four thousand," Leoncio repeated, agog at the staggering sum. "How much more?" The twenty ducats he had been
given three days earlier to delay reporting on Emerenzio's whereabouts, which then seemed more than sufficient to secure his silence,
now felt insulting.

"That hasn't been determined yet; perhaps a great deal more,"
said Christofo, his blue eyes crackling the brilliant light of the edge
of night lightning. "But whatever the amount, the Savii and the Minor Consiglio will want to have a comprehensive auditing of all the
accounts di Santo-Germano has in Venezia, so that some measure of
restitution may be made—assuming such is possible—once we have
Emerenzio in custody. Di Santo-Germano has already pledged to
bring us his own accounts of his businesses here. From what I have
seen thus far, the foreigner has not lost all his money, as Emerenzio
has claimed—far from it: the man is so wealthy, you might think he
coined gold himself." Christofo gave a dry little laugh at his own
witticism.

"I should say so, if he had so much gold to be stolen," Leoncio
seconded his uncle. "More than four thousand ducats! Who would
have thought there was so large a reserve to be pilfered, and from an
exile?"

"Emerenzio, for one," said his uncle, and turned his eyes toward
the door as a servant tapped upon it. "What is it?"

"There is an emissary from Cyprus here to meet with you,
Signor'," said the servant through the door. "He says you are expecting him."

"That I am. Have him wait in the reception hall with the ivory
chairs," said Christofo. "I will be finished here shortly." He looked toward his nephew expectantly.

"Is there anything more you want of me?" Leoncio asked, knowing what was expected of him.

"Only to find out what is your next move, Leoncio?"

"I must unearth more informants, and use their—" He stopped.
"Is there nothing from the Lion's Mouths? Surely there must be
someone other than di Santo-Germano with a complaint against this
man who would entrust it to the Lion?"

"Nothing that I am aware of," said Christofo.

"But there may be," said Leoncio. "Have your clerks look."

"We cannot accept anything unsigned," Christofo reminded his nephew.

"Then you have seen something, something unsigned. Perhaps neither Consiglio can use it, nor the Savii, but I might be able to put it to good use," Leoncio exclaimed. "Won't you tell me what it says?"

"I regret I cannot," said Christofo in the tone of a man used to refusing.

"Emerenzio must have a great deal to answer for," said Leoncio darkly, thinking of the various casette where Emerenzio gambled frequently, and the places he might have taken refuge in the two days since they spoke. "I will go out this afternoon and continue my search."

"Very good," Christofo approved, but without much conviction. "See you are not distracted along the way."

Leoncio ducked his head. "Not I, Zio Christofo. I know where my loyalty lies."

"I should hope so—and that should not be at a gaming table or in the bed of a courtesan," said Christofo, unpersuaded by Leoncio's protestations. "When shall I expect to see you again?"

"Later tonight or, if I find reliable information, tomorrow. If I make a discovery, I will send you word of it at once," he promised, adding to himself that he would get more than a paltry twenty ducats out of Emerenzio to remain silent this time: Emerenzio had misappropriated a fortune, and Leoncio would get his share or he would reveal all he learned about Emerenzio to his uncle and the Savii whom he served—they would reward him for his diligence if Emerenzio would not.

"I shall await your news eagerly," said Christofo, his anticipation as much a warning as an expectancy.

"Si, Zio mio," said Leoncio.

Christofo touched the wen on his cheek—a sure sign that he was considering more than he intended to reveal—and said nonchalantly, "Have you been to the gambling establishments near San Alvise il Vecchio, or Santi Apostoli recently?"

"Is that what the Lion's Mouth—" He hated the thought of an informer knowing about the game he was playing, so he shook his head vigorously. "No. You must not tell me. Whatever you have seen was unsigned and cannot be examined or substantiated. I do understand that. But I am curious why you ask about San Alvise il Vecchio and Santi Apostoli."

"It is simply a question," said Christofo in a tone that did not encourage more inquiry. "The Cypriot emissary is waiting for me. I must leave you, Nipote, to your work."

Leoncio nodded several times. "Yes. Just so, Zio. I thank you for giving me the benefit of your advice."

"Then go and make use of it," Christofo said as he moved to leave the room. "I cannot extend my patience indefinitely. The Doge himself knows of our present investigation, and I will have to tell him something to the point by noon tomorrow."

"I understand," said Leoncio, and held the door for his uncle.

"Do not disappoint me again, Nipote." With that, Christofo Sen left Leoncio standing in the corridor and hurried along to the reception room with ivory chairs.

Leoncio watched him go, and allowed himself the luxury of swearing under his breath. This was becoming more difficult by the hour, and all he had hoped to gain from the protection he had extended to Emerenzio he now saw as paltry amounts for a much greater risk than he had realized he was taking. He lowered his chin onto the umber-damask silk of his doublet, unaware that he had left a smudge of sweat on the glossy fabric. Moving at a steady pace, he left the Palazzo dei Dogei and stepped out into the Piazza San Marco. The hot wind raked the open square, and a number of passersby grasped at their clothing as the frisky air snatched at them. Muttering at the sky, Leoncio hurried along past the Bacino di San Marco to the footbridge that led to Santa Maria del Giglio. As he reached the handsome church, he ducked inside and, after his eyes had adjusted to the dim interior, found himself an empty seat in a rear pew where he could sit and think in relative tranquility. He made an effort to keep his eyes open, so he would not be accused of sleeping in church.

"Are you waiting for the confessional, my son?" asked a priest when Leoncio had been pondering his next move for almost an hour.

Startled, Leoncio looked up. "No, Padre. Not just yet. I am trying to sort out a difficult question, and I hoped your splendid church would help me to—"

"Oh, yes," said the priest, whose face had the weathered texture of a man who had spent many long years at sea. "Contemplate your problems in God's Hands." He sketched a blessing in Leoncio's direction and went off toward the row of private chapels along the side of the nave.

Left to himself, Leoncio found his thoughts supremely blank. No efforts on his part could summon forth a scheme that would benefit him without exposing him to hazards he was unwilling to accept. When the chimes sounded for midday, Leoncio shook himself inwardly and rose, planning to make for the door and the increasing bustle outside. Slowly he made his way to the door and glanced out at the wind-battered throng as if hoping to find some indication of what he should do in the behavior of strangers. "Veneziani," he grumbled as he joined the multitude hurrying to prandium, and then the midday rest.

At San Samuele, Leoncio decided to speed his activities and walked down to the Gran' Canale to signal for a gondola; being well-dressed and having the Sen arms on his dogaline, he was sure he could command one of the sleek Venezian boats without long delay or excessive haggling. When a gondola finally came up to him, having discharged two prosperous merchants across the Gran' Canale at San Barnaba, Leoncio held up a silver Foscar and said, "Santi Apostoli, and two more of the same if you get me there promptly."

The gondolier bowed Leoncio aboard, taking the one Foscar from him, and saying, as he held the boat steady while Leoncio made himself comfortable under the amid-ship awning, "There is a crush of barges and gondole around the Ponte Rialto. If you want speed, I shall have to go around it, past Campo San Angelo, then along to the Merceria, and on from there."

Leoncio sighed. "Do as you must, so long as you move with dispatch."

With a bow that also worked his oar, the gondolier moved off toward his indirect approach to Santi Apostoli, along the busy, narrow waterways to the oddly shaped Campo Santi Apostoli, where he brought the gondola up to the landing and held it steady, allowing Leoncio to disembark. "I have done my part." He doffed his soft cap and held it out for his tip. "No one could get you here any faster at this hour."

At another time, Leoncio would have found a way to keep his coins, but now he cocked his head and handed over the whole amount. "You did well, gondolier, and you have earned this," he said in a rare demonstration of good-will; the last thing he wanted was an argument to draw attention to his presence in this place. "May the Adriatic bring you good fortune."

"And to you," said the gondolier, and shoved away from the landing, bound for the Gran' Canale; his voice floated back on the hot, hard air, calling to the Star of the Sea to look upon him with favor.

"Gondolieri are a superstitious lot," Leoncio said to himself as he stepped away from the landing. Sauntering in an unconcerned manner, Leoncio moved along the narrow walkway that led behind Santi Apostoli to a cluster of buildings near the bridge on his right. Two of the houses were simply what they appeared to be, but the one immediately next to the tavern was something less than a casetta and more than an inn: this was a house of assignation, clandestine and discreet; it was called Le Rose, both for the flower of secrecy and the climbing brambles that went up the walls of the hostelry. Leoncio entered the iron-work gate and stepped into a minuscule courtyard that still carried the perfume of flowers although most of the blooms were spent. Here he was met by an unctuous landlord, who bowed several times and began a long recitation of compliments that Leoncio cut off curtly. "Yes, yes. I am here to see someone."

"Of course, signor', of course," said the landlord, Benedetto Maggier, all but rubbing his hands. "That is one of the purposes of this establishment—to provide a discreet place for private encounters, or for negotiations for uncommon goods. Le Rose is a place for all manner of meetings. Whom did you wish to see?"

Leoncio coughed delicately. "You have a guest—an unofficial guest, as I understand it—a man whose name is not to be mentioned, but who has been here three days; a man who has good reason to keep his presence secret. He is known to be a gamester, and—"

The landlord held up one soft, long hand. "Alas, the man you are seeking is no longer here."

"Not here?" Leoncio did his best not to reveal his annoyance. "That is unfortunate, for I have come with money he is owed."

"That is unfortunate," echoed the landlord.

"Do you expect him to return? Did he mention if he would be

back?" Leoncio could feel cold panic rising in him; if he failed to run Emerenzio to ground, he would lose more than money, and he was unwilling to give up his way of life for the sake of one miscreant's treachery.

"The guest did not inform me; he departed with three men bound for Murano, or so one of them declared." He bowed again, more deeply.

"Murano—how very traditional," said Leoncio: Murano was one of the first-settled islands of Venezia, and some distance from the main part of the city now—famed for its glass-makers, Murano was used by smugglers to avoid taxation on such things as water and wine, fresh vegetables and flour; slaves and runaway sailors took refuge there as well as escaped criminals who could afford to bear the expense of such surreptitious flight.

"He said he was going to the home of his niece," the landlord offered at his most obsequious.

"Oh, yes—Bellafior," Leoncio improvised glibly. "I had forgot about her."

"That is the one," the landlord said, capping Leoncio's lie with his own. "Bellafior."

"Then I suppose I must seek him at Bellafior's house," said Leoncio, and handed the landlord his last Foscari, thinking as he did that wherever Emerenzio had gone—if he had gone at all—it was not to Murano. "I thank you."

"You are truly welcome," the landlord assured him, bowing again before retreating into the interior of the house.

Leoncio did not linger, for he feared he was being observed, and that his inquiries might be noted by those who would use them against him. As obsequious as Benedetto Maggier had been, Leoncio knew he had lied, and that worried him. Deciding that most of Venezia was at table for prandium, he made up his mind to leave while there were few people on the canals and walkways, and his business here could go unnoticed. He satisfied himself that no one was immediately outside Le Rose, then eased out of the courtyard. As he closed the iron gate, he noticed a small boat drawn up beneath the foot-bridge; he slipped into the shadow of Le Rose, prepared to listen, if the boatman turned out to have something useful to impart, and to observe. That the boatman might merely be sheltering from sun and wind did not occur to Leoncio, for there were more comfortable places to do that, and there was no need for such a surreptitious act. So he waited for a quarter of an hour, to be certain the boatman was alone, and then made his way to the edge of the bridge, and called out, "You there!"

The boatman swung around sharply, revealing a pockmarked face and a missing ear. "You want me?" He had a half-eaten apple in one hand and a wedge of cheese laid out on an old piece of linen.

The sight of this ordinary repast calmed Leoncio. "Yes, boatman, I do," he said, moving a little closer. "I have some questions to ask you. I will pay you well for honest answers."

"Ask as you want," said the boatman; his voice was flat and his accent was that of Grado, to the east.

"Perhaps I should come down to your boat? We could speak more privately, and—"

"—we would not be easily observed," the boatman finished for him. "Come ahead if you must."

"Very good of you," Leoncio said as he climbed down beneath the bridge.

"You have something you want of me," said the boatman, a cynical light to his lopsided smile. "Tell me what you are looking for, and what you are willing to pay, and I will tell you if I can assist you."

"I am searching for a man and a woman. They are not together, and the man is the more urgent matter," said Leoncio as he got into the boat. "If you can help me find the man by this time tomorrow, I will give you four ducats for your help." He hated offering so much, but he wanted to convince the boatman that he was serious in his pursuit.

"A fair sum. The man must be a desperate rogue," said the boatman, rasping the stubble on his jaw with his thumbnail.

"He has absconded with—" Leoncio suddenly realized he might be inciting more greed in the boatman if he said too much, so he finished lamely, "—with the funds from a foreign merchant's voyage."

"A shabby thing to do," said the boatman, setting his oars in the oarlocks and beginning to row. "Such things give Venezia a bad name in the world."

"I have been sent to find him, so he may be brought to court," said Leoncio, hoping to impress the boatman.

"Then you may ask what you like." He was a short distance from the bridge by now, moving slowly but steadily toward the lagoon. "If you find my information useful, you may pay me when you have secured that criminal you seek."

Watching the blank-faced buildings, Leoncio had a moment of panic. "Where are we going?"

"We are going where we cannot be overheard," said the boatman. "Isn't that what you wanted?"

Text of a letter from Ulrico Baradin in Venezia to Franzicco Ragoczy, il Conte di Santo-Germano, Campo San Luca, Venezia; carried by footman and delivered the day it was written.

To the most esteemed Conte di Santo-Germano, Franzicco Ragoczy, the greetings of Ulrico Baradin, broker of paper and inks in the Repubblica Veneziana:

I have your order and the orders from Giovanni Boromeo, and I am just about to receive three pallets of paper, each pallet holding four hundred eighty-eight sheets each, of fine-grain heavy stock, rag-based, all sheets suitable for quartering. If you are willing to authorize the purchase, I will need ten ducats to secure the paper, and another ten upon delivery, to cover not only the cost of the paper itself, but to pay my commission for the work I have done. I will accept the equivalent amount in other coinage—florins are acceptable, and reals—should your coffers not be full at this time. Also, I am about to bid on another six pallets of similar weight and content, and sheets twenty percent larger, if this order may be of any interest to you. I will need to have your answer in five days, and your deposit of twelve ducats.

In addition, I have found a supplier of ink that is especially high quality: the density is excellent, and it does not bleed through the paper in spite of its density. The characters it prints are sharply delineated, and it resists smudging once dry. The ink is available in black, red, and an intense blue, all of which may prove useful to Signor' Boromeo, and which I have already demonstrated to him, to show its worth for all of you.

It may be that the inks will not be available next year, for they are made near Zurich and the maker has warned me that he has been informed that he is not to sell to Catholics or to Catholic countries, for fear that what they publish may not be used to the benefit of Protestants. This man has given me his word that he will honor orders placed before All Saint's, but he cannot vouch for his inks being available after Christmas, at least not to Venezia. If you have some means of purchasing inks in Protestant regions and having them brought here, I not only urge you to take advantage of them, I ask you to make such buying arrangements available to me, in return for which I will halve my commission from you.

If you are uninterested in the ink or the paper, please send me answer by my messenger so that I may notify my other clients that these lots are available. Your patronage has been so constant and so generous that I have offered these to you before telling anyone else about them. With summer coming to an end, and the autumn storms about to begin, you will want to have a good supply of paper and ink on hand; you do not want to have a slack winter for lack of supplies, I am certain.

Let me assure you that this offer is accurate and genuine—I am not as gullible as I have sometimes been in the past, and I have been at pains to ensure that my goods are of the quality described, so you may be confident that you will get full value for money. I will not be satisfied with inferior products, and I do not ask any of my clients to be so.

With every surety of my continued dedication to your work

> *And with grateful respect,*
> *Ulrico Baradin*
> *factor and broker in papers and inks*

At Venezia, on the 18ᵗʰ day of August, 1531

5

"But the man is a respectable widower," Pier-Ariana's cousin Marcantonio Rosseli said to her over the dining table. "With my father dead these ten months, I am mindful of my duty to take you in, since you are not sponsored by your patron any longer—more's the pity that his business should fail so terribly, and he be gone—yet you have some money to contribute here from the house you have claim to in Venezia, but I will not allow you to remain here forever—I cannot. You have a duty to your family to wed—at last. Cornelio Paschetti is an honorable man, Cugina, with sufficient money to keep you well enough; he is the best instrument-maker in Verona, and his work is praised everywhere. You would be an asset to him, as a musician." He sat back, the force of his emotion making color rise in his face. "Your mother would expect you to make the most of this offer, if she were still alive."

Pier-Ariana sat very still on the women's side of the table; her face was pale and her mouth was hardly more than a thin line. She felt her cousin's wife nudge her in the side, and realized she had to say something. "I know you mean well by me, Cugin', and I am deeply grateful to you for taking me in, but until I know how matters stand with the Conte, I cannot make such a decision as you ask of me, not without careful consideration, and a better acquaintance with Signor' Paschetti."

"He will come to visit here if I tell him he is welcome," said Marcantonio. "You will not have to decide without knowing something about the man."

"And if I should say I would rather not receive him, what then? Would you decide to require me to accept his suit?" asked Pier-Ariana, moving her hands under the table so Marcantonio would not see them tremble. "Is my willingness to be courted a condition of my continuing welcome in your house?"

The five other women on their side of the table flinched at Pier-Ariana's challenge, his mother-in-law, Tiberia, going so far as to cross herself at such temerity; Marcantonio's oldest step-daughter blushed deeply and looked across the room as if to vanish from the meal.

"No, no, of course not," said Marcantonio, but added fretfully, "But unless you want to be known as a woman of questionable character, you had better encourage the attentions of a well-respected man. Otherwise you will risk gaining such repute as no man would be likely to—"

"To what?" Pier-Ariana waited for a long moment. "Well?"

"You have been in Verona more than two months," said Marcantonio bluntly. "If you plan to return to Venezia, you would do well to leave before the end of September, when the weather changes, and so you can make plans for the winter."

"I haven't made up my mind, Cugin'," said Pier-Ariana with more firmness than before. "If you would rather I go elsewhere—"

"No, no," said Marcantonio. "I won't have it be said that I turned out a relative in distress, and a good Catholic."

"For the sake of my late mother," said Pier-Ariana, "and the two ducats I provide every month." It was the entire amount she received from the Pisan merchant currently residing in the house di Santo-Germano had taken for her, and she paid it reluctantly, for it was the only money she had in the world.

Marcantonio glowered in Pier-Ariana's direction. "If you will not listen to me, then speak to my wife: Serafina is a sensible and worthy woman, whose grasp of such matters is admirable. Since you do not seem to apprehend the perils of your situation, she will explain your circumstances more effectively than I can, and why Cornelio Paschetti has been most generous in his offer." He smiled at Serafina. "She understands how such things must work."

"Because she, as a widow, needed support for herself, her mother, and her children, and so married you?" Pier-Ariana inquired.

Serafina's smile did not reach her eyes. "You and I should talk, Pier-Ariana," she said, with a quick glance at her three daughters: the scarlet-cheeked Giacinta, the deliberately preoccupied Feriga, and the sweet-featured Orsola.

"If you insist," said Pier-Ariana, and rounded on her cousin. "If you will excuse me, Cugino, I will leave the table." She got to her feet and stepped away from the table. "I find I have lost my appetite."

"Pier-Ariana—no," said Serafina. "You mustn't—"

But Pier-Ariana was halfway to the door, and she would not look around. As she closed the door behind her, she heard excited conversation erupt among the remaining diners. She resisted the urge to pause and listen, making for her rooms at the rear of the house. As she climbed the stairs to the second floor, she had to bite the insides of her cheeks to keep from crying. Once in her bedchamber, she gave vent to the turbulent emotions gripping her, but her tears carried with them no release or anodyne solace. She mourned her music, her life in Venezia, her time with di Santo-Germano, her heartache so intense that she could barely breathe. By the time she wiped her eyes, she was in a more desolate state of mind than before she had left the dining table.

In an effort to restore her equilibrium she reached for her virginals and began to play; the melody that wove itself through her fingers was plaintive and sad, turning her thoughts more forlorn than they had been. She stopped her music in mid-phrase and, instead of trying another tune, rose and went to the small window on the east side of the room, where she looked out at the small kitchen garden below. Some little distance beyond the garden wall, she could see the curve of the walls of the old amphitheatre, built long ago by the Romans, rising over this quarter of Verona, and the tall spire on the Capella di Santa Pomona, said to have been a pagan temple before it was a church. Other buildings claimed her attention as the day waned, a distraction from her misery. She remained there until the night faded all the details from soft grays to deep, ill-defined shadows. Returning to her virginals, she lit three oil-lamps using flint-and-steel, and finally resumed playing, carried by her despondency at the bleak outlook presented to her.

As the family came up from the ground floor to go to bed, a tap on Pier-Ariana's door announced the arrival of Serafina. "Pier-Ariana, you and I must talk."

Tempted though she was to send Marcantonio's wife away, Pier-Ariana sighed and called out, "Come in, Serafina."

Needing no more invitation than that, Serafina entered the room, a candle in her hand to show that this was to be an important discussion. "I heard you playing. We all did."

"Thank you," said Pier-Ariana, closing the virginals in case Serafina's remark was not a compliment.

"My husband has asked me to speak with you," Serafina began.

"I am aware of it," said Pier-Ariana.

"Then you must also know what he expects me to say," Serafina said, pulling herself up with all the dignity she could summon.

"He expects you to advise me," said Pier-Ariana with the semblance of humility. "You are here to do his bidding—along his recommendation."

"His and mine are one," said Serafina.

"He expects you to explain the advantages of marriage to me," said Pier-Ariana, trying unsuccessfully to look compliant.

"That he does—and I pray you will listen," she said, and launched into the first phase of her argument. "It must surely be apparent to you that you have put yourself at a marked disadvantage, given your age and your . . . recent distresses, and it is only through the deep concern of your family that any chance for a decent life is still available to you. I beg you, keep in mind what your presence may do to the position of us all." She sat on the end of the narrow bed, for Pier-Ariana was occupying the only chair in the room. "I don't want to prolong our discussion, because it is pleasant for neither of us."

"But your husband has instructed you, hasn't he?" Pier-Ariana asked, doing her best not to sound too indignant at this attempt to coerce her into a marriage she did not want.

"For your sake, yes, and for the rest of us, as well," said Serafina, pausing as if to muster her arguments. "For women, marriage is a necessity, if there is no inclination for the religious life, and no parent or sibling needing a woman's care. You are not crippled or ugly, so you have a reasonable expectation, even now, of making a worthwhile alliance. Signor' Paschetti is a man of good character, one who has much to offer a woman like you. Do not make light of his courtship. Marriage is the path most of us must tread, and many have fared less well than you would with Signor' Paschetti. All women must weigh such advantages against their inclinations; otherwise we bring dishonor to ourselves and our families."

"So I have been taught, and not only by Cugin' Marcantonio," said Pier-Ariana, who had heard this contention since she was old enough to listen: her mother, the local priest, her aunt in Holy Orders, her playmates, her nursemaid, all impressed upon her the obligation to marry as her family wished. Only her father's loss of money and subsequent death had altered these admonitions, allowing her to pursue her musical aspirations. "You don't think you can find many husbands willing to overlook my past in Venezia."

Rather than blush, Serafina gave a single, decisive nod. "I am glad you grasp the nature of the problem. Your patron did well by you when he was in Venezia and had his fortune, but you can no longer rely on his support, nor can you remain here in so ill-defined a capacity. The convent of San Apollonius would be glad to have you as a tertiary, to direct the choir of the orphanage, but you say you lack religious vocation, so it must be marriage, and sooner rather than later. At least Cornelio Paschetti has not spoke of any deep disapproval of your abilities, so long as you abandon your playing outside the family, although he may occasionally ask you to demonstrate his instruments. The sooner your own music is forgotten, the better it will be for all of us."

Pier-Ariana was unable to speak, and so she stared at her oil-lamps, swallowing hard three times as she strove to maintain a semblance of control of her temper. "Suppose," she began, "I had been a widow? Would it then be so hard to secure a husband for me?"

"That is entirely different," said Serafina. "You would have your husband's family to provide you a living."

"Yours didn't," Pier-Ariana remarked. "You married Marcantonio because it was that or penury."

"I have three daughters who must be dowered and wed, and who need a place in the world," said Serafina stiffly. "I cannot provide any of those things for them, nor can my first husband's family, with four dead from Swine Fever, along with my late husband. Your cousin did not have to agree to the match, but he did. I would have been irresponsible and contumacious had I refused his offer." She coughed. "Your cousin is a good man—kindly and generous. I have been most blessed in this marriage, and that, in itself, is reason enough for you to consider Cornelio Paschetti's offer."

"So you wed Marcantonio for the sake of your daughters, which was probably very prudent. But I have no children." Pier-Ariana fell to musing. Finally she said, "There are two books of my songs. They are being sold." She did not mention she had completed part of a third which she had promised to deliver to Giovanni Boromeo as soon as it was done.

Serafina nodded, not comprehending Pier-Ariana's meaning. "That is unfortunate, but I must suppose you cannot withdraw them now; the printer expects to recoup the cost of his printing, and he must do something with your patron no longer in a position to bear those expenses, no matter what it means to your reputation. It is a difficult impasse, to be sure, for the printer cannot give up sales for the sake of your family."

"I will have a little income from the books," Pier-Ariana reminded Serafina.

"But it is a small amount and once the books are sold, it will be gone." Serafina shook an admonitory finger at Pier-Ariana. "You must not depend upon such things, for they will fail you."

"Does Signor' Paschetti know about the two books?" Pier-Ariana asked, hoping this would end her awkwardness.

For the first time, Serafina lacked a prepared answer. "I . . . I believe something was mentioned."

"But you don't know what," Pier-Ariana guessed. "That was the part your husband glossed over, wasn't it?"

"I wouldn't put it that way," Serafina said huffily. "It isn't fitting for me to know about such dealings where you are concerned, given that the relation between us is in law, not in blood. You are not my daughter, or any part of my family: you're my husband's cousin."

With a glint of mischief in her eyes, Pier-Ariana said, "Yes, and for that reason, I should think you'd want this Cornelio Paschetti for Giacinta or Feriga, since he is such a good match."

Unaware of the barb in Pier-Ariana's observation, Serafina smiled; there was a hint of triumph in her demeanor. "Neither Giacinta nor Feriga have any reason to accept Signor' Paschetti: both of them have engagements of long-standing, and each will be married when she turns fifteen."

"So late," Pier-Ariana marveled.

"Young enough," said Serafina, again failing to detect the satiric intent of Pier-Ariana's words. "I think it is wrong to marry a girl off as soon as she has her first bleeding: better to give them a little time to accustom themselves to the world of grown women and the duties of running a household. Those old-fashioned parents who send a bride to the husband's family at eight do their daughters a disservice. Such conduct may serve very well for nobles, who often have to find brides from far away, but for honest merchants and tradesmen, it is not fitting."

"Then you should have approved of all the things my mother did for me," said Pier-Ariana.

"It was well-done of her to permit you to learn music—that is a skill all women should have—but her encouraging you to seek out such a life for yourself was, at the best, short-sighted. She was not thinking of the man you would marry or what the world would believe of you." She was warming to her purpose now, and her words came more quickly. "You are not young any longer, Pier-Ariana, and your abilities, although commendable in their place, cannot recommend you to any prudent man except one such as Paschetti."

"Do you think that he is apt to be a good husband?" Pier-Ariana asked.

"I think that any husband is a good husband for you at this point," said Serafina somberly. "And the sooner you are wed, the better."

"It would spare you embarrassment?" Pier-Ariana opened the virginals and began to play again, noticing that the two lowest strings needed tuning.

"It would make our life here easier, I admit it," said Serafina, as if performing a distasteful-but-necessary duty.

"Even though you would lose two ducats a month?" Pier-Ariana's smile was provocative. "I had no notion I was such a burden."

Now Serafina flushed, her cheeks plum-colored, her forehead the color of new roof-tiles. "I would not mind the loss of those ducats if you would be happily established."

"With Signor' Paschetti," said Pier-Ariana, and began to play more vigorously.

"He is willing to have you," said Serafina. "You must not forget that."

"How can I, with you to remind me?" Pier-Ariana put most of her attention on her playing, offering no apology for her discourtesy.

After listening to Pier-Ariana play for more than ten minutes, Serafina rose from the bed. "Well, I will leave you to think over all I have said. I know you will do what is in the best interests of us all." She started toward the door. "If you refuse this opportunity, you will be the most ungrateful jade in all of Verona."

Pier-Ariana continued to play even after the door closed behind Serafina. Concentrating on the sounds made by the instrument, she deliberately shut out all noises in the house, worried that she would be even more unmannerly with anyone coming to speak to her; so she was surprised when, more than an hour later, there was an emphatic rap on her door, and Marcantonio himself requested that she come down to receive a visitor. "A visitor?"

"He arrived a quarter of an hour ago; he and I have been talking," said Marcantonio. "About your future, Cugina."

"Unexpected, I am sure," she said, striking a jangling chord.

"Most unexpected," Marcantonio confirmed. "He is waiting for you." He cleared his throat. "I told him you would receive him."

Dreading this ordeal, Pier-Ariana finished the passage she was playing, and then closed the lid of the virginals as if it were a coffin containing all her music. "I'm coming," she called out, and started toward the door.

"Make haste," Marcantonio urged her.

"I'm coming, I'm coming," she repeated, lagging as much as she could. She stepped out into the corridor, wondering if she should challenge this obvious ploy as what it was.

"I would have thought you were more curious than this," said Marcantonio, trying to lighten Pier-Ariana's state of mind. "Didn't you hear the horse in the courtyard?"

"I'm sorry, Cugin', I was preoccupied," said Pier-Ariana, starting down the narrow stairs behind him. She went as slowly as she dared, anticipating her meeting with Cornelio Paschetti—for surely the new arrival could be no one else—with simmering rancor. How she detested having her hand forced! What would she say to this man? If only she had the courage to return to her room.

"Pray make yourself more presentable," Marcantonio admonished her. "You don't want to appear unconcerned."

Pier-Ariana pulled at her guimpe in a desultory fashion. "Where have you put this guest?"

"In the parlor," said Marcantonio. "The servants have lit all the lamps and are bringing in candles."

"Such extravagance," Pier-Ariana exclaimed; she was a little startled that her cousin had gone to such trouble for her suitor. Signor' Paschetti must have some money, or be able to provide other advantages to Marcantonio's cousin to merit so grand a reception.

"Try not to look down-cast," Marcantonio chided her.

"Why should I do so?" Pier-Ariana asked with false cheer. "You have gone to a great effort on my behalf."

Marcantonio shook his head. "Tiberia is in the anteroom, to chaperone. She will remain there while you talk with this visitor. I will make sure your good name is protected while you are under my roof." He opened the door and offered more of a bow than would usually be given to a man of equal social position as Marcantonio's. "Mia cugina, Pier-Ariana Salier."

Pier-Ariana stepped into the parlor, noticing how bright the room was—another demonstration of respect; she held her head high and she fixed a brittle smile on her lips. "God send you a good evening," she said, on her best behavior. Behind her she heard the door close, and it seemed as loud as the shot of a cannon.

The man on the far side of the room turned around, revealing a long, black-and-silver riding habit under a knee-length cloak of black wool lined in dark-red silk. "Pier-Ariana," he said.

She stared in astonishment. "Di Santo-Germano," she whispered; she began to shake.

He took two steps toward her, then stopped. "I am so pleased to see you again, Pier-Ariana."

"What are you doing here? of all places," she asked, still nonplussed. She felt as if all the world had slowed down, and she was moving as if through a conjuration. That's it, she told herself. I have fallen asleep at the virginals and this is my dream.

"I came to find you," he said, and held out his hands to her. "I thank all the forgotten gods I have found you."

She went toward him, hesitant to touch him for fear he would vanish. "How did you know I am here?" Suddenly she felt signally calm, as if she had done all this before, and she stopped trembling.

As her hand slid into his, he lifted it to his lips. "I did not know; this is a welcome discovery. I came here because I hoped your cousin could tell me where you had gone."

"Here," she said remotely; the sensation of his kiss ran up her arm like a shock. "I came here. There was nowhere else to go." She moved close to him and leaned her head on his shoulder, holding her breath so that she could bask in his presence without any dereliction of attention.

"I am sorry you have had to endure this on my account," he told her; she could summon up no words for this ineffable moment. He kissed her forehead. "You have to breathe, you know."

She sighed. "I know. But I don't want this to end."

"Is there some reason it should? Why should a breath interfere?" he asked.

"I don't want to wake up," she said, and laughed sadly. "I will soon have to decide to marry Signor' Paschetti, the instrument-maker, and I would so much rather be with you."

"Then you shall be," said di Santo-Germano. "Tonight, if you wish. It is all arranged."

"Arranged?" She began to think she was awake, after all, and that the impossible had happened. "What has been arranged? With whom?"

"With your cousin. I have provided him the means for you to live independently, if that is your wish, and given him extra for the care he has provided you in my absence," he said. "Were it in my power, I would give the money directly to you, but—"

"Marcantonio would have to administer the money in any case," she finished for him. "Marcantonio or a well-reputed priest."

"Lamentably, yes," said di Santo-Germano, recalling the many times Olivia had expressed her dismay at this development, and what it had cost her over the centuries.

"But you have made arrangements, you say," she prompted him.

"I have. You may establish a house of your own where you like, if you do not want to come back to Venezia with me."

She blinked and stared at him. "Are you in earnest?"

"Never more so," he assured her.

"And I am to return to Venezia?" Her smile grew brighter. "Will I have my music?"

"If that is where you wish to go, and what you wish to do," he said, his voice dropping to a low, caressing pledge.

"How would you decide?" She considered him carefully, remembering his admonition about the dangers of gratitude.

"If it were up to me? —to Venezia, to your house, or to mine. I have secured another house for you there, and paid its price, secured you a deed of ownership through the Savii, and you will not have to give up the house, or its staff, at any time in your life. All that is arranged."

"How?" She took half a step back from him so she would not be so overwhelmed with the sight and the sound and the feel of him.

"Through contracts and payment," he said, lightly touching the wisp of hair that escaped from beneath her starched lace cap. "As all things are done in Venezia."

"But your fortune is gone," she said, shaking her head in disbelief. "How can you afford such extravagance?"

"I do not depend on a single city, or a single business, for my wealth, Pier-Ariana."

"Then what happened? There was no money, I am sure of it." She clutched his hand between her own. "Your business factor explained it all to me, most apologetically, but nonetheless—"

"A great deal of money was embezzled from me, but my fortune is still fairly intact. You need not fear that you will be imposed upon again." The grim line of his lips were belied by the warmth in his dark eyes. "I have taken pains to be sure that you cannot suffer such hardships again upon my account."

"But you will leave me again, will you not?" She took the padded sleeves of his riding habit in her hands, holding them with determination.

"It is the nature of my trading and other dealings that I travel," di Santo-Germano told her. "I cannot change that. If you would prefer to return to Venezia but not to more than my patronage, then I will abide by your decision."

Had she not endured her stay in Marcantonio's household, she might have been tempted to challenge him by accepting his terms; but she realized that she did not want to lose any time she might have with him, not after the nightmare of the last seven weeks. "I prefer to enjoy your company when it is available," she said.

He kissed her hand again, this time the palm. "Then I am at your service." He paused. "This time will be five. I have told you the danger of six, have I not?"

Still exalted by his kiss. she wanted to answer him, but thought of Tiberia in the anteroom, listening. "You have." With an urgent cry, she pulled him to her. "Take me away from here, Conte. Take me back to Venezia, or to Alexandria, or Valencia, or the New World."

He held her close to him, astonished at the renewal of vitality within her. "Will you go to a villa for tonight? It is two leagues away, and it will be midnight by the time we arrive there."

"Anywhere, so long as it is with you," she said, and welcomed the promise of passion in his kiss.

Text of a note from Basilio Cuor to Christofo Sen, carried by messenger.

To the well-regarded secretary of the Savii, Christofo Sen, my most devoted greetings.

This is to assure you that I am once again in Venezia, and that I have some information in regard to di Santo-Germano, as he calls himself here, that may be of significance to you. I will deliver it in person to you at whatever place and whatever time you require. There is much we must do if you are to achieve the purpose of your inquiries.

In haste, although entirely at your service,
Basilio Cuor

presently at Le Rose, on the 4ᵗʰ day of September, 1531

6

The young clerk handed di Santo-Germano the copy of his formal complaint. "If this is accurate, please affix your signet here." He indicated a place at the bottom of the page, his manner as officious as his position was subordinate.

Di Santo-Germano read the copy carefully, then offered the clerk a Spanish silver Emperor. "For your good service. If I may have wax?" He was in an elegant doublet-and-dogaline of black-damask silk, the turned-back dogaline sleeves lined in deep-red satin. His hose ended just above the knee and were secured with small silver buckles set with rubies; his camisa was silk edged in lace, of perfect whiteness. Only the thick soles on his shoes were a bit unfashionable, but that was a minor flaw in an otherwise faultless appearance.

"Here," said the clerk, offering a box of hard sealing-wax tapers and a lit candle. "This should serve your purpose."

"Thank you," said di Santo-Germano, selecting the darkest-red wax in the box and setting its wick to burn. "How soon before this complaint is presented?"

"No more than ten days; I am not at liberty to say more than that," said the clerk. "You have powerful friends here in Venezia, and they have urged the court to act swiftly."

"Then I must thank my Venezian friends, for advancing my cause so speedily," said di Santo-Germano, who had already done so. He dropped the hot wax with care and used his signet ring to impress his eclipse device on the wax. "There. The original will remain with you until the case is heard?"

"That is the procedure." The clerk studied the seal. "This will serve very well."

"Excellent," di Santo-Germano said, and glanced toward the window and the shiny fog. "I shall await your notification of when my presence is required."

"The case will proceed whether or not we find Signor' Emerenzio." The clerk pointed to the door, a hint that their business was finished. "That much is assured."

"So I understand," said di Santo-Germano. "I am prepared to wait for my judgment if I must."

"You realize that since you are a foreigner, the state is not responsible for providing redress for the theft, since Gennaro Emerenzio is a Venezian." This last caveat was delivered hesitantly, as if the clerk feared that di Santo-Germano might become irate.

"That was explained to me when I first opened my trading company here, taking over from my cousin, as you will see in your records," said di Santo-Germano, preparing to leave.

"There may be other witnesses at your hearing," the clerk warned.

"I understand," said di Santo-Germano.

"The advocates will be allowed to present evidence about you that has no direct bearing on this case. You understand that, too?" The clerk was speaking as if by rote, and he paid almost no attention to the response di Santo-Germano made.

"As an exile living in Venezia, the court is permitted wider leeway with this case, as it is being brought against a Venezian. I understand."

"Very good," said the clerk, rapidly losing interest in the foreigner, and taking up the tone of ill-concealed tedium.

"Do you require anything more of me?" di Santo-Germano asked.

"If we do, you will be notified by one of our messengers," said the clerk. "There is nothing more we need from you today."

"Fine," said di Santo-Germano, and left the clerk's office, bound for the water-steps and Ca' Fosian.

In answer to his signal, Milano drew up di Santo-Germano's gondola to the loading step, saying as he did, "I believe you are being followed, Conte."

"Very likely," said di Santo-Germano, settling down in the boat. "Ca'—"

"Fosian. I remember," said Milano, starting out of the Rivi Sotto la Piazza and into the Bacino di San Marco where a number of ships were being unloaded—ships with the colors and banners of more than two dozen ports. Milano moved among these much larger vessels with the ease of expertise. "They say three merchant-ships were taken by corsairs, and three galleys. The oarsmen are now chained to an Ottoman pirate's bench, if they aren't dead."

"Has there been any talk of ransom?" di Santo-Germano asked.

"Not yet, but very likely we will hear something soon." He skirted a pair of barges. "If the crews are to be ransomed, all merchants will have to contribute to the payment—foreigner merchants in particular."

"I would assume so," said di Santo-Germano.

"Another charge on your purse," Milano said indignantly.

"I can bear it, if it is not too outrageous a sum." He put his hand to his brow, for the thin fog glared and the water shone so harshly that his night-seeing eyes began to ache.

Milano saw this, and said, "I will keep watch, Conte. You have nothing to fear." He cocked his chin in the direction of a northern ship flying the colors of Lubeck. "Those Protestants will bear the brunt of the cost of the ransoms this time, and with the blessings of the Pope and the Emperor."

"Doesn't that strike you as a fine as much as a ransom?" di Santo-Germano asked.

"Yes, and who better to bear it?" Milano pushed the oar firmly and the gondola slipped across the Bacino di San Marco, toward Ca' Fosian.

"The merchants whose men are captured," said di Santo-Germano. "In the past I have always paid the ransoms asked for my men."

"Except the last time," Milano reminded him.

Di Santo-Germano's demeanor changed subtly, but emphatically. "Yes; a most deplorable consequence of his theft. Of all things, that is the one that Emerenzio must answer for more than the rest: that he let men in my employ die needlessly—" He stopped. "As I shall ask the courts to determine."

"May God favor your cause, Conte," said Milano. For the next several minutes, Milano was occupied with guiding his craft, and kept his concentration on his efforts. He negotiated the narrow space between two other gondole, then moved off down the Gran' Canale.

"How very deft you are," di Santo-Germano said when they were nearing Ca' Fosian. "I should not be very long; Consiglier Fosian asked to have a moment of my time when I was through with the clerk."

"Very good. I will go to La Onda Bianca for a glass of wine." He nodded to the small tavern a short distance from Ca' Fosian. "You may find me there if I am not here."

"Very good," said di Santo-Germano, tossing two copper coins to Milano as he got out of the gondola. "Enjoy yourself."

"Tante grazie," said Milano, shoving his oar to get moving again.

Di Santo-Germano climbed the three steps to the loggia where he was met by the under-steward, who welcomed the Conte to Ca' Fosian and asked whose name he should announce. "I am Franzicco Ragoczy di Santo-Germano here to see Consiglier Fosian. I believe he is expecting me."

"So he is," said the under-steward. "He is in his counting-room, where—"

"Where he would prefer I not go," said di Santo-Germano with unflustered affability. "I would not expect him to receive guests in that chamber; I am not discontented."

"How good of you to understand," said the under-steward as he led di Santo-Germano to a small, beautiful reception room. "Is there any refreshment you would like?"

"I think not, thank you," said di Santo-Germano. He selected a Turkish chair upholstered in fine tooled leather and moved it so that it was not quite so near the window and the water beyond. He sat down, smiling as its jointed frame shifted to accommodate him, and smiled. "This is quite satisfactory."

The under-steward withdrew, returning to his post in the loggia.

In less than half an hour, Orso Fosian came into the reception room, saying as he did, "My brother will be joining us shortly, di

Santo-Germano. There are a few matters we would do well to review."

This lack of formal greeting alerted di Santo-Germano that something was wrong, but nothing in his manner or expression revealed this as he rose to his feet and said, "I am delighted to be a guest in your house, Consiglier, and I thank you for being willing to discuss my pending case with you."

"You may not be when this meeting is through," Fosian said with a deepening frown. "But I ask you to believe that these problems are not of my making—nor, I suspect, are they of yours. I doubt you would do anything so foolish as the claim declares. Were it my decision to make, we would handle this more privately, and with fewer issues brought into it."

"I see that it has caused you some distress," said di Santo-Germano, who had only the first inkling of what Fosian was talking about. "Then you have my full attention."

"For which I am grateful. Some men would not tolerate any mention of such a calumny as this one and would leave my house for saying even this much. You have a cooler head than most, which you will need before this is over." He clapped his hands and told the footman who appeared almost upon the instant, "Bring me wine, the dark-red from Torrecella, and some new bread."

"At once," said the footman, and hurried away.

"He will probably bring glasses and bread for two," said Fosian.

"No matter. You will have them for your brother," said di Santo-Germano, wondering which of Orso Fosian's three brothers was expected: one was on the Galley of Romania and was not likely to return to Venezia for another month, leaving two other brothers in Venezia.

"Yes," said Fosian, continuing as if he knew what di Santo-Germano was thinking, "Segalo will be joining us."

"From the Arsenal," said di Santo-Germano.

"Exactly. His duty there ended a quarter hour ago and he will come here directly." Fosian pulled at his short, gristled beard. Finally he cleared his throat, then said awkwardly, "I am afraid that certain circumstances have . . . have been allowed to become a part of your hearing that may—" He broke off as another gondola arrived. "Ah. Segalo is here."

"I shall be glad to renew my acquaintance with him," di Santo-Germano said, turning toward the door.

"Segalo Fosian," announced the under-steward as he admitted the new arrival to the reception room.

Seven years younger than his brother Orso, Segalo Fosian was dressed in a heavy canvas doublet and leather hose with grieves over his lower legs. He was well-muscled and broad-shouldered; white knots of scars on his hands attested to the hard labor he supervised at the Arsenal. There was a skeptical cast to his features that was not present in Orso's face, and this sharpened as he took stock of the two men in the room. He went to touch cheeks with his brother, then swung around and looked steadily at di Santo-Germano, his face twisted with concentration. "Well," he announced as he completed his swift inspection, "he doesn't look like a kidnapper, I'll say that much. That may be of some help when you appear at the hearing."

"What does a kidnapper look like?" di Santo-Germano asked, bemused.

"Not like a dignitary," said Segalo. "Or like a man able to handle his own affairs without recourse to scoundrels."

In spite of his formidable composure, di Santo-Germano blinked in surprise. "I should think not."

"There are those who say otherwise in your regard, or there would be no reason for concern—men much closer to the Savii and the Minor Consiglio than you are—no insult to you, Orso," he appended.

"I didn't suppose so," said Orso Fosian quietly. "But I had not yet explained to di Santo-Germano what has transpired in the last two days. You stole the wind from me on this, Segalo."

"Oh." He looked from his brother to di Santo-Germano. "I thought you must know by now. I never meant to distress you."

"You have not—not yet, in any case," said di Santo-Germano, moving back toward the Turkish chair. "Whom am I believed to have kidnapped?"

Orso made a fussy gesture with his gnarled hands. "There's time enough to discuss this after we have had some wine and bread."

"Yes, indeed," said Segalo. "You cannot think what a—" He broke off at a signal from his brother. "I have heard," he went on to di Santo-Germano, "that you left an account to pay ransoms for your oarsmen and crews, and it is as empty as all the rest. Badly done, very badly done."

"It was," said di Santo-Germano, "and all the more so because some of those oarsmen and crew have died because of it."

The footman knocked before bringing wine and bread into the room, along with a plate of broiled scallops. He set these on an ornate table from Trebizond, then left the three men alone.

"Take what pleases you," said Orso, reaching for the bottle of wine and one of the three glasses. As he poured, he said, "Some have been saying that you never had money in the ransom account— that you claimed you did, only so men would sign on with you, believing you had enough to ransom them, if that should be needed." He handed the glass to his brother, then poured a glass for himself.

"That would be very foolish of me, as well as contrary to Venezian law," said di Santo-Germano, once again giving no sign of being flustered.

"I hope you will be so sensible in days to come," said Segalo. "You must know that all you do is being scrutinized."

"So I hope," said di Santo-Germano, "for I have done nothing to give countenance to the suspicions you mention."

"You are a clever man," said Segalo, although it was unclear whether this was intended as praise or blame.

Orso clicked his tongue, then held up his glass. "To your vindication, di Santo-Germano."

Segalo raised his glass as well, but said nothing before tasting his wine. Then he looked squarely at di Santo-Germano. "Do you know Leoncio Sen?"

The directness of the question shocked Orso, who tried to intervene. "For the Saints and the Sea! have a little tact."

Di Santo-Germano regarded Segalo steadily. "I believe I know who he is. But am I acquainted with him—no, I am not, although I have a slightly nearer familiarity with the man I think is his uncle, Christofo Sen."

Orso faced Segalo, gesturing for a little less heat from his brother.

"You see? I told you this man has no reason to do the thing he is accused of doing. He is being manipulated for the benefit of someone else. What purpose would incline di Santo-Germano to kidnap Leoncio Sen? What would he gain from it?"

"Money," said Segalo bluntly. "If you will pardon me, di Santo-Germano, a fortune has been taken from you, and you may need to recoup some of your losses as quickly as possible. What better way than a swift payment of a ransom?"

To both Fosian brothers' discomposure, di Santo-Germano laughed. "If this is the result of such a ploy, it makes no sense at all that I should do it." He ducked his head, considering the charge Segalo had leveled at him. "If I were to choose someone to kidnap, it would not be a lesser relative of an important official, as I recall Leoncio is, but a man of high standing and great personal fortune, not presently in Venezia, and without the close connection to the Savii, and the Doge."

"Most interesting," said Segalo. "So you have thought about it."

"Not as a thing to do, no," said di Santo-Germano. "But having paid three large ransoms for my crews and oarsmen—as the Minor Consiglio is aware I have done—I cannot help but think about the implications of kidnapping, and I will apply my conclusions to this situation." He stood very still, his presence made more imposing by his lack of movement. "Even if I were a Venezian, and therefore protected from certain . . . shall we say? . . . oddities of law, I would be reckless to try to kidnap a Venezian in Venezia, where surely he is better known than I am. Leoncio Sen has done nothing to me to warrant my displeasure, so I can think of no benefit I would gain from putting him in harm's way."

Segalo downed the rest of his wine in a single draught. "There could be other reasons for your kidnapping Sen."

"And what would they be?" di Santo-Germano asked pleasantly.

"Leoncio Sen has been known to gamble with Gennaro Emeren-zio, and has won money from him on several occasions," said Segalo, raising his voice and taking a step toward the foreigner in black.

"All the more reason for me not to remove Leoncio Sen from the reach of the courts," said di Santo-Germano. "I want to find Emeren-zio, not give him more opportunity to escape."

Orso refilled Segalo's glass, making an attempt to interrupt the sharp exchange between his brother and his guest without being obvious about it. "Now, Segalo, think. What di Santo-Germano has said is sensible. If he presents his pleading in such a manner to the court as he has to us, he must convince the judges of his innocence of those charges."

"But, as a foreigner, he will have to provide proof of all his statements," said Segalo, a little less belligerently than before.

"So I might," said di Santo-Germano, "and I thank you for telling me what I might expect at the hearing."

Segalo snorted his incredulity. "You are hardly a man to be overwhelmed with gratitude, I would guess."

"Not overwhelmed," di Santo-Germano agreed. "But I do know the value of forethought, and you have provided me that." He glanced at Orso. "I thank you, too, for furnishing me this opportunity."

"I hadn't thought it would be so—"

Segalo glared at his brother. "I think you may want to keep some distance from this man." He stared at di Santo-Germano. "I intend nothing to your discredit; I want only to save my brother from any taint of impropriety."

"Which you fear my friendship may inspire," said di Santo-Germano. "I understand, and I will not subject you to the compromising potential of my presence." He bowed slightly to Segalo and then, a bit more courteously, to Orso. "I appreciate your help in these difficult times, Consiglier. I trust, when all of this is over, we may resume our cordiality." Saying this, he went to the door and let himself out, then made his way to the loggia and the landing steps where Milano was waiting.

"Is there trouble?" Milano asked as he helped di Santo-Germano into the gondola.

"There is trouble already," said di Santo-Germano, "but it comes from an unexpected direction." He pressed his lips together as if to keep himself from speaking, then said, "You and the other gondolieri exchange information, I suppose."

"I will not gossip," said Milano.

"I am not asking you to," said di Santo-Germano. "But if you should hear about a young blade being abducted a short time ago, I ask you to find out all you can concerning the incident, and report it to me, if you will."

"Why should I do this?" Milano asked, curious at this request.

"Because there are those, apparently, who have said I am responsible for it, and if I cannot divert suspicion from me in that regard, I may never be able to press my case against Gennaro Emerenzio," said di Santo-Germano. "This is one thing Ruggier is in no position to do—he is as foreign as I am."

Milano leaned into his oar as he considered this request. Finally, as he maneuvered between a small barge and a fisherman's lanteen-rigged boat, he said, "If I hear anything more than speculation, I will inform you, Conte."

"There are three ducats for you if you bring reliable information." Di Santo-Germano closed his eyes and leaned back as Milano continued to row for the Rivi San Luca.

Text of a letter from Erneste Amsteljaxter in Amsterdam to Grav Saint-Germain in care of the Conte di Santo-Germano, Campo San Luca in Venezia, written in scholars' Latin and carried by business courier; delivered seventeen days after it was written.

To the most excellent Grav Saint-Germain, the greetings from Erneste Amsteljaxter on this, the first day of October, 1531, the city of Amsterdam, with the assurance that I have not sent this to impose upon your most generous nature, not to inform you of any mishap, but to describe our present circumstances here:

I have been to see Mercutius Christermann at Eclipse Press to discuss the possibility of doing a book of tales told by women. I would ask women to tell me their tales; then I would write them down and he would publish them. He said he would only undertake such a venture if I secured your permission first, for which I am now applying. If you are willing to have such a book appear from Eclipse Press, then I would contrive to have the work completed by the end of 1533. I ask you to consider your answer carefully, and to weigh the advantages against the disadvantages in providing such tales to the public. I have made bold to approach you on this matter because of your approval of the folk tales you have already published. Mercutius Christermann has reminded me of all the problems inherent in such a project, so you need not reiterate them for me. But I believe there is merit in this undertaking, as well as folk tales not often recorded that would be of interest to scholars in many places.

At present there are six women living with me in this house: one is still married, but she has sought refuge from her husband, who beats her: her priest has not approved her separation, and so we have said that she is the step-sister of one of the women already resident here, whom she has come to nurse. The others here are widows whose husbands left them without means, and who lack family to succor them. They have no wish to have to beg for their bread. The oldest among them is forty-three, and a grandmother; the youngest is seventeen. Had you not made this house available to me without conditions imposed, I could not have extended my hand to these women, and so I thank you most profoundly for your kindness to me, and by extension, to these women.

Rudolph Eschen has been to visit this house, and he has advised me not to take in any more women until he can present a declaration to the courts that my purposes here are charitable and have your endorsement; one of the Spanish captains has accused me of running an improper house, and has asked that the women be branded as harlots if they continue to live here. I am following his instruction, and I will continue to do so until you advise me otherwise. I have no intention of doing anything that might endanger the function to which I have decided to dedicate this house.

On other matters, I fear my brother has run into another patch of trouble, and I have sent him twenty ducats to provide him support for the next several months, or until he can gain another position. He has pledged to pay me back in full, but this cannot occur until he has found appropriate employment. I ask you, if it is not too great an imposition, to look about for a post he could obtain. I know Onfroi's intentions are of the best, but he has yet to establish himself in the world and until he does, much of his support must come from me—and without you, I would have no support to share with him, so I appeal to you, for my sake and yours, to help Onfroi.

I look forward to your good counsel in these arduous times and ask you again to add your voice to preserving that which you have made possible. A sworn licence from you in regard to my intentions and obligations as approved by you would aid Advocate Eschen in dealing with the Spanish and the courts. Of all matters in this letter,

that is the most urgent, and I trust you will be able to supply Eschen
with what he requires before the end of the year.

With my thanks and my prayers,
Your most allegiant,
Erneste Amsteljaxter

7

By the end of the second day, the storm had reached the height of
its fury; all over Venezia shutters remained closed while waves
slapped and clambered at the landing steps, occasionally washing
into campi, loggie, and kitchens; ships and boats and barges of all
description were secured to pilings, moorings, and docks to keep
them from being battered to pieces. Since the storm began, no
boats had crossed the lagoon from the mainland, and in many
households, food not secured from the sea was running low; roofs
were studded with barrels to catch the precious fresh water even
while the rain was decried.

"I have authorized the cooks to take the smoked geese from the
larder; there were complaints about the crab in cream that was served
today—not enough herbs or onions to make it taste right," Ruggier
informed di Santo-Germano as he entered his study, his entry bringing with it gelid tendrils of air that riffled the pages of the open books
spread out on the trestle-table.

"Until the green-grocers have new stock, and the spice-merchants,
all Venezia may have to settle for blander dishes," said di Santo-
Germano with a sympathetic ducking of his head.

"There are a few tinctures of herbs in your laboratory that could
be used. It wouldn't require much, but it could mean better tastes. I
have already sent to your emporium to secure a box of pepper, and to
the apothecary for a jar of garlic preserved in oil." Ruggier made no
apology for this extravagance, knowing di Santo-Germano would not
object to it.

"Excellent; the staff will have a fine prandium tomorrow."

"They would not eat so well in many another house," Ruggier said. "Being closely confined makes food a strong point of interest."

"So it does. It is a fussiness we may have to deal with for another day or so—by then we may hope the storm blows itself out; once the weather clears, everyone will be less cantankerous about everything; it's being forced to remain indoors that exacerbates their states of mind," di Santo-Germano approved, looking up from the square of paper he had been examining by the flickering light of the oil-lamps. "From the court: another postponement."

"In this weather, I am not surprised," said Ruggier. He had donned his Dutch huque; its lining of marten-fur made it the warmest garment he possessed, so that his appearance was in keeping with the heavy clothing all the household wore during this first tempest of winter. "How many times has the hearing been postponed now?"

"This makes the sixth time," di Santo-Germano said.

Ruggier frowned. "What are they waiting for?"

"I have no notion, and my guesses are only that: guesses," said di Santo-Germano as he put the card down and set an alabaster jar on it to keep it in place. "Still, I *guess* that they are waiting for a witness or intelligence crucial to the matter."

"Or they are looking for ways to discredit your claim," Ruggier warned.

"That is always possible," di Santo-Germano said with nettling urbanity.

"Does none of this bother you?" Ruggier asked, more sharply than usual.

"Of course it does," said di Santo-Germano. "It is supposed to vex me into doing something foolish."

"But who is doing it?" Ruggier pursued.

"Ah—that is the sticking point, is it not," said di Santo-Germano ironically.

Ruggier abandoned this fruitless line of inquiry, asking instead, "Has there been any more information on Leoncio Sen? Or Emerenzio, for that matter? Have either of them been found?"

"Neither, so far as I know," said di Santo-Germano. He, too, was wearing Lowlands clothing: a long doublet of French velvet in silver-shot black, with a chamarre of black wool lined in wolf-fur, knee-length barrel-hose, and tall, thick-soled boots of English leather, for although he, like Ruggier, did not feel the cold, he also knew that it was prudent to give the appearance of warding off chill. "I trust I present a creditable appearance, even in these northern clothes."

"Are you expecting anyone?" Ruggier asked, indicating the garments di Santo-Germano wore.

"No; I am going out; this storm has brought an early winter, but that does not alter my appointments," said di Santo-Germano, and shook his head as he saw the dubiety in Ruggier's countenance. "Do not be dismayed, old friend. I am going to Pier-Ariana's house; I can reach it along the walkways and bridges—I need not take to the water, except that falling from the sky."

"Fortunately you have a new lining of your native earth in your soles, or this storm would vitiate you." Ruggier's face revealed very little of his thoughts. "Rain in Venezia must be a double tribulation."

"That they are," di Santo-Germano agreed.

"I don't suppose you would consider postponing your visit? Tomorrow the rain should slack off, and the winds drop." Ruggier gave di Santo-Germano a respectful scrutiny.

Di Santo-Germano made a gesture of polite resignation. "She is expecting me. She has set up her music room and would like me to see it."

Ruggier made no comment about this plan, saying only, "Have you some notion when you might return?"

"After sundown, and before nine-of-the-clock, unless the winds pick up again," he replied. "You may have one of the pages wait for me, if you think it wise."

"Why should it not be wise?" Ruggier asked.

"We are still under observation, with or without the storm." Di Santo-Germano reached for his long riding-cloak of boiled wool and pulled it around his shoulders. "I will assume someone is keeping track of me when I am outside this house. This storm is not enough to keep the spies away."

"And there are some who keep track of you when you are inside, as well," Ruggier said, a knowing lift to his brows.

"You have discovered something new?" di Santo-Germano inquired, pausing in his departure.

"I have," said Ruggier. "The newest footman—Camillo?—has been asking a great many questions of the other servants, and has been found trying to open the door to your laboratory."

"Are you certain it was he?" di Santo-Germano asked with a suggestion of a weary sigh.

"Yes. I must assume he reports to someone of importance, perhaps one of the Savii, or a Consiglier," said Ruggier. "I doubt he answers to the Doge."

"And I. It may also be he is a familiar of the court, or of the Church." Di Santo-Germano straightened his narrow ruff.

"Yes, my master, for Pompeo, the second cook, is the Doge's man," Ruggier agreed.

For a short while di Santo-Germano remained unmoving, then he said, "Well, whomever he serves, we can do little about it now. Enemy or ally, Camillo cannot be removed without repercussions. You know how to deal with such men—you have done it often in the past. I leave you to do as you think best, for the good of all the household." He pinched out all but one of the oil-lamps, leaving wavering trails of pale smoke rising from the wicks. "I doubt there is much to be done but endure his presence, at least until the hearing is over."

Ruggier ducked his head. "I will manage him as propitiatorially as I am able."

"Thank you," said di Santo-Germano, and went to the door. "I will speak to you when I return." He grabbed his soft seal-leather cap and set it firmly on his head.

"I trust you will," said Ruggier, and nodded his farewell.

Crossing the loggia of his house, di Santo-Germano was aware of two pair of eyes following him; he did not slow his stride as he made for the door onto the Campo San Luca, bending into the wind as he closed the door behind him; his cloak bellied and whipped as the wind-angled rain struck it. The midafternoon was so dark that the only light seemed to come from the glistening rain; the few figures out-of-doors looked like smudges of black amid a world of gray. Di Santo-Germano tugged his cloak more tightly around him as he shoved his shoulder into the wind and started on his way. He crossed the bridge over the Rivi San Salvatore and went along to the Merceria, then turned northeast to the Campo Santa Maria Formosa and an alley on the east side of the campo. He went to the third door along the narrow passage and knocked twice on the door, then waited for an answer.

"Who is here on such a night?" demanded a voice from inside the house. "Whom do you wish to see?"

"It is di Santo-Germano. Your mistress is expecting me," he answered, raising his voice to be heard over the wailing wind and the tattoo of the rain.

"I did not think you would venture out in this weather. Allow me a moment." There was a pause, and then the bolt was drawn back and the door was opened by Palma da San Ghirgione, who studied di Santo-Germano carefully. "She said you would come, Conte."

"I am pleased that she knows me so well," said di Santo-Germano, stepping through the door, then leaning against it to help the houseman secure it against the relentless wind, for he was a small-ish man over forty, and nearing the end of his working days. "Where is Bondama Salier?" He used this most courteous form intentionally, to make his high regard for Pier-Ariana obvious to her servant.

"You will find her on the floor above, in the room on the north-west corner of the house," Palma told him in his best impressive tone.

Di Santo-Germano offered the white-haired man a disarming smile. "Thank you. I will go up to her." He shed his cloak, handing it to the houseman. "If you will find a place where this can dry?"

Palma accepted the cloak with a hint of annoyance. "And your hat, Conte?"

Removing it, di Santo-Germano offered it to Palma. "A fine suggestion."

"I will hang it in the kitchen, near the stove."

Di Santo-Germano indicated his approval before he went toward the stairs and began his upward climb. On the landing he picked up one of two oil-lamps set on a long, narrow table; this he bore up with him, watching the heavy shadows retreat before it. He left the oil-lamp on a table matching the one on the landing before going on to the northwest corner of the house, where he heard virginals being played. While he waited for a silent moment, he smiled, realizing this was a new piece. The music was at once spritely and wistful. When the phrase came to an end, he tapped on the door.

"Enter," said Pier-Ariana, sounding a bit distracted.

He did as she requested, standing by the door once he closed it, watching her write the musical passage on a score-sheet. When she put the pen aside and reached for the sand, he said, "That was a very moving passage; I hope you will play the whole song for me."

She looked up so sharply that she spilled a more generous portion of sand onto the paper than she intended. "Di Santo-Germano! You startled me." She was dressed for warmth more than beauty, her somewhat old-fashioned Padovan gonella made of handsome, forest-green Fiorenzan wool, with the outer sleeves buttoned from shoulder to wrist over a guimpe of substantial Tana cotton. Her red-gold hair was covered with a chaplet of blue-green satin. Looking down at her clothes, she said, "I should have changed into something more suit-able." She got up from the table on which her virginals and her paper were set, taking care not to overset the standish of ink.

"On a day such as this, you are most suitably dressed," he said, coming to her side and embracing her.

"You caught me unaware," she protested, both chiding and flirta-tious as she put her arms around his neck.

His smile made his dark eyes appear luminous. "How should I do that? I supposed you were expecting me."

"I was. I am. But the storm being what it is—" She leaned against him. "I thought you might not come."

"But I have," he said.

All her discomfiture left her, leaving behind a welling anticipation of passion. "Si, Conte mio, you have," she breathed, opening her lips to his as his arms circled her waist, his small hands spread out across her back. Their kiss began temptingly enough, but it developed into a precipitate rush of passion that brought a deepening thrill to their embrace. As she finally broke away, Pier-Ariana was feeling a trifle light-headed. "I . . . I don't know what to say."

He held her easily but in a protective manner. "You need say nothing, Pier-Ariana," he said softly.

"I had thought to spend an hour or so here, playing for you, and then we might retire to my apartments, but"—she looked up at him wistfully—"perhaps we might . . ."

"Retire first, and you will play afterward?" He kissed her brow. "Whatever pleases you must please me."

Color mounted in her face. "Whatever?"

"With the exception of anything that degrades or harms you, yes, whatever," he answered. "To the limits of my capabilities."

Her glance was eloquent, revealing longing, need, desire, and uncertainty. "I don't know what your limits, or my limits, are."

Two thousand years ago, this admission might have distressed him: now he drew her close to him; his laughter was low and tantalizing. "You know the most obvious of my limitations, and that has not seemed to trouble you."

"You mean that you do not . . . take your pleasure of me as most men would do?" She could not bring herself to meet his eyes. "You have given me such gratification as I thought never to find—I fear that I have not returned the same to you." This last came out in a rush, as if she had to speak quickly or lose her nerve.

"Since I share in what you experience, how could I not be wholly gratified?" He lifted the back of her chaplet and touched the nape of her neck, his fingers delicate as petals, yet igniting ephemeral fire.

"You say you seek the blood because the blood is the unique essence of who I am. I hope that is so. God save me! I hope it is so." She kept her head averted, trying not to be distracted by the sorcery his fingers worked on her neck. "And if it is, I could not begrudge you any, if it meant you took all."

"My appetite is small, Pier-Ariana. Half of what would fill a wine-goblet will suffice me," he said calmly. "It has before."

"Still," she murmured. "If you asked for more, it would be yours. I owe you so much more than I can ever repay."

Over the wind there was a loud clatter as something—probably a shutter—fell into the narrow passage outside the house, then clapped its way along the paving-stones.

"Then it is fortunate for you that I will not ask it." There was a note of concern in his words now, and he took her face in his hand to allow him to look directly at her. "I have no wish for your gratitude; I have said so before and nothing is changed."

"You called it poison," she said. "I haven't forgot."

"Then what troubles you, Pier-Ariana?"

She pressed her lips together. "You said I would become what you are when I die, since we have lain together now eight times. That when I died, I would live again, not in Heaven or Hell, but here on earth; that I would live as you live, from the blood and the intimacy with others." She coughed restively, aware of how she must sound to him. "I know you told me what it means to be one of your blood, and I am trying to comprehend it; if that is what must be, then I will be content."

"It does not seem so to me," said di Santo-Germano, kindness in every aspect of his demeanor.

"I don't want to offend you," she said abruptly. "I don't mean to say anything against you."

"Anything you might say, I have heard before," he told her, feeling weariness to the depths of his marrow; he removed her chaplet and stroked her hair. "And worse than you could ever think."

"I am embarrassed," she admitted.

"Because you have doubts about your decision?" He knew his guess had been accurate when he saw the flash in her eyes.

"Yes and no," she said after a brief silence, beginning as she had rehearsed it during the night. "Never doubt I want your love, the exultation of my senses you provide, and I want to know the hearts of men as you do those of women. But I don't know if I can sustain the loneliness you endure. That is what worries me. It is hard enough, being a woman alone, on my own—as much as I may be without money or property. But what happens when my family is all gone, and my friends, and anyone I know or have met?"

"There is anguish in long life, and this is the heart of it," he said, kissing her brow.

She shot him a shame-faced look, forcing herself to continue. "You have done all that you can to ameliorate my situation—far more than I have any right to expect, but the laws of the state and faith declare that there are limits to what I can be given, even by you; therefore nothing you have done for me is wholly in my control, or in fact mine: if another Emerenzio should gain—"

"I have taken steps to be certain that will not happen," said di Santo-Germano.

"If you are not in Venezia, it could—it might," she said. "I would so much rather be making love than—But your hearing may deprive you of your property here, and you may have to leave Venezia—"

"What do you mean?" he interjected.

This was harder for her to answer. "While you were gone, a demanding young man pursued me, threatening to arrange for me to lose everything if I rejected him," she confessed, her stare fixed on the nearest oil-lamp. "I gave him no encouragement, Conte. You must believe I did not."

"I do believe you," he said gently.

She studied his face. "I hope so," she murmured, looking away again. "He said you would not be able to keep me, and indeed, you were not." Before he could speak, she hurried on, "I know it wasn't your doing, but I was abandoned nonetheless, and without my cousin I have no reason to suppose that I would not be reduced to penury. Leoncio said it would happen again, and again, until you were driven from Venezia."

A sustained blast of wind made the windows shudder in their lozenge-shaped frames, and the shutters over them flick together like soldiers' drums or the wings of angry bees.

"Leoncio Sen said this to you?" Di Santo-Germano strove to keep his words composed.

"Yes. And now he is missing, and some say it is your doing." She went pale. "If you are put in prison, I will be cast on the world again. My cousin will not take me back, and no other relative would welcome me after my life here. So there is only the Church left to protect me, and di Santo-Germano, I have no aptitude for the life of a nun."

Di Santo-Germano held her as she wept. "Pier-Ariana, do not fear. No matter what becomes of me, you will be provided for. I have made not one but two arrangements for your housing and care, and if one fails, the other will not." He was glad now that he had sent instructions and funds to Rudolph Eschen designated for Pier-Ariana if anything should happen to him. "But there will be no need for these second funds, I am certain."

She sniffed, trying to stop her tears, her voice muffled by the small kerchief she had taken from her corsage. "It galls me that I should be so frightened; it is because I have so much to lose. I am too old to be a whore, and Signor' Boromeo cannot afford to support me for the sake of Eclipse Press."

"Probably not," said di Santo-Germano, and again turned her to face him. "But you will not be cast, poor and friendless, upon the world: not now, and not after you come to my life."

"I thank you for all you have done," she said, and faltered.

"Do not say you are grateful once more, I beg you," di Santo-Germano said tenderly, his fingertip tracing the curve of her brow, her cheek, her chin.

She almost managed to laugh, but the end of it collapsed into another burst of sobbing. "Oh, I ask your pardon," she managed to say. "What a preposterous woman you must think me. I hate this."

"That you should cry?" He bent his head to kiss her upper lip, lightly but with a heat that matched her own. "I wish I had yours to shed. I lost tears along with the rest when I returned from death."

It took Pier-Ariana a short while to comprehend what he had said. "Truly? You do not weep? Not ever?"

"Not since I came to this life," he said.

"That's hideous, not to cry." She hugged him fiercely. "How can you endure it?"

"Because I must," he said, continuing in a more compelling tone. "That is one of the reasons why I value intimacy so highly, and why I seek it—as you will learn to."

"So I may weep?"

"So you may feel," he said. "So you may not lose your humanity."

She regarded him in silence, still clasping him tightly. "So that is why you do what you do."

"And why I have no need of your gratitude," he said with such compassion that her eyes stung.

"If you tell me you do not want it, then you shall not have it," she promised, and kissed him, all her passion in the kiss, made more intense by its serenity than her tempestuous kisses had been.

"We should go to your apartments," he suggested as she released him.

"No. Here. In my favorite room. With the instruments to remind us." She shrugged abruptly. "Besides, my bedroom is draughty, and today, that wouldn't pleasure me." She reached under her arm to untie the lacing there. "If you'll unfasten the sleeves?"

"Certainly," he said, reaching for the three brooches that held the left sleeve to the garment. He was aware that she preferred not to mix lovemaking with dressing and undressing, so he remained pragmatic while she worked to shed her outer garments. "Where do you want me to put these?"

"On the table next to the virginals," she said, tugging the sleeve down her arm and dropping it on the carpet.

He unfastened the other sleeve and pulled it free; he put the brooches and sleeve on top of the score-paper, then took her gonella as she wriggled it over her head. This he dropped over the back of her playing chair. "Where now?"

"The couch in front of the fireplace," she said, indicating the small hearth opposite the windows. "Take the pillows off the window-seat."

"As you wish," he said, going to do as she asked. Bringing the six pillows of various sizes to the couch, he put them down in a pattern to ensure her comfort. "Will this do?"

"Oh, yes," she said, standing in her guimpe; being designed for winter-wear, it reached almost to her knees. She rushed the couch and flung herself backward on it, the pillows cushioning her impact. "I like this. It is like the decadent East, where women lie about on pillows all day and read poetry."

Di Santo-Germano said nothing to dispel her image of Oriental women; he came to the side of the couch and went down on one knee to be more level with Pier-Ariana; he drew off her house slippers and winter leggings and set them down at the end of the couch, then moved up its length again. "How splendid you are, Pier-Ariana," he said as he pulled the ivory pins from her hair and spread it over the pillow behind her head.

She tried to remain composed, but a hint of a grin slipped out the corners of her mouth. "You are kind to say so, Conte."

Slowly he began to stroke her calves and feet, taking his time to learn the texture and contours of her limbs. "You have magnificent skin." He bent and kissed the arch of her foot, then, ever so lightly, slid her guimpe upward, exposing most of her thighs; while she quivered in anticipation, he bent down and pressed his lips to the inside of her knees.

"Here; let me help you," she said, and pushed herself up on one elbow in order to get out of her guimpe, which she cast onto the floor without hesitation or care. "Now. I'm ready."

"No; you are not," he said, amusement and desire coloring his voice. "In time you will be."

She crossed her arms over her breasts. "But I'm getting *cold,*" she exclaimed.

"That will not do," he said, and moved over the top of her, leaving only a tiny space between them, just enough room to allow him to slide his hand in to caress her, starting with her shoulders and making his way deliciously down to her breasts.

As her arousal heightened, she began to make a low, purring sound, ardent and content at once. Her body became pliant, ductile, and more exoptable than she had believed possible. Gradually his searching of her flesh became more fervid as she gave herself over to the rapture she felt surge within her. It was as if he had ignited tiny, ecstatic fires everywhere he touched her, and as the seraphic conflagration immersed all her senses, she succumbed to a release that began in the core of her body and spread to the farthest reaches of her soul while di Santo-Germano encompassed all her passion in the haven of his arms. She strove to find words for what had just transpired, but could only say, "The fur on your collar tickles."

Di Santo-Germano took off his chamarre and wrapped it around her shoulders, shifting his posture so that they lay side by side amid the pillows on the couch. "You gave me a remarkable gift, Pier-Ariana."

"Nothing you haven't had before," she reminded him.

"No; this time you gave me all of yourself—there is no treasure greater than that."

She mused over this, and said, "Then in some way, I have had all of you, as well?"

"I hope so," he said, kissing her closed eyes.

If she was aware that his response was indirect, she did not question it; she lay back on the pillows, the wolf-fur of his chamarre and his nearness blending with the fire to warm her into sleep.

Text of a letter from James Belfountain in Calais, France, to Grav Saint-Germain, in care of Conte di Santo-Germano, in Venezia, written in English and delivered eleven days after it was sent.

To the most excellent Count of Saint-Germain, in the care of his kinsman, di Santo-Germano at the Campo San Luca, Venice, the greetings of James Belfountain, on this, the 19th day of October, 1531, from Calais, and entrusted to Yeoville to carry to you on his way south to Rome.

First, Count, I wish to reassure you that the strongbox and documents you entrusted to me and four of my men has been successfully delivered to Rudolph Eschen, advocate in Amsterdam. I have his receipt enclosed with this letter, and his acknowledgment of your instructions in regard to various Venetian ventures. I thank you for entrusting me and my men with this mission, for work has been hard to find of late, what with many seeking our services also demanding religious uniformity of one sort or another, a guarantee I am unable to make. Between the demands of those offering employment, and the siphoning off of my men to one divine's army or guard, or the Pope's forces, my Company is sadly depleted. I have not more than twenty men left, and most of them are planning to depart. Your generosity has made it possible for me to send my men away with enough money to assure them, with a little prudence, that they will make it through the winter.

I have been summoned home to England. It appears that my next-older brother has been disinherited and disowned by my father, a development I learned of only a few months ago, and now my eldest brother has died of a fever, and I have become the heir. In order to reconcile with my father as much as I am able to, I am now preparing to take ship, in the hope that when I finally assume his title and his responsibilities, I will have a good understanding of what I must do. Timothy Mercer is coming with me, to be my guard and companion as I make my way to Derbyshire. I will be glad to have a familiar face with me, for I feel I may be a stranger when I reach my native shore.

It will be disquieting to see the family again, for I have not laid eyes upon any of them for all of sixteen years. You, as a much-traveled man, know what it is to be long away from a place, and doubtless you will understand that my elation is mixed with anxiety. I am sure both will pass in time. What might not pass is all the habits I have acquired in the last dozen years of fighting for hire. The family have asked that I make no specific mention of my Company, and I will try to oblige them, but I fear that may be harder to do than anyone—including myself—supposes.

I would like to express my appreciation to you for your open-handedness and your reliability during our various associations. If ever you should be in England, you will always be welcome at Baxbury Poges; I do not suppose you will visit, though, not with King Henry and the Pope at such loggerheads as they are. At least this dispute is about a woman, and not about God's meaning in His Word.

With my assurance of my high regard,
I sign myself for the last time,
James Belfountain

8

Two of the Savii as well as five members of the Minor Consiglio along with three advocates and a dozen witnesses attended the hearing of di Santo-Germano's petition and the accompanying complaint against the Venezian business factor, Gennaro Emerenzio. The room designated for this proceeding was on the second floor, not officially a courtroom, but in the building housing the secondary law courts, for it had not yet been determined what crime—if any—had been committed in the jurisdiction. Emerenzio was represented by Atanagio Moliner; Consiglier Decimo Ziane served as moderator for the presentation of witnesses. Di Santo-Germano had retained Thaddeo Valentin, a promising young advocate with a reputation for meticulousness.

The morning—a fine, glistening autumn day with a rollicking breeze batting puffy clouds over the sky, but with chilly shadows—had begun well enough, with a parade of servants and gamesters all testifying that they had dealings with the absent Gennaro Emerenzio, and knew that when he was short of money, he would come upon a windfall that would enable him to continue gambling. There was a clear connection between the times that various of di Santo-Germano's enterprises suffered unaccountable set-backs and Emerenzio's remarkable infusions of money, while, although circumstantial, was good cause for suspicion, particularly since Emerenzio was no place to be found. In response, Moliner had parried these testimonies with witnesses such as Ulrico Baradin, the paper-broker, who claimed that most of di Santo-Germano's wealth was the result of confabulation among those who did not know him well; then Eugenio, who had served in di Santo-Germano's house and spied on him for the Consiglio, threw suspicion on di Santo-Germano's political sympathies, stating that the foreigner still maintained all manner of ties to foreign places in manners not beneficial to Venezia. The first mate of the *Aphrodite,* one of the Tedeshi's fleet, contended that, contrary to rumor, di Santo-Germano had not paid a full ransom for the crew of that ship when it was taken by corsairs, but only half the nine hundred ducats demanded for the men's release.

Consiglier Decimo Ziane, a man of forty-five with a shock of gray hair and a distinguished manner, listened to the testimony, then consulted the standing clock in the far corner. "How much more of this do you intend to offer to this hearing?"

"We have four more witnesses, and a possible fifth," said Valentin. "You have heard from di Santo-Germano's stewards and his printer, as well as the record-keepers at various gambling houses. I have yet to call Sanson Micheletta of the Casetta Santa Perpetua, and Padre Egidio Duradante, who is—"

Ziane raised his hand. "We are all aware who Padre Duradante is."

Valentin bowed slightly. "Of course, of course. I meant nothing disrespectful." He indicated di Santo-Germano, seated alone in the rear of the room on an upholstered bench reserved for complainants. "I trust you will not hold my inept remark against the man I represent."

"Understood." He looked at the first mate of the *Aphrodite,* saying, "As the men were taken from a Tedeschi ship, I am astonished that di Santo-Germano paid any portion of the ransom, let alone half of it." He nodded to the advocates as the first mate rose from the Witnesses' Chair. "Pray continue." Ziane sat back in his chair, straightening his official cap as he did.

"I will also call Baltassare Fentrin, who was steward to di Santo-Germano's mistress, and knows what hardships she faced as Emerenzio took the monies granted her for his own use." He bowed slightly. "Also, I will call Lilio, her cook, who remained with her until there was no money left, to describe the depredations Emerenzio's thefts made upon her, and the reason he is convinced that Emerenzio has taken all the funds entrusted to him and absconded with them."

"That's four," said Ziane. "Who is the possible fifth?"

"Consiglier Orso Fosian." This statement caused a moment of silence in the room, which Valentin finally ended by saying, "He has agreed to speak on this matter, and on the character of di Santo-Germano."

"Di Santo-Germano must be a commendable foreigner, to have a Consiglier appear on his behalf," said Moliner, raising his voice theatrically.

"Di Santo-Germano has conducted himself in a manner beyond reproach," said Valentin. "Consiglieri should recognize honorable dealings when they encounter such, as an example to others."

"Prego, Signori," said Ziane, "and you, Moliner—whom do you wish to call?" His manner was offhanded but his authority completely clear.

"I have four more witnesses to call, Consiglier Ziane."

Ziane considered all this, occasionally squinting as he assessed his options. After almost five minutes, he said, "We will continue for another hour, and then stop for prandium and the midday rest. We will resume at four-of-the-clock. Call your witness, Valentin."

"Sanson Micheletta: I call Sanson Micheletta of the Casetta Santa Perpetua," said Valentin, glancing over his shoulder at di Santo-Germano to keep from looking at the witness, who rose from his chair and came reluctantly forward. "If you will, take the Witnesses' Chair."

Although he was ill-at-ease, Sanson did as he was told, crossed himself and vowed before God and the Repubblica, as a true Venezian, to speak the truth and only the truth.

"You are the owner and manager of the Casetta Santa Perpetua?" Valentin asked.

"I am the manager; my share in the Casetta Santa Perpetua is forty percent." He tugged on the peplums of his doublet.

"And you are familiar with Gennaro Emerenzio?"

"He has lost a considerable amount at my dice-tables," said Sanson.

"Would you say he lost more than he could afford to lose?" Moliner asked, beginning his turn at questioning.

"Every month," said Sanson, trying to appear more comfortable than he was.

"Why do you assume that, if he regularly loses large amounts?" Moliner made his inquiry sound like an accusation.

"Because he is a business factor," Sanson said as if the answer must be obvious to everyone, "and I know of no other in his profession who can regularly lose a hundred ducats without suffering for such extravagance."

"But he paid his debts," Valentin began to pace, covering the space between the horseshoe-shaped array of chairs.

"Yes—sometimes he takes longer than is advisable, but he has always paid." Sanson cleared his throat and stared at the open shutters.

"Did he make settlements in large sums?" Valentin pursued. "In amounts in excess of fifty ducats, shall we say?"

"Every quarter or so, he would settle all his debts and begin accumulating new ones," said Sanson, adding, "He is one of those for whom gambling is a possession, almost a sickness that he cannot be cured of, no matter what remedy is tried. He ought to be exorcized, for unless he is, he will continue to gamble, though it be for wooden tokens, or pretty pebbles."

"Did he tell you where his money came from?" Moliner approached the Witnesses' Chair, his face determined.

Di Santo-Germano moved forward on the bench, his full attention on what Sanson was saying.

"He had no reason to do so," said Sanson, "although he has often boasted that he has been paid a bonus for his good work. He told me once that he could, if he wished to, ruin more than a dozen men in Venezia, all of them rich foreigners."

"Did you have any reason to doubt him—that he had been paid a generous bonus?" Moliner loomed over Sanson as he answered.

"I know of few men who have so many bonuses, or in such amounts as he has claimed. I had no doubts about his ability to ruin foreigners, either."

Valentin took over once more. "Then—given your understanding of this man and his situation—have you any idea of how he has come by the money he has used to pay debts?"

Sanson shrugged, a gesture made graceless by nervousness. "I thought he was probably raking the trust accounts in his care: that would be the easiest way to line his pockets."

"By raking, you mean he was stealing from these accounts?" Valentin stopped pacing as he waited for the answer.

"Yes. I mean stealing."

Ziane leaned forward, looking directly at Sanson. "Did you suspect this, and yet failed to report it?"

Now Sanson was squirming. "I had no proof, only supposition," he said by way of excusing this lapse.

"I see," said Ziane, and motioned for the advocates to get on with it.

"I have nothing more to ask just now," said Moliner.

"Nor I," said Valentin. "Not now."

"Then we will hear another witness," said Ziane.

Moliner called Christofo Sen, and began by asking him if he had kept any records pertaining to di Santo-Germano.

"Of course. As I do of all foreigners in Venezia," he said crisply.

"Then you were aware that he has a number of business interests in Venezia?"

"I am. We have information on all of them." He nodded to Ziane. "I have presented that material, along with all the rest, to the Doge and the Minor Consiglio twice a year."

"I am aware of your excellent service," said Ziane, and signaled Valentin to commence.

Sitting very still, di Santo-Germano wondered how Moliner had managed to shift the emphasis of the hearing from Emerenzio to him, making it appear that he deserved to have his fortune plundered. He had seen this kind of maneuvering several times in the past, and although it cast him in an unfavorable light, he was able to admire the skill required to have this persuasive impact.

"You say you reviewed di Santo-Germano's accounts—did you discover any irregularities about any of them?"

"He appears to have lost a great deal of money suddenly. But merchants do have occasional high losses; every year, some few merchants endure serious failures. That is the nature of trading." Christofo Sen put his hands together as if to absolve himself from any malfeasance in the business.

"Did you have any reason to suppose that his factor had any part in these losses?" Moliner asked.

"Why should I have had?" Sen countered.

"And at no time did you think it necessary to inspect the manner in which Signor' Emerenzio kept his records?" Moliner all but pounced on the words.

Sen cleared his throat. "I did not."

From the back of the room di Santo-Germano regarded Christofo Sen with intense curiosity, aware that there was something askew about his testimony; he watched the witness, looking for small mannerisms to betray him.

Valentin began his question with disarming mildness. "Why is that—because di Santo-Germano is a foreigner?"

"I would say that is not the primary reason: no," Christofo Sen answered coolly, lacing his hands together. "The man has many diverse investments, and it isn't reasonable to think that every one of them is flourishing." He glowered toward the shadowy corner where di Santo-Germano sat. "I know you have been most generous here in Venezia, and often I have wondered why."

"I will ask him that at the conclusion of our hearing," said Moliner, earning a look of remonstrance from Ziane.

"So it might be that you were less diligent with di Santo-Germano's records than you were with—shall we say—Consiglier Ziane's records?" Valentin bowed his pardon to Ziane.

"I would not say less diligent, but perhaps not so well-informed, given that much of his money was not in this city," Christofo Sen declared. "I have little intelligence on his businesses away from Venezia, except what he chooses to report."

"Did you do anything that might compromise di Santo-Germano in your records?" Moliner asked.

"Not that I am aware of," said Sen, a look of unctuous satisfaction spreading over his visage.

"And you are satisfied that you could not specifically identify the thief as Gennaro Emerenzio?" Moliner folded his hands in a display of patience.

Sen glared at di Santo-Germano a second time, his gaze piercing the darkness as if to bring fell deeds to light. "If there was any theft, I could not determine its source."

Valentin studied Christofo Sen for a long moment, then asked, "Do you have any reason to hold di Santo-Germano in such contempt as you appear to do?"

"I do not hold him in contempt," said Sen.

"But you have said you agree with those who assert that di Santo-Germano had a hand in the kidnapping of your nephew, Leoncio, have you not? For I have a witness who has heard you say that." He cocked his head toward the keystone of the horseshoe chairs, where Consiglier Fosian sat.

"I may have said I counted him among several who might be inclined to harm my family. Why do you ask such things?" Sen stamped his foot, half-rising to do so. "It is hard enough that the lad should be missing, but to know nothing of what has become of him is the cruelest—"

Moliner was about to speak but Consiglier Ziane interrupted him. "What reason did you suppose di Santo-Germano might have to abduct your nephew?"

Sen seemed at a loss for an answer. "I should have supposed it was for ransom. My family would pay a great deal for Leoncio's return, and after all, di Santo-Germano's fortune is sadly depleted. Demanding a ransom for a youth from a good family would swiftly fill his coffers."

Di Santo-Germano saw Christofo Sen's eyelids flicker, and he wondered why the secretary was dissembling.

"And have you received such a demand?" Ziane inquired. "If you have, I have heard nothing of it."

"No," said Sen. "We have heard nothing."

"Don't you find that odd?" Ziane asked as he waved Christofo Sen away from the Witnesses' Chair.

Christofo Sen faltered. "I hadn't considered it," he said stiffly. "At first we all thought that Leoncio had decided to leave the city for reasons of his own. But when he didn't return, we made inquiries. We are still making inquiries, but have discovered nothing."

"You must be fearing the worst," said Ziane.

"I am not fearing anything," said Sen, and seeing the shocked expression on Ziane's face, he added, "I am certain my nephew must be found, sooner rather than later, and when he is, he will tell us what happened to him, and we will take the proper measures to deal with those who wronged him."

With a sardonic slant to his brow, Ziane said, "I am sure all of us share your hope." He pointed to Valentin. "Who next?"

"Padre Egidio Duradante," said Valentin promptly, and motioned for the priest to come forward and take his oath.

"This all seems fairly redundant. I am a priest and enjoined to speak truthfully at all times," Padre Duradante said as he sat down, smoothing his silk-faille lucchetto with fussy little strokes of his well-groomed hands. "But for the sake of formality, I will oblige the Consiglier."

"You know Gennaro Emerenzio, do you not?" Valentin began.

"As a gamester, yes. Beyond that, no." The priest was being wary, and weighing his answers to volunteer as little as possible.

"You also know Leoncio Sen," Valentin said.

"Better than I know Gennaro Emerenzio," Padre Duradante replied, settling more comfortably into the Witnesses' Chair.

Moliner studied Padre Duradante for a full minute, then asked, "How well do you know di Santo-Germano?"

"I know who he is, and I know he has a house on Campo San Luca. I have not been there, but Padre Bonnome has informed me about the household, including his long history of generosity to San Luca."

"Do you know anything about Gennaro Emerenzio's dealings with di Santo-Germano?" Moliner held up his hand so that Padre Duradante would not answer yet. "I don't ask you to reveal anything you have been told in confidence, yet I ask you to consider private discoveries as well as public ones."

"I would not compromise a confidence," said Padre Duradante disdainfully, fixing Moliner with a hard look. "But in this case, there is little to tell: Emerenzio remarked to me, when di Santo-Germano left to go to the Lowlands?—he mentioned that di Santo-Germano had provided lavishly for all his Venezian ventures and dependents; he said all merchants should be so providential. Sometime later, Emerenzo said that the Lisbon earthquake had dealt di Santo-Germano a fearsome blow, and that it could be years before he recouped his losses."

"Would you suppose, from what you know for yourself, or have been told by reliable men, that Gennaro Emerenzio might stand to gain from his position as business-factor for di Santo-Germano?" Valentin asked.

"I might surmise it," said Padre Duradante.

Why, di Santo-Germano wondered, was Padre Duradante willing to offer so much information on Emerenzio's behalf, and so little to his benefit?

"At any point in your gambling with Emerenzio did you wonder about his money, and his losses?"

"I don't usually think about the affairs of those with whom I gamble," said Padre Duradante, retreating into hauteur.

"But you have wondered if di Santo-Germano was in any way connected to Leoncio Sen's disappearance, have you not?" Moliner took up his questioning again, this time with alacrity.

"That I have," said Padre Duradante. "When I heard the fellow was missing, I wondered if it had anything to do with Pier-Ariana Salier, who had been in di Santo-Germano's protection until his fortune was lost; Leoncio desired her for himself, and sought to win her before she left this city to take up residence with a cousin. Leoncio vowed to find her and continue his solicitation of her favors, but that opportunity eluded him. Upon his return to Venezia, di Santo-Germano must have heard of Leoncio's suit, and when young Sen disappeared, I could not help but wonder what di Santo-Germano had to do with it, for Pier-Ariana returned to Venezia not long after Leoncio vanished, once again in di Santo-Germano's protection."

"Is there anyone who could corroborate your observations?" Moliner asked, making no effort to hide his satisfaction at Padre Duradante's answer.

"There is one I am aware of—a rogue of a fellow—a spy called Basilio Cuor." He pursed his lips in a show of distaste. "I gather the man has been following di Santo-Germano for some time: Leoncio told me Cuor had been ordered to follow di Santo-Germano to the Lowlands, and that he did so, providing his uncle"—he nodded toward Christofo Sen—"with reports of di Santo-Germano's activities there, including his assistance to Protestants, and rebellious women, against the order of the Spanish Crown."

Valentin needed a little time to evaluate the implications of these remarks; he asked, "This Basilio Cuor—do you trust him?"

Padre Duradante uttered a harsh laugh. "Does anyone trust a spy?"

Valentin nodded. "True enough—and yet you trust him enough to offer this hearing that man's mission to support your contention: why is that?"

Taken aback by this unexpected inquiry, Padre Duradante stammered, "He . . . he has been in the employ of the Consiglio, and they have been guided by his revelations."

Moliner was ready with his next question, but was stopped when Consiglier Ziane intervened. "A second-hand report on such important issues is not acceptable, even for such a hearing as this one. It appears that we must have testimony from this spy before I can reach any conclusion in regard to the case. Since he is not in attendance here, he must be found and summoned. Therefore we will stop now for prandium and I will send the footmen of the Minor Consiglio out to apprehend this Basilio Cuor, so he may appear before me and explain all he knows. I will have word sent to you as to when this hearing will resume. Be ready for this afternoon, but understand that it may take a day or two to find the man."

Valentin and Moliner exchanged quick looks of alarm as they bowed to Consiglier Ziane, and when the Consiglier had left the chamber, Moliner said, "I thought the matter was finished. Now this."

"The matter isn't finished," Valentin said, and motioned to di Santo-Germano, indicating they should meet in the corridor.

While the witnesses filed out of the hearing room in unaccustomed silence, di Santo-Germano saw Christofo Sen let himself out of the side-door; this perplexed him, for he was not convinced that Sen was answering the summons of any of the Savii. Pondering what else Sen's behavior might imply, di Santo-Germano went into the corridor and waited beneath the tall window that poured light into the corridor.

Valentin came up to him almost ten minutes later. "I apologize for keeping you waiting, Conte; I was hoping to learn something useful about this Basilio Cuor. I am ignorant of the man and his dealings with Sen, and that troubles me."

"And what did you discover?" di Santo-Germano inquired politely.

"Nothing of significance." Valentin paused briefly. "Moliner tells me that he, too, was unaware of the man until now."

"Do you believe him?"

Taking the time to frame his answer, Valentin said, "I believe Moliner did not know how much of a role this Cuor might play in the case, but I also believe he had heard the name before, and had been told a little about him."

"And what—if anything—does any of this have to do with Gennaro Emerenzio?" di Santo-Germano asked.

Valentin put his hands together. "That is what we must determine," he said with an emotion made up of hope, uncertainty, and impatience, "and we must do it before this hearing resumes."

Text of a letter from Gennaro Emerenzio to Christofo Sen, carried personally by Benedetto Maggier of Le Rose.

To Christofo Sen, senior secretary to the Savii da Mar, on this, the 2nd day of November, 1531.

I have done your bidding a month since, forcing Leoncio to follow me until I was able to take him prisoner. Your nephew has doubtless reached the slave-markets of the Ottomites, and will not be returned to you, no matter what pleas he makes, for, as you instructed, I branded his forehead with the mark of a perjurer before delivering him into the hands of the Turks. No matter what he says, or what promises of ransom he vows will be paid for him, no one will believe him.

You promised me when I undertook to work for you that all my debts would be paid or canceled if I shared my gleanings of di Santo-Germano's accounts and rid you of Leoncio; I have completed my part of the bargain, and yet you have not completed yours. I must have your pardon shortly, or I will be wholly without funds. If you think Benedetto Maggier will allow me to remain here clandestinely without the required payment for his silence and his attic, you misunderstand the man. If I cannot pay his fee, he will expose me to the officers of the court, and collect the reward that is presently offered for my seizure by the court.

Do not suppose that if I am captured that I will keep your secret for you—I would use everything I know of your pilferage and your nephew's extortion attempts to ensure that my sentence is kept low, and I would rejoice in knowing that you would be incarcerated with me for hiring me to dispose of your nephew, as well as your accepting stolen money from me. You and I have done damnable things, and for the sake of my soul, I will confess every aspect of my part, as well as the role you played in my raking of trust accounts, as well as the profit you made from my actions. The court will have sufficient reason to charge you with several crimes, as I will testify.

I will wait until midday tomorrow for your response; if I hear nothing after that time, I will go to di Santo-Germano, and ask him to accompany me—I will then present myself to Consiglier Ziane and beg for his mercy. Give this your close consideration, and then send me word of your decision.

In the high regard you deserve,
Gennaro Emerenzio

9

Milano leaned on his oar and sent his gondola gliding out of the Rivi San Luca into the confusion of the Gran' Canale; the day was foggy and dank, with almost no wind to stir the air. All Venezia seemed muffled by the mists, so that shouts were muted, and buildings along the serpentine canal were shrouded and indistinct. A funeral barge, all black and purple, loomed out of the murk, only to vanish into it, silent as a ghost.

"You say Emerenzio hanged himself?" di Santo-Germano asked Milano, drawing his dark-gray cloak around him, for the clammy chill called for such garments as much as pouring rain did. Because the meeting for which he was bound was being held in a church, he had armed himself only with two small daggers tucked into his sleeves, all but invisible.

"That is what the landlord of Le Rose said, and what everyone is saying now," Milano answered. "The word is that the chambermaid found him this morning; he had been hanging there most of the night."

Di Santo-Germano considered this. "Do you believe the story?"

"That Emerenzio is dead? yes—that he hanged himself? that is another matter; convenient deaths always are grounds for specula-tion," said Milano, finding his way to the far side of the Gran' Canale and sliding into the rivi that led past Campo San Polo to San Giacomo dell' Orio.

"That they are," said di Santo-Germano, holding the side of the gondola as the boat rocked suddenly as the wake of a faster-moving craft struck it.

Milano held the gondola steady, pushing the oar to turn into the wake. "Why did Consiglier Trevisan send for you? Do you think it has something to do with Emerenzio's death?"

"He did not say. He asked that I meet him at San Giacomo dell' Orio by ten-of-the-clock." Now that the wake was behind them di Santo-Germano appeared at ease in spite of the pall of the weather and the distress about Emerenzio.

Milano coughed. "Is that why Ruggier was sent off to Mestre an hour ago?"

"Not specifically, no," said di Santo-Germano; he had wanted Ruggier to make sure they could leave Venezia swiftly and without attracting notice, if flight should become necessary, but he kept this to himself. "There is a horse-breeder I wish to meet with; Ruggier is arranging that meeting."

Milano laughed. "Do you expect him to return this evening?"

"I do," said di Santo-Germano, beginning to wonder why Milano asked.

For a short while Milano was busy finding his way along the narrow waterway to the lozenge-shaped Campo San Giacomo; in the thickening fog it was increasingly difficult to make out approaching craft and to avoid the dangers at crossings. Finally Milano swung the gondola to the west; the boat snuggled up to the steps leading up to Campo San Giacomo dell' Orio. "When shall I return?"

"In two hours, I should think; that should give us sufficient time to attend to our business, and to permit me to find out who is watching me now," said di Santo-Germano, stepping out of the gondola and onto the short flight of marble stairs.

"I'll carry a lanthorn, one with two eyes, so that you will be able to find me," he said. "I may pull into one of the boat-alcoves, so as not to be struck by other craft in the fog."

"Excellent notions," said di Santo-Germano, and continued up the remaining two steps to the Campo. San Giacomo was only a dozen paces away, and di Santo-Germano covered the distance swiftly, entering the church after briefly and futilely attempting to see what might be waiting in its shadow. He saw very little through the haze, but he took comfort in the knowledge that no one could see him, either.

The interior of the church was quite dark, smelling of incense, sap, and candle-wax; a solitary monk was placing pine-boughs over the sanctuary, using cords to secure the new-cut branches in their places. He paused in his labor and said, "The Virgin's Chapel. On the east side of the altar."

"Thank you," said di Santo-Germano, and went off to the right, along the gallery behind the altar, to a small chapel with ornate oriole windows, just now showing the milky swirl of fog. Di Santo-Germano crossed himself as a precaution, and was rewarded almost at once by an approving chuckle.

"I have sometimes wondered if you are Catholic or not," said Merveiglio Trevisan as he came out from behind the statue of the Virgin kneeling to Gabriel.

"I trust you are satisfied," said di Santo-Germano, looking directly at the Consiglier.

Trevisan laughed again, his amusement more cynical than mirthful. "I am a trifle surprised, you being foreign and from the east. I had assumed you were of the Orthodox Church, not the Roman one."

"When one is an exile, such distinctions are less stringent than they are for men living on their native earth," said di Santo-Germano.

"Or on our native forest," said Trevisan, and shifted the subject without warning. "I understand you meet regularly with Orso Fosian, and that he has supported your claims from the first."

"Yes; he has been a good friend to me," said di Santo-Germano.

Trevisan gestured his approval, then asked, "Has he told you what the Minor Consiglio has decided in regard to Emerenzio, now he's dead?"

"I have not seen Consiglier Fosian since evening before last," said di Santo-Germano. "At the time we spoke, I gather Emerenzio was still alive."

"Possibly he was," said Trevisan. "I haven't been told the whole of the findings of the court's familiars." He glanced over his shoulder as he heard the monk move his ladder. "We probably won't be disturbed for another half-hour. After that, we must not expect privacy."

"And we may be overheard even now," said di Santo-Germano.

"So we may," said Trevisan. "But I will depend on Fra Rufio to guard us while he attends to his duties." He prowled around the chapel like a caged lion, his head thrust slightly forward, his irregular gait making his movements ominous. "Your advocate, Thaddeo Valentin, was most eloquent this morning when he spoke on your behalf. Consiglier Fosian also provided a statement regarding your probity in dealings with others as well as the quality of your character. A pity you were not permitted to attend, but there! We must now be willing to accept the decisions of Consiglier Ziane. You have much to be grateful for, and most of those things are to Valentin's credit. Between him, Consiglier Fosian's statement, and your manservant's testimony, much of the damage done to your reputation has been diminished. Without Ruggier's eloquence, you might still be under suspicion, but since he spoke so persuasively, and Valentin will be able to produce the spy Cuor, his examination of your man made it clear that you could not have participated in any of the misfortunes that redounded to all those associated with Gennaro Emerenzio. I will assume that Cuor's testimony will corroborate all that your man has said."

"Let us trust he will," said di Santo-Germano. "If this Cuor has been spying on me, I would like to know why, and for whom."

"Do you think it is one man?" Trevisan asked. "With all that has transpired, I would guess it to be the work of more than one man."

"Oh, yes," said di Santo-Germano. "Because with more than one man ordering the spy about, he would have been exposed before now. These things have a way of insinuating themselves into the public mind when there are conspirators rather than a single reprobate, unless the leader of the conspirators is utterly zealous or utterly ruthless." There had been many times in the past when di Santo-Germano had seen secrets unravel because they were shared by too many, and lost their secrecy: from his father's fortress-castle to the Temple of Imhotep, from the court of the Emir's son to Leosan fortress, from the builders in Fiorenza to the docks on Corfu, secrets had been maintained only by the elimination of those who knew them.

"It may be so," Trevisan said slowly, and he studied di Santo-Germano's face for a long moment.

"And if it is, you will want to secure this Cuor as quickly as possible, for I think the man's master must be eliminating any who share his secret in order to escape the consequences of his act." This was the most perturbing aspect of the present situation—that those who had the means to reveal whose secret all this was might soon be removed, and the culprit go undiscovered, leaving official suspicion to remain focused on di Santo-Germano and his associates. He regarded Trevisan steadily, an unfathomable light in his dark eyes. "If the master in this is one of yours, what will become of him?"

"Do you mean if he is a Venezian, or one of the Consiglieri?" Trevisan imbued his question with a quality of incredulity, as if daring the foreigner to answer.

"I mean if he is connected to the government of La Serenissima Repubblica," said di Santo-Germano. "Will the Consiglii support my claim over that of one of your own?"

"We here in Venezia observe the law," declared Trevisan. "Whether it is to our advantage to do so or not."

Di Santo-Germano nodded decisively once. "So did the Romans of old, and strove to uphold the principles they espoused; but often it turned out that those with ties to the Senate suffered less for their criminality than those who lacked powerful friends." He had a short, powerful recollection of Cornelius Justus Sillius, Olivia's brutal husband, who had been condemned only after his ambitions brought him too near the Emperor.

Trevisan gave a short, hard sigh. "Yes. There are abuses everywhere, which is all the more reason for us to extirpate malfeasance wherever it is found."

"Then you will act if you have proof of the culprit," said di Santo-Germano.

"I would hope so," said Trevisan, then lowered his voice. "I would, if I were you, arrange protection for your presses and your . . . other interests until this matter is concluded."

"A wise precaution," said di Santo-Germano. "I will take it to heart."

"But have a care: you would not want to alert your foes by precipitate action." Trevisan folded his arms.

"No, I would not." He waited for Trevisan to speak, and when the Doge's friend remained silent, di Santo-Germano continued. "From which I infer that I am still being watched."

"I would suppose that is a safe assumption," said Trevisan. "Certainly it is better to take precautions than to proceed heedlessly."

"I will keep your admonition in mind," said di Santo-Germano. "I gather from this that you have a certain culprit in mind?"

Trevisan weighed his answer. "Let us say that those under scrutiny may reveal much to us if they are not alerted to our efforts."

"So you would prefer I maintain my usual habits while you continue your investigation. You want my cooperation." He looked directly at Trevisan.

"Yes, Conte, we do." It was as blunt a statement as Trevisan would make, and both men realized it.

"Then, for the sake of my reputation and the protection of my friends, I will do as you ask, at least for the next several days."

"If we require longer, we will inform you," said Trevisan, his manner shifting from formidable to affable in an instant.

Di Santo-Germano knew better than to ask the Doge's friend Trevisan whom he meant by *we,* saying only, "As I will send you word if I become aware of growing peril to my household or associates."

Trevisan smiled. "I am obliged to you, Conte. I trust Consiglier Ziane will settle your case to your satisfaction when your hearing resumes and this Cuor can be examined by the advocates."

"I share your hope," said di Santo-Germano, aware that they had struck a bargain between them.

"Then," said Trevisan, "unless you have any other issues to raise, I presume our business is done?"

"I believe so," said di Santo-Germano, offering a slight bow to the Consiglier.

"I will leave first, with Fra Rufio to escort me to my cousin's house on Campo San Polo. I would recommend that you wait a quarter of an hour before departing. You will find very comfortable benches at the end of the narthex where you will not be disturbed." With those instructions delivered, Merveiglio Trevisan left the chapel.

Di Santo-Germano remained where he was, staying away from the door into the chapel, waiting for the chime on the half-hour. He occupied himself trying to decide what he might do to make sure Pier-Ariana was beyond harm until she came to his life. Little as he wanted to be deprived of her company, her music, and her blood, he knew she would have to leave Venezia for a year or two; if she remained, she would be vulnerable to all manner of attacks. He was pondering if Giovanni Boromeo might require a second location—one away from the city—when his cogitation was interrupted by the sharp, metallic voice of the bell, accompanied by a ragged chorus from the other bells of Venezia, chiming the half-hour.

Fra Rufio had finished hanging the pine-boughs and the sanctuary was framed in branches. Di Santo-Germano half knelt and crossed himself, making sure anyone watching him had the chance to observe this pious act, then he went out of the church, his footstep as quiet as an owl's wing, using the side-door in order to avoid the narthex and anyone that might be waiting for him. As if to aid him in his clandestine departure, the fog enveloped him as he closed the door behind him, leaving him in a narrow passage that led through to the rivi behind the church or back to the Campo San Giacomo dell' Orio at the front of the church. Di Santo-Germano hesitated, considering his choices, and it was then that he heard a stealthy footfall from the campo-end of the passage.

"I know you're there, Conte," came a singsong challenge from somewhere in the obscuring haze. "I saw you leave San Giacomo."

Di Santo-Germano felt his lace cuffs, loosening the hilts of his two small knives. He moved a short distance farther down the passage, away from the voice, then stopped, listening intently; he was rewarded with a faint scuff of an approaching step. Flattening himself against the wall of the church, di Santo-Germano slipped toward the voice, hoping for an opportunity to get past the man searching for him, but prepared to fight if he could not win free.

"You want to talk to me, Conte," the voice continued; di Santo-Germano began to notice the odor of sour wine. "You want to deal with me now." An echoing rattle sounded along the passageway: di Santo-Germano realized the stalker had thrown a handful of pebbles to make him stumble and so give away his location.

Di Santo-Germano resisted the urge to bend and pick up any pebbles he felt, aware that such an act would expose him to attack as sure as a ray of sunshine would. Knowing his pursuer expected him to be distracted by the pebbles, di Santo-Germano moved away from the campo again, toward the rivi at the far end of the passageway. He thought that the man could have a confederate or two waiting at the far end of the passage, and that he would have to deal with two or three attackers, not just this single, jeering man.

The next words out of the stalker were more hollow, echoing more from the stones around them, indicating he was following di Santo-Germano; another rattle of pebbles underscored his purpose. "I have watched you for many months, Conte," the voice informed him. "I know all your secrets. *I know what you are.*" His voice was no louder, but the accusation held more malice than anything he had done or said before this last recrimination.

Stopping still, di Santo-Germano clenched his teeth to keep silent.

"I know you prey on women's dreams. I know what you take from them. *I know what you are, and what your mistress will become."* Covered by his disorienting charges that rioted along the passage, the man was moving closer.

Di Santo-Germano drew the daggers from his sleeves, poised to meet the rush he knew would have to happen before he reached the end of the passage and the small canal beyond.

"You are a very clever man, Conte, I give you that," the voice mocked. "But wait! You aren't a man at all, are you?" There was the hiss of a blade passing through the air hardly more than a handsbreadth away from di Santo-Germano's shoulder.

Ducking below where the sword had passed, di Santo-Germano eased away from where the man was standing, looking for the rise of the bridge over the rivi just beyond this passage. If he could reach the bridge, he would be able to escape without fighting.

"Not that the Consiglio would believe it, but they would burn you anyway, if they knew." The hunter was a suggestion of shape in the dark passage, a place where the fog was less dense and the shadows clustered to form a figure of a large man in a long sailor's cloak.

This time di Santo-Germano knew he had to take a chance: he tucked his daggers back in his sleeves, but with the hilts protruding from his cuffs, then he ran toward the end of the passage, not as fast as he could, for that might be observed, but fast enough to draw the stalker from cover.

"I know you are a vampire," Basilio Cuor hissed as he lunged at di Santo-Germano, his sword raised to strike a deadly, downward blow.

Di Santo-Germano swung his cloak, lifting it from his shoulders and wrapping it about the sword-blade, jerking sharply and pulling the weapon from the larger man's grip; he released the cloak and heard it splash as it and the cloak dropped into the rivi just beyond the walls of San Giacomo.

"I know you are a vampire!" Cuor raised his voice, and the echoes became noise rather than words. "If I testify to what you are, you will be disposed of, and all my crimes will be forgot by all Venezia."

"If you know what I am, then you should realize you are in danger," said di Santo-Germano, almost conversationally. He pulled out his daggers and took a defensive stance.

"I will strike off your head, Conte," Cuor vowed, and moved in on him, a short-sword at the ready. Steel blade met steel blade in a scrape that was marked with sparks. Cuor shifted his position, stepping back into the middle of the passage, becoming almost invisible once again. The sharp intake of his breath warned of his second strike.

"Attack however you like," said di Santo-Germano, then went silently along the wall, keeping pace with Cuor as the man moved toward the rivi.

"If you encounter water, you will be powerless." His laughter was dire. "Why would something like you come to Venezia?—or Amsterdam?"

Unwilling to be goaded into an answer, di Santo-Germano felt his way to the half-round pillar that marked the end of the church-wall. He could feel the presence of water, and he knew his strength would be lessened. He reminded himself: if he reached the bridge, he could escape.

"Running away? I don't think you can, not now." He rushed at di Santo-Germano, swinging the flat of his short-sword in an effort to knock di Santo-Germano off his feet. "How much of your fortune do you think I'll be awarded for putting an end to you?" He was breathing rapidly now, his caution fading in the heady excitement of this desperate struggle.

Di Santo-Germano evaded Cuor's feint, and swung back to face him, his two daggers held away from his body to allow him the widest range of movement. He kept making his way backward toward the rivi and the bridge, his full concentration on the man coming at him through the fog.

With a bellowed oath, Cuor flung himself at di Santo-Germano, his short-sword extended; he felt the blade penetrate the velvet of the foreigner's black chamarre and doublet, then nick a bone as Cuor pushed it through di Santo-Germano's body, and saw the end of the blade emerging from the left side of his chest.

Staggering with the weight of the man behind him and the shock of the wound, di Santo-Germano dropped to his knees, a long, soft gasp underscoring his fall.

"You're dead," Cuor gloated, bending over to pull his short-sword out of di Santo-Germano's body.

"Yes," di Santo-Germano whispered. "I have been dead more than thirty-five centuries." In spite of the grinding pain of the blade, di Santo-Germano sloughed around and half rose, plunging his daggers into Cuor's body just below the arch of his ribs. "And now, so are you."

Cuor gagged, stumbled, and tried to keep from falling; seen in the pallid, mist-filtered light at the end of the passageway, his features were set in a rictus, his limbs beginning to twitch as he collapsed and died.

Very slowly di Santo-Germano got to his feet, and very gingerly he pushed the short-sword out of his torso, pausing when the pain became too ferocious, but keeping steadily at it. Only when the sword dropped to the stones did he bend to pick it up, then, almost fainting, he went to Basilio Cuor's big body and took his still-warm hands to lug him to the narrow canal, where he shoved him into the water, tossing his short-sword in after him. Light-headed with agony, di Santo-Germano moved back into the protective darkness of the passage and leaned against the inner curve of the half-pillar, grateful for once that the fog concealed him better than shadows could. Gradually it occurred to him that he was out of danger, either from the court or the Church, and that recognition proved anodyne, making it certain that he was safe at last. He remained on his feet in an act of will, striving to remain conscious until Milano returned to bear him off to Campo San Luca and the care Ruggier would know to provide.

Text of a letter from Olivia at her horse farm near Orleans to Franzicco Ragoczy di Santo-Germano, Campo San Luca, Venezia, written in Imperial Latin and delivered by private courier eleven days after it was written.

To my most treasured friend and long-time confederate, Ragoczy Sanct' Germain Franciscus, the most sincere greetings on this, the 22ⁿᵈ day of December, 1531, from Atta Olivia Clemens, presently in residence outside Orleans, tending to my horses while the rest of the world is going mad—which should please those seeking the end of time.

I include you in the general madness, for I cannot help but think that by remaining in Venezia, you have lost an excellent opportunity to find a less risky place to live just at present, while the various religious, military, and national interests vie with one another and among themselves to sort out the new form of their world. I do understand that trade is important to you, and your book-making, but to remind you of the warning you gave me twenty years ago: Europe is on the boil, and it will have to explode or overflow; neither will be pleasant. I cannot convince myself that you were in error, and therefore, I am bracing for worse to come, and I trust you are doing the same.

Your escape from attack was fortuitous, and you would be well-advised not to tempt the gods to spare you from another such ordeal; one fortunate happenstance is enough for this century. Had you not been in fog, and had your gondolier not returned to take you back to your house, things might have gone very differently. Rogerian has informed me of the wound you received, and remarked that had the blade severed your spine rather than cracking one of your ribs, you would have died the True Death, which has given me much to worry about. I am sorry you have to have a long, sore recovery, but it is preferable to the end of your life. Do guard yourself more thoroughly, for my sake if not your own.

And speaking of risks, I do applaud you for arranging passage for Pier-Ariana to Amsterdam, where she may still compose and where you have a press to publish her works, but where she will be safer than she would be in Venezia. I know the scholar there—Erneste Amsteljaxter you have called her—will know better than to ask too many questions of Pier-Ariana. Your decision to send her by sea is a prudent one, for the amount of turmoil on the merchants' roads is increasing, in addition to the hazards of bad weather. It is still stormy on the ocean as well, but not so much so that ships will not set out for fear of being damaged, and as you pointed out, there are fewer corsairs to contend with in the stormy season. It would be awkward to have to ransom her; you certainly could not leave her in Ottoman hands, so better a few storms than capture, to say nothing of the awkwardness of wakening to our life in a city built in a lagoon. Not that Amsterdam is much better, but it is on sounder footing than Venezia with its upended logs.

You must feel relieved of a great burden to have both the Venezian Consiglii decide that you were faultless in the embezzlement of your business factor, the man Emerenzio—although why they should think you could be implicated in any way baffles me: you were the one he stole from. No doubt this is a very Venezian way of looking at matters. Still, you are no longer under the shadow of suspicion, not even as regards the death of said Emerenzio, and that has to be an improvement from what had gone before. You say that it was proven by your advocate that the senior secretary of the Savii was giving orders to the man Cuor, who has so conveniently vanished, and that has made it impossible to lay responsibility on you. When a sentence has been agreed upon for Christofo Sen, I hope you will let me know of it. I am curious to know what the Consiglieri mete out as appropriate, given the extent of his crimes.

Let me once again invite you to visit me here, where you could recover in as much comfort as you can find in Europe today. I think back to my living youth and I am struck again with how much has been lost and is only now being rediscovered. I find I miss your company and the comfort you bring me. Not even Niklos Aulirios can console me when solitude is upon me. You have always restored me to an understanding of my own place in this very long life you have given me. If you would like a year or two away from the water—and I cannot doubt that you would be pleased to get some earth, though it is not your native earth, under your boots—you have only to tell me when to expect you and Rogerian, and I will make all the necessary preparations for your visit.

So until I see your face again, I hope this letter will convey

My undying love,
Olivia

EPILOGUE

*T*ext of a letter from Erneste Amsteljaxter to Grav Saint-Germain in care of his kinsman, Franzicco Ragoczy di Santo-Germano, Campo San Luca, Venezia, written in scholars' Latin and delivered by private courier twenty-two days after it was dispatched.

To my patron, the esteemed Grav Saint-Germain, the affectionate greeting of Erneste Amsteljaxter on this, the 29ᵗʰ day of March, 1532.

My dear Grav, I must begin by thanking you for the kindness you have shown my brother! To sponsor a school for him to teach in in the New World, and to provide him with an annual stipend is more than he could have ever achieved on his own. Onfroi is beside himself with enthusiasm, and has pledged to dedicate himself to the people of the New World as well as to the families of the Europeans living in that remote place. From what he has said, a few ships from your own trading company make the crossing to the New World every year and have done so for more than a decade. I cannot tell you how this spares me what I feared must be a lifetime of providing for Onfroi's living. Whether or not you intended it to be so, you have helped me through your generosity to my brother.

You have also contributed to my happiness in another way: Mercutius Christermann has informed Rudolph Eschen that he would like my hand in marriage, and agreed to abide by the terms I have set upon the marriage: that I shall retain my position in regard to your house; that I shall be able to continue to offer shelter to women who are in need of it; that I shall not be stopped from preparing more books for publication—this, in fact, Christermann encourages, which is one of the reasons I am inclined to accept his offer; that I shall keep half of the money you have granted me for my expenses; that I shall have the right to provide education to any children he and I may have, be they male or female. It is to Christermann's credit that he, himself, has added a proviso: that I am to have my full share from sales of my work to do with as I please. When Eschen has made a proper contract, we will choose a time. I fear we must wed in a Catholic church or the Spanish may declare the marriage null and void, and all the provisos abolished, which neither of us want.

I was much saddened to hear of the death of the Venezian woman you were sending to me as a companion. To have the ship on which she sailed blown up when only a day out of port must be a most dreadful sorrow for you. You say the official report ruled that the Golden Sunset was fired upon by accident, and that the war-galley mistook a small merchant-ship out of Tyre on course for Venezia for a corsair, and missed the smaller craft which it was supposed was bearing down on your ship. That the firing was an error does not provide a lessening of grief, as I know from my own life.

I will remember you in my prayers every evening, and I will continue to fulfill my purpose promised to you for as long as there is breath in my body. Were it not for you, I would not have so much to be grateful for, to my own benefit and the benefit of others.

With my sympathy and my gratitude,
Your most devoted,
Erneste Amsteljaxter